Praise for King

To lose yourself in a terrific tale is to live. King has fashioned relatable characters we wish to cheer for into an extraordinary tale tht will have her readers ushering in and out of worlds confined only by their imaginations. ~ Robert E. Kerns, Author of Embers

King's intricate world-building is logically and rooted in every aspect of the tale to immerse the reader in Raven's epic quest, evoking a sense of wonder and awe from cover to cover. ~ KC Finn, Readers' Favorite

In Protector of Legends: Raven's Story, Deanna King has taken the traditions, legends, lifestyle, and folklore of the native Americans and written a page turner. I learned more here about native Americans that I ever did froom a history book. You will be entranced from start to finish. ~Bernadette Longu, Readers' favorite

Ms. King immerses us in a captivating narrative where we travel through time portals transporting us to crucial events in Native American history, creating an enchanting panorama entwining fantasy and facts to delight our imaginations, and keep us turning the pages wanting more! ~ Genevieve West, Owner: Wicked Read Books, Canton, Texas

Also by Deanna King

JACK WEST NOVELS

Twist of Fate
Lethal Liaisons
Vicious Vendetta
Trust No one

KASPER BERGMAN NOVELS

When Good Men Fall

LEGACY NOVELS
Saving A Sioux Legacy

CHILDREN

Gracie's Stories (eBook Only)

Protector of Legends

Raven's Story

Deanna King

Deanna King Writing

ISBN: 979-9856982-6-8

Cover by Chandra Fry – stainedglasspublix.wixsite.com/ppromoting

Published by Deanna King Writing

deannakingwriting.com

Dedicated to the Indigenous Americans – the First People

LIST OF CHARACTERS

Sioux Council Members:

Silver Moon
Meda 'Soft Dove' Clark
Sam 'Running Elk' Johnson
Pete 'White Feather' Johnson
Blackie 'Black Crow' Kangee
Dakota 'Wind Dancer' Kangee
Blaze 'She Cougar' Clark Kangee
Paytah 'Payton' Kangee
Wakanda 'Kanda' Kangee
Chayton 'Chay-Star Gazer' Kangee
Nathaniel 'Nate- Little Wolf/Red Elk' Cooper
Raven Make Kangee Cooper—Raven/Little Bird

Extended Council Members:

Eli Two Suns Harris—Paiute Tribe
Dan Dark Water Jones—Cherokee Tribe
Jon Little Bird- Apsáalooke (Crow) Tribe
Bud Yellow Wolf Parker- Cheyenne Tribe
Henry (Hank) Cooper—Ancestor of T.H. Cooper- Whiteman who lived with the Sioux tribe of
Chief Black Raven- circa1810

Legends (real and fictional)

Cheyenne Tribe- Kingfisher & She Who Sees Truth—Parents of **Chief Dull Knife**
Cherokee Tribe- Annie Shorey grandmother of **Chief Jon Ross**
Apsáalooke (Crow) Tribe- Otter Woman Mother of **Chief Plenty Coups**
Comanche Tribe -**Joe Little Fox Comanche Code Talker**

Miniconjou Tribe -White Cow - Mother of **Rattling Blanket Woman**

Miniconjou Tribe- Rattling Blanket Woman- Mother of **Chief Crazy Horse**

*The *Seven Bands* known as the *Lakota* people: The Miniconjou, Itazipo, Shiasapa, Oohenumpa, Oglala, Sicangu, and Hunkpapa.

Prologue

My name is Raven Maka Clark Kangee, the daughter of Dakota Kangee and Blaze Clark, known as Wind Dancer and She Cougar. My father is full-blooded Sioux, and my mother is half Sioux, half White. What does this make me? Proud. I'm proud of both my heritages.

My mom recounted the tale of how I came into existence. A fairytale I loved—told of her trip back in time to a place where people lived off the land, hunted buffalo, and life was hard. My father told me about our famous Sioux ancestors and the strength they passed down to me. My dad was glad I was one with the animals and with the land. I had a gift. Mom got dreamy-eyed recalling how they made me in the Paha Sapa during a winter storm. Paha Sapa is the Lakota word for the Black Hills, which are in parts of North and South Dakota. Our Council sent her on a journey through time to guarantee a legacy for the Sioux Nation. She'd saved the life of a Sioux warrior named Dark Cloud. If he had died, the famous Chief Sitting Bull would not have been born, and part of Sioux history would've changed.

"There was a battle between some Dragoons who'd run away from the Army to look for gold in the Black Hills, and a general was chasing them."

"Dragoons? Can they breathe fire?"

My momma hugged me, giggling. "No, Baby Bird, they're Army men from the olden days."

Baby Bird was her pet name for me. Her story awed me—how they'd lived in a teepee, traveling long distances on horses, and how scared she was when the Army men were fighting. Other times, I would ask her to share the tale of how she went to sleep in the snow and woke up on the prairie to meet my dad.

Make-believe stories, fairytales, and infantile fables. I loved hearing all the stories—to the same degree I doubted their truth—although what a lovely way to share the story of my Mom and Dad's love for one another and how I came to be. Until the day I discovered the books. Yes, books—four to be exact. Books not on our bookshelves. Books I'd never seen before. Books that fascinated me and, in the end, would enlighten me.

The first book was *The Diary of Blaze Clark Kangee*. My hands trembled as I browsed accounts written in my mother's hand, the same bedtime tales I'd heard as a child, dated from before I was born. How could she have known these stories beforehand? Once more, I repeated the word in my head: stories.

After reading some of her diary, I took the next old book, its rough, yellowed pages bound with tiny strips of thin leather and covered with tanned animal hide. My heart raced, and cautiously, I turned the brittle pages. Crude drawings intrigued me, and the words were written in Lakota—words not foreign to me, since I had long since embraced the language and could read, write, and speak the language of my people. My heart stopped. This book spoke of a supernatural journey to other worlds and times—how a favored one must travel to save people who would cease to exist. Chronicles of a chosen woman sent to save one man and the legacy of her people. I read pages and pages written by an old chief known as Black Raven and how he envisioned this type of enchanted transportation. Stories of how he'd learned to leave his physical body and watch over his people when held captive by Army men in tattered clothing. My hands trembled as I closed the book, and my pulse hammered in my neck. I'd just read the true tale—proof I was the flesh and blood of what I had always deemed a fairytale.

I set this book on top of my mother's diary and opened the next one. The pages were also yellowed but not as brittle, tied together by leather and fastened shut with the same thin leather straps. Words were written in snaky cursive as the writer's hands shook while penning the words: *Book of Dreams—Meda Clark*. My great-aunt Meda Clark, my grandfather Gray Wolf's sister. These were her dreams—dreams with important meanings, visions which had occurred or would occur, in no reasonable order, with no dates. One might consider her past visions to have happened already, but that wasn't how this worked.

While I read, I noted early on she spoke of magnificent black birds—a male and a female—both large ravens. Fascinating, since I'd heard the stories of Chief Black Raven from the 1800s, and my name was Raven. Aunt Meda's reveries and her complex interpretations of what they meant intrigued me, but dreams to me were like tarot cards. I wasn't a believer. If

I had known then how to decipher the meanings, I would've understood her power. Whilst I flipped through her book of scribbles, the question of why we had her book popped into my head—why didn't she have it?

I set it aside and grabbed the last leather-bound book, undoing the straps and turning to page one. The only thing written on the page was "*Undocumented History—Hunkpapa Sioux, 1799,*" and underneath, "*As told by Silver Moon.*"

Silver Moon—our own Siouan legend. An older woman with whom I had strong ties, as did Auntie Meda and my mother. Her handwriting at the beginning was strong, dark, and bold. Over the decades, it grew fragile and less heavy-handed. The words she'd written shifted from cursive to printing, so they were more legible. The information written in Lakota were accounts of undocumented happenings from hundreds of years ago. How was this not in history books? Because if it happened, then it happened, didn't it?

I read and understood. These narratives were too far-fetched. It read like Aesop's Fables. No one would believe this to be true of our people or our history. Magic, time travel, time warps, and spirits moving from one dimension to another to fix time and space. This was craziness—it had to be. I could've dismissed this information as not part of our people's history. However, the facts would stand later, and before long, I'd have to rely upon these very secrets, guaranteeing the lives of many, including my own.

I put the books back where I found them. Funny—it'd been the other way around. The books found me. I hadn't been searching for them. I'd been searching for old family photos in the attic—photos my mother wanted. Did my mother play a trick on me? I supposed it didn't matter, because what was past was past. I kept this news to myself, not telling her or asking questions. A sly smile crossed my face. This could drive her bananas. Oh, I hoped so.

I slept in spurts, dreaming. Tall and magnificent, I'd seen him on the hill, and standing by his side was an impressive-looking buffalo. In my dream, I walked toward him. He awaited my approach. The closer I came, though, the more distant he grew. Once I stood where he had been, his image was all but a wisp of air. Next to my feet, I found what he'd left for me—a thin braid of rawhide, three feathers attached to one end, and on the other, an arrowhead of steely flint rock. The tip of the arrowhead pointed in the direction he'd disappeared.

I picked it up, closed my eyes, and grasped the arrowhead, holding it in my fist. The leather strap dangled, the three feathers blew in a sudden gust of wind, and I gasped as a whirlwind of images, words, and voices flowed through my soul, fitting pieces of history into tight-knit frames. This generated a wonderful yet terrifying saga.

When I woke, my skin was wet with perspiration. My heartbeat thumped loudly in my ears. I was out of breath, like I'd just run a mile without stopping.

I stared at the shadows on the ceiling as the moonlight danced from corner to corner. The curtains on my window parted. I saw the night sky and turned onto my side, staring into the darkness. Out in the country, on our ranch land, without city lights to dim the stars, I saw millions twinkling and flashing. Shooting through the skies—not one, not two, but several—bursting into small flashes before disappearing. Covered with bare, wispy clouds, yet the stars shone so brightly. My breath caught in my throat. I felt as though I might suffocate. With force, I breathed air into my tight lungs. I drifted back to sleep to dream again.

They'd chosen me to make the journey—to flit between worlds, mending a crack that drained our people of life. The Sioux, with a lifetime of heritage—but this also included the Cheyenne, the Crow, the Comanche, the Cherokee, and the Whiteman.

In my imagination, the changes occurred in stages. I was powerless to stop it, my destiny in motion. My world, as I'd known it, was about to fade—bit by bit—into shadows. As if clouds covered the stars without warning, our future might forever change if I didn't set it back on course, ensuring the same outcome and keeping the world from being flung into a tailspin to plummet and burn.

My impending task was to rewind history to stop it from imploding and align it back to yesteryear. I would form allegiances with descendants from other tribes—our worlds rebuilt with the courage of those called together by ancient magic and the hearts of the fearless.

While I slept, my brow crinkled, and I tossed and turned until I became still. I would find love in an unusual partner who appeared, yet I saw no face. A man once my foe would fight alongside me. In unison with the others, we'd put the future back to rights, repairing the cracks within our worlds.

My flights of fantasy continued, and in a magical moment, the clouds dispersed, unveiling a sky filled with a million stars that set the night ablaze with their brilliant glow. The nobleman stood atop the hill, and I stood at the bottom. The buffalo seemed grander than before. He wore the bonnet of a chief, and in his hands, he held a book. His head nodded, his face wearing a pleased countenance. His lips moved to speak, yet I heard nothing until the wind carried his words to my heart—words telling me that through these events, I'd grow a woman's heart and fall in love, continuing my strong ancestral line. My courage would prove my value and my worthiness of life and love. It was my birthright to travel the realms of time to save the legends of the Real People, the First People.

1

"It'll be soon."

At the breakfast bar, she'd been reading and rereading the *Book of Dreams*. Blaze looked at Dakota. Worry filled her eyes. She understood firsthand the fear she'd felt in a world not her own. Her daughter... well, her daughter wasn't her. Raven was part her and Dakota—a force much stronger than she'd been.

Aunt Meda's book told her nothing as she flipped through the pages in search of a sign of what Raven might face. Even in her written words, Aunt Meda was a mystery. With her own special talents, Raven might understand its craziness. Blaze didn't interpret visions. Dreams told her a story, yet she didn't comprehend any deeper meaning. For her, visions were one-dimensional.

With a hefty exhale, she reread one story, and it saw a dark-haired maiden traveling. The journey was her daughter's quest, and she wouldn't be there to guide the daughter whom she loved. This was Raven's chosen path, not hers, for she'd completed her quest twenty-three years ago.

Dakota nodded. "I feel it too, and you're aware our daughter is strong, right?" Over the rim of his coffee cup, he winked.

A tinkling laugh, the one he loved so much, slipped out, and she smiled. "Of course. Who do you think her mother is, my love, my Wind Dancer?" Blaze tried playing it off, but he saw she was worried.

Dakota leaned in and kissed her, tasting the sweetness from her lips. Once the kiss ended, Blaze sighed. "Our baby will face many things, but we won't be there for her."

"Ah, but you forget, my beautiful She Cougar. You were also alone when you journeyed back in time. Our daughter is the same age as you were. Raven is strong. I hate to say it, but she's stronger than you were, and don't forget she's my daughter, too," Dakota remarked.

Her smile not reaching her eyes, she nodded. "You're right, but I'll still worry. Like Aunt Meda worried about me, I'll worry about Raven. There are differences, though. She's aware of her journey, but not completely prepared."

He studied the tabletop. "Raven knows something will happen, sure, but not when nor what. Although she has advantages you didn't, because she can speak the language and knows her people's history."

Blaze's lips curled into a bittersweet smile, contented by her daughter's understanding, knowing something was about to occur, but also filled with unease, unsure of the obstacles ahead. Even the elders weren't privy to what or when her daughter's journey would start or end.

———

L ife as we'd lived it, past and present, shall disappear as the world's axes then reversed, erasing important moments no one ever suspected were important. Raven's task was to make sure those moments didn't vanish. Crucial past events that could cease to occur depended solely on her to ensure they happened as they should, keeping the world right at all costs.

Together, they will unite to revive a world that may never have existed without them. Years before into the future, forever lost, and many important people shall cease to exist, thus changing the world. It was Raven's birthright to prevent this catastrophic calamity.

———

A shawl around her hunched, frail shoulders, she rocked with ease. Her wrinkled hands were no longer nimble. Pulling the shawl tighter, she smiled. Meda 'Soft Dove' Clark, a tribal soothsayer, understood it was time for her grandniece. Raven's life journey, right around the corner. In Meda's heart, she knew Raven possessed a strength even greater than her mother Blaze.

Sounds of footsteps on the wooden stairs brought her out of her thoughts. A slight creak squeaked out as he emerged on the top step. Meda turned to see Blackie 'Black Crow' Kangee step on her porch, making his way to her. Bending, he kissed her cheek.

"Blackie, it's been too long since you've visited."

He patted her hand. "It's been a while. Pete, Sam, Paytah, and Wakanda will be here soon. The others are coming?"

"Yes."

He stood against the porch railing in a relaxed pose saying nothing, as they enjoyed the midmorning sunlight. Blackie noted her house and the area for the umpteenth time. It suited her. He loved this area. It felt like family.

The house, smaller and older, made of wood, set on a pier-and-beam foundation, draped with lattice. Latch doors in four different spots around the foundation served as crawl spaces for plumbing repairs or other needed work. The front wraparound porch—made of wood, sanded and treated with water-resistant materials, painted the color of light oak faded with age, and overlapped around the sides—appeared to encircle the house. The porch, large enough to host a gathering of twenty adults, with kids amassing underfoot, running in and out. Over the years, there'd been weddings, birthdays, funerals, and other tragedies their clan endured held on their massive vestibule.

Ready to embark on the next stage of her life, as a wedding gift, she'd given all her land and her house to her niece, Blaze. She and Dakota built onto the farmhouse before Raven was born, including a new barn, a tack room, and a small cottage for a ranch hand. Over the years, they'd done well raising cattle and a small herd of horses.

Meda then moved in with Silver Moon, her Siouan Spirit sister. Silver Moon had decided long ago never to take a Christian first name or surname. The US government gave her a Christian name, yet she refused to acknowledge the name or answer to it. Long ago, the US government tried to eradicate the American Natives, pushing them into the Whiteman's world. The old woman never wished to be known as Mary, Sally, or Abigail Washington. Silver Moon, a pure Sioux woman, born Sioux, would live and die as a Sioux. No government could ever change this, so there was no reason for her to change her name.

Those two old ladies in one house—a frightening thought. Meda nearing eighty and Silver Moon in the latter part of her nineties, but only a guess. She'd never shared her age.

Had it not been for Silver Moon's unfathomable knowledge of the past and its secrets, the mystery of Blaze Clark Kangee's journey would never have been known.

So much more transpired in our past than what we read in books. The facts you thought were true concerning your history—or any history—were lacking. Certain people knew things never written in a book. Silver Moon was such a person. Blaze had concluded this was a secret for few, and she'd been one of the few. If anyone ever told you some of this history, you'd not believe it to be true. Blaze and Dakota lived within a small circle of those who knew and believed.

In time, Blaze learned her delightful daughter Raven was another special soul who shared this magic within this elite circle. Raven was destined for something unknown, and soon it would come to pass as Silver Moon had foretold.

———

"The screen door opened—groaning and squeaking—and a diminutive woman, with long graying hair pulled into a braided ponytail, stepped onto the porch and ambled toward the second unoccupied rocker. Blackie jumped up helping her into the rocker.

"Pilamaya Sapa Kangi." (My thanks, Black Crow).

"Tanyan Yahi Maza Ska Hanhepi." (You are welcome, Silver Moon), Blackie responded.

The language kept them in touch with their inner Sioux. They'd never forget who they were and how far they'd come as a people. What pained the Elders was their youth—those who no longer understood the days of yore, younger members who'd discarded the tribal ways, losing even the language of their people. For the Elders of the tribe to hear the younger generation talk the way kids spoke these days—in what they referred to as jive, slang, or gangster—wasn't English, but foreign. Its youth massacred even the English vocabulary and, over time, not only Lakota, but proper English disappeared.

Members of the top council and diehard tribal members, those who took pride in their Siouan roots and heritage, never forgot the people's language, and they spoke daily to keep it alive.

Over the years, the tribe's four Elders learned other tribal languages. It would seem necessary as other Nations and their people moved into adjoining lands, forming friendships along the way. The Sioux clan lost members of their community to better jobs, new opportunities, and marriages, and it mattered not what Sioux Tribe you originated from, be it Lakota, Dakota, or Nakota—they welcomed everyone into what they considered only as the "land of the free."

Two generations later, tribal members such as Blaze and Dakota Kangee, and his brother Paytah and his wife Wakanda, enjoyed the old ways, the language, and the customs as did their peers.

How refreshing to have Raven—a youth of today, an old spirit she was, in the young, vibrant body she lived in—embrace the Sioux ways, keeping it alive for her generation. As a born leader, she embodied the Siouan spirit, using her uncanny ability to speak the language, understanding the ways, immersing those around her in the thick culture, making it come alive in others.

Having her in their tribe was a blessing, for young people flocked to her as a moth to a flame. Young Raven would create the glue to put two worlds back together again.

Paytah (Peyton) and Wakanda (Kanda) Kangee's only son would also fulfill his destiny, joining forces with his cousin to restore the stars and bring balance to both realms.

Soft Dove and Silver Moon realized the time was close. Soon, certain worlds would fade—into the winds as never being. Life would spin not only for the Sioux, but for Native Americans in totality. Various tribes would cease to have certain powers unless these events were reversed. The two worlds needed to run parallel, but at no time should they touch. Blaze and Dakota couldn't be there to guide their daughter. They had to relive their own past one last time to keep the world balanced so Raven's journey could begin. At no time could they meet, or it would trap them in a never-ending time loop. Unless their daughter succeeded in her journey, everyone involved in this magic would continue to live in a past that would fade, then never exist.

2

"**N**o one's here."

My heart rate quickened as I led the gray mare out, shutting the gate behind me.

My best friend followed me with his pony, Moon Beam. He was also my cousin, Chayton Kangee.

"You reckon they all went into town?" Chay asked. He was the sensible one of us most of the time, but he'd heard my panicked tone.

"Nope. There's Dad's truck and Ben's. And Mom's Suburban is in the shop. Hold Gypsy's reins while I run into the house, see what's up."

I slithered off my favorite mare, sprinting up the front porch steps and into the house. "Mom? Dad? You guys in here? Ben?" My voice echoed throughout the house.

Chay sat, shaking his head. Raven acting weird and overexcited. Weirder than normal. Never leaving the house. Never seeing friends. In truth, having no fun anymore.

For the past two months, we'd repeated this conversation:

"Rave, come on, there's so much of the world to see."

"No, Chay, here—this land. This is all I need. I love it here and never want to leave."

"At least go into town once in a while."

I was too stubborn, but then who was he to talk? He still lived at home, too. But I was different, because it was all about my Sioux heritage—the life, the culture. Chay, also proud of his heritage, told me I needed to embrace the new world.

My excuses for not having a life were thin, nonexistent. No real reason to keep myself shut out from the rest of our group.

"I can't explain it, but I need to stay close to home. It's what my gut says." I'd repeated this for the past two or three months.

"Yeah, I know. You're an all-powerful Siouan witch who knows things." Chay poked me in the gut. "You need to spew out that feeling and start living."

Chay was bigger than me, but if I got mad enough, I could whip him. At five foot five, around a buck ten dripping wet, I was in top shape. Not a sissy girly-girl, either. At twenty-four and working hard on my father's cattle ranch, I was muscular. Plus, I was smarter and more cunning.

"Well?" Chay asked when I jumped off the porch, avoiding all the steps to grab my mare's reins, hauling myself up.

"Nope. Nobody's home, and no note. That's not like Mom. Dad and Ben, yeah, but not Mom."

I turned Gypsy's head, and for a split second, the back forty flashed into my mind.

"Follow me." I headed toward the back pasturelands at a gallop. Chay followed without question.

———

Two hundred head of cattle grazing on this section were gone. Vanished. Before me was empty land and an old shack I'd never seen before.

Chay was confused. "Where're the cows? I just helped you and Ben herd these cows back two days ago after we'd vaccinated 'em. Hey, and what's up with the old shed? Why did someone haul it up here?"

I eyed the shed. If the wind blew—even a breeze—it'd come tumbling down. It looked like it was a hundred years old.

Unsure what was happening, I tapped Gypsy's flanks, moving closer. The windows were boarded, with a few cracks wide enough to see inside, but we'd have to get down to look.

A new—but old—twenty-by-twenty wooden shed stood flat-dab in the middle of my dad's north pasture.

I circled the small shed again, and fear riveted through me. Panic rose in my throat. First, how had this gotten here? Second, why was it here at all? Then something in my mind snapped, telling me I'd seen it before, and the knowledge I'd buried deep within fought to get out.

A loud whistle sounded, bringing me out of my deep reverie, and when I turned, I saw Chay pointing. Following his finger, I saw what had drawn his attention. My mouth opened, but I didn't utter a sound. I couldn't.

Back on a distant hill stood one lone buffalo, and next to the beast stood a man. No ordinary man. Dressed in full headdress, feathers flowing, painted face, a spear in his hand. Next to him stood a large chestnut-colored stud, to which he held the reins.

My thoughts raced when I saw Chay move his pony forward. I cried out, "Stop! No! Stay!"

Chay pulled back on the reins. "Whoa, Moon Beam—the boss says stop." He guided her backward until our horses were side by side, his eyes still fixed on the vision in the distance.

"We can't just sit here. I am so, so, so—and a million more so's—curious, aren't you?" His gaze met mine, and it sent a chill up my spine.

"Rave, you'd better talk to me, oh mystic girl," Chay said, snapping his fingers, bringing me back to earth.

I broke my stare with the old chief on the hill, but before I looked away, he smiled and gave me a slight nod. Something passed between us, and I was no longer afraid—but troubled, knowing something big was happening, and I didn't feel ready.

"Chay, let's get back to the house."

I raced toward the house on Gypsy, not slowing down until I arrived. Chay hadn't argued and was close behind.

Once inside, Chay sat on the overstuffed chair, propping his feet up on the ottoman, watching me pace—my waist-length hair in a braided ponytail flapping as I turned, walking back and forth in deep thought, mumbling. Stopping, I placed my pointer finger and thumb against the bridge of my nose, pressing inward to relieve the tension causing my head to throb.

"You got a headache from all that thinking and muttering?" Chay averted his focus from the loose thread on his T-shirt to gaze at me. I stared at him like a ghost.

"Listen, Rave, there's always an explanation for everything. There's gotta be a logical one, right?"

I faced him, hands on my hips. "Logical to you, no. But logical to me, yes."

"Is that a riddle? What does that even mean?"

"Let's start from the beginning." I pulled the ottoman out from under him, letting his feet hit the floor with a thud, then sat down and looked him straight in the eye. "You ready for this?" I was a little less frazzled, but a trace of anxiety laced my voice. Chay knew me well; I couldn't hide any emotions from him.

Chay might not be all-knowing, mystical, or as gutsy as the stories of his ancestors. Truth be told, after all these years, we'd figured they'd embellished the stories. He was a here-in-this-century kind of person, preferring to refer to himself as *The New Sioux Breed*, and sometimes he'd mock me and my old soul.

"Yeah, okay. Tell me, my warrior maiden—what gives?"

"If you're not gonna listen with an open mind, then when the feather pillows hit the fan, you'll be on your own!" I huffed.

"All right, already. I'll give it my best shot—make a believer out of me. I'm all ears." He waved his hands with exaggerated motion, giving me center stage.

3

"Well, that's not news to me. I've heard this same story about a million times. Geez, you remember who my parents are, right, you know, Paytah and Wakanda Kangee? Your aunt and uncle?" Chay snorted.

He'd heard the story of how the old chief's journal sent my mom and dad back in time before they became Mom and Dad, and how his mom and dad performed some voodoo spell from an ancient book and the whole pile of baloney.

"You gonna spin that old tall tale again? Come on, we're not kids anymore."

"Now, you listen to me, Chayton Star Kangee."

"Awe, now you gotta start using my full name? Crap, you know I hate my middle name. Geez, Louise!"

Why had they given him the middle name Star? Chay's mom told him that the night Blaze traveled from the past back to her present world, a shooting star appeared in the sky over their house. It had been a sign for her to use the name Star for her firstborn child. His father, with ever so much more ginger in his explanation, said it was because the night he had taken his beloved to the stars was the night Chay's conception occurred. His mom smiled at his dad, explaining Star Gazer was his Sioux name, and this he liked, for it meant he'd never fear getting lost because he could follow the stars.

"Can I just finish the story?" I rolled my eyes in aggravation.

"By all means, please." Once again, he motioned with his hand, giving me the floor.

"So, this is gonna sound nuts..." I inhaled before resuming.

Chay almost said, "What's new about nuts? Our whole family is nuts." But he held his tongue.

"They selected me to go search for our people and make sure changes don't occur in the past that would upset the balance of nature."

"That's it? I'm a tad disappointed. Isn't there more to it?" He huffed. "So, where are the cows? How did you do it?"

"—I stopped at the expression I saw on his face — "what?"

"I can't stand when you begin a sentence with Moreover."

"Anyway." I clenched my teeth. "I'm the selected one to fix what's broken in our world and make it whole again. Chay, will you please be serious? This isn't a joke, I promise, so please trust me."

"Fine, I'll try, not gonna promise I won't laugh an itty-bitty bit."

For now, that'd have to do. I gave him a lopsided smile with the realization that he soon would learn he had to trust me.

"Get knapsacks and bedrolls out of the loft. I'll get canteens, then search for any nonperishables. Wait. Get all the knapsacks you can find. We'll use them for other things like toothpaste, aspirin, antacids, ointment, you know, and other stuff we might need. Dig through the bunkhouse and get some of Ben's clothes. Y'all are about the same size."

I was talking a mile a minute.

"Rave, hey, Raven," Chay shouted. "Holy moly, girl, slow down and wait a minute. What in the fruit juices are you talking about?"

"Humor me; make believe we're going on a long camping trip via horse-back. Pretend with me because we don't have a lot of time." Something in my eyes said, don't argue, and he touched my arm.

"On one condition."

"What condition?"

"Explain more to me while we ride?"

"Absolutely." This was my reply as I hurried upstairs, shooing Chay to the barn and bunkhouse.

———

I gathered beef jerky, peanuts in bags, dumped dry cereal out of boxes into large Ziplock bags, and grabbed a box of granola bars, anything I thought might last on a long trip. Afterward, I pulled all the bottled water out of the fridge. I was glad to see Mom had purchased a fresh case, which sat on the floor in the pantry. As an afterthought, I took a large box of powdered milk and laughed. You had to have milk with cereal.

As I rummaged through a large junk drawer, I found a few packages of rubber gloves, and for some odd reason, I stuffed them into the knapsack. I continued to dig for matches, lighters, anything to start a fire with. Then, I made a mental note to get the small kerosene lantern from the tack house, then discarded that idea. We'd have to cart kerosene. Two flashlights rolled from the rear of the drawer, and I grabbed them. Flashlights, better bet. With a smile, I dug around in the junk drawer for extra batteries.

Packhorses. I ran to the front door and collided with Chay, who'd run in with four backpacks, one filled, and three more that were empty.

"Crud, sorry," Chay panted, out of breath from all the scurrying around in the barn and bunkhouse. He bent to gather the flashlights and batteries he'd knocked out of my hands after we'd collided.

"It's okay. I was coming to tell you to bring Sadie and Jumper. We're gonna use them as packhorses. You find Ben's clothes?" I nodded to the filled knapsack.

"Uh-huh, but I ain't using the old guy's toothbrush. Y'all got new ones for visitors?" I thumbed. "We gotta hurry. We need to ride out to the back forty before we leave. Once we get this stuff gathered and loaded, it'll be after three, and won't be long before dark."

He didn't understand. Ride back for what? Chay thought this was stupid of him for following along with this foolishness. Hey, though, what was a cuz-slash-best friend for, if not to follow in the craziness of the other? One day, if it ever happened, he hoped his wild, yet extraordinary cousin would follow him—if he ever was the one leading. He raced out heading to the barn to get Sadie and Jumper ready to haul whatever his cousin had been stuffing into the other backpacks.

I grimaced. We'd need more supplies, but we had no more room. Ascending the stairs three at a time, I ran to my mom's room, yanked the desk drawer open, and pulled out her diary, the ancient diary of Chief Black Raven and Silver Moon's undocumented history book. Rushing to my room, I pulled open the top drawer of my bureau and freaked. Aunt Meda's Book of Dreams was gone.

4

C hay found me in a mess of clothes and shoes, with boxes from my closet covering the floor of my once nice, neat room, my hands covering my face, sobbing.

"Hey, what's going on in here? Looks like you tossed the joint, Bugsy?" He snorted, but I persisted in weeping into my hands and hiccupped. "I can't find the book, and I've looked everywhere." Wailing, I sniffed up more tears.

"What book? I'll search for it," he offered.

In between the sniffing and hiccups, I explained, and Chay looked through the mess but didn't see what I'd described.

His brows furrowed, then a light came on over his head, and he sniggered to himself because he could see the cartoon bulb pop on as he snapped his fingers.

"It's not funny." I sniffed, blowing my nose on the nearest t-shirt laying on the floor.

"No, not laughing about this. I was, well, never mind." Deciding to forgo the cartoon in his head, he said, "I know where the book is. Your mom had it out in the kitchen this morning. She was looking at it, and I saw it after she went to get your butt outta bed."

I jumped up and wiped off my teary face. "Thanks, Chay, you're tops." I hugged him. He shrugged it off as nothing, sliding down the banister and out of my sight, heading to get the book I'd been boo-hoo'ing over. Following him, I realized my mom had been looking through it—this in itself might confirm I had to have her book.

I took the book Chay handed me, along with the other books, and slipped them inside the smaller red-and-yellow-flowered backpack, then slipped it on. These books could never leave my sight.

He watched her, hoping she had a tale for all this rigmarole. He loved his cousin like a sister, but she was a loon! When she took a rifle off the gun rack and a handgun, he gave her a stare of caution.

"Really, Raven? Guns and stuff, you think we are in danger? Come on now." He gestured his disapproval.

"I'm not sure we'll need guns or ammo, but I won't take any chances and be unarmed. I'd rather have and not need, then need and not have. Chay, I'm uncertain what we're facing. Besides, like you asked me, I'll try to explain when we ride into town, but we gotta get finished up. Please, trust me."

She was unruffled, yet frightened, acting as if they were heading into a war. She knew it worried him because he knew her and she wasn't joking around.

With guns in play, I had his full attention now, if I hadn't before. We got the gear packed on Sadie and Jumper and the saddlebags stuffed with extra things, tucked both rifles into the scabbards, and I tucked a small handgun into my waistband.

When he saw me do this, he nodded, tucking one into the back of his waistband, even though I'd yet to explain.

"Leave Sadie and Jumper tied here at the house. Let's go to the hill where he is."

"What do you mean by 'is'? You think he's still there?"

"I'm not sure what the exact sequence is. He might be there, he might not. I need to go see something."

Like before, I took off, and Chay followed me, no questions asked.

———

The old building was still there. It looked like it'd been sprayed with white paint. There were white blotches in random places on the roof and around the bottom. Out of nowhere, trees sprouted, growing in areas of the once empty acreage. Weeds grew next to the shack, and bushes had piled up on the corner by the front door.

I'd stopped to gaze at the shack with notable changes, and Chay almost crashed Moon Beam into Gypsy's rump. His eyes on this unfamiliar sight, his mouth hanging open, not believing what he was seeing.

"What the devil sort of voodoo is this? I mean, what the—" He pulled the reins back to keep from bumping Gypsy, then turned his head to say something, and he saw it, too.

The older man with the war bonnet had vanished, and only the buffalo was there at the top of the hill. The massive beast stood, his head stooped to the ground as he grazed. A lone buffalo, and I wasn't afraid.

Dismounting, I held Gypsy's reins, looking on the ground, searching for something, but not what I was seeking.

Chay watched, then he turned to glance at what now looked like a country wilderness amidst flat pastureland. Where there had once been nothing but pasture sat a ramshackle shed. Land that had been cleared now filled with trees, bushes, and weeds. He shivered in a shimmy, recalling me telling him I'd heard when you shivered it meant someone was walking on your grave. Why was he spooking himself?

He was getting worried, awaiting my explanation, or to hear me say "ta-da!" then tell him how I pulled this hoax off. However, he watched me knowing this wasn't a trick, and the hairs on his neck bristled.

I squatted, running my fingers over a patch of taller buffalo grass, finding what my fingers sought, and with care, I collected the old beaded, long leather braid, which had three feathers attached, and on the other end an ancient arrowhead. I smiled.

"Pilamaya, Tunkasila, wana sota hanyewi, ehangini, Egogshan," I said loud enough for Chay to hear, my words carried into the wind, to the ears of the ancient past.

He hadn't understood a word because he only knew a smidgen of Lakota, but I was fluent. I'd begun learning to speak it at an early age, amazing everyone.

"Uh, Rave, you wanna translate?" he called out.

"I said, thank you, Grandfather, one of many moons ago, until we meet again."

Again on my horse, I tucked the feathers in my pocket. They were the sign I'd searched for. Straightaway, I knew what the old rickety structure was and why it appeared.

"Let's go, Chay." I turned Gypsy around.

"Now hold on a minute. You wanna explain, please?" He pointed to the old shed. "Where did all the shrubbery come from? What's the white stuff? Looks like paint."

I exhaled. "You know the story, Chay; you said you've heard it a million times. Think."

It took him all of five seconds. "You mean, this was where Aunt Blaze was? That's the mill shed? You gotta be joshing me. It can't be true, that shed was in South Dakota, and you're telling me it's here now and with snow appearing on it? Shut the front door. That's preposterous. Shi...uh, stuff like this doesn't happen, ever!"

"Go ahead, you can say it. This is stupid, and you think I am batshit crazy, but hey, it's there, and you see it with your own two googly eyes. Up to you what you want to believe. You'll be a genuine believer later. Wait and see. Let's go get Sadie and Jumper. Need to get to town, if we can, before dusk sets in."

I turned to leave, knowing Chay would listen once we made it to the township. There may be things he needed to see first. Afterward, a long explanation would be due.

S oon I would call Chay, Star, or Star Gazer. Some would refer to me as Little Bird or Black Bird throughout this amazing journey. I am Raven Maka Clark Kangee, conceived long ago, in an older era, but born in the twenty-first century. My preordained destiny: save the mothers of heroes or the hero, not just for the Sioux Nation, but for the nations of the Real People and for those who would save many.

5

"Why are we stopping? It's only about two more miles to town." Chay surveyed the area.

He hadn't pressed me for the story, trying to comprehend what he'd just seen. Chay knew in time I'd tell him, so as he'd done his entire life with me, he waited, and unexpectedly, I felt his impatience.

We found ourselves facing an abandoned farmhouse which had seen its last days of human habitation, and a barn no longer the red barn of yesteryear, which sat back off the main road on a narrow dirt path, overgrown with brush, trees, and weeds. This place was where we'd hung out when we were teens—played music and enjoyed peace away from our chores and our parents. The old barn had plenty of room and held tons of teenage memories. Memories our parents never needed to learn about.

I got off Gypsy, walking her and Jumper toward the barn.
"Chay, bring Moon Beam and Sadie. We're gonna keep them inside, let them rest."

"Rave, we might want to make sure the barn doesn't cave. It looks worse than it did five years ago. Don't want the wind to topple it on top of our horses' heads, do we?"

"It looks stable. Don't be a pansy."

Sometimes following his girl cousin was a big fat P-A-I-N, he thought, sighing, but followed anyway.

"We'll be inside, and it's off the road enough for hiding, plus it still has doors and we can shut them." I looked around inside and saw a loft and a ladder, then checked it out, making sure the wood hadn't rotted. I climbed up to peer out and see beyond the small farmhouse to the road.

This place had sat empty for fifteen years. The owner died, and his children never wanted this life or to embrace the Sioux heritage which had been their birthright. It saddened me, thinking how at one time in my mom's life she hadn't wanted to know about her history—who she was or where she'd come from. Had it not been for magic, I wouldn't have been born.

"How's the view up there?" Chay asked. He ascended the ladder, hoisted it up, and set it to the side.

I frowned.

"Just making sure we can get down in case the ladder falls while we are up here." He scooted on his backside to where I sat, still frowning at him. "Also making sure my weight doesn't cause the floor to cave in. This barn's old—could have wood rot. Both of us up here, not good if we fall through." Chay puckered his brow when he heard boards creaking. "See?"

"Old wood creaks. Doesn't mean it'll give way." Sometimes my cousin is a scaredy-cat.

I kept looking beyond the house and the trees to the road. This paved two-lane county road was the main road for everyone who lived here. Today was Saturday. Most Saturdays or weekdays, a truck, car, tractor, or flatbed would usually be coming or going. I thought it way too calm.

"You gonna just sit there gazing, or you gonna talk to me?" Chay disturbed my thoughts.

"Chay, don't you think it's odd there's not one truck, tractor, or flatbed on the road? We didn't see a soul on the way here either. Nobody's working in the fields, no kids riding today or outside playing—nothing?"

He pondered for a half beat, then shook his head.

"It's strange, but hey, we're not always out and about either. There are times we're at your place, riding or herding cattle, or in the barn or whatever, and no one sees where we are, and we don't see anyone else...so what?"

I didn't answer, but I crawled over, dropped the ladder, then slipped down. Chay followed.

"Let's go," I said, and headed to the open barn door.

"Walking? Are you serious?" he asked, standing beside Moon Beam, ready to mount.

"Jiminy Cricket, Chay, it's only two miles into town. You're a healthy man. Stop being a crybaby. I told you we're gonna hafta stay in the shadows until I see something. Lord have mercy!" I rolled my eyes, waving my hand for him to come on so I could shut the barn doors.

"This way," I instructed. "Keep close to the fence line. We're gonna walk through the pastures."

He complained several times—his feet ached, the sun beat down too hot, whatever he could complain about to annoy me. Only I didn't rise to the bait, staying silent. This was punishment for him. He loved to talk, and he was tired of hearing his own droning voice.

"Fine, okay. If you talk, I'll shut up. Tell me a bit more about what all this crap is, would'ja?"

I couldn't help but laugh.

"Uh, before you do, can I ask a question? Why don't we just walk on the road? Especially since you feel no traffic is gonna drive in either direction."

"Because," I said, "if we have to, we can jump a fence or run for cover in these side fields. I am not saying we will, but we should stay alert."

Chay was aware he still had the handgun tucked into the waistband of his jeans, taking note I had mine tucked in as well. We didn't have to run. All we had to do was pull out guns, but right now he didn't want to remind me of this. He blew out a big, long, overdramatic breath.

"Okay, spill."

Chay became silent, waiting for me to tell him something plausible—only I knew he'd have to wait a long time to hear something believable, because what I was about to tell him he'd never believe.

"It was in the books my Aunt Meda passed along to my mom. Chief Black Raven's journal and a dream book Aunt Meda wrote. See this." I pulled out two chains from under my shirt. Each held an amulet. I fiddled with both, trying to decide if I should just tell him everything or wait.

"Well, what is it?" he pressed. "And if you don't quit dropping into la-la land, I'm going to shake you until your teeth rattle. Got me?"

"Let's keep walking," I said, holding one charm to show him, tucking the other one back under my T-shirt. This could wait until later—one thing at a time.

I showed him the amulet. It was significantly larger than a silver dollar, however smaller than a coaster, with a solid backing and a Plexiglas cover to keep it protected.

"This is a replica of the feathers of power," I said. Eagle feathers, once worn by Chief Swift Eagle; the dark-colored raven feather, worn by Chief Black Raven; and finally, the hawk feather, worn by Warrior Dark Cloud. These feathers, added with the powers of our tribe, create a vertical line to the powers of each man. "You know what I found on the hill? Where the old man stood with the buffalo?"

"No, what?"

I stopped walking to fish into the front pocket of my jeans, pulling out the braided leather band, showing him the feathers which dangled on the end.

"This."

"You sure you're not trying to pull a fast one and you already had it in your pocket?" He gave me his are-you-kidding-me stare.

"Chay, with serious things, do you recall me ever—and I do mean ever—lying to you?"

"You've pulled pranks, I gotta admit, but never ones this elaborate." He searched my eyes for a glimmer of a joke and saw I wasn't kidding.

"Alright then, you're serious. What does this mean—do you know?"

I stuffed the braided leather strap into my pocket and slipped the chain under my shirt, shaking my head.

"Not sure. Only I've an idea we're getting ready for a journey—one which might be dangerous, one our people will depend on us completing for the sake of our existence, as well as the continued existence of others."

My tone firm, my jaw set, and I must've had an expression he'd never seen before.

Chay nodded, and I knew he wasn't one hundred percent sure this wasn't a ruse.

Chay's eyes darted over to see her as they walked in silence. His cousin acted serious, and he'd give her the benefit of the doubt for now. He didn't know what he was walking into because he knew she wasn't telling him everything, but no matter—he'd stand with her. If need be, fight alongside her for the sake of what he too loved—the Sioux.

Even without knowing what he faced, I knew Chay would stay by my side, seeing our journey to the end.

———

We were approaching the main road of the small town. Nearing the five o'clock hour, we hadn't seen a soul. Once on the main road, Chay's head swiveled in every direction—left, right, front, back—and as he looked around, he saw only a smattering of people, but the place was small. We live outside of a rural area that rolled its sidewalks up right at five-thirty to six o'clock every night.

"It's quiet, but it is getting late, and ya know the sidewalks will roll up any second," Chay remarked as we stood next to a boarded-up shop on the corner of Main and Second Street.

I gestured. "Follow me, I need to see something."

Making sure no one would see us, I stayed in the shadows alongside the storefronts. The stores already closed for the night and wouldn't reopen until Monday. Tomorrow was Sunday.

Chay followed me as I ducked into an alleyway between two shops—a small packaging store used as a post office and a dry goods store selling sewing needs and artsy craft items. I walked to the back alley toward the old tack and feed store, then stopped.

"Hey, Mr. Elkin's dumpsters are all gone. Who would steal dumpsters?" Chay laughed.

My eyes scanned the alley, narrow and empty—nothing behind any of the stores. No dumpsters, no empty pallets, no boxes, no scattered trashy debris. Oddly, I smelled a powerful horse's scent.

A bewildered look on his face, Chay saw everything I did—or rather, didn't see.

"Come here, help me up." I kept my voice low.

He walked to where I stood under a small opening in the rear of the shop.

"Is it my imagination? Are these buildings all wood? What happened to the bricks and stucco? They were made of that, weren't they?"

"I don't know what you're talking—" I stopped. When I looked up, I saw the wall was no longer stucco, but made of wood—untreated wood, painted with whitewash.

"Here, help me up so I can see inside."

Chay linked his fingers together and lowered them so I could put a foot in, and he hoisted me up to see inside what we used to know as Elkins Feed and Mill Supplies.

"Uh, Rave, are we fantasizing or are we dead? Are we in some weird Progressive Insurance commercial—you know, the one where everything turns white before their eyes? Only this is one where everything's turning back into another era?"

"Let me down. We should head back to the barn."

"You gonna tell me wha—"

I shushed him. "No, not now. We've got to go."

With a very heavy sigh, he shrugged his shoulders. "Fine, lead the way, then."

I stayed next to the building and rounded the corner toward the main street, with him on my heels watching his own feet, so when I stopped, he ram-butted me.

"What the hell, Raven—" he began, but stopped short. Neither of us could believe what we were seeing. It was impossible.

The road was no longer made of asphalt but dirt. No curbs or cars—just hitching posts and horses. Not a breathing soul around.

I looked over my shoulder at Chay, whose mouth was gaping, and when his lips moved, I put my finger to my lips to shush him. "Back away."

He did, and after a few steps he turned. I followed at a hurried pace until we were in the alleyway again.

"Lord Almighty. What in the hell is going on? And I'm not moving an inch until you explain!" His whisper was so forceful, spittle sprayed from his mouth. It pissed him off—and more so, it scared him.

"Go back to the barn. Then I can explain, I think."

"You think you can explain? Are you telling me you might not?"

I knew this Chay—the getting mad, upset Chay—and I didn't want him flying off the handle.

"I'll do my best. Just follow me. Don't talk and stay out of sight." My eyes implored him.

Not happy about this, not one bit, Chay clammed up and followed.

6

It took us fifteen minutes to go behind the shops and down a path. A fresh path of regular dirt leading us back to the farm-to-market road. The area looked the same, yet different. The old tree at the city limits sign was still there, but smaller. No longer the hulking oak it had once been, but a younger sapling. But the telltale sign was the large boulders stacked a few feet from the shrunken oak tree. Same place it had been for years, more years than they'd been alive. Chay stopped. He stood on his toes, climbing up so he could see on the other side.

"The vein's still there," Chay remarked, satisfied he knew where he was, still in this world.

"Yeah, the tree appears to have shrunk. It makes the boulders seem like a mountain."

The boulders, stacked by nature, were big enough for two or three kids to sit on top of, and they'd called it the Rock of Dracula. A thin line ran across the top rock, which they thought resembled a blood vein stained with a bluish hue with two dark spots, where they imagined Dracula had sunk his fangs. They'd made up stories for years, saying it had been a pile of petrified bodies the Count had killed after drinking their blood. Stupid stuff, Chay said rocking back on the balls of his feet, but Dracula he no longer feared because these newer occurrences were scary, and I didn't blame him. I was both eager and nervous. We'd seen movies about time warps and make-believe time machines. Movies such as *Back To the Future* or *Somewhere in Time, Kate, and Leopold*, even *Avatar* had these fairytale elements, but honestly, neither one of us thought we'd be living in a real one.

"Let's go," I said.

Chay looked around and nodded. "Okay, which way?"

I looked around, squinting. "That way, I think." I pointed. "It looks different now, though, doesn't it?" My right index finger at the tip of my mouth, I chewed on my fingernail. My nervous habit Chay always scolded me about, but I feared we'd gotten turned around with all these changes and was unsure of myself and my prowess with directions.

Chay Star Kangee stood up straighter, feeling something inside of him he'd never felt before and in the beginning, it scared him. Something took hold filtering through his every being. His skin, his veins, his head, and his heart; it ebbed in and out of him. As if someone was cleaning his spirit and refilling it with something. He shuddered and then went still.

Chay stared at me and I was still in deep thought. "Raven," he said, "I'll show you the way. Follow me."

In slow motion, I turned when he spoke. I heard something. Something different from the Chay I knew. The clown, the forever doubting, always playing around, zany cousin. What I'd heard was the voice of Star Gazer, a Sioux spirit of the stars, the pathway of the people.

I stared at him, my jaw dropping, and I snapped it shut, smiling.

"What are you smiling about?" he asked, pointing which way to go.

"You, Chay, I'm smiling at you. You're Star Gazer, really."

"Don't get mushy about this stuff, but yeah, I felt a … a change inside. But never think I'm not the same Chay you've always known. Maybe I just got indigestion and smart simultaneously," he kidded.

I laughed, and we walked, him directing me over new lands which popped up in our pathway. A dense over treed area appeared which was not there when we'd passed earlier. It amazed me. The land had plainly changed. Even now, the town behind us was still changing, moving backward to yesteryear.

Chay led me over a stream which appeared by magic. It had never been there in our lifetime. His voice took on a sudden, urgent sense of concern. "Do you think the barn and our horses are there?"

"Yes, I do. Don't ask me why, though. I picked this barn because there has been a barn here since time began. Well, not since time began, of course. That's not possible." I held in a laugh.

"From what I learned, there'd been a structure since around 1815, or it was 1825. I can't remember the date. Anyway, it wasn't always a barn, but it was something. I read about it in the dream book my Aunt Meda gave me."

"Your aunt dreamed about the barn?"

"Not the barn, Chay, the land. The Sioux once occupied this area before the settlers came. In her visions, she said the Cheyenne tribe lived in this area, or at least frequented the area when they hunted buffalo. She was told a Raven would leave supplies and means of travel stored there, and hunt for a town. Weird, huh, because my Aunt Meda had this vision before I was born. She dated some of them, so I'd know when she dreamed them."

"Oh, yeah? When we get to the barn you might want to, uh, enlighten me about some of these fantasies, you think?"

I ponder this. Chay may need to be knowledgeable about what could happen. Although I wasn't even sure what was going to happen. All I knew was changes were imminent, changes spinning both of us around in a million directions, and it would be dangerous.

7

It'd taken us longer to get back. The path wasn't as easy, nor as simple, as it had been the first time. It surprised Chay how the land could change over what he was sure was a hundred or more years. He'd never considered himself a tracker, but he was tracking and guiding—something he never knew he could do, and he was full of himself.

Our light was dissipating. Just past dusk, with a full moon rising, and with so much land without towns or structures obscuring them, the stars were bright—in hordes of thousands—lighting up the darker skies.

There it was. The barn. A place we'd started in, now a crude-looking building, the wood rough, and the doors held shut with a sliding rail. I lifted the rail, tossing it to the side to let the door swing open, and Chay rocked his head back and forth, then grabbed the rail and tossed it inside.

"Wow, weird. When we left, there was hardware keeping the doors shut, not a rail. And I wanna keep it fastened when we're inside. Besides, we don't wanna get trapped inside in case someone's out here."

He had a point.

What a relief to find all four horses unharmed. What we weren't prepared for was the very pregnant Native American woman who came out of the shadows, and behind her a larger-than-life Native American man. Both dressed in authentic clothes of the period, very real-looking.

We stood there, four sets of eyes boring into each other, the interlopers sizing up the situation—me in total awe, and Chay needing a clean pair of boxers.

Time stopped. I'd been holding my breath for what felt like a lifetime. Then I relaxed enough to breathe. Chay, had I not touched his arm, might have keeled over for lack of air.

The man, spear in hand, a scowl on his face, gave me pause before speaking. I had to make sure not to irritate or scare him. I knew this woman was his woman, and she was carrying his unborn child.

He spoke first, "Nit'uwe hwo?" (Who are you?)

"Kangee, emaciyapi yelo. My name is Raven Kangee. In Lakota, the word Kangee is the word for crow/blackbird."

He gestured with his head at Chay, and I explained he was my relative; his name is Chay Kangee, known as Star Gazer.

He nodded at Chay and looked back, asking me if I were Cheyenne or Lakota.

"Lakota."

"I am Cheyenne, but I understand your tribe's words. My woman, She Who Sees Truth," he said, gesturing to his wife, who had taken a very short step back, hiding behind the foreboding man. "I am called Matsenestse (Kingfisher)."

He stood straight, proud, and unafraid. Chay and I, dressed in modern-day clothes, should've scared him; it would have scared me if I were him.

I smiled, and Chay, still speechless, took a step forward, which wasn't a bright move on his part.

"Stop!" His words were screamed in Cheyenne. Kingfisher lifted his spear and aimed it at Chay, who froze, one foot still in the air.

Speaking in rapid-fire Lakota, I told Kingfisher we meant no harm.

Then I addressed Chay. "Step back before you get us both killed. He's scared for his wife."

"What! He's scared? Holy cow, I just about peed myself," Chay said between clenched teeth as he stepped backward, standing beside me. His eyes were on the man with the spear. He asked, "What do you suggest we do? Man, this guy is going to think we're evil spirits. What are you going to say? Our clothes and how we're dressed, we don't fit this time era—not a smidge!"

My hand on his arm to ease his qualms, I spoke to Kingfisher in Lakota, happy we had no communication problem.

"Your Wee-yah (woman), when does your hoksicala (baby) arrive?"

His gaze moved to She Who Sees Truth, and I saw tenderness in his eyes which had shown my cousin threat.

"One full moon."

The woman nodded.

Wow. This would be weird. I'd never seen a human baby born. I'd seen calves and a foal's birthing, but this would be more amazing.

"Is good? We help?" I asked.

"No, no man see, not even me."

I looked at Chay, then Kingfisher. Holy cow, I'd have to help, or She Who Sees Truth was going to bear this baby alone. Jeepers Creepers. This was a nightmare! Then I wondered if they'd still be here. A moon was a month. How long would we be here, and what about Kingfisher and his wife?

"You wanna fill me in, and can I move? I feel like a statue and my bones are aching." Chay did a sideways talk out of his mouth, like Clyde talking to Bonnie in a gangster film.

"Come, sit so She Who Sees Truth can rest." My hand gestured to the center of the barn, encompassing the hay and straw scattered around on the dirt floor.

Kingfisher nodded and took a confident step forward, unafraid, leading the woman to sit behind him. He protected her, which I admired in him.

I acted as the protector, while Chay sat behind me, his eyes never leaving the other man's face.

I tried not to laugh but couldn't help it, which caused Kingfisher to raise an eyebrow in curiosity. "Why do you protect the man? Has he no courage?"

"What did he say about me? I know you two are talking about me," Chay huffed.

"He wants to know why I protect you because you're the man," I cackled again, this time with too much mirth, or so Chay thought, because he poked me in the side and I jumped.

"Chay, stop poking me."

"You can tell him what's going on and that I'm not his enemy. Tell him I'm part of your tribe even though I don't speak Lakota, even though I am full-blooded Sioux, because this is pissing me off. And..." His voice rose a notch. "I'm due a freaking explanation, don't'cha think?"

I nodded. Chay had never spoken to me that way, especially regarding the issue of being pure-blooded. It stung a small degree, but I'd get over it.

"How about I explain it to you both, but it will take me some time, since you can't speak Lakota nor Cheyenne, so I'll need to tell the story twice," I ground out between gritted teeth.

He ducked his head. "I'm sorry about the full-blooded thing, Cuz. Honest, I didn't mean to piss you off. I'm...well, yeah, I can say it, I'm scared because I don't even know what's going on or why."

With a nod, I patted him on his knee. "It's okay, I understand. I would be too if I were you. Heck, I'm me and I'm scared too because I still don't get it either. So, come up here, sit beside me, be the valiant warrior I know you are, Star Gazer."

He conceded and scooted up, crossing his legs and staring at the other two, trying not to look defiant or threatening—or like a scared bunny rabbit twitching to run down a rabbit hole and hide.

———

I had them spellbound with my tale, and several times, Kingfisher's jaw dropped, but he snapped it shut just as fast. The woman, whose mouth had dropped open, stayed open in a full-on "catching flies" expression. Once I'd finished, I turned to Chay.

"I've caught them up to where we are."

"Which is where?" Chay asked, miffed.

"I told them a shortened version of my mom and dad, you and your parents, and Aunt Meda's book, the old chief, and the buffalo on the hill, and how it was my ancestral grandfather from many moons ago, and how things are reverting to the past before our eyes, and I don't know why. Also, I told them I don't know why we're here."

Kingfisher stood. "Horses safe, hidden in thicket; we come to rest. Our hunting party camped near Tatanka, but many White men come; they hunt Tatanka too, but for hides and sport, not for winter survival, food, and clothing. Not prepared for Whiteman to fight, not afraid, but we are few, and I fear for our unborn child."

The proud Cheyenne looked at his wife. "She Who Sees Truth traveled with midwife in case her time comes, but we separated from the others and here we stopped so she can rest before we go back to camp near Black Hills." He looked down on the top of his woman's bowed head.

Chay, now no longer afraid, thought he was an amazing-looking man. Kingfisher was six feet tall, lean and muscular, with a rough etched face, squared jawline, long sloped nose, smooth brown complexion, and long black hair pulled into two tails bound with leather. His eyes were piercing black, and he wore leggings with fringe down both sides, boots made of buffalo hide, and a leather slip-over-your-head shirt lined with fringe. Kingfisher carried a large knife in a leather belt with a pouch dangling from it, and a sling of beads. Chay wondered about their horses.

"What'd he say? And where are their horses, or are they on foot?" Chay eyeballed me.

"They have horses, two of them. They left them hidden in the back thicket. Seems they were heading to a new winter camp and Whitemen were out hunting. As far as I can translate, they were only a small group that had been the last to leave. To avoid a skirmish with the Whitemen, they left the area and somehow became separated from the rest of the small group, including the midwife. They're on their way to the winter place in Montana, and he claims it's only a four- or five-day ride from here."

Chay let this seep into his brain. Then he had the look on his face I'd been awaiting.

"Uh... I...what the...well, hell! All I can say is we're not in Kansas anymore now, are we?"

I shook my head. "I know, I know. When we started out today, we were forty-five miles outside of Standing Rock Reservation on the South Dakota side; now we're in North Dakota, near the Montana border? Did the earth shift and dump us North, because we aren't even close to Kansas, Toto?"

"So," he leaned in whispering, and I sucked up a laugh.

"What's so funny?"

"Uh, we're speaking English and they can't understand, so why ya whispering?"

"Oh, ya, right. The old mill shack in the back forty was in South Dakota, the one your mother had hidden near the day they used a mystic spell and she went back in time, right?"

"Yeah, and she ends up in North Dakota, and that's where—"

He cut in on me, "Yeah, it's what I was getting at."

"So that's how we got here. It sorta fits, I guess."

But neither of us passed out and woke up in a different time like my mom had. This sort of just happened to us while we were awake. We sat whispering to each other, trying to piece it together when She Who Sees Truth said something to Kingfisher in Cheyenne. He helped her up, walked her to the back where there was a single door, then turned to stand guard, his eyes driving into Chay.

I pinched my lips together to keep from laughing because I'd understood just enough to know what was happening. Even if someone didn't speak Cheyenne, any woman would understand a pregnant lady's needs, at least some of them.

"What?" he asked, eyeing the Cheyenne, then me.

I lifted my hands in a shrug and twittered. "Nature calls and Kingfisher doesn't want you calling on her as she calls on nature, I think."

"Well, I would never in a mil—oh screw it, this sucks. I need to communicate too; it'd be a lot easier if I could!" This frustrated Chay.

I agreed and then thought about it. Black Raven's journal had magic. Perhaps that magic traveled with us and I could find the words to help; then I thought, nah, I wasn't magical. Even my mom had the elders helping her; were they at work helping us? I did know that after today's occurrences, anything was possible.

8

It was getting late. Communication was lacking on Chay's part, and I noted the woman was tiring. Then I heard Chay's stomach growl and laughed, because I was hungry too—and wondered if our new guests might be hungry.

Kingfisher stood and helped his wife to her feet. Looking at Chay, then at me, with a partial scowl etched on his face, he said, "We go, make camp by horses."

He turned to leave, but I stopped him. "No, wait. Stay. Your woman—she can sleep inside, here." I waved my arms in a sweeping motion, showing him they should stay here. It would be safer.

"No, must get horses and food."

I chewed my bottom lip, shaking my head. In my heart, I felt they shouldn't leave.

"No, you and Star Gazer, go get horses. She Who Sees Truth needs rest, and it is dark. You go get your horses. I'll stay here with your woman."

Kingfisher gazed at me with a somber expression, then looked at Chay, long and hard. He wouldn't leave his woman with the man. The woman who spoke Lakota was a different matter, and with me, he felt his wife would come to no harm. He regarded his pregnant wife—she needed rest—and the day for their child to arrive was nearing. She'd lost two babies at birth, and he wouldn't take the chance.

"He not talk Cheyenne or Lakota. How we talk?"

I looked at him, then at Chay, who'd stood up, dusting his backside off.

"After you tell me where the horses are and how far, I'll explain, and then you can use your hands like this." I gestured, walking with my fingers, showing silence by placing my hand over my mouth, and motioning for him to come along.

Time stood still as he thought about it. He glanced at his wife, who nodded and, in Cheyenne, said she needed rest, water, and food.

I saw Kingfisher's internal struggle and felt certain he'd yank the woman up and leave—fearful of what he shouldn't be fearful of—hoping he wouldn't endanger his very pregnant wife.

"You wanna fill me in?" Chay almost ordered.

"Go with him. Help get their horses. His wife can stay here and rest. I explained you can communicate through a sign language of sorts. It's the only way, okay?"

His eyes grew as big as flying saucers. I almost doubled over in laughter, and would've if the situation hadn't been so dire.

"From what he's told me, the horses are a quarter-mile away, hidden in a dense thicket of trees. We know Whitemen live near the area if this ramshackle barn is here, so just follow him and help him bring their horses back." I glanced at the woman. "Chay, she's about to pop with a new baby and needs rest. I speak Lakota, and she can understand me, at least enough. So if anything were to happen, I'll be here for her. Besides, you wanna stay and take care of the woman?"

"You have a point. But..." Chay jabbed his thumb toward Kingfisher. "I'm sure they think we're from Mars. I won't feel safe until I get back. Not an ideal situation for either of us, not at all."

A tiny grin played at the corner of my lips as I tried to calm him. "What other choices do we have? Besides, if something happens to either of you, the woman and baby will live, and deep down, my gut says it's very important. The thing is, he won't leave her if I go with him because he sees you as a threat, so best if we eliminate those feelings." I cocked a brow at him. "You good with that? And Lord, Chay—Mars, are you kidding? I'm sure he has no idea there's a solar system, except for the sun, the moon, and the stars."

Eyeing Kingfisher and the very pregnant woman, Chay looked at me and curled his lips.

"Alright, I'll go. And listen—don't pick at my words, because you know exactly what I meant."

"Yeah, I did."

Chay let out a very audible exhale. "Terrific. Ask him again where their horses are and a landmark or two if you can while I'm fishing in our knapsacks for a flashlight." He turned around, then back. "And please explain to him what a flashlight is, because it's gonna freak him out, and I'd rather not get speared tonight or any night."

This time, I doubled over in laughter. When I looked up, Chay's arms were crossed, a scowl on his face, looking every inch as fierce as Kingfisher, and my smile dropped.

"I will. Seems I'll be explaining a lot of things, won't I?"

His eyes closed, and he sighed. "Guess so." Then he headed to Sadie and took a knapsack off her back, digging for what he needed, while I gave it my best effort to explain the firelight in the metal tube and how it would shine a light like a fire stick. Although it took more explaining on my part for the Cheyenne to believe me, I had him convinced we meant them no harm.

———

I t took them an hour and a half to bring back three horses—not because it had been far. According to Chay, they'd butted heads over the best way to return.

"Honest to God, I thought he'd run me through with his spear. When I mimed a shorter way and didn't follow him, he thought I was trying to steal the horses. The guy's a loon—it took me half an hour telling him in crude sign language I wasn't stealing his horses. It was like pulling teeth, grueling."

Boy, Chay talked a mile a minute, wound up tight, and the man called Kingfisher sat there, not too happy.

"Kingfisher," I spoke to him, but looked at Chay. "He is called Star Gazer. He has countless knowledge of the stars. Understand?"

Kingfisher jutted his jaw, giving Chay a tough-man chin salute, his lips pressed together in a thin, flat line, grunting at him. It was the best my cousin was going to get, for now at least.

"We better eat, all of us, or we're gonna keel over from hunger."

Chay was several things—tired, hungry, and agitated because he couldn't speak Lakota, knowing only a few basic words, and would've liked to communicate like I did. He worried more because he had no clue what was happening. Chay also needed answers, but I had none.

With a nod, I went to get things out of the knapsack—things I'd have to explain. My hope was they would eat and drink the supplies we'd carried into their time. Into their time—this still amazed me, and I pinched myself to make sure I wasn't daydreaming. Nope, and I was more excited than I let on because I knew Chay wanted no part of this, but he was stuck. I felt like I'd burst at the seams with anticipation. It had all been true—my mother's story—and it both scared and thrilled me, knowing I had a path similar to hers. But, same as her twenty-four years ago, I hadn't a clue what my quest was.

9

One Day Earlier in Present Time

From the Sioux Tribe, Meda Clark (Soft Dove), Blackie Kangee (Black Crow), Sam Johnson (Running Elk), Pete Johnson (White Feather), and Silver Moon sat, waiting on the others to arrive. Representatives from the Cherokee, the Paiute, the Cheyenne, the Crow, and the Whiteman would be joining them.

"O-si-yo`, Silver Moon," he greeted in his native tongue, then turned to Meda. "Hello to you, my friend. Good to see you again."

The once very tall Dan 'Dark Waters' Jones of the Cherokee Tribe, still handsome as ever, had aged a bit—slightly shorter than in his youth—but his smile remained charming, and his eyes still held the sparkle of mischievousness. He and Meda had been friends since their youth. She smiled upon seeing him.

"Wonderful to see you as well. It's been too long. Come, sit; I see others arriving."

He took a place to the right of Meda and left of Silver Moon, sitting between what had been two of the prettiest Sioux maidens of their day.

"Ah Kahee`, my friend, how are you?" Silver Moon asked.

"Kahee`, I'm well, I'm well," Jon Little Bird of the Crow Tribe said, turning to Sam. "It's been too long since we've talked, my bachiialaxpe, my friend."

"Yes, way too long. It'd be fantastic if we could go fishing soon."

Sam and Jon, though from tribes who had historically been at war, had been two proud young men who almost hadn't formed a friendship. No one had ever heard of a Crow and a Sioux being friendly. Years of past hatred and youthful stubbornness had cost them time, but they'd forged a steadfast relationship between themselves—not their tribes. They both loved the outdoors: fishing, hunting, anything that took them into the wilderness and the land. As time passed, they had seen less of each other, and now it was time to reconnect before one or both were called to the gods in the sky.

"Haaahe, Blackie Kangee," Bud 'Yellow Wolf' Parker of the Cheyenne called out, walking up the stairs to the porch. As always, Yellow Wolf, a smiling and jovial man, still had a spring in his step and laughter in his heart. He grabbed Blackie's forearms in a traditional handshake, which turned into a hug.

"I have missed the days of playing cards and talking about the old times!" Bud grinned. "We need to do more before the gods of our past call us home."

Blackie hooted. "Yes, but no cheating!"

"What, me cheat? I would never." Yellow Wolf cackled.

"Yes, you do, but it's never stopped me from whooping your butt," Pete said, slapping his knee.

When Silver Moon spoke, the laughter died down.

"We wait on Paytah, Wakanda, and Two Suns—uh, Eli Harris, our Paiute friend—and Henry Cooper, the Whiteman who has also joined our close-knit group. Once everyone has arrived, we shall begin."

———

S ilver Moon was ready, but tired, and felt the spirit gods hovering about her. She needed this meeting accomplished to ensure her work on man's earth was done. She had lived long and seen much, and all she feared now was not having enough time. After discovering the journal penned by Chief Black Raven hundreds of moons ago, and the Book of Dreams that she and Meda had written, she understood the stakes. The two books wove a tale no one would ever believe.

The history she documented over the years—events she knew to be authentic—would, if not played out correctly, shift time itself. Many would not live, others would never be born, and the future could be altered. She was not creating a better or different world, but ensuring the existing one stayed intact. The domino effect of an alternative timeline had to be stopped—and soon.

Silver Moon had considered this for many years. As a young maiden, she had foreshadowing abilities and knowledge she kept to herself. She watched, worried about having enough time to do what had to be done. If she failed, those alive today—including herself—might never have existed. Completing this task would also free her and Soft Dove, ensuring life would continue as it should. A new traveler in time for the Sioux was foretold to emerge, keeping history on its proper path.

P ayton and Kanda arrived, followed in an old, beat-up black Chevy truck by Eli 'Two Suns' Harris.

"Ma-nah-hoo," Eli called out, a friendly Paiute greeting. Meda rose with a smile, one she never thought she'd have for this man.

"Good to see you, Two Suns."

The history between them had been strained for years upon his arrival in North Dakota. It was odd that he'd ended up so far from his people in Western Nevada. His distant relatives had traveled here long ago, seeking a new life among the Sioux. These ancestors had married Sioux maidens and chosen to stay, spreading family ties across the country. Eventually, he reached out to Meda, and their friendship grew over days of talking about the Old World and traditions. Forty years later, they were bound by heart and spirit.

"I'm glad to be here, Soft Dove, my wise friend." He bent, kissing her cheek, then turned to the other woman. "Silver Moon, so good to see you."

"You too, Waha'yoo Taba," Silver Moon said, using his Paiute name meaning Two Suns.

"You remember Paytah and his bride, Wakanda?" Meda asked, standing beside Blackie Kangee.

"Ah, yes, I do." Eli smiled, nodding to everyone else, mentally taking roll. "Who are we waiting on?"

"Henry Cooper. He'll be here soon," Pete supplied.

"It's always the Whiteman—last to arrive!" They laughed, as they often did. Their private joke: the Whites were always last, but there were no grudges between tribes or men.

Henry Cooper was well-liked and considered part of the family. A direct descendant of a man who had helped free Chief Black Raven, Cooper's ancestor was invited to live among the Sioux and take a Sioux bride, cementing his place in the Sioux family tree.

"**H**ere he comes," Sam said, pointing. Dust kicked up as the wheels of Cooper's jeep flew down the dirt road and swung into the gravel drive.

Despite being fifty-five, Cooper was still a handsome man, defying his age. His blue eyes shone with life, his light-brown skin bore the marks of both Whiteman and Sioux heritage, and his dark hair was streaked with silver. Though his nose was slightly stubby for a Native American, his high cheekbones, and firm jawline made him striking. Tall and energetic, Cooper had military ancestors, including Dragoons and the first Cavalry. His grandfather had saved a Siouan chief, and Cooper's admiration for Native Americans—especially the Sioux—was deep and enduring.

He hurried from the truck to the porch where everyone waited.

"Sorry I'm late. Had a flat tire on the way and had to go to the...well, y'all don't need to hear that," he said, out of breath.

Silver Moon stood as Blackie helped steady her. "Nice to see you again, Cooper. Now we can begin."

10

In a Reversing World

Explaining the basic processed foods had been fun—or not so fun. It made me happy when Kingfisher allowed the woman to try the peanut butter crackers. She smiled, nodding at him as she chewed. The bottled water wouldn't last, but the looks on the faces of the two Cheyenne had been priceless. Chay enjoyed the rigmarole I went through to explain everything, and in Lakota, which was some feat. Most things we'd brought had no Lakota translation, so I struggled to create a word equivalent for Kingfisher to comprehend. My assumption was he'd given in, as the hour had grown late and his poor pregnant woman was hungry and tired.

"After they're fed and bedded down, we should talk about your book, or whatever it is we need to discuss, so I can understand what's happening," Chay reminded me for the millionth time.

"Bedded down? I'm not their mother, geezer, Chay. They're adults. They'll sleep when they want and where they want. Besides, I don't know if I can interrupt these books." His whining was exasperating me. Also, I wasn't sure how my brain would function without some needed sleep. I loved my cousin, but I was ready for him to shut up. "It's not like there's an instruction manual explaining how to decipher these prophecies, or a key code."

"Eat, I think you're hangry, then let's talk." Chay shoved a granola bar my way and a bottle of warm water, and I gladly accepted, telling him to eat too. At least if he was eating, his mouth would be full, and he'd stop yammering questions my way.

S he Who Sees Truth slept. Kingfisher sat near his sleeping wife, covered in a blanket, and it didn't appear he'd sleep, but I understood and told him in Lakota he had nothing to fear with Chay or me. He nodded; however, he didn't sleep right away.

We took a spot and got as comfortable as possible on the dirt floor with straw padding as our mattress. Chay sat, leaning his back against the old plank wall, me next to him, and we covered our legs and feet with a light down blanket I'd packed in one of our saddlebags. My butt hurt from the hard floor, but I was just going to endure.

"I can't believe this is happening. Are we living a nightmare?"

"Keep your voice down." I looked over at our visitors, who slept like logs on the dirt floor, unbothered by the lack of creature comforts we took for granted in our future.

Chay pointed the penlight at the books I held on my lap, the Book of Reveries and Chief Black Raven's journal. I skimmed through the pages, unsure of what I was looking for.

"Here. This might be what I'm looking for. There are passages here about a baby called Morning Star, born to a wandering couple. At least I think it means wandering. Right here it says," I showed Chay. "They have headed home, amidst perils and lost from the others, and the blackbird shall lead them home."

"First, I can't speak Lakota. Second, I can't read it either. And how in the heck can you make any sense out of that? That... that... what is that?" He jabbed his finger on the page I was reading. "Hieroglyphics?"

My shoulders shook as I held in my laughter, and it took me a few seconds to compose myself before I spoke.

"Yes, hieroglyphics of sorts, crudely drawn. Aunt Meda has a shaky hand. She's what, over eighty? And—" I stopped talking while my eyes scanned the page. "What's this? It's dated. Forty years ago, so nope, it's not because of her age; she would have been in her forties. Ain't the reason it's shaky." Thinking back to something my aunt said about her book, it clicked.

"Chay, she was in a trance when she drew this. That's why it's all fuzzy, shaky, or whatever. She told me peyote induced her visions, but they were true visions. Also, a lot of her visions had already happened before she had them."

"Your aunt does drugs?"

"Come on, Chay, no, she doesn't. Back in the day, that's how visions occurred. They sat by a campfire to inhale the fumes of the peyote." I snickered and then grew serious. "They did this in a way that hypnotized a person, I think. It was how she foreshadowed certain events—not all the time, but sometimes. She had a lot of actual revelations which weren't peyote-induced. See?" I showed the clear and detailed drawings on the pages where she wrote her visualizations and events which either happened or were yet to occur.

"You need to get into one of those books and find the spell they used to give your mom the uncanny ability to suddenly understand and speak Lakota. I need this, and soon."

I nodded because deep within, I knew this was vital in case time were to separate us. The prospect of me not being there for Chay was a concern. I needed to make sure he could handle any situation. I knew he could, as long as he could communicate.

We searched until neither of us could focus, me on the words and him on the pictures.

"Chay, we have to rest. We don't have any clue what tomorrow will bring." I yawned.

As if on cue, he yawned too.

"So, what do we know so far?" He slid down, resting his head on a backpack.

I blew out a long sigh. "Not a lot. I think I'm here to help these two. I'm uncertain how, but I've got a sneaky suspicion I'm going to become a midwife in the future—or shall I refer to it as the past? In the book it says a blackbird will help them. My name's Raven, and since a raven is a blackbird, my guess is it'd be me. This can't be a coincidence, can it? This unborn Cheyenne baby is a key point here. The name Morning Star could be a boy or a girl. We're going to find out the gender soon. Until we know more, we'll help them get back to the Montana border."

"Is that all? Shoot. I thought we'd be challenged," Chay groused, then looked at his wristwatch. "Has the time change happened, ya think?"

"Oh, yeah, I'm sure the time has changed." I held in my giggles, said good night, and closed my eyes. With a grin on my lips, I dreamed about the birth of a baby boy.

11

Same Day, Present Time

They sat in lawn chairs, in a circle near the rear of the house. The campfire blazed. Although it was a sunny day, the campfire was symbolic for them. It was time to put ancient histories, stories of wars, and past transgressions between any or all of the represented tribes behind them and work together—a feat they could do knowing it blessed them to be chosen for this new world and its powerful enchantment.

"He will need this magic if he's to help her," Kanda said.

Meda held the circle-within-the-circle charm. "Have you wondered why Blaze and Dakota aren't present?"

Henry Cooper said, "I think I know, Miss Meda. Shall I enlighten them?"

Her brows lifted into her wrinkled forehead. What did he know the others hadn't figured out?

"Yes, Mr. Cooper, please."

"It's Henry or Hank, Miss Meda, you know that," he laughed. "Mr. Cooper was my daddy."

"Of course, Henry it is then, and I'm rather curious to see if you know."

He cleared his throat. "I know my granddad's stories and his granddad's stories, so I would imagine, for reasons I can't fathom, they aren't here because they're back in the past where they first met, on the prairie sometime in the early 1800s. What I don't know is why. I was hoping to get this story today. Am I right?"

Silver Moon's laughter bubbled from her throat, and she looked at Cooper with eyes that twinkled.

"You're right, Henry. Now please enlighten the others how you came about this knowledge," Silver Moon prodded him. She knew how he knew, and when the others learned, it would be a shock—especially to Meda.

Henry sat, his hands lying in his lap. He leaned forward, his head bent as he pondered his next words. His eyes went from face to face, landing on Meda Clark. Then he said, "Because I dreamed it."

Meda let out a deep gasp, and her jaw dropped open. She stared at him. It was true—not just tales she'd heard—and Cooper had the gift of prophecy.

His face beamed, and he blushed. "Silver Moon knows, because when it began it scared me, so I went to her, and she told me the story and explained it's part of who I am."

"Why have you not told me?" Meda asked.

His glance darted to Silver Moon, who spoke. "I instructed him to keep this between him and me until this day arrived." She looked at her dear friend. "It was hard to keep this from you, since you know things too."

"And may I ask the reason I couldn't know?"

Everyone looked from Meda to Silver Moon, anticipating her explanation.

The older woman's shoulders lifted and then dropped. "No reason except to see the shock on your face, my Sioux Spirit sister," Silver Moon said. "It's rare to see you shocked or surprised."

Meda huffed, crossing her arms, then rolling her eyes, and said, "Good. You have your laugh. Can we get back to why we're here?"

"Don't be mad, Miss Meda. You're still the vision queen," Hank Cooper remarked.

The others kept their chuckles down to a low roar, and Meda was soon laughing with them.

"Henry, you and I will have to talk in depth one day," Meda said.

"Some of my visions I can't tell you about, if you know what I mean." His brows wiggled, and he had everyone in stitches again.

"Tsk-tsk," Meda clicked her tongue. "You're shameful, Henry Cooper, just shameful."

Silver Moon clapped her hands to get their attention again. "You may know the story, but I'm going to tell it again—the story of Henry's ancestor and his role in our tribe."

Without further ado, they sat back to listen to Silver Moon, a fabulous storyteller, one who knew more undocumented history of the Sioux Tribe than any living soul.

The Story of Hank Cooper's Ancestors as Documented by Silver Moon

"T. H. Cooper, a Whiteman who lived with Chief Black Raven's tribe, was an unusual man. When She Cougar traveled those many years back to live with the Sioux, she'd been unaware Maka, Swift Eagle's wife, had a younger sister named Ehawee, meaning Laughing Maiden. Four moons before we sent Dakota back using the spells written by the old chief, Ehawee and a group of women were at the creek filling water containers when a group of Pawnee men came upon them. They abducted Laughing Maiden and one other maiden by the name of She Who Sits, and by pure luck the others were able to flee.

The tribe assumed Laughing Maiden and She Who Sits were dead, or worse, captives of the Pawnee. Maka never told She Cougar the story. To speak of the dead would be impolite. And so, the chief had another daughter you might not have known about. The chief was heartbroken but refused to retaliate and call an act of war on the Pawnee. His command was no more loss of life. Two moons later, the chief got captured by renegade Dragoons, where he continued to grieve in deep silence. And you all know the story of Blaze and Dakota, so I will bypass that.

Now, a full moon after Dakota returned home into our world, Sioux men scouting the area found Laughing Maiden alone on the prairie. These Sioux men carried Ehawee back to camp. Poor child—the Pawnee beat her, and no telling what else the poor thing endured. Near death, this devastated her older sister, Maka.

Even though Laughing Maiden survived, she was fearful of men, even those in her tribe. It mattered not, because the males who had tried to woo her before her abduction no longer desired her as a bride. As a good older sister, Maka took her into their home to protect her, but her sister was no longer the Laughing Maiden she'd been."

Silver Moon looked at Henry. "The Whiteman they called Cooper felt bad for her and befriended her. Their friendship blossomed into a romance—one to beat all romances in the tribe. They were allowed a tribal marriage with Chief Black Raven, thus joining Cooper to the tribe by blood ties, and I might add, these were tribal chief blood ties."

"My ancestral great-grandfather Cooper from long ago was a lucky man," Henry interjected.

The others murmured, all agreeing, and then Silver Moon proceeded with her story.

"Cooper and Laughing Maiden had four children. Three of them lived—two boys, Fire Starter and Beaver Claw, and a daughter whom they called Wild Rose. Their fourth child didn't live past five moons. Her name had been Butterfly. Wild Rose married, joining Dark Cloud's son in marriage, and Fire Starter married a Sioux maiden called Ee'-ay-E-hahivbee. Ee'-ay-E-hahivbee means She Dreams, and although never given the title of Prophetess, she was one no matter what. Her visions befell greatness and did many things for our tribe. It was uncanny, as the chief had penned: Ee'-ay-E-hahivbee had visions stronger than his own daughter, Maka, who by all rights was deemed a true Prophetess by their clan."

Everybody nodded, for they all knew of Maka's magnificent stories, including the ones told by Blaze 'She Cougar' Clark Kangee, mother of Raven, who had traveled back to make certain the Sioux legacy continued in Chief Sitting Bull's line.

Silver Moon went on with the story. "Henry comes from that family line. The truth is it began with Laughing Maiden after her abduction; this drastic occurrence in her life brought about her abilities. At first, her nightmares scared anyone she told them to. After the nightmares subsided, she foresaw things about their enemies—not terrifying dreams, but visions about how to defeat them or how to avoid a war. Her dreams changed several times to visions of people in the tribe, to those not part of the Sioux. After a period of several moons, Laughing Maiden changed her name and became Ee'-ay-E-hahivbee Mai'Pay, meaning She Dreams Deep."

Again, Silver Moon looked at Cooper. "You have had this greatness passed on to you, and if I recall, something traumatic happened in your life, then your reveries began. Is this true?"

With a tiny wry smile, he nodded. "It began when I lost my wife, Shirley, five years ago."

"Then you're one in the spirit with us." Meda now understood more about why Henry Cooper would be with them on this important passage.

Meda held up the charm of two circles again. "These circles which cross, overlapping one another, signify our past, present, and future. One over the other, over and over and over, meaning you couldn't have a future without a past, a present without a future, and if we have no past, then we have nothing."

12

Back as Time Changed and Reversed

I was awake and restless. Careful not to wake Chay, Kingfisher, or She Who Sees Truth, I grabbed the old journal and the dream book. Then I snuck out to the rear of the cowshed and found a clump of bushes so I could turn on the penlight we'd been using earlier. Lord knew it pleased me to have a few creature comforts from my era. What I feared was that everything was changing—and what if everything we'd brought into this time warp disappeared? I needed to keep those thoughts at bay and dig into this book for answers. Why hadn't Meda, my mom, or Silver Moon spent more time with me discussing or at least warning me about all of this? I was sure they knew, and it miffed me.

As I thumbed through the pages, hoping something—a word, a phrase, even perhaps a picture—would jump into my brain and tell me something, I grew discouraged. It wasn't until the desperate third thumb-through that I saw it. I'd just missed it.

Aunt Meda had drawn two spheres, one semi-overlapping the other, like two rings lying side by side but stacked on top of each other, almost not touching, and a line that dangled down and then back up from each circle, like a chain. Auntie Meda's charm looked, to some degree, like my mother's charm and a bit like mine, but the three had slight differences.

I recalled the day I received my charm from my mother, Blaze.

"Wear it always," my mother said.

She handed it to me. I took it, holding up the long, thin silver chain. Attached were two circles, one laying by a hair's breadth on top of the other—one for the past and one for the future, she'd told me.

"But, Mom, it is so special to you. I can't take it, really. This is the one Aunt Meda gave you. You need to keep it," I'd protested.

"Honey, I have mine. It's right here." She lifted it by the chain and showed me her talisman.

"Then what's this, a replica?" I had trouble keeping the disappointment out of my voice.

"No, my sweet daughter, it's not a replica. It's one of a kind, too." She hugged me. "This is even more special. When I spent time with Silver Moon, before I knew I was pregnant with you, she'd given hers to me. She told me one day I'd have a daughter, and here you are."

I studied both talismans and found the differences. Aunt Meda's was a circle inside a circle—the inner loop represented the past, and the larger outer ring represented the future, meaning the future would always swallow up the past. My mother's was two round spheres lapping over one another like two rings hooked together, meaning the past and the future were connected, as you couldn't have one without the other.

I lifted the long silver chain from under the collar of my T-shirt, and at the end dangled my special charm. Two circles, but different from my mother's—and I hadn't noticed the differences before. Mine was a tad bigger than my mother's. Still two loops, though. However, I hadn't seen the two tiny—very tiny—spheres lapping over the bottom and top parts of where the two silver rings crossed each other. It was hard to describe as I sat staring at it, laying in the palm of my hand.

The overlapping areas of each larger sphere again overlapped at the middle of the cross points. This point formed an X in the center of the larger circles, top and bottom. The two tiny discs held the larger loops together. My mother explained that the past and the present would always touch. But then future events would hold them in place, change them, or obliterate them if time gave it a way to do so.

Those two petite, thin discs representing future events were my destiny—one I'd been born for—and it would come to pass one day, Silver Moon told me when I was fifteen. Well, one day was here. Deep down, I knew I wasn't as well prepared as I felt I should've been. The charm of my destiny lay in my palm as I looked at the skies.

P resent World, Early Morning Before Raven's World Began Reversing

They sat, all of them, around a roaring campfire, and Meda Clark chanted, as did the rest, all in their own native languages.

Somewhere in the past, under a large tree on a hill, Blaze, wearing her magical necklace underneath her buckskin dress, stood with Dakota just before the loud clap of thunder struck, giving her the mysterious ability to understand Lakota but not speak it. Even further back in time sat Raven, who held her charm of past and present, connected to change or destruction—each woman waiting on the mystical plan of Chief Black Raven.

The thunder clapped, and Dakota and Blaze looked up to the sky. Meda, Silver Moon, and the others gathered also looked up as the skies grew dark and the campfire glowed brighter. Then the darkness lifted, and the fire dimmed.

I felt a slight shudder—or I'd shuddered. I wasn't sure. When I looked up into the sky, two very opulent, very distinctive stars were spinning in the heavens like balls of kaleidoscopic white fire. Shaking my head, I held the charm between my forefinger and thumb.

"Wichahpi angeni, Star Spirit."

The words slipped from my lips in Lakota. Yes, this was it—the sign I'd searched for.

13

Present Time

The campfire dwindled, the embers burning down to a dim glow as no one stoked the fire, letting it burn off, and the chanting had stopped.

"It has happened," Yellow Wolf spoke.

"Meda, do you think it worked?" Blackie asked, hesitant to doubt—but who was to say it worked as it had before?

Silver Moon spoke, "Yes. Don't forget Blaze is there now. We've heard her accounts in her own voice. So yes, it worked as it did twenty-four years ago, and we know She Cougar and Wind Dancer's history. Remember." She pointed to herself. "This old woman knows, so do not doubt."

"Miss Silver Moon, how old are you?" Hank asked, drawing the evil eye from the others.

Silver Moon's lips curled in a secretive smile. "One day I shall tell, but not today. Come. We have other work to do before nightfall."

Sam poked Hank in the ribs. "You're one daring man, white or not, asking a woman her age."

Henry Cooper gave a weak shoulder shrug. "You don't ask, you don't get an answer. You ask, and someone could tell ya it ain't any of your business. Can't hurt asking, I always say."

Sam expressed his amusement. So did Blackie and Pete, who were of the same mind. However, none were as brazen as the Whiteman called Henry Cooper.

They'd had a successful night, and spirits were high when the fire died away to ash.

Two days later, magic occurred, and the past was re-lived.

———

C hay woke, his shoulders sore and his back aching like an old arthritic man. He stood, stretching his neck left and right, then rolling it from front to back. He lifted his arms, stretching them as high as he could until he heard a pop. Well, he thought. One kink; he had about a hundred to go.

He looked over where they slept and saw Kingfisher standing, spear in hand. She Who Sees Truth was gone, and Chay figured she was outside. He gave Kingfisher the up-and-down once-over, and it pissed him off. Kingfisher looked rested—not an aching bone in his body.

"Oh, you're awake, good. Listen, I was outside last night, looking through the book, and..." I stopped talking and poked at him. "Hey, I need your attention here, okay?"

"How long has She Who Sees Truth been gone?"

"Wh-wha-what did you say?"

"I asked you how long She Who Sees Truth has been gone."

"Chay, do you realize you just spoke to me in Lakota?"

It dumbfounded me when Kingfisher responded. "She be back soon, walked to stream to wash."

"Good, just wondering," Chay said, and Kingfisher looked at him, a question mark on his face. "How do you speak Lakota today, but not yesterday?"

I wanted to know, too, and was just about to ask when I remembered the two shining stars from last night and lifted my chain from beneath my T-shirt. "This," I said in Lakota. "The chief's magic." I looked at Chay and in Lakota said, "And with the aid of Aunt Meda and Silver Moon."

"Well, snap!" This time, he spoke in English. "I understood every word you just said!"

I lifted my eyes toward the ceiling and almost wanted to shed happy tears. "Oh, philamayaye Wichahpi angeni," was all I said.

Kingfisher and Chay looked at each other, then at me.

"Why you thank Spirit of Stars?" Kingfisher asked.

Just then, She Who Sees Truth walked in, her face distorted in fear, and in rapid Cheyenne told her husband they must leave—and leave now!

Kingfisher took up his spear and made to leave, but his wife stopped him, her hand on her swollen belly. She cried that their baby needed a father, and she wouldn't let him leave her with these two unattended.

Chay, now fluent in Lakota without explanation, only caught bits and pieces of the rapid-fire Cheyenne, so I explained and then turned to She Who Sees Truth.

"What is the matter? Tell me, please. We will help; I swear to the Sun Gods we will."

"Whitemen come. They bring guns, and more come with them, but not Cheyenne, not Sioux. Our enemy, the Crow, comes with many men." She looked at her husband. "They hunt for us, and the rest of the tribe."

No time for a history lesson. Not if their mutual enemy, the Crow, was coming from one direction and the whites from another. We'd get massacred. I knew this wasn't supposed to happen.

Without talking, we gathered our knapsacks and gear, got everything loaded and tied on the horses, and in less than fifteen minutes were riding away, headed southwest, around the backside of the Paha Sapa, the Black Hills, southwesterly, as Kingfisher allowed Chay—now his equal as Star Gazer—to guide them out. True to his name, Star Gazer led us through a wooded area, the trees and shadows our only cover.

We rode for what seemed like miles before reaching a river called Minne Sosa, meaning Muddy Waters in Lakota. From there we'd proceed along the muddy embankment, horses stepping through the water, Kingfisher instructed.

"Horse's feet in water, no horse tracks. Brilliant idea," Chay said.

"Star Gazer do fine job. Now I lead past river," Kingfisher acknowledged Chay with admiration this time, without loathing. I was relieved. We were now a team of four, no longer two against two.

"Ahem." Chay cleared his throat and then addressed Kingfisher as he rode up beside him.

"Le mita pila le mita cola Wo'glak a Lakota, Ee'-yay Cheyenne. (My thanks, my friend, to talk Lakota, and not Cheyenne)," he said, with the voice of someone who was proud.

Chay was proud of his Sioux heritage, but he hadn't embraced it as I had. I'd never held grudges against anyone, White or Native American, but inside me was an Old-World soul. Chay never felt the same way. My being conceived in a time forgotten and born in this century was why I had such old, deep traditional feelings. I had been told countless times I was an old soul.

"Humph," he grunted, nodding. "Kola, tany'an yah ksto yelo." (Friend, good you came.)

Star Gazer fell back, letting Kingfisher take the lead—happy to have an ally in this magnificent Cheyenne.

"Chay, I need to stop calling you Chay, and start calling you Star Gazer," I remarked when his horse fell into step with mine.

"You do, and I won't ever speak to you again." He beamed, happy with today's new outcome. "You know, Rave, being able to communicate with them is fantastic, and if—I mean a big if—we make it home, I trust it sticks like it did with your mom. She can still understand and speak Lakota, and I hope I do, too."

"Me too, Chay. Me, too." It'd stick. I knew this much, but getting home—well, this was an uncertainty in my head.

As far as we could tell, no one followed. But we stayed on high alert. The Muddy Waters River was just a trickle of water ending at the base of a small dried-up water hole. Chay looked around and then rode up to Kingfisher to discuss directions, while I sat next to She Who Sees Truth.

"You are well. Can I help with anything?" I asked the poor girl. It hadn't occurred to me until then, but she was from this era, used to hardships. I wondered how one survived pregnancy in ordeals such as this.

"I'm fine, but need to have a private moment." She blushed. This was personal information she hadn't wanted to share with me, a virtual stranger.

Turning her pony, she headed to a very low but thick area of brush and gingerly dismounted, tied her reins to the brush, then disappeared behind the clump to void.

I looked over at Chay and Kingfisher, who noted his wife's departure, and his eyes stayed glued to the brush where she squatted. Seeing this warmed my heart. I hoped one day to find someone like him.

She Who Sees Truth came back feeling better, smiling. I saw how beautiful the smile made her face—albeit puffy from being with child—but she radiated from impending motherhood. Her eyes were a soft brown, with black flakes making them appear the color of a leopard's skin. Her hair, jet-black, long, hung in two braids reaching past the middle of her back. The braids, tied with leather strips adorned with some type of shell and beads—the same as those Kingfisher had dangling from his leather belt strap. I wondered where the beads came from—a trade with a Whiteman, one who had been friendly. Not knowing what year we were in, or if trading posts were around, or if the Whites and Indians had a few amicable meetings.

"How did you come to be named She Who Sees Truth?" I asked.

She thought about this before answering.

"First, they called me Kishori, Young Girl. To me this means I knew nothing, as a young girl knows nothing, and I didn't like it. Then I saw truth in the ways of the older women, who understand the man more than most. I was the only girl child in my family. So I learned from men I needed to be tough. My mother died. I was only five moons old, raised by my aunt, who," she hooted, "was more man than some in our tribe. When I saw what I felt was right, I spoke out. Aunt no longer thought the name Young Girl fit and said I was old spirit; I always saw the truth. She renamed me, She Who Sees Truth."

"What do you see now? Do you see a future?" I asked, not expecting the explanation she gave me.

"No, I don't see visions; I see truth in those around me. You're true, and you're who you say you are. I don't understand this magic you have, which is strong; I have heard stories but cannot, in truth, say I understand. A vision came to me one moon ago. I've told no one." She looked at me, and something flitted in her eyes. It appeared to be a deep sorrow, so deep I felt a chill sweep through me.

"You cannot speak of this to Kingfisher, I beg you."

I nodded. "No, I'll let it lie here with me, once you have spoken." I pointed to my heart. Whatever She Who Sees Truth was about to say was the reason I was here.

"You will care for my baby. I envisioned a beautiful blackbird come as my birthing time drew near, and my baby needed protecting. The blackbird swooped in to make sure my baby was safe to live to be an important man. You, you're Raven, another word for Blackbird, and you're a handsome woman, one with a smile of beauty and eyes with compassion."

Shocked and speechless at what she'd just revealed—while flattered by the compliments—it scared me senseless to think this woman thought I would care for her baby. Where in the heck would She Who Sees Truth be?

"You are mother, you will care for baby; I'll be glad to help," I voiced.

She shook her head, her eyes filled with an almost physical sorrow. "No, I go to spirit world when baby comes, see baby short time, and then spirits must take me. This prediction comes three times since the last full moon. I see truth and accept what the spirits wish. Nothing else I can do."

I wouldn't accept this as truth, but neither of us had a real say. The future, or past, would happen. I knew some things were unchangeable, no matter how hard I might've tried to make them right.

14

"The darkness will come soon. Stop, eat, and rest. We start again very early." Kingfisher took charge of the group.

Chay agreed. Not only was he hungry, his rear end was aching. Neither of us had ridden like that in years. I conceded, knowing She Who Sees Truth needed to rest. She looked exhausted.

Chay pointed at a thick grove of short trees. "There's a decent place. We'll have cover and a stream. We can tie our horses nearby."

The tall Cheyenne nodded. "Is good," he said, sliding off his horse, taking the reins to She Who Sees Truth's mount, and leading them into the denser treed area. Kingfisher helped her off her mount and got her comfortable.

"Horses need water." And off he went, so we followed his lead.

The sun began its slow descent behind the small mountain range to our rear, and the night air set in.

"No fire," I said, pulling off a knapsack and digging in for food. When I pulled out a package of beef jerky, I stifled a laugh. Processed beef jerky would be different from buffalo jerky, and I hoped they would like it.

Kingfisher and She Who Sees Truth enjoyed the bottles of water. Even at the tepid temperature, the water tasted crisp and clean—not at all like the creek, stream, or lake waters they were used to drinking.

"No sediment," Chay said, taking a hard pull on his bottle.

"What is what you say? Sediment?" Kingfisher asked, chewing the beef jerky I'd given him, smiling with each bite.

I admitted Chay's command of the Lakota language was impressive. He had it down with all the accents in the right place and any guttural sounds, as I listened to him explain sediment to the Cheyenne man.

She Who Sees Truth, full of water and peanut butter crackers, lay down beside her sitting husband and fell fast asleep in minutes. I eyed her, thinking about the conversation we'd had, and prayed she made it through childbirth. I'd read about pioneer women dying in childbirth, and this scared the devil out of me. What would we do if she died on the trail? Would Kingfisher carry her body back? What would happen to the infant with no mother to feed it? For the first time since these strange happenings, I was petrified of what was to come.

———

We spent the day riding hard, then resting at night for brief spurts. At the break of dawn, Kingfisher had us up and not wasting any time. I saw the admiration Chay had for him—they'd formed a bond, talking as men do—and I was feeling left out.

"You and Kingfisher are getting along," I stated to Chay in English when the Cheyenne man went to guard She Who Sees Truth on her private moment. The woman's feet were swollen, as were her face and hands, and I worried; she didn't seem well at all.

"Yeah, I like him. For a man with zero schooling and book learning, he's smart. I misjudged him at first. Did you know they tell boys to stay away from girls early on so they can train and learn their skills? The others judge them on their horsemanship and fighting abilities. It's also imperative they're courageous. They must win the approval of the tribe as a warrior. Until a boy proves himself with his abilities, the higher chief won't allow him to take part in a buffalo hunt. I gotta say, it'd be so cool if I went on a buffalo hunt like my Uncle Dakota did. Even more interesting, at age seventeen, he's considered a man. After this is when they go out of the village and search for their guardian spirit. Even if the man never went into battle, he could still hunt for buffalo. And yeah, premarital sex is forbidden, and sometimes the guy must court the girl for years until he has enough horses and a satisfactory war record. Ridiculous, huh? He might not get married until he fights in a war!"

I couldn't help but smile. Chay was rambling a mile a minute, happy and enthusiastic, so I let the fact I felt left out alone. They hadn't left me out; I was here, wasn't I?

The minute I lay my head down, I was picking it right back up and we were traveling again. Keeping a very cautious eye on She Who Sees Truth, I'd become anxious and withdrawn, keeping my thoughts to myself. Chay noticed and called me on it at the next stop.

"Hey." His words were low and in English. "You okay? You're not acting like your usual self. What gives?"

His whispering got me tickled.

"Well, at least she still laughs. You want to tell me what's so funny?"

"You are, Chay, still whispering like they understand English."

"Oh, well, guess I forgot. Anyway, what's up with you? You've been as nervous as a cat and quiet as a church mouse. What gives?"

I struggled for a minute, deciding I had to trust him because I couldn't bear this alone. At least he'd be there for me psychologically, since this was all I'd expected of him.

"Chay, She Who Sees Truth thinks she's going to die after the birth of the baby, and she says I'm here to save her baby and get it back to their tribe. I just can't do this. I mean, I can help her, but I can't care for a newborn. That's crazy. And I don't want her to die."

My eyes filled with large unshed tears, and when I blinked, they trickled down my cheeks. I swiped them away so the woman wouldn't see me weep.

"I can't let her see me cry because she'll know I told you. Listen, has Kingfisher mentioned how close we are to their winter camp?"

"We haven't discussed it, but I can ask. See if he wants to go with me to scout the area for tomorrow's ride, then talk to him about the trail. Find out how far he thinks, while you girls set up camp?"

I put my hand on top of his before he got up to leave.

"Chay, you've been amazing, and in you, I've seen a Sioux man come to life. You're not the goofball I always thought you were. And, uh, thanks for being here and being my cousin and best friend."

"Love you too, cousin, and, uh..." He raised his eyes upward, stuck his tongue out, and said, "I'm still a goofball, just one who can speak and comprehend Lakota."

Then he let out the noise of a black crow and smiled. "For you, Raven Kangee, the Black Crow has called out."

A shiver shot up my spine. I knew, with that sound, my reason to be there was to save not just a new life with the impending baby to be born, but to make sure his mother made it back to raise him. How prophetic

Chay was—and without knowing it, all with the melody of a black crow, he had helped me see my destiny.

———

D ay six.

When night fell, we stopped to rest. Chay and I sat alone on the bank of a small creek. Exhausted from worrying about She Who Sees Truth, sleeping with one eye open all the time—meaning I never slept.

Chay stretched his neck and arched his tired back. He'd just returned with Kingfisher after they'd scouted the surrounding area.

"Kingfisher's an amazing tracker, Rave. Seen nothing like it," Chay said. "The man sees broken limbs, grass, or weeds pushed down by horse hoofs or men's feet. He can pick out the paw prints of a jackrabbit or a beaver. The best news is we are close. We're going to follow a river called Unzinzintka in Lakota and Heneneohee in Cheyenne. Cool, huh? Me learning his language?"

"Rosebud Creek is a river?" I remembered a history lesson about the Battle of Rosebud Creek. Although I wasn't sure what year, I knew Rosebud Creek was in Montana Territory. We'd been gone six days; I'd kept count. I doubted we'd been in the Dakotas when we met these two Cheyennes because it would've taken at least two weeks to go that distance.

"Yeah, guess so. That's what he said. It is about a half mile up to the mouth of it, so, guess we are really close, huh?"

"Raven, Star Gazer," Kingfisher's voice raised as he spoke in rapid Lakota. We turned, surprised because the man never yelled.

Scurrying, we headed to the campsite, Kingfisher gathering hides, then tossing our knapsacks on Sadie and Jumper.

"What's going on?" Chay followed Kingfisher's orders and began loading the packhorses at a frantic pace.

"Men, come. Not know if Indians or White, but know not far; go now!"

She Who Sees Truth was already mounted, her horse already moving. Kingfisher instructed her which way to ride, giving her a head start.

"It'll be dark soon; we ride up those hills, into the mountains. Come," Kingfisher beckoned. He mounted his pony, took hold of the packhorse's reins, and took off at a gallop, sending dirt flying as he did. We weren't about to question how he knew, so we followed.

The Cheyenne man led us out of the dense treed area and up a narrow path toward a small area of hills, leading us into a higher mountain range—a range I knew would be difficult to maneuver, especially in the dark.

Without mishap, we cleared the smaller mountain range and headed down. It felt like someone dropped the four of us between two mountains as we rode in a valley passing between a narrow and rocky area—but manageable, and safe to stop. Although the night was black, we'd been fortunate enough to have an almost full moon shining to light the way.

Kingfisher told us in a low voice we were in the mountain's spirit, so we made camp nestled in fir trees and evergreens near a rushing full stream fed by melted snowcaps.

"What mountains are these?" I watched ahead.

Kingfisher looked up in the darkness, the moon visible, and said in a hushed voice, "Nahkoe' Onene Hohohaeve`omenestse."

"Bear Tooth Mountain?"

"This stream." With a jerk of his head, he motioned behind us. "Part of Rosebud Creek. My people over the next mountain range." His words were in Cheyenne, but I understood him, which surprised me.

"What'd he say?" Chay asked me.

"He said the stream is part of Rosebud Creek. His tribe is on the other side of this next mountain range."

"Wait a second. You understood him?" Chay's eyes narrowed.

"Yes, and I didn't know I could either. Strange, isn't it?"

"Yeah, but not for you, dear cuz. Seems there's nothing you can't do."

I wasn't sure how he meant that. Was he mad or envious?

"Hey, give me a minute to talk to Kingfisher in Cheyenne. I need to test something."

Chay shrugged with apathy. "Hey, do what you need to do."

I spoke to the Cheyenne in his own tongue, and satisfied, I reverted to Lakota, thanking him so Chay could understand.

"So, more sorcery, I'm guessing? I mean, now you speak not only English and Lakota, but Cheyenne, too. How about that? I'll be Jack Sprat." Chay smiled—not seeming jealous, well, possibly just a tad.

Kingfisher then told us what happened, causing us to flee. He awaited She Who Sees Truth to get back from the bushes while he stood watch and saw one horse and rider in the distance. The rider was too far away, and the night falling meant he couldn't see well enough to know if it was his enemy and didn't want to chance it.

No one slept, except She Who Sees Truth. Carrying an unborn child took all the wind right out of her sails, and Chay was envious she slept so peacefully.

"Geesh, I'm gonna need a Rip Van Winkle nap once we're back in our own time. But funny, I'm tired but not tired, because, well, I think it's the adrenaline, you think?"

Yes, it had to be adrenaline. Otherwise, I could've joked and told him we'd set our clocks back too far. This had been something Chay had already joked about a few days ago—or was it just a few days ago?

15

The Second Ceremony, the Very Next Night, Present Time

Bud "Yellow Wolf" Parker took the lead, chanting in his native Cheyenne tongue. After three minutes, the others joined him. Yellow Wolf led them, and although the Sioux representatives outnumbered the others, no single voice drowned out another. The vocals blended in perfect harmony, sounding as one, synchronized, and breathtakingly beautiful.

Cherokee Dan Jones, Jon Little Bird of the Crow, and the Paiute, Eli Harris, each chanted in their native tongues. Every so often, an individual sound rose above the others, giving each man's voice a distinct quality as the chanting soared skyward.

Silver Moon, head bowed in prayer, chanted as she shook a paddle adorned with beads of varying lengths hanging from leather strands. The beads clacked against the thick wooden paddle, adding a percussive rhythm. Meda sat, head bent, chanting while holding the supernatural powers of two circles in one hand and shaking a rattle made from a turtle's shell filled with dried corn in the other.

Just past dusk, the campfire burned with intensity as the wind picked up. In the distance, the mountains seemed alive. Birds flew up and around, trees swayed with the wind, and if one had stopped to listen carefully, the sound of a flowing river could almost be heard.

As the group chanted, Wakanda, Paytah, Black Crow, Yellow Wolf, and Hank Cooper rose, never missing a beat, and danced around the campfire. They dipped and circled, hands raised, hands lowered, repeating their motions in perfect rhythm. The dance and songs, resurrected from the long ago past, fused past and present into one living moment. Enemy tribes and allies alike united in this ritual, creating the magic and the deeds the Sun Gods and Mother Earth demanded. Tonight, a miracle of two lives would occur.

I woke with a jolt, sweat on my brow, and inhaled as deeply as I could. My lungs felt drained.

"Holy cow!" I muttered under my breath, wiping my brow, trying to get my bearings and adjust my sight to the nighttime. I stood. What I needed was a walk to the stream to splash cool water on my face—but not alone. I carried my shotgun with me, then headed to check on the stilled horses first. I had to get a handle on this feeling of impending... whatever it was. Possibly doom? I didn't recall dreaming because I'd slept hard, though my subconscious might have shaken me awake.

I stood next to Gypsy, stroking her soft gray muzzle and cooing that things would be all right. A noise made me tense. I turned, afraid it was not a member of our group. Nothing. Just my imagination. Relieved, I returned to cooing to Gypsy, thankful the gods of time travel had allowed my precious mare to come with me. She comforted me with her familiar presence, and I also silently thanked the gods for Chay's presence.

My thoughts wandered until another bush shook nearby. I aimed the shotgun at the noise, thrilled the gun had made it into this era, yet hoping I wouldn't need to use it.

Moving as soundlessly as I could, I unlatched the safety catch, pulled the hammer back on my 12-gauge, and used the barrel to move the brush aside to see what—or who—was hiding.

She Who Sees Truth lay balled up under the brush, sweat soaking her face, teeth clenched, letting out a low guttural moan between pinched lips. I lowered the hammer, put the safety back on, and laid the shotgun on the ground.

"Your time is now?" I asked.

She nodded, holding back a scream as her body tensed in pain.

I panicked—but only for a fleeting second. I had to help. I was determined She Who Sees Truth would live—and live long enough to see her baby grow into adulthood.

I recalled every detail of childbirth I'd learned in Health and Biology class and from watching calves and foals born on the ranch. My mom had discussed birth with me once I was old enough to watch my first calf. At the time, I'd thought it was gross. Now I marveled at how miraculous birth was. My resolve strengthened: this baby would come into the world healthy, and She Who Sees Truth would survive.

Dragging her out of the brush, I got her as comfortable as possible. I ran back to the packhorses, retrieved a blanket, brought it back, and rolled her onto it. Then I hunted for a stick, washed it with creek water, and brought it to her.

"Bite down on this for your pains. If you yell and someone is tracking us, they will hear you. Understand?"

She bit down on the stick so hard I thought it would snap in half.

"I'll be back. I must tell Kingfisher and Star Gazer. If I need them, they must be near us, you understand?"

Her eyes grew wide, and she opened her mouth to speak—but a sudden contraction seized her. She bit down on the stick again, a low moan rising deep in her throat, her hand waving for me to stay.

I grabbed her hand, surprised at her strength. As she crushed my fingers, I almost needed a stick myself to chomp down on. Once the contraction ended, she held my hand fast and panted, giving me a moment to speak.

"No, no husband," she began—but another contraction gripped her, and again my fingers were held in a vice. Once it ended, she looked at me.

"No males to be here when baby is born. It is our way, please." Another contraction came. She panted.

I got her to release my hand. "I need to tell them, so if something happens, they will know. But they won't be here when the baby comes—just me and you, okay?"

She nodded, and just then another contraction began. By my calculations, they were three minutes apart. I needed to hurry.

———

Same Time in Present Day

The chanting intensified. The participants were so absorbed that even a gunshot or an earthquake would have gone unnoticed.

The campfire blazed as dancers revolved in a loop, one dancer after another, increasing the pace with fluid motion. Spirits of the past rose, spinning in a vortex of colors like the Northern Lights encircling them. Hues of every color surged upward, cloaking them as the flames grew red-hot, then colored smoke billowed skyward toward the gods of the moon.

As quickly as it began, it slowed. One by one, the dancers sat cross-legged in the lotus position, still chanting in hushed voices, leaving one dancer—Yellow Wolf of the Cheyenne Nation—dancing alone. He moved slowly, fluidly, heart and soul embodied by the spirits of life.

As the others stopped chanting, the paddle of beads and the turtle-shell shaker fell silent. Yellow Wolf's soft chant grew distant, until all that could be heard was a faint whisper. He stopped dancing, bowed his head, and became noiseless. The night was still, the embers faded, the wind unmoving, and the distant mountains quiet.

Each person was spent. Silver Moon breathed a heavy sigh.

"It is now out of our hands. We have given it to the gods of the moon and sun, and to the keepers of time. Wankan Tanka, of htalhen, Hechetu," she acknowledged in Lakota, entrusting it to the spirits of time. Translation: Great Spirit of Yesterday, so be it.

16

C hay would've laughed if this hadn't been such a serious matter. He watched Kingfisher pace between two short prickly bushes, like an expectant father. What was missing was a TV in a corner on the wall with other people, including medical staff going in and out of a room. A loudspeaker paging a doctor or a nurse to a nursing station or a room, a Mr. Coffee Maker on a sidebar with Styrofoam cups, canisters of creamer and sugar, and trash balled up with crushed cups and full ashtrays. He half expected to see a box of cigars clutched in Kingfisher's hands as he paced, ready to hand out the celebratory cigar after the baby arrived healthy and safe.

Kingfisher stopped pacing to glare at Chay, who had a stupid grin on his face. His half-worried, half-quizzical frown gave Chay a warning.

"Yes, time to be serious, but to celebrate. You bring a new life into your world, another life, and you're going to be a father. Are you not happy?" Chay asked.

He grunted, bobbing his head. "I thank the Gods, yes, but worry tribal women not here. Raven is alone and we travel. We need to return to the tribe before others catch up." Kingfisher was once again pensive, wondering what was happening behind the bushes with the woman called Wife and his unborn child.

———

S he was sweating, and her mouth was dry. I knew from old movies and words of wisdom from my smart mother that she could only have ice chips, nothing to drink. I had an idea, so I tore a piece of cloth from a thin blanket, dipped it into the stream—water from the ice caps of the mountains, colder than normal—wrung it out, and let She Who Sees

Truth suck on it for a minute, then swathed her sweat-laden face, cooling her off as much as I could.

The woman nodded her thanks and tried to smile, but a new hard and long contraction came, and she bit down on the wood, leaving her definitive teeth marks on it as she did so.

I lifted She Who Sees Truth's buck-skinned dress and saw her time was closer than I'd realized. My heart jumped into my throat, my pulse sped up, and I prepared myself for the onslaught of bringing a new life into this world and saving another. The head was coming out first. Relief washed over me, and I let out the breath I had been holding. Since I'd watched heifers in breech births, meaning buttock first, and the agony a cow was in, I had hoped this wasn't the case. I was sending up a prayer of gratitude she wasn't breech.

She Who Sees Truth pushed and pushed, but the head wouldn't budge. Not sure what to do, it occurred to me the woman could need leverage to push. In a rush, I grabbed blankets and the knapsacks. I made her roll one way then the other, getting them under her lower back.

"Okay, bear down, plant your feet and push as hard as you can," I said in her native Cheyenne tongue, "like you're squatting."

She Who Sees Truth took a deep breath. "You speak Cheyenne," her words panted; she pressed her lips together, holding in a scream using both hands to support her upper body and her weight, and pushed.

The head moved out as I pulled, rotating the baby's shoulders, and the rest followed. Then I dislodged anything in the baby's throat, mouth, and nose, making sure he was breathing. He whimpered. I was thanking the stars he hadn't cried out. I took a soft t-shirt I'd stuffed in my knapsack, wrapped the baby, laying it at She Who Sees Truth's breasts, cut the umbilical cord, pinching it off with a rubber hair tie, and ordered her to push again. She did, and I scraped it into a shallow hole, covering it, hoping wild animals would stay at bay until we were gone.

I thought I'd handled it well and had no time to consider how unsterile it all was. But again, this was how it was in this era. With stream water, I cleaned up the baby and the mother as best I could, then I fetched Kingfisher and Chay.

"You're hoksicala is a boy!" I called out.

"She Who Sees Truth is well?" Kingfisher asked as he brushed me aside to go to his wife and new baby son.

"Fantastic work, Rave, now you have midwife for humans, not just cattle to put on your resume, huh?" Chay hugged me, squeezing tight, then we followed, and Chay beamed as bright as the sun when he saw the baby and the new mother.

———

There was no time to waste. Traveling by horseback was not an option for She Who Sees Truth after birthing a child, so Kingfisher began making a travois. He explained to Chay how to help and how he'd hook it to his horse, allowing him to drag it behind, carrying mother and baby.

He was a lovely baby, not crying, just sleeping at his mother's breast, as she hummed. Kingfisher instructed Chay which trees to cut and strip, and gave me the duty of gathering strong reeds by the stream, then showed me how to weave them to make a hammock-type carrier.

"Must work fast, must leave soon," Kingfisher said.

About the time we'd connected the mat weaved from reeds to the tree poles, the baby began whimpering, and I went to check on them. She Who Sees Truth was asleep, so I shook her. The woman didn't move, so I shook her more aggressively, calling out her name, and she still didn't move. I panicked, feeling a pulse, and then raised her eyelids to see her pupils. Thank God she was alive, but unconscious. The only thing I could imagine was she'd lost too much blood, or perhaps she'd passed out from pain. Either way, somebody needed to tend to the baby, because his whimper turned into a full-fledged cry.

I snapped up the babe, bellowing for Chay.

"Bring me the purple backpack off Jumper, grab a bottle of water, and hurry!"

Chay ran toward Jumper, spooking him, and the horse stepped back, slipping on the mossy stream bank. Jumper's eyes grew wide in fear. Just as the horse lost his footing, Chay grabbed the reins, pulling hard, forcing the horse to scramble upward, his hooves clamoring against the flat rocks. He snorted and whined.

"Whoa, boy, I've got you, big fella," Chay calmed him, pulling the reins and leading Jumper to a flatter area, stroking his gray muzzle.

As I bounced the baby, trying to shush his cries, Chay tied the horse's reins to a bramble bush, jerked the smaller, red-flowered backpack off, grabbed a bottle of water from one saddlebag, and darted to me and the crying infant.

"What do you need me to do?" Chay exhaled, his breaths puffing out.

"Get powdered milk out of the knapsack, and—" I began.

He cut my words off. "Powdered milk, why would you—"

"Just do it!"

He brought the box over, and I instructed him to open and pour it into the bottle of water.

"Be careful, Chay. We don't want to waste any. Make the water milkier ... perfect. Now put the lid on. Now dig in the bottom of the purple bag. There's a pair of rubber gloves. Get one out, cut off the pinkie finger."

"Rubber gloves?"

"Don't ask questions." I shook the bottle, bouncing an unhappy baby. One worked as the powdered milk and water mixed; the other not so much, and the baby cried harder but muffled because I had him pressed to my breasts.

Chay got out a glove, took his pocketknife, and sliced off the pinkie finger. "What now?"

"Dig in the smaller pocket of the backpack, find the rubber bands, get me one."

"You brought rubber bands? Why?"

I huffed, exasperated. "Just do it and hurry, please."

He dug and found what I wanted.

"Here." I stopped when I realized he understood what I was aiming for.

Chay saw a safety pin attached to the flap of the smaller backpack. He pricked three tiny holes in the end of the rubber fingertip, then took the water bottle, uncapped it, put the end of the rubber pinkie on top, and wrapped the rubber band around the threads to hold on the makeshift nipple.

I took the bottle, shook it again, and tiny droplets of milky water spurted. I popped it into the baby's mouth, wiggling it around, giving the bottle a small squeeze, and once he got a taste, he suckled with vigor.

Kingfisher, working on the travois, noticed when his son stopped wailing and smiled at me. I smiled back.

"Hey, about the powdered milk and rubber gloves, how'd you know to bring them?" Chay asked, his heart rate lowering to about two hundred.

"I bagged up dry cereal, so hence the powdered milk. And the gloves," I snickered, "were in case I needed to touch something I might not want to touch."

"Yeah, okay, makes sense." Chay's brows dipped. "Rubber bands, though, why'd you bring them?"

"I grabbed them on an impulse from my mom's big junk drawer when we were gathering stuff."

"Huh, there are three things I'm thinking here, dear cousin. You're either very smart, lucky, or blessed by the gods," Chay remarked.

"I hope we are smart, lucky, and blessed, because we're gonna need all the karma we can get."

By dawn we'd completed the basket weave, lashing it to the travois, and hooking it to Kingfisher's extra packhorse. She Who Sees Truth lay unconscious, strapped in with the sleeping baby next to her bosom.

"Need to get to tribe. My woman need medicine man, and spirits to wake her," Kingfisher said. Determination laced his voice; nothing was going to stop him, nothing.

Chay took point, while Kingfisher rode center, his extra horse following him with the woman and infant pulled behind. I brought up the rear with our packhorses, Sadie and Jumper. The path was narrow and rocky as we rode out of the area, staying on the flattest land possible. My eyes on the travois, a rough, shaky ride carrying mother and child over hard rocky ground, which would've been painful for She Who Sees Truth, had she been conscious. As for the baby, it bounced him to sleep.

By midmorning we rode on less treacherous, softer, grassier land. We sped up our pace, and I moved to ride beside Kingfisher, letting Chay take up the rear with the packhorses.

"You name baby?" I asked.

Over his shoulder, he glanced back at his wife and infant son, his heart blessed.

"We will call him Wahiev, Morning Star, because baby born before the morning, under the stars. One day, my boy be a powerful man of our tribe," he said, crossing his right arm over his heart and thumping his fist.

I knew he'd be a famous chief once I heard what they were to name him. In history books, I'd already read about this child as a man. I'd just helped with the birth of a chief. Chief Morning Star, who, long from now, my Sioux tribe would call Chief Dull Knife. If memory served me, during a battle against the Sioux, Chief Morning Star tried to pierce through a buffalo hide shield of a Lakota warrior. Not able to put his knife through the hide and because of the incident, he'd acquired the name Dull Knife. The Sioux warriors had cried out in Lakota, *Tamela Pashme*, which translated to Dull Knife.

I decided this wasn't a story I should share with the father of the new infant called Morning Star but nodded. "Fine name for your hoksicala."

N ighttime fell. Even with a newborn baby, who slept without waking, calmness enveloped the night. I slept for the first time in days and dreamed.

Clouds swirled about in my sleep, and I felt like a feather floating high in a breeze, then swirling down again. In my slumbering visions, it carried me to places unknown, with faces of strangers going in and out of focus. Wisps of shadowy images and a few faces I recognized—my Aunt Meda and Silver Moon. Otherworldly specters hovered over me, and I could almost feel them touching me, soothing me, saying things would be alright.

A long, lonely trail formed in my vision, and people, some too tired to walk, fell, weak and crying, leaving the young, aging, and ill to perish. The days were hot and cold, the path treacherous, food and water sparse. Graves dotted the land as forced feet moved forward, day after day after day.

The weeping of souls caused me to jerk in my sleep, waking me. Not yet dawn. The moon overhead was all the light I had. Looking around, I saw Chay asleep. But no Cheyenne man called Kingfisher. No woman on a travois with a baby.

Getting up, I looked about and saw our horses—Gypsy, Moon Beam, Sadie, and Jumper—but nothing else. I did not want to wake up Chay, but I knew something wasn't right. The block of trees where we'd camped behind wasn't as thick, the mountain range not the same.

With a deep inhale, I gathered my courage and walked out of the thicket. The moon illuminated the land. I saw three horses, two riders in the far distance. As I stood in the moonlight, these figures rode into the daylight, and I reached out my hand; my fingers swept through a haze, like cobwebs. I knew what I saw wasn't real, but a vision in my head.

Then I watched as Kingfisher and She Who Sees Truth, with a bundle strapped to her back—the baby, Morning Star—rode away. In my peripherals, I saw other riders advancing on their flanks. Other Cheyenne had joined them. It was akin to watching a movie with the sound off. I heard no noise, no horse's hooves pounding the ground, no wind, nothing.

In a tranced state, I watched, knowing their people had come for them, and She Who Sees Truth would raise her child and have many more. Morning Star would survive, and he'd become who he was meant to be, fulfilling his destiny. A smile flitted on my face before I crumpled to the ground, passing out with a coldness sweeping me away.

17

C hay rode back toward us after scouting the intended destination.

"Smoke from campfires ahead, faint, ten miles or so. I can't gauge distance, sorry," he said with a shrug.

My heart quickened. I wanted to urge the horses forward, but the travois dragged behind, and the packhorses added weight. Help for She Who Sees Truth was so close, yet so far. Ten miles with a weighted travois and three packhorses would take another four or five hours. We'd already been riding at least seven, factoring in stops to clean the baby and feed him while his mother remained unconscious.

At each stop, I checked She Who Sees Truth, praying she wasn't bleeding inside. I had no medical training, and my concern for her outweighed all else. We needed her to reach the tribal woman, and I hoped they'd know what to do.

"We stop soon, rest horses, get water, care for baby, then camp," Kingfisher said, knowing we had to preserve our strength.

"Kingfisher, we must—" I began, but his raised hand silenced me.

"No. We go to the stream. You wash She Who Sees Truth's face, check her breathing, look over the child, give the horses water, rest. We move at first light."

I complied, shielding my eyes from the scorching midafternoon sun. Clouds were gathering behind us.

"Storm coming in behind us," Chay observed. "Find a windbreak and trees."

Kingfisher sniffed the air, scanning the land. He pointed to a small grove at the backside of a hill.

"Go there. Take horses, Black Bird, use trees for shade. Star Gazer, set up camp. I go hunt food." He vanished toward a rise, leaving Chay and me behind.

Chay turned to me. "I'm tired. My butt's worn down to a blister. Can your spell book tell us what's next?"

I smiled faintly. "I wish, but no. For now, I'll do as he asks: get She Who Sees Truth in shade, uncover her, wash her face, tend to Morning Star, then try to rest. Go gather firewood and come back. We haven't slept since night before last."

Chay huffed. "Jumping Jehoshaphat, alright, already, I will, I will!" He watched me disappear into the thicket.

The trees offered some shade, but it remained hot.

She Who Sees Truth didn't stir as I undid the leather straps and removed the blanket. I carefully lifted the sleeping baby from her chest, placing him on a hide from Kingfisher's packhorse. The infant was safe and covered; now I turned my attention to his mother.

Her brow glistened with sweat. I took water from the sack we carried and wiped her face, then felt her forehead—hot to the touch. She was feverish. I wrapped her in two more blankets, hoping to help her sweat it out.

Morning Star began to stir and whimper. I cooed softly, uncovering him, finding his plain white tee soiled. The infant needed cleaning. Kingfisher only camped near water, and I could hear a small brook beyond the thicket.

Checking the comatose woman, I grabbed a backpack and took Morning Star to the water.

I dunked the soiled tee, set it aside, and tore another with my teeth—balancing a baby and t-shirt in my hands.

I dipped the cloth into the water and bathed him. He shivered at the cool temperature but didn't cry.

"You are indeed a chief, tiny Morning Star. You will serve your tribe well. Wakan tana kici un, wee-chah' Thami'laphe'sni," I whispered in Lakota. "May the great spirit bless you, Chief Dull Knife."

I could've sworn he grinned. Either way, this tiny not-yet-chief warmed my heart.

I wrapped him in a large t-shirt from Chay's knapsack, chuckling at the faded words: Go Redskins, 1983 Super Bowl XVII Champs. If this wasn't an omen, I didn't know what was.

"Someone will see the smoke, won't they?" Chay worried about the campfire.

"No. Crow not follow. Cheyenne sacred burial ground not far—they fear it. Whiteman not follow. Safe now."

Chay relaxed and dozed off. I held the baby, rocking him as he slept. She Who Sees Truth remained unconscious but was no longer feverish. Wonderful news. Kingfisher lay beside his sleeping wife, eyes closed. The man had to be exhausted.

"Kingfisher's right, Chay," I whispered in English when he woke a few hours later. "We're safe. I feel my job here is ending."

"What's next? Go home? Does your dream book say anything?" He peeked at the sleeping baby.

"Don't know. My gut says my travels aren't finished."

"Well, I don't care for your gut. I'm tired. I hope we're done."

"Don't think we have any say."

"We or you? I'm not part of your destiny, but somehow you've sucked me into this crap." He closed his eyes.

Kingfisher woke, got up, bent over me, and peered at his son. I handed the baby to him.

"You are Morning Star, son of mine, son of She Who Sees Truth. You will be a valiant warrior one day." He handed him back to me and walked away.

"Where is he going?" Chay asked.

I shrugged. "Some things I just don't know."

Chay huffed, reclosing his eyes, and soon he was fast asleep.

18

"Wow, best night's sleep I've had since this ordeal started." Chay yawned, stretched, and rolled upright, noticing we were alone.

"Hey, She Who Sees Truth and the baby, where are they? Did she wake up? Does this mean she's going to be okay? Where are Kingfisher and their horses?" Chay rubbed his eyes, focusing on the obvious but missing the bigger picture.

"They're gone." I sat cross-legged next to a burned-out campfire.

"How? When? And man, Rave, why didn't you wake me so I could say goodbye?"

"Hey, I didn't get notice of their leaving either, so get your nose out of joint. Over there." I pointed.

Chay's eyes followed my finger and his jaw dropped.

"Uh, okay, who moved the mountains?"

"I would suspect we've left Kansas, Dorothy. Well, I don't know where we are. It's the only fact I do know."

Chay jumped up, scanning the area, bewildered.

"So, we've moved on while we slept? To another era still not our era, and you don't know where, when, or why, correct?"

Before I could reply, he repeated what he had just asked in Lakota.

"Whew, just checking." He let out a sigh. "Wanted to make sure I could still speak and understand the language. I have no idea how this time warp stuff works, just needed to make sure I didn't lose the new abilities I've acquired."

"Yeah, and who knows what new stuff we'll be adding to our repertoire of supernatural powers?" I said. It sounded funny, but I wasn't trying to be comical.

"Alright then, oh Mighty Oz. Where do you think we are, and what do we do now?"

"Chay, I was kind of hoping you'd know. Can Star Gazer come out and play? Tell us where we are, you know, be our guide?" My tone carried a touch of concern, something he'd never heard from me. This was his turn to be strong.

He paused, thinking. First, he told himself he needed to calm his cousin and be strong for her, as she'd always been for him.

"How about we dig in the knapsacks, get breakfast, and chill for a bit? We've been riding hard, and you've worried about the baby and She Who Sees Truth. Now it's time for you to rest."

I nodded, chewing on my index nail, my nervous habit, and Chay swatted it away.

"How about we eat granola bars and you stop eating your hand?"

"Yeah, sure. And boy, I'd love a Diet Pepsi."

"Here, how about diet water?" He handed me both a granola bar and a bottle of water.

Chay unwrapped a granola bar, hoping for a sign, or his intuition to kick in, or for Star Gazer to appear and save the day. He had to lead us, but he didn't know what to do next.

*

Present Day, The Night Before

The ceremony complete, the fire long burned out as they sat; no one wanted to leave the camp circle. Bud Yellow Wolf wiped the sweat from his brow.

"He's safe. And the gods have seen fit to keep She Who Sees Truth alive to raise him into the man he shall be. His father will teach him the ways of the warrior, to be a man who shall lead his people. Chief Dull Knife's legacy will continue to appear in the history books."

"It is as it should be, and the Cheyenne legacy will flourish; they saved your line, Yellow Wolf," Silver Moon said. "Wakanda, your Chay is strong-willed, and he has grown. I feel it in my soul."

"Thank you. I feel it, too." Wakanda stuck out her hand, clasping it with Paytah's, and she squeezed.

Meda put her hand to her chest, a pained look in her eyes. "My prophecies tell me certain things, and I feel tears forming in my heart."

Stories of the Trail of Tears—the Cherokee, Choctaw, Seminole, Chickasaw, and Creek Tribes—came to mind. Death, anguish, starvation, and illnesses almost destroyed each tribe.

Dan 'Dark Waters' Jones stood, addressing all of them. "The suffering our families endured made each tribal nation powerful today. Meda, as you have said, our past brings us to our present. Jon Ross was a remarkable man, called Guwisguwi, the Cherokee name for a large heron-like bird. Elected principal Chief of the Cherokee Nation, he resisted the Cherokee Removal Act until his death in 1866. We honor him today."

Meda nodded. "Therefore, we gather to ensure his legacy lives on."

*

Back to the Unknown

Water gone, granola eaten, I felt sick. Nothing in the books popped. Nothing made sense. I had no clue what to do next, where to go, or anything. I wondered if we were stuck in a time loop, never to return home. At least my mom had stayed in one place with one tribe, not tossed about the universe. My mood darkened.

"Glad the horses made it with us," Chay remarked.

I said nothing, sitting with my knees pulled up to my chin, staring into space.

"Fall colors, you think? I mean, it's not too cold, and feels like we're still in the mountains?"

"I don't know," I hummed.

Chay kept at it with questions, frying my last nerve.

"What do we do? Sit here and wait, or leave?"

I stood. "How do I know, Chay? I don't have a crystal ball! I don't know where we are, or what year, or what season!" I stomped my foot, turned, and walked off.

"You're a bit of a grouch in the morning, aren't you?"

"Give me a few more minutes, and I'll show you just how grouchy I can get," I called over my shoulder. Tears came—anger, fear, all rolled into one.

I checked my watch, wanting to scream or laugh. Straight-up twelve. Noon? Midnight? Who knew? Daylight was here, but back home, I had no clue. The watch was silent despite a new battery. Time wasn't my friend.

A massive boulder came into view. I walked toward it, finding a stream on the other side. The boulder was flat enough to lie on, so I curled up and drifted to sleep, dreaming as voices wafted into my ears.

" A h, she is in a soundless sleep."

        "She is fearless, like you."

"I wasn't fearless, Dakota. You were courageous while I was afraid."

His hand reached over, tucking her long hair behind an ear.

"For any woman from the modern era jettisoned into the eighteenth century to survive as you did, my She Cougar, is more than courageous. There's no other woman like you."

"Oh, yes, there is. She sleeps there, on the boulder we sat on, remember?"

His arm slung over her shoulder, pulling her closer, kissing her neck. "Yes, I remember. We must get back; we've seen our daughter's first trip, and we need to finish our quest so she may continue to exist."

Blaze leaned over her daughter's sleeping head, brushing lips against her hair. "Be safe, my love. See you in three centuries."

Dakota's lips touched her sleeping daughter's cheek. "Fulfill your destiny, my beautiful Black Bird."

———

T he wind blew, leaves rustled, and a branch cracked, waking me. I touched my cheek—wet and warm, as was my heart.

No longer afraid, a new power surged through me.

I sat up, stretching.

Downstream, I could've sworn I saw a man and woman walking side by side.

They faded from sight as if they'd never been.

19

My short trek to nowhere special renewed my spirit, and I walked back to where I'd left Chay and the four horses. No Chay. No four horses. The only proof I'd been in the right place were the two empty water bottles and the smashed granola wrappers.

I was alone. No one hiding behind a tree, no neighing of horses. My heart quickened, my vocal cords seized up. My gut told me shouting for Chay wasn't an option. Tons of what-ifs dashed through my brain. What if Chay was being held captive? What if he'd disappeared into another time dimension—or worse, was dead and some jackass had stolen our horses and supplies? Worst-case: Chay was playing a prank. That would be fine after I whipped his butt.

My foot tapped the ground as I thought, my nerves winding into knots. I had to wait this out, but not in the open. I gathered myself and almost screamed at my predicament, then decided against it—any sound would give an unseen enemy my location. A small clump of trees was to my right; I resolved it was safer to hide there. I urged my feet to move.

"This is ridiculous. I can't just sit here." Talking aloud to myself made it even sillier. If Chay was playing a prank, I'd look like a dummy just sitting there. "Use your head," I grumbled. "Think, what would Mom do?" I rolled my eyes, then told myself to stop talking and do something constructive.

Tracks. Search for tracks. Chay or the horses had to have left impressions. Wrong. No footprints, no hoof marks, no bent grass, no broken branches. Did Chay vanish into another realm? If so, and I caught up to him, we'd never separate again.

With lead-filled feet, I began walking, scanning the ground, the sky, left and right, focused on my surroundings. My feet were tired, but thankfully I'd worn hiking boots, or this rocky terrain would've beaten them up.

My stomach growled. I was hungry, thirsty, and dispirited. I followed the sound of what I believed was water flowing.

The books were gone. I hoped they were still in the backpack, in Chay's possession. Without them, I had no clue how to get out of this mess. I kept my eyes on the ground as I trudged along, thinking about what if I never found Chay or the horses—or never got home. Tears stung—not from fear, but sheer exasperation. I wiped them away, then missed a large tree limb. My toe hooked, and I stumbled, hitting the ground hard. My hands skidded through dirt and pebbles before my head smacked a rock. Lights out, again.

———

An ache pounded my right temple. My hand came up to feel a sizable knot. "Klutz," I muttered, standing and assessing my scraped, filthy hands. My nails were cracked and caked with dirt. Ugh. Once home—if home still existed—I'd deal with them.

I walked on, head throbbing, listening for the water I'd heard before. Any wetness on my lips or down my throat felt like salvation. I moved carefully, paying attention to the path and my surroundings. I wasn't alone, and I wasn't the last person on Earth.

Finally, I heard it: the rush of a waterfall. My dirty, aching feet welcomed the thought. Slow and careful, I pushed through a small stand of trees—and almost walked off the mountain!

"Holy moly! Whoa, girl!" I grabbed a tree limb. Terror gulped down my throat as I stepped back ten feet. The mountain stretched before me, breathtaking and scary all at once. The water roared below, pouring into a stream.

"Okay, now you need to climb down, since you must've been climbing up," I told myself. I turned back, and everything was different—the landscape, the sky, even the path. Funny, I didn't panic. Step by step, I moved, and then I raised the hem of my dress... Wait. I wasn't wearing a dress. Blue jeans—my favorite, worn, comfy pair.

Looking down, my hiking boots were gone, replaced by stiff, ugly shoes. I hung my head and saw an ugly brown dress, a white shirt tucked beneath it, and a wide sash at my waist. I reached behind me, feeling a fastener, like the catch on a satchel.

Lifting the hem a little more, I saw thick, muslin-colored stock-ings—pantaloons, or what I called "old granny's underwear." My shoes were stiff, wooden-heeled—not for hiking or modern life. Not the wide silver buckles, but thin, overlapping cloth stitched through each side. I wasn't a fashionista, but these looked like something from the Pilgrim era.

It all had to be a daydream. My head spun, the world blurred, and my eyes closed. "Oh, holy crap, not again," I muttered—and passed out, face-down, the world going dark once more.

20

"Raven. Raven, open your eyes."

The voice was faint; my ears strained to hear, but I dared not open them. I'd had enough surprises... or had I? Was this all a freaky nightmare?

A cold cloth lay against my forehead, and it felt wonderful. Cold and damp; my achy head stopped pounding so hard, and the pain subsided some. My lips were dry and cracked, my throat parched. I wanted a drink of fresh spring water. I had some, didn't I? In a saddlebag, on my mare, Gypsy—yes, I did. Oh, Gypsy, Jumper, my beauties... where had you floated off to? Did Chay float off with you? Was he on Moon Beam, riding in the north pasture dragging Sadie along?

"Chay, please, hemaca nuni, I'm lost; iyeye me, find me, oiykpaze, the darkness, please, I'm scared," I mumbled in Lakota and English.

With a cool, wet cloth, he caressed my face; my eyes stayed closed.

He looked at the lump on the side of my head, which was as big as a chicken's egg, turning purplish. "Wahi yelo, Kagi Taka (I'm here, Raven)," Chay said in Lakota, worry lines etching his face.

"Will she be okay?" a female voice asked, hunkered down, watching me.

Chay glanced at this new member of our traveling party and shrugged. "Pretty sure she will. She needs to get up and walk. By the look of this bump, she's gonna have a headache."

"Mmm, Oooh, my head." My eyes fluttered open, then shut, then re-opened. "Chay? Chay, is that you? Or am I fantasizing?" I stirred, touching my head, and winced. "Ouch! Darn, that hurts like all Billy heck."

"Lord have mercy, girl, you scared the holy hell outta me. Where in the heck have you been? I've been hollering for you for an hour or more. You walked off and, well... shit..." His eyes glanced at the new person. "Sorry about my language. I've been worried about my cousin."

"Oh, my, I understand. I've heard menfolk say worse, I promise you."

I opened my eyes, but everything was still fuzzy. I could see two people—one I knew was Chay—but who was the girl? Where had she appeared from?

"Chay, help me sit up, please. Can you get me some water?"

"Tell me where the water sack is. I'll get it," the girl offered.

Chay helped me up, giving me a fleeting look I understood. Recently, this look had become common between us. Was it necessary to tell this person, whoever she was, about our tale of time and space travel? All I needed was water and food. Strange water and stranger food we carried into this time warp.

"We don't have a water sack, Annie. Help me get her to the stream so she can drink."

"What, Chay? Yes, we do, we have—" He shot me another look. Loud and clear: shut up.

"Let me run to the stream with my jug. I'll fill it while you help her up, get her comfortable, and check the bump on her head," Annie offered, grabbing an oddly shaped jug from her bag and darting to the stream.

"Chay," I asked, "where and when are we?" My fuzzy brain was slowly firing neurons back to life.

"The Colony of South Carolina, from what Annie tells me."

"You said colony... as in eighteenth-century colonies?"

"Uh-huh, exactly. This will be Tennessee someday."

"Who's Annie? And what year are we in? Did you ask her?" I struggled to comprehend why I needed to be in the eighteenth century.

"I don't know a lot yet, and hush—she's coming back." Chay stood. "Thank you. This will help her feel better."

Annie returned with the jug, which looked like a scooped-out gourd, and it was. The water was welcome on my parched throat; I sipped, then gulped.

"Wado (thank you)," I said, handing the jug back—not realizing I'd just spoken Cherokee.

"Gvlielitseha (You're welcome). You speak Cherokee?" Her face beamed.

"Yes, I do, and Lakota too. I'm half Sioux. You are?" I left it open-ended, letting her introduce herself.

"I'm Anna Shorey, but call me Annie. My Pa is William Shorey, Senior—he's from Scotland, and my Momma is Ghi-goo-ie, though Pa calls her Peggy. Easier to pronounce. She's Cherokee, from the Red-Tail Hawk Clan. That's why I speak English and Cherokee. I'm afraid we must go now. The night is falling. I must get home. Chayton said you're traveling. Come have supper with us, and you can tell us of your travels."

Who was I to argue with a hot meal—or a roof over our heads, at least until Chay and I figured things out?

"Chay, uh... where are the horses?" Lord, I sounded melodramatic.

"You have horses. Where are they?" Annie clapped as she looked about. But there were no horses.

"No, we're traveling by foot in the mountains. We, uh... left the horses in, uh—" Chay had no clue.

"Yes, I remember," I said, rubbing my head. "Guess I bumped it harder than I thought."

"Let's get moving. Don't want Pa out hunting me, and we don't want to miss Momma's rabbit stew and cornbread."

Annie led the way. Chay and I followed, neither knowing what came next.

———

T he girl led us on the mountain trail. I couldn't help but admire how strong a young woman she must be to live in this century and manage on her own. Clearly, she was guiding us for a reason. I was certain we were on a backward journey to make sure the past didn't alter our present.

What if whatever we were supposed to correct had already happened? How would I even know? No guidebook, no directions—and who was Annie Shorey to me, or anyone?

I guessed she was seventeen or eighteen, based on her voice and spryness. In a whisper, I told Chay to stay back while I got friendly with her. "Let me chat with her, girl to girl."

He shrugged noncommittally. I caught up to Annie and walked beside her.

"Annie, you've lived here long?"

"Every day of my life, for eighteen years come this next spring. I hope to live another eighteen because I love the mountains... except—" She paused.

"Except what?" I prompted.

"At first, we were friends with the British. I was thirteen when a few Cherokees were accused of stealing horses. Can you imagine a war over some measly horses?"

I didn't want her to know I'd kill for my horses. All the same, moot point here and now.

"No, I can't," I said.

"Anyway, Chief Moytoy led raids on the Yadkin and Catawba rivers. The Garrison killed sixteen Cherokee Chiefs, and afterward our people retaliated. It... didn't end well for the men at Fort Loudoun." Her brows furrowed. "Why don't you know this?"

"I, well, I'm not from here. I'm from far away." Should I tell her who I was? Could this get us burned at the stake?

Annie slowed, cautious. "Where are you and your cousin from, if I may ask?"

I didn't want to lie, but I didn't want to tell the truth, either. "I'm from far north of here, uh... the Dakota Territory."

"Oh, yes, we've heard the French and the Spaniards fight over that territory. Have you seen many wars?"

"No, I haven't." Well, I'd never seen a true war.

"Pa is an interpreter for Ostenaco. Soon he'll attend a conference in Williamsburg."

"He is an important man then, your Pa?"

Annie shrugged. "Well, he is for Chief Ostenaco. The chief cannot speak English. My pa's Scottish, an interpreter, a master with the Iroquoian language. The Cherokee people adore him."

I understood matrilineal and patrilineal lineage. My clan was matrilineal, so my mother's line determined my place in the Sioux tribe. My mother's mixed heritage hadn't mattered; they accepted her as full-blood Sioux. Annie, likewise, was full-blood Cherokee because of her mother's line.

Though I understood, my brain struggled. Chief Ostenaco meant nothing to me. Nor did Annie Shorey. Yet here I was, in wooded mountains with her, headed to her home for supper.

———

T

hey welcomed us warmly, offering heaps of stew and corn-bread, and pleasant conversation with Ghi-goo-ie—Peggy—and Mr. Shorey—Will.

"So, young Chay, have you ever battled up north?"

"No, sir. I hope I never have to fight."

I jumped in. "We would fight for our countrymen if called upon."

"You, a lass, you'd fight?" His hearty bellow made me pause. Chay's hand pressed my arm, and I stayed silent.

"Annie," Peggy said, "you must go to the neighbors; bring food and blankets. They've been ill and need aid." She handed me a basket laden with cornbread and bean soup. "Chay, accompany her, get her home safely."

"I'll keep Raven entertained until you return."

"Yes, Momma, of course. Come, Chay, carry the basket. I'll get the blankets while Pa lights the oil lamps."

———

Just me and Peggy. The woman studied me; her stare hard, face pensive. She didn't speak. Deep inside, I suspected Peggy had the eyes of a soothsayer—someone who could see your soul, who knew things.

"You travel far?" she asked.

"Yes, very far."

"You know our history?"

"The British and Cherokee war?"

"No, other wars—years into the future. I see things. You do too, don't you?"

"I dream, yes. But not like you see."

"It's the same," Peggy said, leaning back, closing her eyes, rocking and humming. I sat silently, afraid to breathe. She recognized I wasn't part of her world.

Then she opened her eyes. "Do not be afraid, little blackbird. All is well. You will do what you came for, and it pleases me. For now, I worry not that my line will end, for today you bring me peace."

She rose from the wooden rocker, patted my hand, and left me in the dim oil-lantern light, alone.

21

"Really, the barn's fine. Hay and blankets are better than dirt and rocks on the mountain," I argued, not about to put them out of their beds.

"Take extra blankets; the night air gets especially frosty," our gracious hostess, Annie, said, shoving several more blankets and two down-feather pillows at us.

"Thank you, Annie," Chay rejoined, a gleam in his eye.

That's when I realized I'd need to talk him down from his sudden infatuation with a woman 265 years older than him. When I did the calculations internally, I stifled a giggle.

Tucked away in the barn, we were alone, with no outsider's ears to hear us, and relief flooded me. We needed to discuss what had transpired.

My first question for Chay was, "Okay, where are the horses and our supplies?"

"Can't say. You got your nose bent outta shape, and I can't remember why. Then you said you needed to take a walk. When you didn't come back, I got worried."

"Gee whiz, Chay, how long was I gone?"

"Half a day, dang it. I walked all over looking for you. After I got back, I sat and waited, then fell asleep, I think."

"Well, let me ask you this, Raven Kangee. Do *you* know what happened to you?"

No, I didn't—and I needed to keep my long-ass pantaloons outta my butt crack.

"When I woke up, Annie was looking at me as if I were an alien. She was petrified. I saw our horses were gone and figured someone stole them. At any rate, Annie helped me find you. End of story."

"Oh, lordy, I hope it's not the end," Chay backpedaled.

I recounted my ordeal—how I seemed to have stepped back in time. Next, I told him about my conversation with Annie's mother. His eyes widened.

"What's that face for?" I asked.

"Annie asked if I was here to save her. I asked her what she meant."

"She wished for horses because it'd be an effective way to escape quickly."

"I don't get it. Four horses disappear into thin air. How does that happen?" Chay asked.

"Alright, I'll tell you how—if you can explain how we're here, three hundred years in the past. Nothing seems impossible now, does it?"

It seemed nothing was impossible. Could you dream a dream with another person and have it feel this real? Dream-walking into another person's head was an interesting idea.

Present Day ... The Next Ritual Begins

In the living room, devoid of furniture save the chairs they sat in, they formed a circle. Silver Moon took the lead.

"Our She Cougar and Wind Dancer have sent their little blackbird on her way. They are completing their tasks to ensure her birth and Chief Black Raven's prophecy. By this time tomorrow, they shall return. The sands of time flow hastily for their reappearance to complete our power group."

Two chairs sat empty between Meda Clark and Blackie Kangee. Once the circle was complete, no one could break it; the power was immense.

Hank Cooper, sitting on Meda's right, shivered.

"Henry," Silver Moon's upper body rocked forward, then back. "Tell us, what do you see?"

"A war is near; many suffer, many losses."

"Many perish at the hands of an enemy. Multitudes take their last breaths across the ocean."

His eyes closed, a tear fell as his hand covered his heart.

"Our brothers—the Yankton Sioux, Choctaw, Cheyenne, and many others—put themselves in harm's way for many."

"We have no representation of Choctaw or Navajo, but they too played an important role," Jon Little Bird said.

"Take hold of your spirit animal," Silver Moon said. "Let him loose to help guide our two on the journey next, once they've saved the woman's line that begat Cherokee Chief John Ross."

Each person—from oldest to youngest—began an internal, silent chant. Their spirit animals rose, ready to guide Raven and Chay through the realms of time.

———

I was tired; the work in this century was hard yet fulfilling. Time had no domain in my life—it could've been weeks, even years, that passed. Chay and I were unaware.

"I've got blisters on top of my blisters. Just how did these people survive?"

"Stop complaining, Chay. Why don't you pray to a higher being—ask Him to get us out of this flipping century?"

"You think I haven't?"

"Hush. Here comes your girlfriend."

"Nope. She's too old for me." Chay rolled his eyes.

"Morning to you both. Listen, since my Pa's passing," Annie began.

All I heard was *her father had passed*. I needed to speak to Peggy Shorey about this. The man was her husband. How would this affect her?

"So, we're headed to see these men about furs and trading. Momma and I would be pleased if you'd accompany us."

I remained quiet, mouth gaping. Chay spoke up. "We'd like that, Annie."

She clapped her hands and went in search of the Widow Shorey.

"Her father died? Good grief—when, and where were we?"

"Now that you mention it, Annie does appear older. Is time moving us forward, and we can't see it happening?"

Man, oh man, I couldn't wait for this nightmare to end. My hope was getting the horses and books back in one piece—praying they would explain this phenomenon.

Back in my real time, the forces of power were working their magic—propelling our travels.

———

Annie walked a gelding and an older mare out of the barn—the same barn I'd just exited. *Kiss my foot.*

There hadn't been horses in there five minutes ago. This had my full attention, but I couldn't just ask, *Hey, where'd you get the horses?*

The cabin door opened, and Peggy stepped out, dark shawl wrapped around her shoulders. She waved me over, smiling.

"Come inside; we shall talk."

She ushered me in, shutting out the cooler weather. After tea, we sat. She let the air blow from her lungs as she rocked.

"It is nearing the five-year anniversary of my William's passing, and time is growing short."

My gut wrenched. *Five years.* Had we been here five years? I'd seen my reflection in the stream and didn't look older—but how did time travel work?

"This surprises you; I see it in your eyes. Am I right?"

All I could do was nod.

"Consumption took him. He was ill before reaching England. We grieve, but the Cherokee people are sorrowful more so. My husband was a thorough master of our language. Annie's Pa may have been born a Scotsman, but his soul was Cherokee."

She paused. "Baby Bird—"

I caught my breath. "Why did you call me Baby Bird?"

"Raven, you're tiny but an enormous force. Your aura speaks to me. Have I offended you?"

"My mother calls me Baby Bird. No one else ever has."

Peggy patted my hand. "You're smart and cunning, like the bird. But different."

"Oh? How?"

"In our world, a raven may signal ill omen—death or loss. You, though, are here to keep the future on track."

I exhaled slowly, watching her eyes.

"So you have visions to know my purpose here, Ghi-goo-ie?"

"Yes. My heart tells me you watch over my Annie."

"Guard her from what—and why?"

"The river flows deep, as does her love for a man. This must come to pass without interruption."

A light burst inside the cabin—star-like. Peggy didn't see it. I did.

As she spoke of Annie and grandchildren, I spoke instead to the swirling apparition above her.

"Tell me, Ghi-goo-ie, why this matters so much."

A second form rose from her body—tall, proud. "Because to the Cherokee people, it means everything..."

The voice was my Aunt Meda's.

I reached out. My fingers touched the swirling form. A jolt raced through me—then calm.

Peggy shuddered. Her fist pressed to my chest, then opened. Two joined circles lay in her palm.

I removed my charm. The spheres melted.

"No—do not touch!" the voice warned. "Let not the rings be pulled apart. Maintain her in your sights. Keep her safe."

Déjà vu struck. I had to talk to Chay before we left for the fur traders.

22

I found Chay in the barn tending to the horses.

 I paused, reflecting on our first meeting here at the home of the Shoreys. There had been mules and no horses, which had been odd since a horse was the mode of transportation in this era.

"You miss Moon Beam?"

Chay kept brushing the mare's coat and nodded. I understood—because I was missing my beautiful Gypsy. More importantly, though, I was missing what Gypsy carried on her back: a pack with my books in it.

"Listen, Chay, let me tell you what just happened in the cabin with Peggy."

His eyes grew large. "Really? Do you think it was your Aunt Meda in her body talking to you?"

"It sounded like her. Afterward, Peggy went on like nothing happened, and our conversation went back to just how it started. I knew something weird had happened. The part about killing if he must—man, this scares the you-know-what out of me. Chay, I can't kill anyone, no matter who it is."

I sat down on an upturned crate, my shoulders sagging in defeat.

Chay stopped brushing the mare, his expression hard. "If it meant losing you, Annie, or Mrs. Shorey, I could."

I drew a sharp breath.

He was dead serious. Inside my head, a voice spoke: He'll protect her, not to worry; after this, his journey is complete.

My kneecaps jumped in fear. Once this was over and we'd done what they'd sent us to do, Chay would be gone. I would be alone.

Is this what the voice meant? Oh, I hoped not—because right now, this very second, I didn't feel I could do this alone. Even my mother had my father and was never, in all honesty, alone.

I kept this new supposed knowledge to myself. Putting an extra burden on Chay wasn't an option. I knew he had a colossal task ahead, and I deliberated on how I would help him.

"Rave, did you ever wonder why there were only mules instead of horses when we arrived?"

"Yeah, once I saw their horses, I was curious."

"I asked Annie, but didn't mention the odd fast-forward of the years, which still astounds me, you know—"

"Chay, the horses," I cut in, getting him back on track.

"Uh, yeah, my bad. So when we got here"—he did a half-grunt laugh—"like a week ago," he sneered with a puff-out chuckle. "Sorry, just can't believe all of this, even though I'm standing right here. Anyway, Annie said once the British and Cherokee went to war, they'd lost the horses and kept only six mules."

"Makes sense, since mules can pull a wagon, are as strong as horses, and have more endurance. Our mules—they..." I stopped talking and wondered if I'd ever see our mules again.

"You will, you know."

"I'll what, Chay?"

"Get home. Once this is done. Your mom and dad did, and so will you, and so will I."

All I could do was nod. I dared not tell him he'd be home sooner than me.

"Chay, Raven," we heard Annie calling.

"In the barn, Annie," Chay hollered back.

"Will you hitch the horses to the buckboard? We need to leave. Mamma doesn't want to lose any daylight. Tonight, we'll camp by the South River, since she doesn't want to travel at night. I'll go get the food baskets and bedrolls and blankets. Raven, will you help me?"

I followed Annie to the cabin, leaving Chay to hitch the horses to the buckboard.

———

The Overhill Cherokee Settlements sat along the Tanais River (known in the future as the Tennessee River), with places called Toque, Tuskegee, Tommotley, and a larger Cherokee metropolis called Chota.

And the Trader's Path, also called the Great Indian Warpath (GIW). The Cumberland Trail and the GIW crossed in the foothills of Lookout Mountain.

You might ask how I knew this, but it hadn't been me; it was a surprising turn to discover Chay had this knowledge.

"I had absolutely no clue, Chay Kangee, that you were a geography buff."

"You think you're surprised? I'm more surprised because I didn't know I knew this stuff."

My eyes crinkled up. "What'dya mean?"

"My dear cousin, geography and math weren't my strong subjects in school. I might just be talking out of the blue for all you know."

"No, you're right, Chay. Those two trails cross paths, only we aren't going that way," Annie said matter-of-factly as she loaded another bedroll on the flat wagon.

I glanced at Chay, who did a facial shrug, then I mouthed the word magic. He nodded.

It had to be the only explanation. Funny—this was our pat explanation these days. Magic was at work: strange and miraculous happenings coming from our people in the future, helping us in our journey through the past.

———

Wagon travel.

I'd prefer a nice soft seat in an air-conditioned car, truck, or plane! Even on horseback, the jolting wasn't as bad—only I'd never gotten a splinter riding a horse.

My admiration grew twofold for these women. They had to be tough, ready, and capable of working and fighting hard. I was sure they loved just as hard and took nothing for granted. How soft we were in comparison.

"The traders have lovely furs, and I hope to get a rabbit fur, and Momma wants beaver pelts," Annie chattered, her voice rumbling and pitching as the flat wagon rolled on the hard ground.

I was worn down, not knowing what was going to happen and when. A lifetime had passed, or so it seemed, and to be honest, this felt like a wasteful journey.

Chay leaned in, his hand on my arm, and whispered, "Raven, have faith. Go with this, for there's no changing our destiny."

My ears heard him; my heart, not so much. But Chay's words resonated—back to things my mother had said long ago. Things like: "Remember who you are and where you come from; keep strong in your beliefs; never deny your heart, for it will lead you in your life's journey."

Right then I exhaled, letting my body relax. I became one with the center of time; no longer did my insides jar and bounce as the wagon moved. It calmed, and like my ancestor Chief Black Raven, I let my soul free and my essence roamed the mountainside. I searched for my answer—to no avail.

Chay looked at me. Only I wasn't aware, and had I been able to read his thoughts, I would've heard him think how envious he was that I could sleep on such rough terrain in an old buckboard wagon.

———

I saw it—a small campfire and several men, rough looking, neither Cherokee nor British, and not fur traders. Four men, six horses, and two packhorses.

Voices were faint; I strained my ears to hear—but couldn't.

Was all this my imagination? No—because I could feel my heart beating as I got pulled back into my physical body. A hand grabbed my shoulder and jolted me awake.

"God, cuz, what the heck? I've been trying to rouse you for a minute now. Man, you sleep like the dead." Chay's eyes held concern as he hung onto my arm.

At that moment, I experienced the bumping and jerking of the buckboard. A wheel had snapped, and we were on a downhill slide with mules braying. The front left wheel was no longer on the wagon, with Peggy pulling hard at the reins.

"Whoa, boys! Whoa." Words called out over the sounds of a half-dragging wagon and traumatized mules.

Annie was holding her mom's arm to keep her from tumbling off the buckboard, and Chay was holding onto me.

Had it not been a life-or-death incident, I might've laughed at what it would've looked like—a comic scene with words in bubbles above our heads.

Forever is a long time—and that's how long it felt as we tumbled down the mountainside.

I watched Annie let go of her mother's arm, stretch her entire body over the front end of the wagon, reach a release strap, pull it, and the mules went flying.

We went skidding in dirt, weeds, trees, and over rocks. Hysteria bubbled up in my throat. No kidding—I think my life passed before my eyes as I closed them, praying.

"Everyone okay? Is anyone hurt?" Peggy's worried voice called out as she shook like a leaf.

"We're fine, Annie. Are you hurt? Did you hurt your hand?" Chay asked, seeing blood trickling off one finger.

Peggy grabbed her daughter's hand, making sure all her fingers were still there.

"I'm fine, Mother. Let's get the mules before we lose them. Chay, help me. Raven, you help Momma with the wagon. Check for any items that might have gotten tossed off during the ride."

Annie was quick to take charge, and again, my admiration for her grew.

This woman was worthy of this adventure.

Yet how would we help her, as strong as she was?

What was our purpose?

23

Mules corralled, no belongings lost, no one hurt. The four of us moved the buckboard to a flatter parcel of land and laid large stones near the operating wheels, supporting it in place. Chay and I hunted for the wheel that had snapped off so we could haul it to town and have it fixed. We'd need tools or a man to repair the darned thing. I couldn't fix a wheel, and Chay was useless at repair work.

"Wow, having a so-called flat tire here is a ride, ain't it, Rave?"

"Like the first roller coaster in the eighteenth century. Although not a pleasing ride, I'd suspect our hosts wouldn't want to repeat or pay for it," I remarked.

"You okay? Are you sick?"

"Why do you think I'm sick?" What had gotten into Chay? Why was he such a worrywart all of a sudden?

"Such a deep slumber, thought you were sick, that's all."

"Been a while since I've slept so soundly," I lied, not wanting to enlighten him on my out-of-body experience. Just one more thing on my list of what I could achieve that Chay couldn't.

Peggy gathered twigs and limbs, and I pitched in and helped while Chay went to help Annie settle the mules for the night.

"We have no choice but to camp here tonight. It's too far to town, and the trail is treacherous at night on this part of the mountain. A fire will keep coyotes and other animals away."

Coyotes didn't worry me; four-legged beasts we could scare away. My concern was the four beasts who walked on two legs. I kept this to myself. Tonight, I wouldn't sleep much, if at all.

Try as I might, my eyelids were too heavy, and I poked Chay.

"What?" Chay's voice garbled; his eyes still shut.

"You need to take watch. I'm about to drop."

"Hey, you promised me a few hours' shut eye."

"Listen to me, Chayton Kangee. If you don't wake up and take watch, I'm gonna roll your hind end down this mountain, I swear."

"Ah, shoot, and you would, too. Fine, I'm awake, I'm awake. But here's the deal: when I think two hours are up, I'm waking you to take the next shift, understand?"

I responded with a yes and made him switch places with me. Then I requested he put more limbs on the fire to keep it stoked, unless he wanted his legs to become coyote food. Either way, this woke him. I smiled, ready to get a few winks of sleep—or hoped I would.

*

It hadn't been the howl of a coyote startling me awake, but Peggy shaking my arm and Chay's voice.

"Get up. You've got to help us."

"What? What's going on?" I rubbed my eyes, pulling myself up to stand.

"It's Annie. She never came back," Chay hissed.

"Came back from where? Where'd she go?" I was fully awake, and the four men jumped to the front of my brain.

"Annie woke me up to tell me she was going to the creek for some personal time. Chay said he saw her go that way," Peggy pointed. "But she never came back."

"Get the oil lantern, Peggy, and I'll go hunt for her. You two stay here in case she comes back." Chay was on the move, and I didn't miss the fact he'd put his revolver in the waistband of his pants. My heart stopped, and these words rang in my head, spoken in the voice of my Aunt Meda as she'd encircled Peggy Shorey in a thin stream of misty air:

"If you must kill, then so be it, but maintain her in your sight and keep her safe."

Annie was in danger. She wasn't in our sight and therefore not safe!

Seconds, then minutes passed. Those moments turned into at least half an hour or more, and we'd heard nothing. No scream, no gunshot, no coyote howl. Not the hoot of an owl, nor the chirp of a cricket sounded in the darkness, illuminated by a partial moon as the small fire burned out.

We kept our voices low so as not to pinpoint our location, in case others were near, and I said, "It's been too long. Perhaps we should get the other lantern and look for her."

Peggy shook her head and, in a hushed voice, said, "We shall give Star Gazer more time, as the skies and his heart guide him."

She couldn't see my expression, of course, and I wondered if Chay said anything to her about being Star Gazer. Surely not.

In the darkness, her hand covered mine. "Ah, you wonder if he told me, don't you?"

"Yes," I whispered.

"He told me nothing, but a woman came to me in my sleep, so vivid, so strong, with long dark hair and beautiful eyes. A woman who loves Star Gazer and has loved him before his birth, and she told me to trust in him. Trust him for my child's safety. She assured me my line would continue in my only child, Anna, who would bear a daughter, and she'd bear my great-grandson, who'll be a leader for the Cherokee for many years."

My Aunt Kanda came to her in a vision? Impossible. What in the world made me question this as impossible? Wakanda Kangee, Chay's mother, had been the one who they'd thought would go back to save the Sioux Legacy, not my mom—but this hadn't been the ultimate plan. Wakanda, her name, a Sioux name, meant "magical." She was Chay's protector, as Aunt Meda was for me.

Then I wondered about my parents and where they were in this entire realm of travel. My heart gave a jolt because I knew! While I was here in 1766 or 1767, my mother and father were somewhere in 1828, saving a man whose line would beget Chief Sitting Bull. Again, my pulse sped up. Somewhere in this path of time travel, would I pass my parents, see, touch, or hear them?

The rock—the place I'd taken a nap before Chay found me. I'd seen the shapes, shadows of two people walking away, hand-in-hand. Had this been my parents? Oh, so many questions. I sure hoped I'd remember them and could ask questions when I got back to my future... if I got back.

The gunshot echoed in the mountains. Birds flew up out of tree branches; crows cawed, and any animal within a thousand yards scattered from where they hid and slept. Peggy's hand clutched my forearm, my hand covered hers, and we froze; neither of us breathed. The glee my heart felt when I saw Chay hauling Annie by the hand out of the trees, him waving for us to get up, filled me to my toes.

"Go, go hide, now!"

Chay didn't have to tell us twice, as we raced behind him and Annie into the trees beyond our camp and past where we'd tied up the mules.

When we'd gotten out of sight, Chay got us hunkered down in a small clump of prickly bushes, but nobody complained. We were all terrified. Annie spoke first, and what she said was funny.

"What in the world? How did that gun do that?"

"It's, well—" Chay started, but I interrupted him.

"Anyone hurt?"

He put his finger to his lips. "Shush."

Peggy, Annie, and I held our breaths when we heard feet pounding the dirt.

"I know he came this way, Clyde," said Amos, "and we gotta get him. He kilt Luke, and he's gonna pay."

"Well, you stupid clod," said Bert. "If you hadn't 'a grabbed the girl, no one would be dead. You always gotta be causing us trouble. The man shoulda kilt you, and then we'd not be worrying about this. Just bury your brainless carcass, and we'd be on with business."

They walked past our hiding spot, and none of us moved, breathed, or blinked. Their footsteps turned, growing fainter as they hiked further up the mountain. When Chay felt it safe, he whispered for us to sneak back to camp.

"Grab what you can, douse the campfire with dirt, then get the mules. We're gonna ride them down, and don't worry, mules have remarkable night vision."

"Chay." Annie's hand shot out, grabbing his arm. "Thank you for coming for me. I don't know, they would've... oh, Lordy." She choked back a sob.

"Annie, it's gonna be alright, but we need to go." He said nothing else as he led us back to our campsite, and we hurried to make a quick exit.

Six mules. We each rode one, headed down the mountain at a treacherous incline in the dark, but our choices were to stay and face the three dangerous men, or roll downhill with a mule. The mule seemed safer.

Once we were further away and on flatter terrain, I rode up to Chay. The half-moon had moved overhead, and the lighting was better. He had a terse expression on his face and seemed upset.

"Chay," I started, not fathoming how to ask, so I blurted it out, "Did you shoot a man? Did you kill him?"

"I did, and I'd do it all over again if I had to. He had Annie on the ground, and I shot him when he turned around and saw me. He had a knife at her throat and was going to violate her. I couldn't let that happen. You know I couldn't," Chay rambled.

"I'm proud of you. You did the right thing, and you showed a lot of courage going in by yourself."

"I killed a man. Am I a bad person now?"

"Absolutely not, Chayton Kangee. You're a hero. This was your destiny, and you saved a woman. It is her family line for the Cherokee, one which cannot change without disrupting the future."

After telling him what Peggy had told me about her vision, Chay beamed. His family, like mine, was amazing, and for the first time, Chay Kangee felt the old ways of the Sioux were just as important as the new. No longer would he mock my old soul.

―――

O nce we'd crossed the river at the bottom of Lookout Mountain, exhaustion had settled in. The rising sun had ascended, creating a spectacular sight. Rays of sunshine, like a prism, brilliantly danced over the mountain peaks. Peggy and Annie rode ahead; Chay and I brought up the rear. As I turned to say something, Chay's face faded out into a puff of smoke, and the mule he'd been riding trotted down toward Annie's, and she grabbed the reins as if she'd dropped them by accident.

"Oh, Pete, you naughty mule, don't escape."

Below us, I could see a town, teepees, and people—Cherokee families bringing their morning alive. A man called out in Cherokee, "Osda Sanalei (good morning)." Peggy answered back, and Annie waved with enthusiasm. No one acknowledged me, and I wondered why until I blinked. The scene was below me, and I was in the clouds, no longer part of the group, but a watcher.

24

"Be at peace now, Dan, for Chief John Ross shall live," Silver Moon said.

Dan 'Dark Water' Jones of the Cherokee Nation exhaled, bowed his head, and murmured a word of thanks.

"Where is our son?" Payton Kangee stood, his hand on his wife's shoulder, worry on their faces.

"In time he'll return. For now, he wrestles with his heart to accept what he had to do; but this won't haunt him. Have faith in my words," Soft Dove said.

"Is my boy drifting alone in time, Meda?" asked Wakanda.

"No, his spirit hovers with Raven, and his physical body slumbers beyond the mountain ridge. Chayton's life force will stay with her until she settles into the next realm. Then he'll return to us when his time has come. This is all I have knowledge about."

Payton and Wakanda Kangee worried about Chay, for he was their only child, but they knew this was part of their heritage—this spiritual inner circle. This was also Chay's preordained destiny, as were the risks of traveling through time and space, keeping history preserved.

The front door creaked, and footsteps of two new arrivals padded down the hallway to the main room. Everyone turned to gaze at the entryway.

"Blaze, Dakota, we welcome your arrival." Silver Moon nodded at them.

"Right on time, too. Are you rested?"

"Yes, Aunt Meda, we are." With a smile, Blaze took Dakota's hand.

"Feels like we've been gone for eons, but it's only been a few days." Dakota squeezed his wife's hand.

"It's been a lifetime, packed into a few days, nephew." Blackie stood to shake hands with Dakota.

"Uncle, good to see you," Dakota responded. "Wonderful to see everyone."

"All went as before?" Hank wondered if any small thing—movement or word—had changed. His concern was anything that might upset the balance.

"It was odd." Blaze shrugged. "Even though we were there, we were only spectators watching ourselves, like watching a movie."

Jon Crow sat forward. "You mean you didn't repeat it? You only watched as it unfolded?"

Eli Harris of the Paiutes' head bobbed in spurts. "That's how it should be. If there's ever a need for either of them to retrace these steps, they, too, will watch themselves as ghosts. Like you were in spirit, so shall they be."

"I don't understand why?" Hank Cooper scratched at his chin, his brows dipping in a deep V.

A small hand rose, and she patted the air. "Shush, I'll explain. Once we've been in a past date, altering what was necessary, keeping history on course, we can never go back again. Our power is only to correct small occurrences, making sure the historical outcome stays the same."

"Ah, I see now. So this can't be reversed, can it?" Hank understood what she meant.

"If one tries using this magic to benefit their ancestors or to change the outcome, making it more favorable for them, our world's history would explode."

"Meda's right, and our task is to keep it from changing, making sure it stays the same for the people of our tribes. We cannot alter anything else," Silver Moon voiced. If she had the power, she'd erase the unpleasant things for every person in the world. This wasn't her call, though, but the call of a higher being.

Somewhere in a Time Loop

Here I was again, my feet not on the ground. This was getting old. I had no control over, well, anything.

I watched below as everything began fading away. But where the heck was I? In a cloud, in a fantasy, or in a nightmare?

No Chay, no horses, no provisions, and no darned dream book, diary, or whatever! If I'd known this would be my fate, I might've begged to get someone else. Would it have been possible?

I kept revisiting my mother's adventure. Mine was nothing like it—not at all. Here I was, flitting from place to place and growing tired of it. What was next?

As I sat alone on an invisible cloud, which I couldn't jump off or walk away from, I contemplated my dilemma. Chay had gone somewhere different, and I considered a fact I hadn't thought of before. Perhaps he had his own purpose to fulfill.

"Boy, oh, boy, you sure are narcissistic, thinking this was solely about you," I said to the air. I clicked my tongue, just like my Aunt Meda admonishing me. "Raven Kangee, are you really that self-involved? Do you think you're the best thing since sliced bread?"

Right then, I didn't like myself and was ashamed. As soon as the word "ashamed" trickled through my thoughts, I felt the dizzying effect again and blew out a breath.

"Uh-oh, here I go again." I passed out, falling through the darkness.

To a Future Century Not Yet Born

"You beautiful filly," Chay said, walking toward Moon Beam. He rubbed her soft muzzle, cooing at her. "I'm relieved to see you, Jumper and Sadie, all still in one piece. Y'all are a sight for sore eyes."

Chay rested his hands on his hips, scanning the area for the fourth member of their equestrian team, Gypsy, and for his cousin.

Hmm, just him and the horses smack-dab in the middle of where? He swiveled his head in all directions, then directed his gaze at his feet.

The road was paved, and this worried him. Hadn't he just been riding a mule down a mountain with Raven and two other women? They were... uh... he couldn't remember the names. He placed two fingers at his temple, tapping, and then he remembered. "Ah, Annie and Peggy Shorey, and we were heading toward the trading post."

However, they were gone, the mountain disappeared, and so had Raven—for a second time! The backpacks were still on the horse, and he was famished, so he dug in, eating cheese crackers and dry cereal, washing it down with tepid water, and it tasted superb.

He stuffed the trash in a side pocket of a knapsack, then linked Jumper and Sadie together with a pack string and hopped on Moon Beam. Last time he waited; this time he'd search for her, hoping he made the right decision.

As he rode, he noted he was holding his head higher and felt more confident. Something had changed inside him, and his brows knitted in thought. What had transpired on the mountaintop?

The sound of cannons rang in his ears. Yet there were no cannons for miles—only land, trees, and a paved road. His hand went to his waistband,

and his fingers touched the cold metal of his revolver. As his hand gripped the butt of the gun, he remembered. He'd shot a man.

A mean man had been about to harm the girl, Annie. This couldn't happen. A tear slipped from the corner of his eye and he let it fall. He wasn't regretful, for he did what he had to do: taking another's life. Would this haunt him?

Chay let Moon Beam have her head, staring forward at a clear blue sky—a sky soon to change to black and orange with strange new visions as the horse carried him into another world.

25

Facedown, eating dirt, the sounds of hoofs exploded in my ears.

Once I raised my head, all I saw was rusty powder swirling in tornado fashion, the reverberations of countless horses hammering dry, hard ground getting closer.

My heart thudded. I had to move fast or get trampled!

My eyes cut left, then right.

I flipped myself over onto my back, rolling until I had fallen six feet over a narrow ditch. The dust plumes rose, and I coughed, holding my hand over my mouth to keep as much grit out of my lungs as I could, to avoid choking to death.

The noise was unbearable—the screeching, yelling, whooping, and the horse hooves kicking up soil, leaving divots as they ran full speed at... what?

I didn't know. All I knew was I felt like I was in a Wild West movie, and I suspected Chay was going to pop up and, as always, be late to the party.

I prayed something would spirit me away, sending me on my way to my purpose.

Once the screeching, whooping, and galloping hooves faded, I pulled my jumper over my face to keep dust out of my mouth and nose.

Hands over my ears, eyes shut, I counted to one hundred.

I removed my hands and pulled the bottom of the jumper off my face, sputtering wet dirt, inhaling, hoping the clouds of dust had died down.

Under my breath, I muttered something about water and a drink, and a hand shot out with a water bag.

"Here, betcha need a drink after all that, don'tcha?"

His eyes cornflower blue, he stood over me as I lay covered in muck, my hair tangled, my clothes more than travel-weary. The jumper pulled up, showing my muslin-colored pantaloons and old-lady underwear.

It didn't bother me; I wasn't showing him teeny bikini underwear or, Lord knows, a tiny thong.

"You gonna take the bag or lay there like a discarded rag doll in the dirt?"

Not worrying about pomp and circumstance, I sat up, grabbed the pouch, and chugged water to wet my dirt-parched throat. As the water ran down the sides of my mouth and onto my white cotton shirt, I jerked the jumper down to cover the old-lady panties, then dried my mouth with the corner of the dress.

"Wow, I wasn't sure you'd get out of the way in time. I tried, but there were more of them and only one of me." The young man laughed, took the water bag, slung the strap over his shoulder, and reached his hand down to help me out of the ditch.

I refused his hand, getting up by myself, scowling. Who was this guy and why was he here? And where in tarnation was Chay?

"And who are you, and who were they?" I thumbed in the direction the riders had torn off.

"My name's Nate, and thank God—"

I cut him off. "Nate—Nate who?"

"Henry Nathaniel Cooper, but my great uncle goes by Hank, and I didn't wanna be Hank, so they call me Nate."

My nose wrinkled in thought, my forehead crinkled. When I was about ten, I had been familiar with a boy named Nate. He was one or two years younger, spent time at his uncle's farm, and his uncle was friends with my Aunt Meda. Cooper... Cooper.

Then I remembered.

"You're Hank Cooper's nephew? Same Hank who's friends with my Aunt Meda?"

"Is she the lady who lives with the other scary lady, the one with the silver hair?"

"Silver Moon? You think she's scary?"

His shoulders lifted indistinctly. "Sorta. At least I used to think so until all this crap." He waved his hand over the area.

I was puzzled. Why was Nate Cooper here? Where was Chay? And, for the love of God, where were we?

"Fine, I see you don't get it, and me neither, except she told me I had no choice, and I—"

My hand shot up. "Wait! Just wait a flipping second, would ya? First, you know me, do you? Second, who said you had no choice? I'm confused."

"Silver Moon said this was my fate. I swear I didn't know until Uncle Hank told me the story of his great-great-great... oh, crud... I don't know how many greats. His grandpappy from way back met your mom in a time warp or something like that, and I know you because we've met, you dork."

"We have? When?" My head was about to explode. No matter how hard I tried, I could only remember him when he was ten and I was twelve or thirteen.

"Two or three years back, one summer when I was visiting my uncle. We were at a Town Hall meeting and chatted, right before your mom had to haul you off to see about a mare dropping a foal."

Gypsy. It was when my horse was born. How I wished she were here now so I could ride off!

"You don't remember, do you?"

"No, I don't, sorry. But I remember that night. My horse, Gypsy, was the foal, and I gotta tell you, she's out here in this time warp, as you call it, floating somewhere with provisions on her and some books I very much need."

Nate's right arm came up, pointing a finger. "Oh, you mean that horse and those knapsacks?"

I turned to follow his finger and was filled with joy.
My beautiful gray-and-blackish mare, carrying everything, including saddlebags and backpacks.

I ran up to her, stroking her soft nose, telling her I loved her and how glad I was to see her.
Secretly, I was happy to have some far-into-the-future delights: bottled water and food. Oh, my heavens, I had food, and I was starving.

Unbuckling a saddlebag, I brought out a bottle of clear spring water, uncapped it, and chugged, not letting a drop escape.

"And they say coffee is the nectar of the gods, and whoever they are is dead wrong; water is glorious."

I patted Gypsy on the hind end, then pulled out a bag of honey-roasted peanuts, tore them open, and poured them into my mouth. I'm sure I looked like a chipmunk storing nuts for winter when I saw Nate watching me.

Again, I admonished myself: this wasn't all about me. With my mouth full, I waved him over, dug into the saddlebag, and grabbed him a bottle of tepid but very fresh water.

"Thanks, appreciate it. Creek water is okay when it's not too muddy, but this will be like heaven." Nate drank long gulps and aahed.

I chomped the peanuts, handed him the rest, and swallowed before asking, "How long have you been here?"

"Not sure," he said, crumpling the peanut bag and shoving it in his back pocket. I noticed his clothes—period correct, or so I assumed.

"You have a horse?"

"I did, but during the last raid, he got caught up and ran, and since I was hiding, I couldn't go grab him."

"Uh, where did my horse Gypsy come from then?"

"That's odd, too. I saw you flat on the ground from the hill over there. You just sorta appeared. After I knew the riders were gone, I hightailed it over to you. Man, I'm glad you weren't hurt."

"Um, still doesn't tell me when Gypsy appeared." I didn't respond about me being unharmed, instead reaching into the saddlebag for water, pouring some into his empty bottle, and handing it to him.

"Thanks," Nate said, taking the water. "Once you stood up, the horse appeared. You think it's the magic they're doing?"

"They? Who is doing what magic?"

Nate arched his brows at me. "You mean you don't know?"

"I guess not, since I'm asking you."

My ire was up. I sounded snotty, but I didn't care. Never knowing when or where I'd disappear—or if anyone such as Chay, my horse, or a stranger would accompany me—was frustrating.

Okay, in all fairness, Nate wasn't a stranger, but I didn't know him very well either.

"See the tree up there on the hill, about three hundred yards, or as some might say, about three football fields away?"

I nodded. Using a football field as a measuring reference might be funny, but I didn't feel humorous. Later, I might chuckle.

"Let's head that way and sit in the shade and talk, okay?"

Despondent, I stuck a foot in a stirrup, hauled myself into the saddle, then held out a hand for him to grab. He did so with ease.

A foot into Gypsy's flank, and she moved forward. His hot breath on my neck, one hand on my waist to steady himself, disrupted my senses. I felt unsettled, off-balance.

Once at the hill, I tied Gypsy's reins to a low-hanging branch, retrieved two more waters from the saddlebag, and we sat under the tree.

Internally, I pondered... we might—wait, I had imagined him and me as "we."

Wow.

Now this was a change of pace—not thinking only of myself, as I had been doing.

"This hill, this tree, your mom would know it, so would your dad."

I looked around. Prairie land, a hill, some trees, weeds, tall and short grasses—not too special. Inside, I huffed. *What the heck was wrong with me?*

"Oh, yeah. And since you've been here all of... wait, you never said how long you've been here." I stared at him, wondering why I was being such a disagreeable donkey's butt.

"All I've had to mark time with has been this tree."

My eyes squeezed, my nose wrinkled like someone smelling something horrid. "What does that even mean?"

He moved away from the tree, pointing. "I started marking the days on the tree, but at the rate I was marking, I was gonna kill the tree."

The poor tree trunk had slashes all around the base and upward.

"I'd count them, but I'm sure you know the number, right?"

Nate let out a deep breath and nodded. "Yep. To my best guess, I've been here almost a year now."

"A year, oh, my Lord—"

"Waiting for you."

"Waiting on me?"

The grimace on his face told me it hadn't been pleasant.

"Yeah, and you landed a few feet from where they said, about ten months later, too."

Nate put up his hand to keep me silent. I closed my mouth and nodded, letting him speak.

"Silver Moon told me you'd be here, the day and time. To say it's been easy... well, it hasn't. First, look at me—a Whiteman in this territory. My dazzling blue eyes got me nowhere, and I was terrified, at first anyway. This is Crow Indian territory, and I got damned lucky to find a tribe who wasn't bent on scalping me!"

"Scalp you? Heaven help me."

I feigned terror, punching him in the arm. "So, about this magic... you gonna spill or what?"

I knew about some of this from the books. But what did he know? Who told him? I imagined Silver Moon had. But what had she told him, and why were we together in this time?

"My uncle is Hank Cooper, and my ancestor from, oh, I guess 1820—or heck, I don't know the actual date—but in the early 1800s, T.H. Cooper met your mom. After her story happened, he lived with the Sioux, in Chief Black Raven's tribe, even married into the tribe."

"Nate, please, I know all this. Don't rehash. Just tell me what I don't know—like this tree, this hill, and, well... you."

"You landed in the same spot your mom did. This hill was where your father was sitting the first time he saw her."

"Oh, yeah?" Fascinating. The thought of my parents being here when they met, neither remembering, was... oh, no. Could it be?

The story was her and my dad knew each other—but didn't really know each other, even though they'd met a few times.

Nathaniel Cooper and I knew each other, but didn't know each other. We'd spoken a few words years ago, same as Mom and Dad, and... oh, holy Toledo, was this like match.com for time travelers?

"Uh, yep, same thing I thought."

My head spun. "Hey, did I say something out loud?"

"Nope, but your expression." He bit his bottom lip to keep from laughing. "Told me what you thought. You don't have a poker face."

I huffed. "I don't play poker, I don't gamble."

"Oh, yes, you do—you're here, aren't you?"

Darn him. He was right. I stuck out my tongue, not very ladylike, and let loose a hearty laugh.

"Okay, Nate, what's our next move? Did Silver Moon mention why or the purpose of our being here?"

"What? Other than us hooking up? Nope, not a word."

Hookup—my big fat foot!

Whatever they thought they were doing in our future to make this happen in the past was ludicrous.

They wouldn't control me, and I told him so. Nate agreed, albeit a mite too passionately, which offended me slightly.

How could I have known my wounded feelings were just the first of many?

26

"How about we get back to my place?" Nate wiggled his brows just as I took a swallow and spurted water down my chin.

I sopped up the water with the front bib of my jumper and shrugged. "Sure, I can't wait to see the creature comforts. Come on, I'll drive," I said, making my way over to Gypsy and hauling myself up.

Nate stood there, arms crossed, a scowl plastered on his face.

"What?"

"I can drive a horse, Raven, and since I know the area, in case we run into something or someone we hafta outrun or escape from."

So what? I was an excellent horsewoman and could ride better than most men. My pop used to say I'd been born riding. For crying out loud, I found myself doing it again... always about me, myself, and I. When was I gonna stop?

I slipped down and handed him the reins with less grace than I wanted to, but a smirk of a smile curled my lips.

"Excellent point. I should be grateful. Our lives will depend on you and what you know about the area."

He didn't miss my snarky emphasis on the single word *you*.

Nate climbed on Gypsy's back and reached his hand down for me.

I wanted to ignore it—but didn't.

As I fastened my hand into his, he jerked me up behind him. I didn't want to put my arms around his waist—but thought better of it in case we did ride into trouble. I sure as shooting didn't want to slip off the back and have him be miles away before he noticed.

We rode without talking, and I just looked around, wanting something to be familiar, but no luck. It looked like any other wide-open space of undeveloped land, yet different.

The wildness saturated the air. An untamed essence of beast and man drifted in and out of my nostrils and into my soul. I experienced a sense of peace I'm not sure I'd ever felt before, and it was a wonderful sensation. I felt like I belonged.

Inhaling, I relaxed my body, leaning into Nate's back. My hands dropped to the curve of his hips.

My eyes closed as I imagined my parents here in this time period, meeting and working together—falling in love as they fulfilled their destinies. One of which was me—and my purpose—whatever that was.

Nate rode, his back straight, and I evaluated his head. Light-golden brown with flecks of darker brown. It was not the longish hair of a Native American and was a tad shaggy, needing a cut.

Hmm, I mused, imagining the only option for a haircut involved a sharp blade and a potential scalping. Yikes! How awful—I shook it from my thoughts.

His shoulders were broad and firm, his arms not ripped, although I was sure he was strong; he was a healthy young man, after all.

I glanced at one of his feet, which was clad in some kind of boot made of softer leather and worn.

His feet—not large, but, well, I suppose—looked man-size. I'd never really thought about feet until I looked at mine. Darn. I needed some jeans, or any sort of trousers, because this ugly jumper wasn't my style. I liked pants, but in this era, I was sure they weren't proper for females. When in time was I, anyway?

"Do you know when we are, Nate?"

I saw his shoulders shrug.

"I was decent at history, and my best guess—remember I said *guess*—is around 1825, 1827, and to answer your next question..."

"Who said I had a next question?"

"Girls always have a next question. And the answer is, we're in Crow Nation and you're Sioux, so yep, like oil and water mixing."

I thumped him in the ear.

"Ouch! Why'd'ya do that?"

"Because you're a stupid boy and a smartass. And because that was my next question."

Nate's shoulders shook, and he tried to hold his laughter in, but let it bust loose.

"Silver Moon said you were your mother's daughter, so I gotta ask—are you?"

It was a funny question to my ears.

Was I my mother's daughter? I was my mother's daughter, but I knew what he meant, yet I pondered this for a moment.

"It's okay, you don't have to answer. It's a stupid question."

"Oh, shut up, will ya? Yes, I'm both my parents, rolled into one. I've always loved my heritage. My mom had to learn to love it. My father is a proud Sioux man. We all know that each tribe sacrificed significantly to get to where we are now. As far as if I'm like my mom—yeah, I'm stubborn and fierce."

"Thick-skinned, too?"

"What? Why? Are you gonna start slinging insults at me?"

"No, worse. I'm gonna own you."

My hands instantly dropped from his physical body, and I scooted my butt backward, locking my knees inward to keep my balance on Gypsy's backside, then said, "The devil you are. What the heck are you blabbing about, Nathaniel Cooper?"

"You're Sioux, dressed in white woman's clothing, and we gotta fix that right away. We're on our way back to the Cliffs with No Pass, which I know in our future world as somewhere near Billings, Montana."

"We? Who's we?"

"The small band of Crow men I've been riding with, and we're—"

"Stop a second. Who were the men that just about trampled me?"

"They were Sioux."

"My people? Are you serious? Can you take me to them? Turn, go back where they are—oh my goodness, this is wonderful!"

Nate shook his head, kicking Gypsy in her flank, setting her into a full gallop. I had no choice but to hang on for dear life.

What in the blue blazes was he doing, and why were we galloping at breakneck speed? My head jerked backward with his forward momentum. I had to swing my head to the side so I could see, since I was too short to see over him. All I saw were dust plumes right before he veered to the left, taking a path through a thicket.

"Keep your face at my back and covered so you don't get an eye poked out, and don't ask questions until we stop, got it? Wrap your arms around my waist and hold on tight."

I muffled an okay into his back, doing as he asked—happy I did.

The ride into the dense brush was brutal. I was thanking God for the long dress with the ugly long-sleeved white shirt, muslin pantaloons, and god-awful shoe-boots.

In the broad scope of things, they saved me from a million and one injuries, some of which might get infected. I never expected to need antibiotics on my unplanned, forced-on-me trip.

Time was impossible to track, and the ride seemed endless until Nate slowed Gypsy.

"You okay back there?"

"Yeah, I suppose barring a few welts from limbs snapping back at me, I don't think I lost an eye or any blood." I was sarcastic.

"Marvelous, and I'm happy you stayed on. Thought a few times you were gonna bounce right off."

"Speaking of off, can we stop? I'd like to get my bearings, if you don't mind. But only if we're out of whatever danger you thought we were in."

He stopped and got off first, reached his hand up to help me, and again, me being me, I ignored him, slipping right off Gypsy's sweaty back.

"She needs water. You think we can get to a watering hole since you know the area and I don't?" Again, I was sarcastic and didn't care.

I hadn't seen one soul in front of us, nor heard anyone behind us, so why had he taken off like the Devil himself was chasing us?

Nate nodded his head to the left. "There's a small stream over yonder. Come on."

I took the reins and led Gypsy, Nate beside me. "You gonna tell me what all that was about or not?"

"Give it a second, will ya?"

"Give it a second. Really? A second for what? I don't understand you, Nathaniel Cooper. You talk in circles."

My mare's head dropped into the shallow water, and she drank. Lead a horse to water, and mine will drink, especially after being run like her tail was on fire. I figured Gypsy might need a break from her saddle and began unhooking the cinch when Nate stopped me.

"Not yet. We won't ride; you can lead her through this next area quietly."

I could hear it in his voice as we tramped ahead—how he admired the wide-open prairie. Once we'd reached a hill, Nate scaled a minor incline, then disappeared over the side.

27

A t Meda and Silver Moon's House

"They are learning each other," Meda said.

"Our daughter is headstrong and stubborn." Blaze looked at each of them, her eyes landing on Hank Cooper. "I don't know your nephew well, Hank, but Meda says wonderful things."

"Nate's a decent kid and smart, too. He isn't like the others of his age. Nate is respectful of the history and a believer."

Silver Moon nodded, then said, "He's also part of us, by blood."

All eyes turned to her, some in question. "He has an ancestor in the Sioux family."

"Of course. T.H. Cooper was his ancestor, just like Hank's," Blaze acknowledged.

"Yes, and on his mother's side he has Sioux blood, too."

Hank's surprised expression didn't escape Silver Moon's attention, and she questioned, "You knew?"

"I did. Just didn't know you did. His mother didn't talk about it to anyone."

Silver Moon's head bobbed. "I understand, but it is what it is."

Everyone seemed confused except Silver Moon, Meda, Hank, and Eli, also known as Two Suns.

Eli asked, "May I?"

With a wave of her hand and a head gesture, Silver Moon gave him the floor.

"When the Ghost Dance Movement began, it spread. We all know how that ended," Eli said, his voice low. "Sitting Bull's death was by the hand of a fellow Sioux, Red Tomahawk. This is who Nate's mother's long-ago ancestor was."

"How did you come to know this, Eli?"

"My ancestor's lineage goes back to Wovoka, also called Jack Wilson, the man who started the Ghost Dance religion. Nate's mom really didn't like being in the line that killed Chief Sitting Bull, and she sort of blamed the Paiute for it."

"Eli," Wakanda spoke. "You said *was*. Is Nate's mother dead? I just saw her a month ago at the county feed store."

"Reva is his stepmother. His biological mother died when Nate was a year old in an auto accident, so he never really knew her. His father and Reva married a year and a half later, and she's the only mother he's known."

"Does Nate know? I mean, about his actual mother and how she felt?"

"He knows she existed, but no, he doesn't know this story. His father never told him and forbade any of us to tell him. When his mother—her tribal name was Walks in Hope—was growing up and this information got out at her school, the other Sioux children shunned her because her ancient relative had killed the distinguished chief. When Nate was born, she said she didn't want that stigma on her child. Her baby boy, she said, had enough to deal with being Sioux and Caucasian," Hank clarified.

Blaze spoke. "I understand more than most, since my mother was a white woman and my father Sioux."

"It will be a suitable pairing and—" She didn't get to finish her sentence before Dakota cut her off.

"Pairing? What do you mean? Raven and Nate will, uh, they'll..." He looked at Blaze and shook his head. "You knew about this?"

"No, I'd like to know, too." Her scowl showed her displeasure as her eyes burned right through both Meda and Silver Moon.

Meda spoke first. "It's not set in stone. It's only a possibility. You know, anything is possible. Look at you and Dakota."

"Us? We're so different. We—I mean, him and I—we..." Blaze faltered.

"Well, God help Nate, because Raven's ten times worse than her mother."

"Dakota Kangee!" Blaze slapped his arm, but in her head, she saw grandbabies with Raven's dark locks and Nathaniel's cornflower-blue eyes, and her heart melted.

"Yes, they will be beautiful children," Meda winked. Once again, frightened at how easily Aunt Meda could just read her thoughts.

Silver Moon got them back on track.

"Now it's time to discuss our next move to help these two along in their journey, for the Apsáalooke People (the Crow) and Sioux will soon make war to battle for land. It will catch them in the middle as they work at completing the task to save another. We will retire to our separate lodges tonight to seek visions in our own unique ways. We meet again in five days."

No one left in a hurry as they mingled and chatted, catching up and laughing at old stories. Pete Johnson touched her on the shoulder.

"Blaze? A word, please?"

In a corner of the large room, they stood, and her heart pounded because she sensed something was wrong.

"Pete, is everything all right?" Real concern etched Blaze Kangee's face.

"No, I—well, it's Sam. He needs to go for an operation, only he won't leave until this is over. I'm afraid this is too much for him."

"Does Aunt Meda or Silver Moon know?"

Pete shook his head, looking worried. "He won't let me mention it, and me telling you—well, I'm breaking my promise. But I need your help, please."

Blaze caught a glance at her Aunt Meda talking to Sam 'Running Elk' Johnson. She gestured to where they stood talking.

"I'd imagine my Aunt Meda already knows, and you needn't worry about breaking your promise."

"That woman," Pete said, relieved. "How your aunt does that, I'll never know, but I'm glad she has her special ability."

"If you knew how often she's read my mind, you wouldn't." Blaze hugged Pete with a chuckle.

———

M eda's hand came up, touching the older man's arm in a gesture of caring.

"If the doctors say so, then you must."

His bushy, dark brows crinkled in concern. "But it's vital to keep our powers whole, our spirits together."

"You worry too much, although not enough about yourself. Follow doctor's orders and get well."

Sam's face was grim. "It can wait until we are done. Anyway, the doctors give no guarantees of life."

"Your cardiologist is a well-known physician, and she's Oglala Sioux, isn't she?"

"Yes, I admire and respect her."

"As a Sioux woman? Or as your physician?"

"Both, of course."

"Do as she asks and get well."

"A double bypass has no guarantees. I could die on her operating table, and if it's my time, then so be it."

"Sounds like you've already cashed in your chips, and that's not the man I know." She clicked her tongue at him. "So no more of this talk. Have the surgery and come back to our people. If you don't, I shall cast my evil eye on you."

Sam's brows arched. "Ah, it's true then. You do have a bit of Siouan witch living inside of you."

Meda's sly grin popped up as she patted Sam's arm.

"One never spills all of one's secrets. Now, I must tend to a few other guests before they depart. Tell Pete to call me once you're in recovery."

"You're pretty sure of yourself, aren't you?"

"Take care of your health. And know this: you'll always be a part of this inner circle. Even when you're not here in physical form, your spirit will attend."

Sam Johnson watched Meda walk away to speak with Eli Harris of the Paiute tribe.

The old woman had something up her sleeve. He was positive—but what? She hadn't said a word, but she spoke volumes with what she didn't say, and Sam's gut told him he'd see her in his dreams.

She had that way about her, and he smiled. One thing he knew was certain—with Meda 'Soft Dove' Clark, a person was never alone, for she got inside your head and stayed there as long as she wished to visit.

Day of Sam Johnson's Surgery

Soft Dove and Silver Moon sat in a small sitting room they'd created in the fourth bedroom of their spacious house.

Photos of Sioux life, relics of the old days, hung on the walls. A double bookshelf held books and odds and ends of each woman's past lives—photos, cards, books, and childhood knickknacks—the important things not obvious to the naked eye, but to them, they knew the value.

Rising from her rocker, Meda gathered the old buffalo-hide-covered book—her own book of magic—and her talisman first, and then she found Silver Moon's amulet and a small pouch, handing them to her dear friend.

"I have always loved this room. So full of spirits and blessings, yet I've felt fear."

"Meda, don't dwell on what we cannot change, but on what we have the power to change. I'm old and growing tired."

"Ah, but Moonie, you say this like your time is over," Meda said. She only called her friend 'Moonie' when they were alone.

"Not yet. But I'm an old woman and have lived too many years. More than the Maker planned, I fear."

"It was His plan that you should live long, or you'd be with your ancestors in the clouds. So shush. Here's your pouch and your amulet. Let's begin."

Meda dimmed the lights before taking her place in the rocker next to Moonie's. Seated, they rocked, closing their eyes as they chanted.

As their singing intensified, Meda held aloft her talisman, and a simple stream of light appeared out of the shadows to shoot through the hole at the top, which created a rainbow prism on the opposite wall.

Silver Moon, still rocking and chanting, opened the pouch without looking and extracted two vials. Her eyes opened. She uncapped one vial, chanting in Lakota about an old forgotten past, about the empty but full lands, and the people and their way of life.

She took a pinch of the amber-colored powder and flicked it into the air toward the beam of light made by Meda's talisman.

Something occurred miles away, in a sterile room—cold steel tables, white sheets, gowns, masks, and the smell of disinfectant. Hands skillfully at work, voices talking to one another. The man lay supine, his eyes closed, his breathing regular, his chest open for the spirits to see, and he felt the power surge into his soul.

Fort Yates Hospital

The door to the outer family waiting room of surgery opened. Dr. Brownstone came out. Pete Johnson stood.

"How'd it go?"

The demeanor on her face said what words didn't. Pete feared the worst.

"Have a seat, won't you?" She waved her hand at the chairs.

He sat. Then, "Well?"

"First, the bypass was a success."

"Good to hear, Doctor. Now what aren't you telling me?"

"Mr. Johnson—Pete—your brother went into a coma. His vitals are stable, his heartbeat strong, his breathing fine, as is his blood pressure, and it has us—well, me—stumped."

"It's not the anesthesia, is it? Sam has a tough time waking up after being under. Might take him a minute longer," Pete said, hopeful.

"I've done thousands of procedures which require anesthesia. This has never happened—ever. I'm stunned. The ether should have worn off by now. Sam's been out of surgery long enough, but he won't respond to any stimuli."

Pete swallowed hard. "Now what? Just wait it out?"

"Right now he's in the ICU, and we'll keep a close eye on him. I promise, Pete." Her hand covered his.

With this news, he headed to the main floor's waiting room to inform the others.

I nside the ICU room, Sam Johnson lay in a coma. The bypass surgery was a success, yet the older gent hadn't woken from the anesthesia.

Sam's eyes moved in REM; his lids fluttered, albeit a tad. However, they fluttered, and no one was there to see. His heartbeat thudded inside his ears—he could hear it.

The beeping of machines, the ticking of a clock on the far wall, voices in the hallway, wheels rolling on a tiled floor. His hearing was keenly acute.

A beam of light flooded him behind his eyes, and other voices took over in his ears—older voices, ancient voices—some chanting, some whispering.

A fire crackled, and he smelled prairie grass and horse dung. The scent of pemmican and jerky invaded his nostrils. He felt starved, ready for the old days and the delicious food.

An old chant rose from the ground.

The clouds moved out, and he opened his eyes.

He saw the land—the mountains, tipis, campfires, and children scampering and playing as women worked. Men prepared for a hunt, crafting spears or purging themselves in a sweat lodge.

But far away, in the distance over a hill, over open prairie land, standing in the green grass, was the massive bulk of the Sioux Nation's survival. Sam saw Tatanka. (Buffalo)

28

In a Different Era, Centuries Before

We made it to the place he called Crag Rock, a large rock formation at the base of the mountains Nate said was part of the Rocky Mountain Range near the Yellowstone River. The river just trickled in a small stream—not deep, but enough water for Gypsy to quench her thirst, with a small patch of grass for her to munch on.

"Wow, this is beautiful."

The one thing I knew: this area was just as untamed in our present world and still gorgeous. I suppose there are some things time cannot change, and this land we'd one day consider a national park—or rather, several national parks—Yellowstone, Glacier Mountain, and the Grand Tetons—protected by the National Park Service.

"Yes, it is. Makes you wonder about the prominent Creator, doesn't it?"

I could hear in his voice how he marveled at this range and the land as he climbed up a small upper embankment and disappeared.

"Nate, hey, where are you going?"

"Tie Gypsy's reins to a tree and come over," he called back to me.

I did as he asked, not bothered much by his orders, as I felt it was less of an order and more of a request—at least my less stubborn side argued.

My hands pulled me up, and I so wanted different clothing, not his ridiculous, horrid girl's long overalls with no legs, the thing they called a jumper. What in the heck was Annie Oakley wearing today? That's what I wanted. Pants, boots—heck, even a shirt with fringe would be better than this pioneer-days crap. My head came over the top, and I saw him standing on the cliff's edge as I hauled my entire body up and over, then stood.

Nate stood, his arms crossed, his head moving from left to right and right to left. "Beautiful, huh?"

So gorgeous and surreal.

Below, I saw a large watering hole, a lake perhaps, nestled between sloping grassy land, hills, and valleys. The area was dotted with loads of trees, and who knew the names of all the wildflowers?

However, the most glorious sight was a herd of buffalo.

This wide expanse of undeveloped land was covered with the majestic beasts—large bulls, most of them six feet tall from the top of their humps, two thousand pounds of mass, with an excellent sense of smell but not of eyesight.

Cows with their calves focused on munching green grass as I watched this huge, ominous-looking beast. Knowing he was a vegan, I giggled.

"In my lifetime, I never thought I'd see this many of them in one place. You know, Nate, we've seen pictures, yeah, but this... well, this is the bomb!" I maintained a soft voice, and I'm sure he heard the awe in my tone.

"Thank God for the National Forest Preserves and the animal sanctuaries, or this magnificent beast would be extinct."

I agreed with him, thankful the buffalo numbers were increasing in our time.

I scrutinized the limitless stretch, and in my imagination, I could see them blazing across the plains, digging trenches as wide as the Grand Canyon. It left me pondering the question: Had the once prehistoric buffalo trenched it out? This made me smile.

"My mom recounted to me the story of the buffalo hunt my dad went on when they were back in this era, and how he had ticked this off his bucket list. Oh, boy, it sounds weird, doesn't it? Anyway, it wasn't for sport but for survival, and it had thrilled him to be involved."

"Yeah, it's a once-in-a-lifetime experience and unforgettable."

I turned to see him and saw the happiness on his face. "You've hunted, haven't you?"

"Yes, after I got here, but not with guns or bow and arrows."

"Oh, so they invited you to the hunt, then?"

"Uh, sort of. When they found me, I was less than cooperative, and at first I thought I was a dead man walking, so I ran like my life depended on it because, well, I thought it did."

"And you're alive, here to tell me the tale. So?"

"Once they saw how fast I ran, they allowed me into the tribe as a runner on the hunt." The delight in his voice made me smile.

Of course, I had to ask what he meant, so Nate explained the way the Crow hunted buffalo by driving them off an embankment. It didn't seem very sporting until he explained the dangers and how a herd could trample a tribe in a matter of minutes, their heads down and all their massive weight charging at you at thirty-five miles an hour—or a bull goring you with his horn, tossing you about like a rag doll.

I was about to remind him of how we did it in our time, skipping to the supermarket carts out of a store and the dangers of the parking lot, when we heard a loud cry and rounded to see three Crow men behind us, spears at the ready.

My heart stopped.

I listened as Nate spoke to them. It was odd for me not to understand what was being said, and it made me uneasy. This was out of character for me. I was never ill at ease with any Native American—I was now.

I then understood how Chay felt, just like my mother must have felt when she went back in time and couldn't speak or understand Lakota.

Within my thoughts, I chanted to myself, *Give me the knowledge, oh wise ones, give me the understanding, please.*

I stopped my thoughts and listened. Well, it'd been worth a shot, so I continued to listen and not understand.

Without forewarning, Nate grabbed my arm and jerked me over, saying something to the three men, and he laughed.

As his eyes cut to me, I saw in them a pleading look to follow along, so I did.

I looked up, giving them my scared look, and they fell for it. Nate nodded, saying something in Apsáalooke.

"Akeè Bìakaate kala," the taller man said with a smirk. (Own girl now, meaning the girl who was me was Nate's property.)

"Yes," Nate smirked back and said in their language, "I own Sioux woman and will do as I please."

The sort of laughter emitted from these men made me cringe, just like the bawdy mirth in locker rooms, with the hoots and catcalls of adolescent boys or immature men.

My back stiffened, and the hairs at the nape of my neck stood on end. Had I been a cat, you would've seen me arch and spit with a hiss, pushing my claws out.

Okay, so that's how I felt on the inside, but I stood straight as a rod, calm and unmoved.

The four of them chatted for a few more minutes, and I heard one word of the Apsáalooke words I understood—*bishèe*, which meant buffalo.

Were they out scouting for buffalo?

Had they seen the buffalo Nate had shown me and were on the way back to the tribe to report?

I couldn't wait for him to be done so we could talk. I was also very pleased we'd tied Gypsy to a clump of trees farther back, or questions about the different knapsacks and the red-flowered one would be hard to answer.

Nate forcibly shoved me back, jutting his chin up at the others. Of course, saying things I couldn't understand, they guffawed, then mounted their ponies and left, leaving Nate and a stunned me alone. When we knew they'd ridden off far enough, he glanced at me and shrugged.

"Sorry."

"For what? Talking about me in front of my face and me not understanding a word? It can't hurt my feelings if I don't know what was said, now can it?" I feigned indifference.

"Well, I told them you were my captive. That's why they laughed. Then we discussed the buffalo herd they found grazing about ten miles from here."

"How on earth did you explain the way I was dressed?"

"You'd fallen ill, and settlers were caring for you when I found you."

I eyed him, wondering how much stock to put in what he was saying, and then asked, "What else did you say? Because my gut says you said more to the three than you're letting on."

First, he looked at his feet, then straight at me and said, "Told them I could do as I pleased with you."

My neck hair didn't just bristle—it prickled with fire, and my eyes tapered into slits.

"I have never, ever," I began, and then I couldn't help it as the laughter bubbled from deep down inside, reaching my lips until I could contain it no longer, and it burst out, with me doubling over, holding my middle.

"You find this funny, do you? I just told you—I told them I owned you and could use you at my pleasure, and you're laughing?"

Once I composed myself and wiped the tears from my eyes, I faced him, glowering.

"First things first: no man will ever own me. It will be up to me and only me if I ever give myself to a man. Second, you and me? I find it truly ridiculous."

In my head, I'd already had this conversation with him when we'd discussed this hookup business. Here I was again, passionately saying I'd never be at his beck and call or whatever, and it could be I was protesting too much.

Is this what Nate thought, too?

I had to make a quick exit from this, so I cleared my throat and said, "We know how this works. It's all a ruse, so don't get any wrong ideas, understand? I mean, if I go along with this charade, you know it's just pretend, don't you?"

He made his way back to where Gypsy was tied without saying a word.

"Nate, you understand, right?"

"Oh, yeah," he said as he mounted Gypsy, stuck his arm out for me, and I grabbed hold, him lifting me onto the saddle with him. "This isn't in any way real, all pretend. Shoot, you aren't even my type."

Of course, this frustrated me—and then again, I didn't witness the sneaky grin on Nate's face as he tapped Gypsy's flank and got her moving.

29

It'd been a while since we'd talked, and I missed having a watch—or a Fitbit, even a cell phone—all of which communicated time. A horse also had no odometer, so I had no clue how far we'd ridden; and even though I was used to riding on horseback—just not behind anyone—my rump was feeling the ache.

I poked Nate. "Hey, where're we going, and how much further?"

"Not gonna get there before dark, so we'll have to camp. Then leave at first light."

"You're kidding, right?"

"You have provisions in these backpacks. I mean, not enough to last a lifetime, and there's a bedroll, so what's the deal about camping under the stars?"

"Fine, alright, we camp—but we aren't sharing a bedroll. That's how misunderstandings start, you know?" I wasn't about to be placed in an awkward situation of fear which turned into passion that I would regret the next morning.

"Sure. I've been roughing it longer than you have out here, so I can sleep under a tree. Let's pray it's a clear night."

We rode until Nate came to a patch of trees, and he rode through, this time slower so tree branches weren't cutting and poking the snuff out of him or me. I dodged limbs, and he swerved to miss low-lying branches.

Once he passed the thickest area, he came out on the other side in a clearing where the sight left me breathless.

Mountains in the foreground, and the orange sun just began its descent behind the peaks. Areas of green grass and tall prairie grass, wildflowers, and trees of every size and shape framed the land. I could see, in the not-too-far distance, a creek and the muddy area where the rains had landed and the creek had risen, then fallen.

Leaves blew in and around the area, floating in the air and on the water. In my mind, I thought of fall and wondered what season it was here right now.

We stopped, dismounted, and I walked into the scene, enthralled at the untouched beauty of the area. This piece of land instilled calm and underlying wildness in my soul, and my inner self gloried at the wonders created by a higher being, which flourished despite man and what he'd do in the future to the lands.

I left Nate with Gypsy, and he began unsaddling her and lifting the weight of the backpacks and gear so she, too, could get some rest, and I walked to the creek. Shucking my shoes and the ugly muslin stockings, I stuck my feet in the water, and boy, it was cold!

I stood, shivering from my toes to my nose, until my feet and ankles got used to the temperature, and then I padded with caution down the side a few feet, watching my every step and looking up every so often to keep my eye out for strangers, which included wild animals and snakes.

As I squatted and dipped my hand into the water, then cupped them to take a drink, I found the fresh spring water quite satisfying as it cooled my parched throat. I stood, with my hands confidently on my hips, and surveyed the area again, amazed at the beauty, and wondered what was here in the twenty-first century.

A town? A road? A farm?

If there'd been a way to photograph the area or put a marker that would still be in place in my real world, I'd have done so, so I might revisit this area hundreds of years into my true future to see where I had stood today and the differences. But this was impossible, so I sighed and headed back to where Nate had set up camp for the night.

"Beautiful area, isn't it?" Nate asked.

"Yeah, and to know one day man and progress will destroy it. What a shame."

"The wilderness is wonderful, but so is progress, Raven, so enjoy this as much as you can for the time you're here."

Funny, Nate never asked what I'd been doing before he found me and where I appeared from; perhaps he thought they'd whisked me right out of the twenty-first century, and he thought I was a pansy. I supposed I should enlighten him on my recent travels to prove I was no pansy, wimp, or a fraidy cat.

"Nate, you've been here, you think, a year. Let me tell you where I've been."

Then I explained Kingfisher, She Who Sees the Truth, Peggy, and Annie Shorey, and the ordeal with them, and about Chay.

"So, you're clueless about the time you've been gone, right?" asked Nate.

I moved my head from side to side and tried to think about time and said, "Clueless about sums it up. It could be hours or even years. I haven't any idea."

Then my head jerked toward the piles of knapsacks and Gypsy's blanket and saddle.

The books!

In a panic, I jumped up, took a step forward toward the pile, but my stupid foot caught on a small divot in the ground, causing me to almost face-plant onto Nate's lap.

"Hey... hey! Whoa! You okay?"

Nate's hand flattened against my right shoulder, pushing me backward to keep me from landing chin-first into his left thigh. He used just enough force to propel me back, but my body was already in a forward motion. My knees hit the ground with the full power of my weight. I yelped as my hands groped for his shoulders to steady me. I caught him, but not as my upper body slid down and I ended up with my face flat on his upper thigh, thanking the stars he was wearing buckskin breeches.

As I garbled my apologies with my mouth pressed against him, I heard him laughing. With as much dignity as I could muster, I moved off his leg, stood dusting off my hands, and then my knees.

"Uh, you okay there?"

A vast sigh blew out between my somewhat closed lips. "Yeah, just clumsy these days. Sorry—hope I didn't hurt your leg with my face."

"Takes more than a girl's face to hurt these legs of steel, I promise."

It was hushed for a minute or two, and then the words we'd just said got me tickled, and soon we were both in fits of laughter.

I think I chalked our stupid giggle fest up to weariness of time travel. I mean, it had to be worse than jet lag, didn't it?

After I got the books, I sat next to him—not touching him, of course—because, well, that wasn't gonna happen. At least this was what my brain told me. But the other parts of me had a small niggling of *what if...* it was here and now, and what if?

Shut up! I told that part of my brain controlling other parts of me. Focus on the books, not on him.

This was sorta funny because it was like, in the back of my head, someone had pinned the idea of him and me on a corkboard, and I couldn't unpin it. I wanted to smack Aunt Meda and Silver Moon on their respective old-lady heads; this was their fault for planting a darned seed!

As I flipped through Aunt Meda's book, my brain kept thinking about them hooking him and me up, and I had to bite my bottom lip to keep the gurgle of laughter from bursting out when the slogan *Time-Travel-Matc h.com—Find Your Soulmate From Any Era* popped into my head.

Nate must have seen me biting my bottom lip when he asked, "Is it that bad?"

Shaking my head, I said, "No, I have other things on my mind I'd rather not share right now." To tell him my thoughts might be admitting something or give him the wrong idea altogether, so it'd be best if I never mentioned this ad slogan I'd concocted.

He watched me turning pages, and I became focused on the task at hand.

"Nate, do you think you can read Apsáalooke, or just speak it?"

"I've never seen it written, so guessing not. I mean, I don't think I can, anyway. Why?"

I pointed at a few words. "I can speak and read Lakota and some of its sister language. Plus, I can speak Cheyenne well enough to get by, but not read it. This is Lakota: *oìhanbleta miyé tuwé o-iyàgle k'un ehàke kȟaŋǧ itȟáŋčhaŋ*; it says, *In a dream I'm the one which leads to the last Crow Chief.*"

"Wow, you're good, because it looks like Greek to me," Nate praised me.

"Yeah, well, not that good, because these next words aren't in Lakota, and I can't read them."

Nate looked, studying the letters and the accents with focused concentration, and then read aloud with perfect accents on each word: "*Alaxchíia Ahú bishé áatchile akhawassdáawe axpée isahké ammilaxpáake iisakusseé.*"

"Sounded perfect, but I've got not one inkling of what you just said. Do you even know?" I asked, my eyes on each word.

"It means 'Chief Plenty Coups to be born traveler save mother's life soon.' Best I can interpret." Nate rubbed his chin, his eyes lingering on the words with multiple vowels, consonants, and accent markings.

I watched him, admiring his humbleness, because anyone else would've puffed up knowing they could read such an old language, do it without hesitation, and understand what it said.

"I'm wondering here if it's you or me who is the traveler."

I gave him a facial shrug of an *I don't know*, then turned the pages in the book, looking for what I wasn't sure.

"Do you know who Chief Plenty Coups is?" Nate asked.

"Hmm, I guess he's a famous Crow Chief, since the message is in Crow."

"Apsáalooke."

"What?"

"They call themselves Apsáalooke; it's the Whiteman who came up with the tribe name of Crow." Nate leaned back on his elbows and looked at me, waiting.

"You expecting me to riddle you with questions?"

"Yeah, I am, since I know these people better than you do—at least this century."

"Don't hold your breath, my new friend. I just want to figure out what we're here for, because the other two incidents I described—well, it was to keep something in the past from making a drastic change and altering the Native American world. This darned book about visions is useless, as is this crappy diary."

With a snap, I closed the book and flung it onto the ground near me.

It frustrated me.

Any history lesson I'd learned back in school wasn't helping me decipher anything. We learned stuff, but I can tell you the kids in our future didn't care about the past—not at all. I suppose as a kid all we cared about was playing and not recollecting anything about the past unless it was an hour ago.

Teenagers—since I was one once—cared about the opposite sex and fun, sports, and if our school teams were on a winning streak. I knew about the Hunkpapa Lakota history because my mom and dad made sure, but not as much about other tribes because they weren't my heritage.

"Nate, did you know anything about any of the other Native American tribes before this?" I wondered how much he knew about his Native American side.

"You mean other than the Cowboy/Indian stuff on television, or genuine history?"

"Funny. You're a funny guy. No, the actual stuff, you dork."

His laugh was genuine, and I laughed too, punching him in the arm. "No, really, tell me what you know, and I'll give you a lesson on the Hunkpapa Sioux."

As I enlightened him on my Sioux history knowledge—in the book, pages past the ones I'd searched—words darkened.

I felt a slight wind blow, chilling me as we talked. I brought my knees to my chest, hugging them. Nate saw and took the blanket from the bedroll, then draped it over my shoulders.

We talked long into the night about cultures and the way our world had turned inside out, separating people of every origin and imploding on verbal impact. Accusations and turmoil created by people who were leaders, movers, and shakers of every color, creed, and nationality.

We did not discuss our current situation and what it held for us—our plan and what we were to do and when.

Neither of us verbalized the other issue, either.

The one we both felt.

A strong current, like unseen electricity, grew between us the longer we talked, getting to know one another.

Fears we should've faced head-on, but neglected to do so, festered as the book implemented an unseen magic that would affect us in ways we weren't expecting.

30

When I woke—the sight, oh my, almost indescribable.

The sun's golden rays shone across the mountaintops, prisms of yellows, reds, and oranges bursting outward like a giant starburst, casting sparkles on the dewy-topped grasses. I imagined how a supernova might perform—imploding from within, casting a million-and-one shards of tiny light speckles, filling the sky with such brilliance it would hurt your eyes and be beautiful all in one fell swoop.

How does one describe the warmth you experience when you see such a magnificent view, as your heart fills with this splendor?

My hand touched my face. I caressed my lips, touching the smile there, feeling happy. What a way to wake up in another realm of life. I looked down, ready to say good morning to Nate.

He was gone.

My eyes searched near the clumped trees where he'd tied up Gypsy's reins.

She was gone, as were the backpacks.

"Don't panic," I said to no one, fists on my hips, turning every direction and searching for signs of him and my beloved mare.

The dazzling sunrise and the scene it created were far from my thoughts now. It sorta ticked me off because, for once in my life, I was stopping to smell the roses, as they say.

"Nate, where are you?" Low words muttered under my breath. I gathered the bedroll with the extra blanket, tying them up and taking them to a tree.

I sat and waited, hoping in my heart he hadn't just scampered off with all my things—and my horse, too.

Pissy because I wasn't able to gauge time. Tired of waiting, I got up, slung the bedroll over my shoulder, and walked, hoping I was going in the right direction.

My aim was toward the large mountain range, and not to run into trouble.

———

S ure, the sun—a dazzling beauty in the morning—was just getting started, but the farther I walked and the higher the old ball of fire climbed, the hotter I got, and not just my flesh. Inside, I seethed because my feet were killing me and I felt like I'd been walking for days, getting nowhere.

What I wished for was food and water; even a stream would be nice to dip my achy feet in and get a darned drink.

At my best guess, I suppose I had a fairy godmother—one named Meda Clark, or perhaps Silver Moon. I could hear water rushing and climbed toward the sound, praying it was an area not only peaceful but also not a watering hole for any wild game. Deer, fox, or rabbit I could handle. Even a coyote. If he was far from the pack, I could scare him away. But a mountain lion—or even a bear? Nope. I'd be breakfast.

The waterfall wasn't Niagara, but all the same, the water was cool and inviting, and I thanked my lucky stars for a glorious sip not from a nasty creek, and for the coldness on my burning, achy feet.

Once again, here I was—shoes and my torn, snagged, dirty muslin stockings off. I hated these stockings but was grateful I had them to cushion my feet inside the ugly shoes.

With my feet in the water, I hiked the jumper up to my knees and splashed water on my legs, washing and cooling them. That was when I heard a man's voice in the distance calling out.

My head snapped up as I cocked my ears, listening, and a familiar shiver went up my spine.

With hurried movements, I stepped out of the nice, cool, refreshing water and dropped the jumper to cover my legs. I grabbed the stockings and tugged them on, then slipped my feet into the shoes, all while looking around for a place to hide.

Few places—but I took the most logical one and scampered back into a clump of bushes, whimpering a few expletives after getting poked and scratched by thorns from a berry bush—blackberry, huckleberry, or whatever. I wasn't a botanist or horticulturist and wasn't about to eat any berries unless it was strawberries; those I knew.

He was closer now, and I heard him, so I peeked out between the limbs, my kneecaps jumping like mad from fear and anxiety.

"Hiŋhaŋni wašté," ("Good morning"), a man called out in Lakota.

His eyes searched the bushes, and I knew he was looking for me—but how, why, who was he?

"Kňkípňe šni ye/yo, don't be afraid. I mean you no harm."

Lakota and English? He spoke distinctly, and I craned my neck to see him better. Tall, lean, older than me by twenty—thirty years, I'd guess—wearing traditional buckskin breeches, a breastplate made with strips of leather and shells, and beaded moccasins.

There was one feather in his long black braided hair, and he carried a bow with a spectacularly decorated beaded quiver slung over his shoulder, holding many arrows.

In a matter of seconds, my heart rate dropped to normal, the fear whooshed out of me, and a calmness overcame me. I straightened and called out—first in Lakota, then in English—"I'm here, and I greet you with peace. I'll come to you."

He nodded, his face devoid of a smile, but not his eyes, and I was no longer frightened. There was a vague familiarity about this man.

"Why are you here?"

"To find a blackbird."

Spooky, since my name's Raven. Could he be scouting the area for his tribe's enemy, the Crow? I hesitated to tell him who I was.

"Are you searching for many blackbirds?"

"A single female bird, and my task will be to guide her to her nest."

Could he be looking for me?

But how did he know about me—or where to find me? It wasn't like he had a GPS, and I wasn't tagged with a homing beacon.

"Let us sit by the water. Please tell me more about this blackbird," I said in English, testing his vocabulary.

"Yes, come, we shall sit by the cool water," he answered, his English impeccable.

After sitting, he told me of a dream—of bright lights, of a hand that pushed his heart to beat back to life, of how he thought his time on man's earth was over.

In his sleep, a white dove with a silver ring encircling it told him not to fear and to let his soul fly into the light. He released his soul, which floated until it landed upon soft prairie grass, and then he woke and walked until he reached this place. His arm came up, waving over the area, and his gaze locked onto me.

"You are Raven?"

He had me there. I was her and wouldn't deny who I was.

"Yes. It's my Sioux and Christian name. Tell me—what do you know of me?"

I sat with my legs crossed in my best lotus position, watching a few leaves drift atop the narrow stream—the product of the waterfall a few hundred feet away—and listened to this Hunkpapa Sioux man talk.

"As I slept, I saw black clouds circling and crowding the skies, with rains falling like a waterfall as the winds blew with the mighty breath of the gods. It was then I witnessed a mountain crumbling, sliding into the river to disappear. A big blackbird will soon swoop in to save a young maiden."

It sounded like a storm would happen and somehow he was telling me I would save a young girl. Add in what Nate had read in Aunt Meda's book, and I wondered who this young woman was in history—and why she was so important.

Nate!

Where in the devil had he gone off to, and had this man seen him?

With as much detail as I could recall, I described Nate and my horse, Gypsy, leaving out items such as red-flowered backpacks and canvas knapsacks.

"No, but he's near," the man said. "My heart says so, and so does yours—if you will listen."

He closed his eyes and softly began humming a chant, the words inaudible at first. I listened harder.

First, he sang about a bird of power, a bird of prey, and dark days to come. He sang about men who fought and died in years long gone—and in years to come.

His words touched on love and death, heartbreak, and happiness, birth, and when men grew old.

Then his words crescendoed, and he cried out to the gods of time to let him repeat his life—to see his people and know the land. None of it made sense to me, but hey, I was just his audience.

His voice grew faint, his words unintelligible, turning into a near growl deep within his chest. He reopened his eyes and looked at me—but I swear he didn't see me.

"Are you alright?" This time, I spoke to him in Lakota.

"I am good. We go."

He stood and held out his hand to assist me, and I smiled. When I took hold of his larger hand, something odd happened.

Memories flashed through my head like a rolling movie—me, my mom and dad at Aunt Meda's house, celebrating something with Aunt Meda's friends—and this man was there. He was in my future. His name was—his name *is* Sam Johnson, also called Running Elk, and he was part of our Tribal Head Council.

I swallowed and closed my eyes, tightening my grip, and he did the same.

We both felt a jolt so electrifying it tingled to my toes.

Once it stopped, I reopened my eyes and Nate stood there, holding my hand, Gypsy neighing in the background.

"What the devil? I was just—hey, where did he go?"

I snatched my hand back, my head nearly swiveling in a full circle as I searched for him.

The man had vanished.

With my back to Nate, hands on my hips, the air whooshed out of my lungs in defeat.

Not happy.

I wasn't happy at all.

Running Elk had gone without telling me why he was here. His words about a bird of power and dark days to come ... was he talking about me? I wondered.

All this talk about birds and my name being Raven—heavens. Was I just being dramatic, making it sound like I was more important than I really was? His last words were strange, requesting the gods to allow him to experience his life once more so he could see his people and the land.

Nate tapped me on the shoulder. "Hey, are you seeing ghosts? Because it's just us and, uh, the horse. No other people are here."

"A lot you know, Nate Copper. A man was here, and when you appeared he vanished, and now I'm, well..." I held my hands up, at a loss for words, which for me was a miracle.

Nate put his hand up to my forehead as if he were checking my temperature, and I slapped it away.

"Stop it. I'm not sick, nor am I a loon. I swear he was here just before you showed up, and he was holding my hand. Then *you* were holding it, and he vanished."

My determination was to make Nate understand I wasn't crazy, nor sick and seeing things.

"Did you know him, or did he know you?"

"Not at first, but once we'd clasped hands, I remembered him from my aunt's house. His Christian name is Sam Johnson. He has a brother named—"

"Pete," Nate said, cutting in. "They're part of the Council. Them and Uncle Hank are friends, I think. Anyway, it's funny because I had a dream about his brother Pete last night."

My eyes widened. "You did? About what?"

"Something about a war—like an old-time war—but it wasn't clear. There were tanks, guns, soldiers in old-fashioned uniforms ... almost made me feel like I was watching an old movie."

I plopped down with my back against a smaller tree and closed my eyes with a loud exhale. Nate sat across from me, his legs stretched out, ankles crossed.

I rubbed my temples. "All these riddles are giving me a big fat headache."

"Did you bring any aspirin in your arsenal of crap from the future?"

Yeah, we'd brought all kinds of stuff, and I'd forgotten about it with all this strange stuff going on every single second, keeping my head spinning and me off guard.

Who knew what would happen next? That question filtered through my thoughts as I heavily sighed and pushed myself up off the ground—just to take one step and trip over a rock, or heck, a blade of grass.

I tumbled on top of Nate for the second time since I'd known him. What, all of two days?

This time, he didn't push me back. His chest broke my fall, and we ended up nose-to-nose.

As my head dropped, with the crown level to his upper chest, I closed my eyes, mumbling, "Sorry," and my hands pushed against his arms as I tried to regain my balance and get off him.

"Stop fighting it, will you?"

"I'm not trying to fight you, Nate. I'm trying to get up."

My hands pressed while the toes of my feet pushed, trying to move myself off him. As I shoved away and started to regain my balance, his hands came around, grabbing me by the waist, and he pulled—landing me with both knees between his thighs, again nose-to-nose.

"Nate, I need—" I started, but he stopped me.

One finger on my lips, he said, "To shut up for once."

The kiss was soft, close-mouthed, and warm.

His lips rested against mine, pressure building, and with one finger he traced my jawline in such a seductive way. I opened my mouth to protest, and that's when his tongue slipped inside to tease mine.

I was under his control, my response automated and devoid of any personal power. I relaxed—but only for a minute—before something in my head told me to snap out of it and get off the man.

When I pushed him away, his hands didn't restrain me, and that somehow angered me. He gave up too easily. Did I want him to keep kissing me or not?

I stood. So did he. We were silent for a few seconds before I coughed and apologized.

"My fault for throwing myself at you on accident, and I guess you thought ... well, whatever it was you thought, was wrong." I frowned, but the anger didn't reach my eyes as hard as I tried.

"No, my bad," Nate said, scooting back, then crossing his arms over his chest. A small frown line wiggled on his forehead. "I guess I got the signals mixed up, so don't apologize. I'll make sure it never happens again."

A hard swallow slid down my throat and my mouth dried some, but I nodded and got my tongue working. "Fine. So now that we've got this cleared up, I'll go get the book I need—it's what I was going after in the first place."

I dusted off my hands and knees for the umpteenth time and walked toward Gypsy to get the books. I wondered why my legs felt a smidge like Jell-O and my insides first felt quivery, then hollow.

31

All the way to my horse, I grumbled at myself for taking all this passion stuff too seriously and for reading into what wasn't there. I chalked it up to tension and the moment in time, then giggled.

"Love to hear a joke if you've got one," Nate called out.

"No, I don't know a funny joke. I just thought of something, and it made me laugh, and—oh, never mind. You wouldn't understand it anyway," I lied.

I unbuckled the flap of the knapsack and pulled out Aunt Meda's book.

When I returned, I sat against the tree for support and asked him to come sit beside me.

"You sure I won't scare you? I mean, I don't want to breathe on you wrong and have you think I'm trying to seduce you."

"Suit yourself. Breathe as hard as you'd like. I won't get any wrong impression since we understand each other."

Okay, so the words came out sorta catty, but hey, I was keeping an even-keeled head on my shoulders because I, for one, knew I hadn't made this time-warp trip to meet him and fall at his feet like a love-struck teenage girl.

What we were to do was the only thing on my mind, and him—well, he was a guy; anyone could do the math.

I also argued with myself that whatever happened here in this past era wouldn't affect me in my future; then my parents came to mind, and that's how I came to be.

Oh, man. Me, conceived sometime in the 1800s, yet born in the modern twenty-first century. Was this supposed to be the plan?

Meet Nate, fall in love, and bear a child?

Well, darn it, where was my head? I was supposed to be looking something up in this book, and here I was, daydreaming.

Heck, it didn't matter, because in this silly scenario I'd fallen in love with Nate, gotten pregnant, and had a child.

Holy moly. I needed to shake this off.

Nate must have wondered where my head was when he said, "For the third time, Raven, you gonna read that book or go into a trance?"

"Uh, sorry. Guess my head is elsewhere, and I—oh, shoot, never mind."

My thumb flicked the book open, and I licked my finger to turn each page, not sure what I was searching for, but when I saw it, I knew I'd know.

As I did this, I didn't see the sly smile twitching on Nate's face, or the spark in his eyes as he watched me.

He knew something I didn't know—or wouldn't admit; it was inevitable. Any dunderhead could've seen it, and Nate could wait, for time was something we had more than enough of—over one hundred years and counting.

When I turned the page, I saw it, and my heart fluttered.

I pointed. "See here. It says, *dark clouds shall descend, the waters torrid, and the ground will slip away.*"

"Sounds like a terrible rainstorm. Or flash flooding, you think?"

He looked into the sky, and there wasn't a cloud—not a single puff of white cotton floating above. "But it's not gonna happen today. Not a darned cloud in the sky."

"What about the vision Running Elk told me of? The one with dark clouds and rain like a waterfall and the side of a mountain sliding into a river? This is what my aunt wrote, and it's dated—see?"

I pointed at the top corner of the page, where Aunt Meda had written *September 14, 1978.*

"You realize she wrote this before you were born—what—forty-three years ago?"

"Yeah, and how did you know it was forty-three years ago? Do you know when I was born?" I gave him a frowny side glance, then looked back down at the page with Meda's chicken scrawling.

"Uh, yeah, because our birthdays are four days apart."

My eyes rolled up into my head. Of course he'd know when my birthday was, and I wouldn't know his, so I said, "I'm older than you, so we're not four days apart—more like years."

"You're the most aggravating, argumentative person. Your birthday is on the fourth of the month and mine is on the eighth—only four days. As far as years, if I'm not mistaken, you were born in 1997 and I was born in 2001, so you're an old lady to my young-guy status!"

I heard the intake of a chuckle and elbowed him.

"Back to the reason we're here, okay, Nathaniel? And since I'm older, you need to listen to me."

"Nope, no can do. But I'll admit you could be—and remember I said *could be*—wiser, so I can listen, but don't have to agree. We good?"

After I stuck my tongue out at him, then blushed, hoping he didn't think it was a flirtatious invite, I cleared my throat, only a little embarrassed.

"All right, young pup," I kidded, then got serious. "Aunt Meda's and Running Elk's nighttime fantasies are too close to not be the same, and it means something—but not a rainstorm. I think it's metaphorical. I've been wracking my brain about old history and can't come up with anything. What about you? You have any thoughts on this?"

"What if it meant a war? That could be a dark cloud, and what if the mountain crumbling means the losses a tribe suffers?"

Nate's answer surprised me, and it made sense. And here I was, older and wiser—ha!

"If we knew what territory this was and what year, it would be helpful," I stated.

"Uh, I hate to even say this, but I think this war is between the Apsáalooke and the Sioux, and if memory serves me, it didn't end well for, uh... my team."

"What the devil do you mean, *your team*? Your ancestors are the Sioux, not the Crow. Are you going to fight against the Sioux?" The steam in my ears built as my anger festered.

"No, and neither are you. We're not here to prevent a war that is unavoidable, and don't think you can try to make peace. That ship sailed long ago—long before we arrived. Listen, what I think is—" Nate stopped, raising a finger to his lips to keep me shushed.

He got up without making much noise, then helped me to my feet, pointing at the short thicket of briar brush.

With a noncommittal shrug, I nodded and followed, and we squatted behind the prickly bushes.

Then I leaned into his ear and whispered, "Did you hear something, or are you yanking my chain?"

Before he could answer, I heard horses' hooves clomping in a slow gait, and my eyes widened.

"Gypsy," I mouthed. "They'll see her."

Peeking out from the brush, Nate got eyes on our unknown visitor, and I felt him exhale. Then he angled his head toward me and said in a muffled voice, "It's a girl—a young teen—and she appears to be alone."

"Huh. Well, maybe she's a decoy. Hey, I don't want to get captured or killed today, so what's your plan?"

Fear gripped my insides and held on tight.

The unknown was scary, and here, in this place and time, Nate and I were more than clueless.

We were defenseless.

He glanced again, evaluating her, and observed her dismount. She went to the tree, secured her horse, and sat. Leaning against the tree, she drew her knees up, then lowered her head, hugging them.

My voice lowered. "What's she doing?"

"Crying, I think," said Nate.

"Whatever in the world."

I stood and looked over the bushes to see what he saw, and sure enough, she appeared to be sobbing.

My heartstrings pulled, and I went to her, with Nate telling me to stay put. Me being me, I ignored him.

Down on my haunches, I tapped her arm, and the girl jumped at least a foot, brandishing a knife—scaring the hooey out of me!

Okay, not the wisest move I'd made, but hey, my heart was in the right place. I'd about swallowed my tongue trying to get Lakota words out to say I was a friend, not foe, hoping she spoke the language.

The quizzical look on her face told me one of two things: she didn't speak Lakota, or she questioned how I appeared like magic.

O-M-Gee. Now I felt like that silly leprechaun, although right this moment I didn't feel too lucky.

The knife pressed at my throat, the pressure bearing down. I'd be dead soon. Holy cow, I prayed Nate would find it in his bones to pop up and save me.

His words were strong as he spoke to her in Apsáalooke. With a sneer, she shoved me backward, sending me flat on my backside with a resounding thud.

I jerked my head up, frowning at Nate. "Just what did you say to her?"

"If she valued her life, then she'd better let the Raven go—or words similar."

"She's Crow?"

Nate nodded, reaching his hand down to assist me up. I obliged, then dusted my backside off.

Geez, Louise. I was always dusting part of me off, and this was getting tiring.

"Humor me. Why would she back off? Does she know me?" I side-glanced the girl.

"No, not you per se, but the folklore about ravens being mystical birds—shapeshifters or tricksters—is common among most American Native tribes."

"Huh. As hard as she pushed me, it doesn't mean she's afraid of me—raven or not!"

I looked at her, furious that she'd held a knife to my throat with every intention of doing me in, and then I saw the tearstains on her face and her red-rimmed eyes.

In Lakota, I asked if she could understand me, and she nodded, saying, "Only some."

Then it was Nate's turn to ask me, "Well, what did you say to her?"

"She understands Lakota, but not much. Boy, I wish I knew the Apsáalooke language—be a lot easier."

When the thunder clapped, we all jumped and looked up, expecting the sky to open and drown us. There wasn't a cloud in the sky, and no rain fell.

Present Time, Seconds Before the Thunderclap

Jon Little Bird's words rang out as the others swayed with the beat of the drum. Then Blackie Kangee stood, shaking the old, lacquered gourd filled with tiny pebbles and shells of time, as they were called.

He shook it from right to left—right signifying present time, left symbolizing the past—moving the power from today to the past.

The words Little Bird chanted reflected the wish for those in past times to comprehend the words of one's enemies.

The others chanted the same plea in hushed tones in their native tongue until they chanted no more.

Silver Moon stood.

Her eyes focused on the wall just outside the main room.

Blaze followed her stare to the enlarged photo depicting a scene from the old days.

Members of a tribe—standing, squatting, and working.

Men, women, and children photographed as they lived daily: working the land, hunting, fishing, and communing with the spirits. Tipis sat in the background, several campfires smoldering out.

Women carried baskets or bison bladders filled with water to begin the day's cooking. Horses were tied to makeshift hitching posts, dogs milling about, and in the far background stood the Black Hills mountain range, with free lands stretching as far as the eye could see.

The old woman shuffled her feet as if the photo beckoned her, and everyone watched in silence.

When Blaze saw her falter, she went to her, giving the old lady her arm so she could balance herself. The elderly woman never broke her stride in her diminutive shuffling, and her eyes never veered from the photograph.

Blaze stood next to her, steadying her, and Silver Moon's face was inches from the photograph. Using her free hand, gnarled with arthritis, she pointed to the photo and said, "Kȟaŋǧi tȟáŋka" (Raven).

Once the thunderclap sounded, they knew it was complete.

"The understanding is complete. There is no longer a language barrier for those who've traveled to the past."

Blaze continued to watch Silver Moon's finger as it moved over the faces in the picture.

Her ancestors. Her people—the Lakota Sioux of long ago. Her hand tightened on Blaze's, and she gestured for her to come closer so she could whisper.

"Words only for you, She Cougar, not for the others. You understand?"

"Yes."

"See here."

The old lady pointed her finger back to the photo.

"There are many changes, many ways to understand. Your Raven is a communicator—one for the Real People, all the Real People with whom her path crosses. Not just the Lakota Sioux, but other Native American tribes too. Do you follow my meaning?"

"That my daughter shall know more tribal languages, speak them, and recognize the words?"

"Yes. And she will not lose this ability once she returns to her time. She will need it again one day—perhaps in the future. For she will travel again."

Her bent, arthritic finger pointed to another figure in the picture's background, a bit blurred.

"There. What do you see, and what does he wear?"

"A man, wearing four feathers, and around his neck—a bauble."

"And next to him?"

"A woman with dark eyes, holding an arrow."

"The bauble is his amulet. Look at it and tell me what you see."

A gasp escaped Blaze's not-quite-closed lips. "A golden feather," her words hushed. Then she pointed at the woman and said, "This is you, isn't it?"

"The man is a young Running Elk, and yes, I stand next to him. We have been called by the higher gods, and soon he shall answer, as shall I. Do you know what I mean?"

A single tear dropped from the corner of one eye, and Blaze nodded.

Silver Moon's face was stoic as she peered at the picture, then a tiny smile played on her lips.

"You cannot reveal what you know, and do not be sad, child, for I need you to be strong. Soft Dove knows, and she too will receive the same calling. You are the next in line, as Raven shall be your successor, and as the family line continues, so shall this duty."

"Me? No, I can't. I'm not strong enough, nor do I have the wisdom, to fill your or her shoes." The words choked out, and Silver Moon's grip tightened.

"Yes, you will. But for today, worry not, for it is not today. There is more to do. Remember—speak of this to no one. You shall know when it is time, but until then, heed what I say."

Blaze nodded, wiping the tears from her face with her free hand.

"Running Elk, he is..." Oh, she couldn't bring herself to say *dead*. She just couldn't.

"No, my child. He sleeps and travels. He visited with your only child to give her a message. He will need to visit her once more and then come home again—but only to leave his earthly body one last time."

32

C irca 1828

A loud, ear-splitting bang rang out.

"Wow, did a cannon just go off, or is one of the mountains a volcano? There's not a single cloud in the sky. See how blue it is—so blue it almost doesn't seem real," I said.

My eyes glanced upward, then widened as a small herd of deer flew by, and I thought the noise had spooked them. I didn't see Nate's hand shoot out to pull me back just as an arrow whizzed by; then chaos ensued.

First, he grabbed my hand, then hers, yanking us both face-down into the dirt.

My heart pounded, not knowing what the Sam Hill was going on, thinking we were being attacked.

He spoke to the girl first and told her we needed to leave. We were on Sioux hunting grounds, and they were hunting. If they saw her, they'd take her captive, for she belonged to the enemy tribe, the Crow.

Nate turned to me and began in English, but I cut him off. "I understood every word, so you don't need to repeat it."

"No way."

So, to prove it, I repeated it back to him, then asked, "What now? Do we get up and run?"

I eyed the girl, who kept her head down as another arrow flew over her.

The young girl gave me the worst stink-eye I'd gotten in a long while, like back in junior high over a stupid boy.

In Apsáalooke, he instructed us to crawl as fast as possible—me to Gypsy, and him and the girl to her mare.

I didn't have time to ask him why he was riding with her. A teeny-weeny green-eyed monster deep down in my subconscious poked its ugly head up and bore daggers at the young, pretty Apsáalooke teenager.

We rode hard toward the base of an unknown mountain range. I looked back several times to see if we'd been followed or were being chased. My heart rate slowed when I saw we weren't.

Nate slowed the other mare, and I caught up to ride beside them, and the younger girl spoke to me for the first time.

"You not Apsáalooke. You spoke Lakota to me first. How can you understand my language now? Are you a shaman?"

My eyes cut over to her, and I wondered how much trust I should put into this girl who had wanted me dead—or so I assumed she did. Who holds a knife to another's throat not wanting them dead?

"Why do you not think I already speak your native tongue?"

Two could play at this, and I was willing.

"He speaks to you in Whiteman's language, not mine, and you speak Lakota."

"You know the Whiteman's words and some Lakota. Tell me how." I found her intriguing and less scary when she wasn't threatening me with a knife.

"I learn from White Woman in our village, and an old Sioux woman."

Okay, intrigued wasn't a strong enough word. This news had me captivated.

First, I wanted to learn why a white woman was with their tribe, and then next, who this old Sioux woman was.

"What are you called?" I asked her.

"Otter Woman."

"Why do you cry, Otter Woman?"

Her chin lifted. "Not cry, I—"

I pointed at her and put my hand to my face, then pointed at my eyes.

"Yours are red, and there are tearstains on your face, so yes, you cry—but why?"

Before she spoke, Nate did, jolting both of us out of our private conversation.

In Apsáalooke, he said, "Get off the horses, both of you."

He reverted to English. "Raven, yank the knapsacks off—anything from the future—and hand me the mare's reins." Then: "There are riders coming over the hill. Run into the thicket. Hide."

He pointed. "Do it now—and quick!"

Otter Woman slid off the back of her mare, while Nate stayed mounted.

I jumped off Gypsy, grabbing knapsacks, flinging them at Otter Woman to help me carry. I spoke in rapid-fire Apsáalooke, and she, in utter confusion, did what I said, and we hightailed it to the thicket. Our arms filled with bags, bedrolls and all, we dove in headfirst, not bothering to check for thorns or wild animals.

We peeked out, both of us breathless, and if she knew what adrenaline was, I'm sure Otter Woman would agree hers was raised to new levels.

In the far distance, we could see Nate on her mare, but Gypsy was nowhere to be seen. I was about to come unglued because he'd let my beloved mare just prance off into God knows where, and the thought occurred to me she could've been caught and thus belong to someone else—the old finders-keepers scenario.

I prayed Gypsy loved me enough to go hide, and felt dumb for the thought, but she was mine—had been mine since the day she'd been born.

We watched Nate guide the other horse up the mountain and disappear into the dense treed area. I swiped a tear from my face. All because of a horse, I was a blubbering dork. Otter Woman patted my arm and told me the man would be okay; he was smart and cunning.

I looked at her like she had two heads, because I wasn't worried about Nate, and here again I was thinking it was all about me. Me—always me-me-me and what I wanted.

When we saw the two riders pass the thicket, headed to the area Nate had ridden into, we stayed still, waiting for more riders, but none materialized, and we felt safe enough to stand and assess the area.

I frowned at her and asked, "Do you know him—the man?"

Had she and Nate met before?

Why would she say he was a smart and cunning man?

"We know of him, from the other Crow tribes; they call him Chía bacheeítche."

They called him To Be White Chief. I wasn't sure whether I was impressed or jealous.

In my rights, I was born from a line of famous chiefs, and Nate was, well, not.

What is my problem these days?

Why did I feel as if I had to be all-important?

Okay, yes, I was an only child, and yes, my parents had doted on me—but not spoiled me, at least not by giving me everything I wanted, not that I wanted much. Growing up, my parents made sure I understood the importance of family and our heritage, encouraging me to embrace my individuality with a sense of pride.

However, at present time, I was ashamed of myself for being self-centered, without showing concern for Nate and his safety, and why this young girl—a mere teenager—had been crying.

I inhaled and shook my head to toss off the uneasy vibes, then asked her to sit beside me to wait for Nate's return. I was glad she now felt comfortable with me and hadn't stuck her knife back in my face.

"Otter Woman, why do you cry?" This time I crossed my arms and gave her an older-girl-to-younger-girl look, my mouth set firm, wanting an answer.

She let her eyes wander the area, and I watched her mulling things over. What had made this woman cry?

And yes, I called her a woman even though she was still a teen; however, in this period she'd long ago become a woman in her clan—one who worked as hard as the others and did her fair share of the work.

Native American tribes were a lot alike in how the man-woman structure went; my mom told me about her time living with the Hunkpapa Sioux and the work the women did. It was the females who kept the home fires burning, so to speak, and without modern conveniences in a life considered not just hard but sometimes cruel.

"I wish not to marry," she said, hushed, her head bowed in dishonor.

This was a universal thought for most girls her age, to have a life before marrying, but this was a different time. Not sure how to approach this, I just dove right into the meat of the matter.

"The boy—you do not love him?"

"He is not boy, is old man, and I love another."

Okay, this took me by surprise, knowing love didn't always enter the equation with tribal marriages. Many tribes based unions on a man's wealth—such as horses, guns, furs, and so forth. He could buy a bride. My guess was this older gent had the wealth, and the younger man didn't.

"Who is the other?" Would Otter Woman consider this prying? I was older than her, not by much—maybe eight years—and perhaps she had no one close to her age to confide in.

"He is Shoshoni and Apsáalooke, not wealthy, but my heart beats for him."

"He is younger, like you?"

Otter Woman nodded, and she patted her heart. "He lives here and works for more horses, and I wait for him to build bride purse."

"Your clan approves?"

"Grandmother pushing me. Mother listens to her, and I run away. He comes for me, but now alone, and this worries me. Sioux are near. You're Sioux—my enemy."

Well, now we were getting somewhere. She'd run away in fright with nowhere to go, and here I was, her sworn enemy, part of the Hunkpapa Sioux.

"I'll let no harm come to you."

"Not good, for the men who might find us—they not be kind."

After wrapping my head around those words, I realized she had a point. Time to get the heck out of Dodge.

I poked my head up, looking in every direction, and saw nothing.

No animal. Nothing stirred—which I found odd—but hey, right now nothing was normal, at least not for me. I stood and then took her hand, pulling her up.

"We will leave. Go hide up higher in the hills."

I slipped the biggest knapsack on, then the next largest to my front, cinching up the straps to tighten it. After that, I put a medium-sized one on her back and showed her how to tighten the straps.

This was funny—but not the time to laugh.

Next, I hooked two packs together with a carabiner snap hook, which got me another inward chuckle at her expression.

She might have a lot of questions later, but now wasn't the time. I fashioned those to her front facings and latched them to the pack on her back.

Otter Woman looked like she was headed for combat, and I squeezed my lips to keep from smiling at the look on her face as she tried to see it all hanging about her.

I took the last one and hooked it and the bedrolls on my front pack.

"Let's go." I grabbed her by the hand so we'd not separate, and she resisted.

"We must wait for White Chief."

"No, we must go now. He'll find us. White Chief can follow our trail up the mountain where we will hide." It sounded good, but I had no idea if he'd find us. Although deep down, something told me I hadn't seen the last of Nate Cooper.

33

The climb was steeper than it looked, and Otter Woman and I were panting as we continued uphill. I had let go of her hand, and we were both grabbing anything we could find to help pull us up, so neither of us went sliding back to the bottom into potential danger.

The other hindrance was the backpacks we had strapped to our backs, as well as the ones we had dangling from our arms. Once Otter Woman began firing questions at me about the knapsacks, I had to tell her in not-so-kind words to shut up and move her tail end!

I chuckled inwardly at her expression for me speaking to her in such a manner. It was something I was sure she wasn't accustomed to, but I was confident she'd bossed others younger than her around. Otter Woman seemed like a decent kid who gave her parents little worry—until now.

She stopped about four feet above me, her foot dangling in my face, and I inhaled. I was tired, and my arms were achy.

"Otter Woman, why do you stop? We must go higher, get to the ridge—it's not much farther," I called out in Lakota, forgetting for a minute she was Apsáalooke.

Her words crisp and clear, she said, "No Sioux. Am Apsáalooke. You forget this."

She was right, and I was a dope, so I repeated what I said, but this time in Apsáalooke, still amazed I could speak and understand her language. I gave a tremendous internal shout-out to Aunt Meda and Silver Moon.

She answered, "I stop because this... this bag is tangled, cannot pull off."

A heavy sigh of exasperation escaped my lungs as I pulled myself up higher so I'd be beside her.

One problem was I hadn't yet looked down, and my heart stopped when I did. It was a plummet of several hundred feet, and it would kill either of us if we lost our footing.

I reached my hand up, grabbed the plastic buckle on the arm strap, and yanked it loose from the broken tree limb. Then I realized she had the pack with the books.

Lordy, if something were to happen to her and the books were lost... well, I dare not think about it. Those books needed to stay with me.

"Please straighten your arm out so I can slip the little pack. It will be easier for you."

She was a tiny thing, and I figured she wouldn't argue, for I was lightening her load—but oh no, she was gonna pull her weight.

"Not weak. Am strong and young. Not child." Her brows crinkled in anger at me.

No time to argue, so I motioned for her to continue upward with a jerk of my head. She harrumphed at me, then went on, tugging herself up with the next overhanging limbs.

It was an absurd statement, but it felt like the mountain was growing taller as we climbed, and our destination was getting further up into the clouds—and we'd never reach it.

Mumbling under my breath, I said, "Time has no concept in the era—or for me it doesn't. I feel like Alice in Wonderland, but in a backward sort of way. Will it ever end—for gosh' sake? Are we supposed to climb this ridiculous mountain forever and ever, or does it have a top?"

Now, I hadn't whispered and spoke in English—not Lakota, not Ap-sáalooke—so I'm not sure what caused it to happen, but it made my head spin.

Darkness overshadowed one edge of the mountain as we climbed, and looking up, we saw the thick black clouds swirling and developing.

In the blink of an eye, all I thought was tornado as they began whirling around and around.

Then rain smacked me right in the face—not just a drop, but like a bucket of water was thrown directly at me.

I saw Otter Woman ducking her head to keep the pelting rain from stinging her eyes and flooding her nostrils.

The gusts intensified at speeds faster than a freight train, and I feared both of us would be blown into the air and then plummet to our certain deaths if we didn't hang on tight and work together to get to the flat landing.

"Put your head down, grab the next limb, and hold on until I reach you."

The wind was so loud I scarcely heard her acknowledgment as I pulled up faster and got as level with her as I could, so we were almost face to face.

I looked down at what had once been such an exquisite sight: trees filled with green, amber, gold, and rustic-colored leaves. In the valley, green grasses mixed with wildflowers of every color, with a background of mountains in assorted sizes lending an element of splendor to the scene.

Now all I saw was fear and death, as the winds picked up and the rain pelted down harder.

Otter Woman and I were soaked to the bone, and in the fierce, howling winds, I screamed, "Move faster! Get to the raised ground! Hurry!"

I pushed her up, my hand against her back, and my heart raced. I feared for her life, not mine—this girl couldn't die.

Our destination loomed above us, and no matter how hard we pushed, the climb seemed to grow, and safety eluded us.

"I cannot make it. Arms too tired," Otter Woman called down.

"No! Don't stop! Keep going—you must."

Now I felt panicked, because if she gave up, she'd slide down and take me with her, and I knew I wasn't strong enough to carry her, with or without the knapsacks.

What had started quickly stopped even quicker, as the wind no longer howled and stilled, yet the darkness overtook our sight.

All I could make out was Otter Woman's form above my head. What a dumb idea I'd come up with—hiding up in the mountains. We could be paying for it with our lives.

Present Time

The Circle of Power worked as Silver Moon and Blaze stared at the old photograph..

"Her fears echo in my ears like the sounds of many drums beating, as does her heart. She fears not for her life, but the life of another," Little Bird said.

Wakanda, her eyes closed, spoke, "Her woman's heart is near complete."

"Raven grows stronger; her spirit will fly," Blackie pronounced.

Little Bird began his chant in Apsáalooke, a song for the many who died, and the many who would live to carry on the crest of his clan.

His baritone voice built into a vibrating crescendo, then softened.

He sang of a woman who, urged by a powerful blackbird, fought to save herself to fulfill her destiny—becoming the mother of a famous chief.

Despite the downpour, she has pulled herself free from the earth and soared above to meet her love.

Little Bird's song faded, and he hummed until he hummed no more, and was stilled.

"This birth will now come to pass," said Soft Dove.

"Born to be the last to be called Chief of the Crow Nation," Blackie Kangee acknowledged.

Jon Little Bird spoke with pride. "His birth name will be Buffalo Bull Facing the Wind, but the world will remember him as Chief Plenty Coups."

The room and the ambience calmed, knowing the Apsáalooke man, a legend in Native American history, was saved. It was time for Blaze's daughter to move on and continue her quest.

Aware of the calmness in the other room, Silver Moon turned, and Blaze took her arm to steady her as they walked back to the group.

Settled into her rocker, the old Sioux woman closed her eyes and began humming, then she sang in her native tongue.

No one spoke as they listened to the haunting words.

Her song translated into words about men frightened in the dark as well as in the light of day—enemies all around and the evils of men who follow evil men. Her song ended, and all eyes were upon her.

"For them, it has not begun, but for one, she must call upon her strength and her courage. Of the many things our world has endured, not by the hand of the Real People or our White Counterpart countrymen, but by the hands of men who follow one who is considered a crazy man."

Silver Moon's sad words dripped from her down-turned lips as she continued. "Our losses on the Trail of Tears and in battle were many, as our battle was for the land—and what the land gave back to us. Then, with the discovery of the yellow rock, greed became our enemy. Those who cower now in darkness do so not because of land or the yellow rock, but because they are unclean in the eyes of those who feel superior, and because of their faith."

She stopped, her eyes cast downward, staring at her hands, and Blaze saw the single teardrop—then another.

Something nudged at Blaze—not physically, but an inner strength burst as she continued the woman's story.

"Silver Moon speaks of the tragedies of those who were different, weaker, disabled, or who were poles apart in religious beliefs. They did no harm, hurt no one, and had no one to defend them, until our country came to their defense. My Raven shall be there, this time in more harm's way than she has ever been, and she needs our support and guidance."

She looked at Hank Cooper. "Your Nate will be there too, and will be the strong shoulder she'll need, and then, as two, soon they'll share one heart."

Hank Cooper nodded. "Nate will experience war firsthand, and this saddens me. I worry for his safety."

"War?" Dan Jones asked.

It was Wakanda who answered, "Yes, Dan, war—the one where millions on top of millions were executed just because they were of different faith and considered unclean by one man who brainwashed a nation."

"Are you talking about Hitler?" Dan's brows crinkled.

Blaze spoke, "Yes, she is."

"Wait, our people weren't involved, so why will Raven and Nate be involved?" Payton finally got into the conversation.

"Raven is our protector of legends, and although we have no Comanche representative in our group, she'll be there to protect a man from the Comanche tribe—a man who must not die and who must live long. Now is the time for moral men and women to act," Blaze spoke to the entire group as a member of the community, but not a Council representative.

Silver Moon stayed silent, listening to the interaction between the council members and the members of the tribal community.

With a side glance, she smiled at Blaze, her voice low, "You are knowledgeable, She Cougar, like I told you. My heart and your heart are one, and you will continue this work."

A sly smile twitched on the younger woman's lips. Silver Moon was indeed a trickster. She'd imparted her knowledge, and unbeknownst to Blaze Clark Kangee, she'd picked up the gauntlet for the next phase of her life as the newest leader of the Tribal Council.

"Welcome, new leader of the inner circle," Aunt Meda smiled.

Blackie Kangee, Dan Jones, Eli Harris, Bud Parker, and Hank Cooper all stood, and one by one each said, in their native tongues, "We welcome you as the new leader for Real People, for our tribal commune."

Elated yet sad, they knew time was short for those older leaders who would go to the gods in the sky, but would forever live within their hearts.

At the Cliffs-with-no-Name, Circa 1828

The rain was now just a light drizzle, with the clouds dissipating, yet the darkness still ominous.

"At top," Otter Woman called out.

Then a bright light poked through a dark cloud, and I saw a prism of rainbow colors sparkling over her head as her arm went up, her hands clawing at the dirt to pull herself onto the flat section of land jutting out.

After this experience, I swore mountain-climbing was no longer on my bucket list of things to accomplish—then I chucked because I had accomplished this feat, just not on the mountain I had set my sights on.

As I looked up, I saw Otter Woman's feet and then gasped as I saw a hand reach down and encircle her wrist, pulling her up and out of my sight.

"Otter Woman!" I screamed, and she didn't answer.

Oh, my heavens—who the heck had been up there waiting on us?

What was I going to do—go back down the way I came up?

Try to escape?

No. I couldn't leave. I had to follow her, make sure she stayed safe. I'd worry about the consequences later because, well, I was stuck. It was too far down and too dangerous.

The hand which had grabbed her reached for me—a dark-brown hand, a large hand, the hand of a man. Better I cooperate than die, so I let his strong fingers grip mine and pull me to safety or death—I wasn't sure which.

Once on the flat land, I mustered my courage to peek at either our rescuer or our captor. His smile was bright, his face young.

Otter Woman stood next to him, her clothes soaking wet, her hair plastered to her head, and a smile as big as the ocean on her face.

"This is Medicine Bird, my love, and our union will be good."

"How did he get here? Was he here waiting all this time?"

Otter Woman pointed to a horse set back a ways, and said, "He follows my heart to find me."

I was standing there, also soaking, with a frown on my face, hands on my hips—not a happy camper.

We'd just risked life and limb to climb this stupid mountain, and this man—this Medicine Bird—was already here? How had he gotten here? Did he fly?

So, I asked him.

First, his eyes met mine, then turned to Otter Woman, who nodded he could trust me.

"I go for vision quest, seek help from the gods to answer my questions about Otter Woman."

"And did your answer come to you?" I asked.

"Yes, in my visions I see many horses come to me and then be rich like Man Who Travels. Then I see a large black raven who brings Otter Woman to these cliffs, saving her from death."

Otter Woman nor I had told him my name, so this wasn't just a coincidence—or so my gut said.

But I hadn't saved her life, or I didn't feel like I had.

My eyes went back to him, and I watched him size me up, then eyeball the bags we carried, especially the one with the red flowers. I'm sure his brain was working overtime trying to figure out what they were.

Otter Woman let the backpack with the flowers drop off her arm, then slipped out of the one attached to her back, dropping them in a heap beside her.

She walked up to the cliff's edge, peering over to see if her enemies had followed.

Even though I didn't want to fall off the mountain, I wanted to see if anyone was down there too, since the daylight had resumed its brilliance.

The rains had soaked the earth, and I felt the squishy mud under the ugly, clunky shoes—and I realized neither Otter Woman nor Medicine Bird had thought my attire was weird.

My speaking both Lakota and Apsáalooke native languages seemed just matter-of-fact to them as well. I wondered what they'd think if they knew I also spoke Cheyenne.

We both peered down, then I felt the earth give way, so I grabbed Otter Woman's hand—and the earth beneath her crumbled—and slipped down the mountain, nearly taking her with it.

I held on tight and pulled with all my might.

Her feet were dangling dangerously close to the edge, and she fought, digging her heels into the soft earth, working her way backward in a crawl to get away from the perilous precipice and certain death.

I used every ounce of strength I had, as I was able, to get my other hand around her wrist, and even though I feared I would yank her arm out of socket, I tugged. I felt another hand grab mine and looked to see Medicine Bird kneeling and pulling. Every muscle in his body strained as he yanked us to safety.

Mud-caked feet, our backsides heavy with sludge adhered to our wet clothes, we stood, shaking.

"You... you saved me. I owe you my life," Otter Woman's voice trembled.

"My woman, you saved her. You're the Raven in my visions. What is your name?"

"Raven Maka Clark Kangee, born of the Sioux," I rejoined, wondering how he'd take it that I was from his enemy's tribe.

To my knowledge, most male Native Americans of this era didn't show affection to others—not in the way we do in our time, like hugging.

Medicine Bird I counted as one of those types.

I was wrong.

He stepped up, enveloping me in his arms, hugging me as a sister, thanking me.

There have been few times in my life in which I'd been rendered speechless, and this was one of them.

About to speak, I felt my body pulling upward, and as I went higher, I could see below.

Otter Woman and Medicine Bird riding on horseback through the trails of the Cliffs-with-no-Name, with no memory of me ever being there.

My task was completed, and now a child would be born from their union—and he would be known to the world and to history as Chief Plenty Coups of the Apsáalooke.

34

Have you ever felt like you were falling through space?

Did the perception of floating in air and falling at the same time ever happen to you?

It was something I had never encountered before, and the sensation it evoked was indescribable.

I was as light as a feather, much like a ball of cotton floating on a whipping wind, then a few seconds later I felt as heavy as a burlap sack loaded with rocks as I plunged downward with the speed of a freight train.

My eyes opened. All I saw was the earth below coming up to hit me in the face.

I had no conscious thought of time in my head as I woke, keeping my eyes shut.

This diving in and out of space, fading in and out of time and eras, was wearing thin on my once-steady nerves.

One thought was being alone.

In the beginning, I had Chay with me, then Nate, and having a person to keep you grounded and just to be there was something I'd never considered before.

As an only child, I'd been accustomed to being alone, and occupying myself for hours on end using my imagination. Therefore, I never felt lonely.

Now, before anyone gets the idea I had imaginary friends, I didn't, because I'd never gotten lonely until right now.

As I lay face down, keeping my eyes shut, the smell of dirt filled my nostrils, so I acknowledged I was outside.

With my right hand outstretched, I swept the area, then repeated with my left. No trees, bushes, or rocks—just flat ground. Was it day or night?

Don't be a coward. Open your eyes, my inside voice said in my head.

I peeked.

It was neither day nor night, but rather dawn or dusk, and I couldn't see if the sun was going up or down. My hands flat against the ground, I pushed, bringing me to my knees to steady myself, and just as I began moving upright, a hand shoved me from behind, sending me back, face first, into the dirt.

"What the..." was all I got out as a hand covered my mouth. His heavier body atop mine, and in one fell swoop he'd rolled me over four times, and with him still on top of my back, we lay in a ditch. My eyes popped wide open, and all I saw was reddish dirt.

Whoever held me from behind whispered in my ear, and I barely heard him for all the sudden commotion around us.

"Shush, don't move, and be quiet."

Fear gripped me as it never had in my life, and then I heard it—the rapid fire of machine guns, heavy artillery, and the ground shuddered with bombs. Overhead, I heard planes, then explosions.

One thing was certain—I was no longer in the wide-open space of the prairie where buffalo roamed and the Native Americans thrived. There were no fur trappers or traders and no cavalry coming to my rescue either.

From the sounds, I'd landed in a war zone. But which war? And even then it didn't matter which war. War was war, and I was terrified.

Was this person holding me in this ditch the enemy? My heart pounded, my mouth dry as I buried my face in the dirt, praying to get out of this mess.

As the noise lessened, time passed, and my arms, legs, and back ached from lying in the same position. I jiggled a foot trying to get the feeling back, lifting my shoulders a little to work out a kink, but his weight held me down. I was scared to speak.

The sounds of a brief silence ensued, and he placed his lips next to my ear and said,

"Stay still, I'm gonna get up and check. Don't move."

My eyes almost popped out of their sockets. In the now semi-silence, I recognized the voice.

"Nate?" My words were almost inaudible. "Is that you?"

"Yeah, now be quiet," he shushed. "I'm getting up to see what's happening. Be back in a jiff, but you don't get up no matter what, you hear me?"

I nodded, but I wanted to jump up and holler. It was Nate! He was here, and I wasn't alone!

The deafening noises of war sounded overhead once more, and I dared not raise my head for fear of getting it blown off. For me, not knowing what was going on was murder, and once I almost inched my head up, then thought better of it.

I counted first in Lakota, then in Apsáalooke, getting to the highest number I could, then in English. When I got to 350, Nate reappeared, and squatting, he tapped my back.

"All clear. You can stand up."

I pushed off from the ground, and his hand reached in, grabbing my arm to help me up. Then, I looked down at my clothes and almost laughed—and you had to just love magic.

Finally, I was wearing pants. Army issue, drab olive green, and an undershirt of the same color, with a jacket to match. I glanced at my feet, which were now clad in old-fashioned brown lace-up Army boots. It might not be fashionable in my time, but it was so much better than the jumper dress, muslin stockings, and clunky shoes.

"Nate, oh, Nate!" I hugged him. "I have never been so happy to see a friend in my life, and I..."

He stopped me by pushing me away. "Come on, we've got to get moving."

He turned, and I supposed he expected me to follow. Well, at this point, I had no choice, so I followed, subdued, because he wasn't as happy to see me as I was to see him.

Upright, I saw the time of day was dusk. The sun was going down, and a chill filled the air. Nate, not in a talkative mood, I let him be, hoping later, when his disposition improved, we could talk. I wanted to ask questions like: where were we, what year was it, how'd he get here—you know, the regular questions one had daily when you lived my life.

The boots were an improvement, but it didn't mean my feet hurt any less. The terrain was littered with debris from bombings—houses and shops blown to bits sprinkled the area, wood, concrete pieces, bricks, and such strewn everywhere.

I tried to comprehend the period I had stumbled upon, struggling to make sense of it all. All I saw in my mind were the old war movies of yesteryear. I wondered why I had been sent back to this moment in time. Did Nate know, and if so, was he gonna let me in on the plan?

We were in an era where timepieces were a current part of our dress, so I checked to see if I had a watch. Huh, I did. Silver, a stretchy band with a round face, and if it were keeping the correct time, it was now six-thirty.

This was the only jewelry I wore—no rings, no earrings. My hand felt under the shirt; my necklace was still there, thank the Lord.

Nate was still not talking to me, and I'd be darned if I was going to start a verbal exchange; he had been a jackass, and he'd have to be the one who started a conversation.

My eyes grew accustomed to the dim lighting, and I became familiar with my surroundings. Amongst the debris, I couldn't make out much, and Nate had us following the sides of buildings, ducking in and out to stay hidden from, I'd guess, enemy eyes. My heart raced, my eyes darting in every direction.

"Over there. Go inside. Wait," Nate instructed in short, two-word phrases. Either a man of few words, or not happy about having to talk to me.

I did as he asked, wondering all the while: what if he decided not to return? What would I do?

This sudden change and the chaos of war exploding in my ears made me forget some things.

First, where was my mare, Gypsy?

Second, what had happened to all the knapsacks, especially the red-flowered pack, the one with the books?

Dang it! I needed Aunt Meda and Silver Moon's books. There had to be something in one of them to tell me where I was and why.

Crouched down, I peeked out around the doorless doorway and squinted, trying to see as best I could, hoping to recognize something. But nothing looked familiar, and when I made to stand up, a hand reached and grabbed my ankle, and before I could scream, another hand clamped over my mouth.

"Don't scream, lady. Please don't scream. If you promise not to scream, I'll uncover your mouth. Do you swear it? If you do, just nod, and don't run either. It's too dangerous out there, you promise?"

I nodded, and he removed his hand and let go. I plopped down on my butt and turned to see him. He was a boy—a teenager, about sixteen, at the most seventeen, his black hair cropped short, his dark eyes scared, and his face smudged with dirt and remnants of ashes.

"Who are you?" he asked first.

"I'm Raven. Who are you? And where are we?"

His brows dipped, and his face wrinkled in distrust. "You don't know where you are?"

I shrugged. "It's a long story, and we don't seem to have time for long stories. I'm here, and how I got here I can explain later, so please just tell me where we are, okay?"

"You're American?" he asked me.

"Well, yes. Aren't you?"

"Are you Native American?"

"Yeah. So?"

I was getting miffed at this dig into my heritage. I mean, he had the looks of a Native American too, but I wasn't getting all up into his family lineage or questioning him because he had a look about him.

"What tribe?" His distrust was apparent in his tone.

"What the devil does it matter? I'm Sioux. So?"

"My people call me Little Fox, but here I'm called Joe."

"And who are your people?"

"Comanche, descendant of Chief Ten Bears."

"Alright, Joe, now that we have each other's names, can you please tell me where we are?"

"You truly don't know, do you?"

I shook my head.

"France."

"What the—France? Are you pulling my leg?"

I wanted to poke my head back out and see, but then again, I also wanted to keep my head from being blown off, since there seemed to be a war going on ... and... war... holy cow, I had landed in the middle of World War II, and it was 1940-something.

"Joe, what year is this?"

His expression was priceless when a deeper voice spoke behind him. "It's 1941."

Joe turned his fist at the ready, about to clock Nate, but Nate halted him.

"Hold on there, I'm not the enemy. Tell him, Raven."

I looked at Joe, lifted my brow, and smirked. "Much as I'd like to see him get a bust in the chops, no, he's not the enemy. Joe, this is Nate Cooper."

After a few, and I genuinely mean very few, pleasantries, Nate was all business.

"I found a spot for the night, but we need to move—and move now. Joe, you can share your story later. We should get moving."

"Nate, 1941, has Pearl been hit?"

He gestured a no, and then the scowl I gave him had him stop short and stick a finger in my face. "And no, no, we can't change it. Don't even get that idea in your head, got me?"

"How do you know we can't? Maybe it's why we're here."

"Just listen to me. I left you with Otter Woman because I had to lead the Sioux away. She had to be saved, and this was your job. It was your destiny."

I looked at him frowning. "Fine, and now here we are, so I don't understand why we can't save more lives?"

"When I came back and you were gone, so was Otter Woman and Medicine Bird, but the backpacks were still there. I looked for the books and read one story, and it was about me."

"You—why you? You aren't even a Sioux..." I stopped when I saw the hurt expression on his face.

"Nate," I said, my hand on his arm. "I'm sorry, I..."

He stopped me. "I know my place, so don't worry." He looked at Joe. "Do they call you Little Fox?"

Surprised, this rendered Joe speechless, and he nodded.

"Are you Comanche, line of Ten Bears?"

Joe regained his voice. "Yes. How did you know?"

Nate looked at me. "I read it in a dream book; the story said I'd find you in France to help you. Now, let's get going. It's gonna be pitch-black in an hour, and we must get to a safe place."

35

In the air, there was a chill as Nate led us in and out of what I thought might have once been back alleyways, to structures that were no longer buildings but heaps of rubble with doorways and partial stairways—too dangerous to climb.

Sounds of sporadic gunfire in the distance grew faint as the night darkened.

War didn't sleep; it just settled down a bit when one couldn't see their enemy, as men needed to recharge and rest while others stood watch to protect their comrades.

Heck, what I knew about war you could fill a Dixie cup with. I was no combatant, and it had nothing to do with my being a girl either, because believe me when I say, if I had to, I'd shoot first and ask questions later.

Nate stopped, halting us, and Joe and I watched him as his eyes scoured the area.

How long had he been here?

It was odd to know that just an hour or two ago, I had been in the Cliffs With No Name, in what might have been 1820, and here I was—121 years later—in France during World War II.

No one would believe me, sans those who traveled with me, like Nate and Chay, and the few people involved in my real future.

What an amazing tale I'd have, yet I could tell no one for fear of being construed as a crazy person.

Nate stopped and turned. "Stay close. See the brick structure over there, the one with the front door still attached? That's our target. You two go around that way, stay near the wall, and don't stop until you're inside. Follow the main corridor until you get to the next-to-last door, find the hidden staircase, and wait for me. Stay hidden. Got it?"

"Where the devil are you going?"

Nate looked at me, then at Joe. "If I don't come back, you need to get Joe to his squad. Do whatever it takes, hear me?"

Joe opened his mouth to protest, but Nate stopped him.

"Don't argue, and if she tells you to do something, just do it."

He turned his attention back to me again. "Raven, take this and don't let anyone get it. Wear it around your neck until I ask for it back."

Nate handed me a braided leather rope necklace, and on it were four objects: one rock, shiny with copper and gray variations, a hole bored through the end; a dark silvery flint stone shaped like a crescent moon; one small rose-colored crystal; and, last, a tiny leather pouch, which he informed contained teeth of a wolf mixed with sage.

I slipped it over my head and tucked it under my shirt.

"Where'd this come from?"

"It's been in my family for hundreds of years. It belonged to T.H. Cooper, who got it from Chief Black Raven, who gave it his magic—or so that's the story. Please take care of it until I ask for it back."

"You going to answer my first question?"

"I'm going to get the backpacks I was able to carry with me. I hid them when I went looking for you."

"Looking for me? Why on earth..."

"Not now. Please, just wait here."

"What if..." I couldn't finish my thought aloud, but he knew I wanted to ask what we were supposed to do if he didn't make it back.

"The amulets and talisman will guide you; trust in yourself and you'll get the answers you need," Nate said, then turned to Joe.

"Be safe and remember to talk the talk; it will save lives." He shook the young boy's hand, then turned back to me, looking long and hard at my face as if he were memorizing it.

"What?" I asked.

Nate shook his head, and a sly smile tugged at one corner of his mouth. "Just considering my options and whether it'd be worth it."

"It? What would be worth it?"

He had me at a disadvantage. I hadn't a clue what he was talking about.

"Kissing you"—he paused—"no, don't think it's worth it. One day it might be, but not today."

He gave me no time to respond and turned to leave, then looked back at us. "Get going," he instructed, then disappeared out of sight behind the skeleton of what was once someone's place of business or home—and who could say in this destruction?

———

J oe and I made it without mishap, and when we entered, it felt surreal.

We'd entered an aged cathedral, and although the outside was banged up, the inside was still intact. The lofty ceilings and stained-glass windows—some of the panes broken out or cracked—the wooden pews upturned, moved about, or broken in half, and the massive statues of saints I had no names for, marred with chunks missing from being bashed.

A large wooden crucifix hung sideways at the back, and a fountain, which no longer spilled water, stood nearby.

On the walls not as damaged were angels painted in flight with cherubic faces. Behind where once stood a podium was a statue of the Virgin Mother, knocked over and smashed.

The place had been looted and torn through, and it hurt my heart to see such beauty destroyed.

Mine and Joe's breathing was labored as we'd run to our target, hoping no one saw us.

My heart pounded, knowing enemy eyes could be watching us.

Women weren't sent overseas in this time frame, which was an oddity. If captured, what was I going to say? "Hey, let me tell you how this ends. Maybe you should give up now?" In my heart, I wished it had been that easy.

"There." I pointed. "That hallway—let's move."

Without reservation, Joe followed me, scared to death, so I tried to keep him from seeing how frightened I was.

We found the second-to-last door and went in, and I shut it behind us.

The room was nearly empty. Crates of books sat on one side, and boards were piled against an opposite wall with broken chairs and rocks. I saw the outline of a door—the crease in the panel almost invisible to the naked eye.

"Help me move this pile of stuff away from the wall," I instructed.

After we'd moved the junk, I pushed on the wall. A panel creaked and popped out, and I stuck my fingers in to pull it open. It was dark and smelled musty.

"Is it a tunnel, or what?" Joe asked.

I shrugged. "It's too dark to see, and I don't have a light."

"Wait, I got us covered." From the pack he wore, Joe produced a 1941 Army-issue flashlight.

"Here." He tapped me on the shoulder, bringing me out of my thoughts about why Nate was thinking about kissing me.

"The batteries are low. Don't know how long it'll work."

Pressing the button, I shined the light and found stairs leading to... where, who knew? But Nate wanted us here too, so this is where we'd be.

Joe followed, and I told him to pull the door shut and prayed we'd have a way out in case we had to leave. The staircase carried us into a basement—or a small bomb shelter; I had no idea.

"Musty smelling," I remarked, taking caution with each step, not knowing what we were walking into.

"Yeah, smells like our dirt cellar back home."

"Where's home, Joe?"

"Long way from here. Lawton, Oklahoma. My parents have a ranch."

A ranch, like us. I liked this kid. "You use the dirt cellar for tornado safety?"

"Never had to, but my mom likes to store potatoes, turnips, and stuff in our root cellar, along with what she cans from her garden."

"How old are you?" I began shining the light around as we got to the last step.

"I'll be seventeen in five months. How old are you?"

His asking my age made me giggle, and I had to stop to turn to see him. "Didn't anyone ever tell you it isn't polite to ask a woman her age?"

"Hey, right now, in this place, with a war going on, don't think it matters much, do you?"

He was right, and I could say my age was a negative number and I hadn't been born yet—not in his world. If I did, he might claim he was older; therefore, he was the boss, or it would scare the kid to death.

"Twenty-four, so yep, I'm the boss 'cause I'm older."

The beam of the light revealed our haven to be a dirt cellar with walls supported by wide, thick beams. Makeshift shelving on one wall held broken and empty jars of what might have been edible food.

This had me thinking about the last time I ate a meal, and for the life of me, I couldn't remember.

The place was about ten by ten, and looking up, I saw tubing, which had to be ventilation, and I mumbled a "thank you, Lord."

On the floor in the far-left corner were blankets. Somebody stayed here before, and I guessed it'd been Nate, since he told us about this place. But why weren't the backpacks here?

Ooh, the man was becoming a splinter in my backside.

"Well, here we are in a pit of dirt: no food, no water, and no idea when Nate will be back."

The batteries in the flashlight were weak, and the light was dimming, so I scanned the room again to get an idea of the layout, and my eyes fell on an old kerosene lantern. Picking it up, I shook it—full.

Good. However, I had no way of lighting it.

"You have any matches in your pack?" I prayed for a yes.

Fishing inside his jacket pocket, he pulled out a box of matches.

"You smoke?"

"Nah, I don't, but I'm a Boy Scout—always prepared."

This made me chuckle as I took the matches and got the lantern lit so we might save whatever battery life was left in the flashlight. After it was lit, I turned it down low, hoping to save fuel because I didn't have a container with extra kerosene.

Joe leaned against the wall of dirt, arms crossed. He stared at me. "I'm confused about all of this. How about you tell me who you really are and how you got here?"

Eyeballing him, I wondered how much I should tell him. Besides, how much would he believe?

We had a long night ahead of us, so why not tell him everything? Even if he figured I was spinning a tale, what did it matter?

So, I began with the dream book and the first incident, right up to this day—and him.

———

Finished, I waited to hear him say I'd just fed him a load of bull-crap, then asking me to prove it. Yet his next statement shocked me.

"My grandfather is—I mean was—a shaman. He passed into the skies when I was ten, but he told me of a bird who traveled hundreds of years ago and about a Cougar which lived in a woman's body in the Black Hills, and how her bravery saved an extraordinary chief."

As I listened to Joe, I knew he was speaking about my mother and the story of how she went to the Black Hills through magic to save the lineage of Chief Sitting Bull, and how a traveling bird crossed the barrier of years to be born in the modern day.

"This bird my grandfather told me about was called Tuhcorpiauku, which means Raven in my language. You're the Raven he spoke of, aren't you?"

I nodded, feeling weird about being in a story his grandfather knew about, and how I had been made into a legend—but as Silver Moon would tell me, this was planned for me long before my mother went back in time, long before she was born, and nothing could change one's destiny.

36

"You believe me?" Joe pulled a face, then his brows dipped. "Yeah. You know, after all these years, I thought my grandpa was just spinning a story to entertain me. Only thing is, why are you here?"

"What a brilliant question, and I'm hoping when Nate returns with Aunt Meda's book, we can figure it out. Tell me, why are you in the Army, Joe? You're just a kid?"

"Because I'm Comanche and I felt the need to do my patriotic duty."

"What in the world does your being Comanche have to do with anything?" I was stymied.

"Do you speak Lakota?"

"Uh-huh, and I also speak Apsáalooke, Cheyenne, and Cherokee. Why?"

"Wow, you can speak all three. Amazing. Did it take long to learn all three, gosh, the dialects are tough I bet." Joe was impressed with my language abilities.

Well, I could let him believe I was super smart, but I wouldn't, not my style.

"By magic, not by me being all-powerful or talented. The only language I came by, as you would expect, was Lakota, because we use it daily in my house. I've just only mysteriously acquired the gift for Cheyenne, Cherokee, and for Apsáalooke, so don't be too impressed. Now, back to why being Comanche has anything to do with you joining the Army and lying about your age."

My comment about acquiring the talent for other native tongues by magic didn't faze him in the least; this also shocked me.

It was then I understood Joe was a genuine believer of the mystical, time travel, and the other side.

"The Germans can't understand Comanche, so we can get messages out and confuse them. You ever heard of the Choctaw code talkers from World War I?"

"No, I guess I haven't."

"Too bad, because in World War I, the Choctaw, Cheyenne, Comanche, Cherokee, Osage, and Yankton Sioux were part of the code talkers who helped the allied powers defeat the Axis powers."

My eyes widened. His use of the words "Allied" and "Axis" powers. He was a smart kid. It could be I'd underestimated him.

"You did a lot of studying on this?"

"I like to read and I like history. Anyway, back to my point. Being Comanche and fluent in Uto-Aztecan language I wanted to help, so yeah, I lied about my age, but I'll be eighteen soon enough."

I understood his desire to do his patriotic duty; but he was here, alone, so where was his platoon?

Was he my reason to be here, or Nate's?

"What happened to the others? Joe, why are you alone?"

He moved his head from side to side. "Can't explain it, cuz I'm not sure what happened. Once we landed, we moved forward to the outskirts of this town, and when the firing started, we scattered and I found myself alone, so I hid. "

"When was this? How many days ago?"

He stared at me as if I were crazy. "Today, early this morning, about the time you got here."

"So, you're my reason for being here, and I need to help you?"

"You, help me, come on, I'm the man in the Army, you're just a ... just a..." He didn't finish.

"Yeah, right, I'm just a girl. Look here..."

The door above creaked.

As fast as I could, I blew out the lantern and we froze, my heart pounding, and if I were to place my hand on Joe's chest I was sure his was pounding just as hard.

I grabbed his hand, and we held onto each other in the darkness.

In the stillness, I heard someone breathing and their soft padded steps when they descended the dirt-filled framed staircase.

Then a whisper croaked, "Raven, Joe? Are you down here?"

"Nate, heavens! You scared ten years of our lives off. Why didn't you just yell down? This is where you told us to come. Why wouldn't we be here?"

My hands fumbled with the flashlight, and once I got it on, I shined it toward Nate to see him.

"Oh, my God!"

One hand came up to my face to cover my mouth, the other dropped the flashlight, and it bounced around until Joe grabbed it and stood up.

"Man, how bad is it?" Joe asked, shining the light on Nate while I fished out the box of matches and relit the lantern, my hands still shaking.

"It's a through-and-through, and pretty sure it missed vital tendons and muscles, but it hurts like the dickens."

Blood saturated the upper left section of Nate's shirt. He'd been shot, thankfully not in the chest or he wouldn't be standing there.

"Here."

He handed me two knapsacks, then he plopped down on the last step, out of breath, I assumed he was in a lot of pain.

As I dug into the backpack looking for anything to help with his injury, I asked him what happened.

"Just as I crossed the road about a mile back I got hit by a stray bullet because I didn't see a soul anywhere and there wasn't any gunfire fight going on; it's crazy how quiet it was until that shot rang out and I got hit. The silence, eerie when you know men are out there, but you can't see or hear them, yet you can feel eyes on you all the same."

I pulled out some Ace bandages and a bottle of rubbing alcohol.

I hadn't even recalled putting this stuff in the knapsacks. But when I was packing I hadn't any idea what all I'd packed; I'd just grabbed anything in my sight, or what my head told me to grab.

Was this just a few days ago?

... a few days ago...

This made my head swim.

How long had it been? I had no calendar—

This was going to be a question I was gonna hafta try to remember to ask Aunt Meda and Silver Moon ... how did time move when you traveled in time?

"Take off your shirt," I said, then blushed. "I mean, so I can tend to your wound, dummy," I supplemented when I saw the lecherous gaze he gave me. Then he winked at Joe, who grinned.

It was as he thought—a clean shot—and me, not being a nurse, did a respectable job of cleaning it up, then packing it with the end of the Ace bandage, and then wrapping it up tight with the remaining part of the bandage. I dug out some Tylenol, but we had no water.

"Can you swallow these dry?"

"Yeah, I think," he remarked, then Joe handed him an old metal canteen, and I chortled.

"What's funny?" asked Nate.

"Our Boy Scout, Joe." Then I expounded on the matches, and how he had the canteen.

"What about food? Got any in your belt of tricks?" Nate asked after handing him back the canteen.

"Nah, Toledo Park was packing most of the K-rations."

"Toledo Park, that's a real guy?" I asked.

"Uh-huh, he's from Ohio. His first name is Yves, but he'll slap your socks off if you call him that."

"Let's get some shut-eye, then we won't think about food," Nate said. His eyes closed as he rested his head back.

I was hungry, and I fished inside my packs, coming up with bagged peanuts, two packages of cheese crackers filled with peanut butter, and one pack of mini oatmeal cookies.

It was a feast.

We split it and then washed it down with what was left in Joe's canteen.

***

The noise was muffled, but consistent, and dirt particles dropped on my face, waking me.

Disoriented, I shook the sluggishness from my head and wiped nonexistent cobwebs from my face, waking in half a stupor.

My shoulders ached as did my neck from sleeping sitting up, with my neck bent in an awkward position. Half asleep I yawned, and as I stretched my arms out in the dark, I encountered another face, my fingers grazing a nose and a mouth, and I heard a voice.

"Hey, you're poking my eye. Stop it, will ya?"

"Nate, gosh, sorry, didn't mean to."

I smelled sulfur when Joe lit a match, then the kerosene lantern.

"Not much fuel left. Be good idea if we got out of here. I can hear the shooting and the bombs getting closer."

It hit me that last night we hadn't read the book; we'd attended to Nate's gunshot wound and ate, then slept.

It hadn't taken me long to drift off. Exhausted, I chalked this up to time travel, jet leg, something else I was gonna try to remember to ask about.

Then wondering if I was going to do this type of travel the rest of my life—something else to find out about when I got home.

Home—was I ever going back?

Another question in a line of questions?

"Nate, the book. We need to look this up."

"First, we gotta get outta here. Joe's right, the war sounds like it's moving closer and will be on top of us soon. Let's go."

I saw him wince when he put his left hand, palm-side down, and pushed himself off the ground, and I went to his aid.

"Here, let me help you."

I stuck a hand down and he took it without argument, and when our hands clasped, my heart fluttered and that was unexpected.

Still in pain, his smile was of thanks only, nothing more. My heart hurt a little knowing that smile wasn't for me.

Just as *they* say, sometimes things must get worse before they get better and whoever *they* were,

I wanted to punch *them* in the nose!

Out in the open, I looked at the watch on my wrist.

Four o'clock.

The sun was just cresting, and the day filled with smog, or it was the vapors from gunfire and grenades.

Knowing the history of this war, years after it happened, and being here as it occurred, well, there weren't words to explain how it made me feel.

Although I longed to turn back time and fix things, the impossibility of it was a bitter truth.

I needed to leave, as was my preordained destiny, or this would devour me; reducing me to cinders.

***

How we dodged bullets and being seen was a miracle, or it was fated, I didn't care which; I was just thrilled we'd made it to a deserted bunker seeing no casualties of war.

My heart ached at the thought of happening upon dead soldiers, and I so longed to leave this epoch behind!

Inside the bunker, we hunched down and opened the book, then Nate passed it over to me.

"Here, hunt for dates. She dated her dreams. Search for 1940 or '41. Joe and I gotta find water."

"You're leaving me here alone?"

"Just read, trust me, I'll never leave you, I promise."

Then he left already breaking his promise in my mind. I watched as he and Joe disappeared, and my hands shook as I opened the book, searching for answers.

37

Time passed, and I became focused on this book, reading and engrossed in the stories.

So much of my Aunt's life. Her thoughts, ideas, her wishes—her real-life events were amazing. She'd traveled years and years backward to meet Wahunsenacawh, Chief of the Powhatan. And the dates she'd penned were 1606–1610.

She is lovely—the chief's daughter. Full of energy and mischief. If I must lie down my life for her, I would do it, for she's a star amongst the stars with her liveliness. One day, as she and I were walking the river, she slipped into the rushing waters. Her head went under, and my heart raced. I knew it wasn't yet her time. My destiny was to keep Pocahontas alive; and once I'd pulled her from the rapid waters of the river, I floated upward into the clouds. I looked down and saw her and heard her say to her brothers, "An angel saved me."

Pocahontas! I never knew, and I intended to scour this book when I had more time, but not right now. Although I was itching to delve into the stories, I needed to find my story first.

As I thumbed further into the book, I was getting discouraged. Nothing was popping up—no date reflecting 1940 or World War II. I shut the book with a tremendous sigh, closed my eyes, shaking my head, thinking this wasn't helping.

Drawing in a deep breath, I laid the book on my lap, letting it fall open on its own, and my gaze drifted down, and the first words I spotted: Joe and Nate are in... the next word was trouble. My pulse sped up, and I kept reading:

Into a deep hole, they lay covered with boards and dirt, and the bird will fly to distract others so they may run, and Little Fox will dash into a hole where his clan will be waiting. Then he listens to the other fox speak his language, and the message will not be lost. Search for empty arches; there you will find your quarry.

It took me only seconds to realize I was the bird, and I must be the distraction to save them.

Joe Little Fox belonged to the Comanche Code Talkers, and he had to get the message. And he was the only one who could translate it; this was what my heart told me.

If and when I ever got back to my real world, I was going to read about these courageous Native American men who used their unique language skills to help win wars.

*

With fear coursing through my veins, I kept my head low, my ears and eyes open, moving as quickly as I could.

A blast sounded.

I dove face-first into the ground, splayed out like a flattened pancake, staying still until I could feel my pulse slowing—then I moved again, repeating the action.

One, two, three...

I counted in my head to twenty at a steady pace, and then I looked up and assessed the area. If my estimation was correct, there were about fifty yards to cover to reach the open archway.

With each breath, I steeled my resolve. Then sprang forward into a dead sprint.

Speed was never my forte, and I'd never won a footrace, but today, I felt a burst of energy and was ready to challenge the fastest woman.

By the time I reached the archway, my knees were jelly. My heart pounded in my ears.

I gasped, bent over, pressing my hand to my ribs to ease the painful stitch.

When I heard another blast, I dove headfirst into the open doorway, landing with my hands flat, just inches from a board with nails which would've pierced my palms.

I stayed put, waiting and listening, and the quiet was scarier—like the eye of a storm—knowing it was there but not knowing when it would burst out.

After a forceful exhale, I pushed off the ground and flew towards the doorway on the right.

The room was intact, with one window, just a gaping hole, no framework, and no glass. This had to be the archway, and I peeked from the edge of what had once been a window to search the area.

No other place had an entryway resembling arches.

This had to be it.

My feet moved backward until I was out of the room, then I turned to peer into the interior.

A hollow room, a large lobby. Once this had been a pleasant inn, but today's guests weren't welcomed.

Startled, I backed away when I heard a muffled cough; then I listened to see where the coughing had come from, and it sounded again, so I followed the noise, which led me to a pile of boards on the floor.

On my haunch, I cocked my head closer to listen. Faint voices were whispering, but I couldn't make out the words.

A giggle bubbled in my throat as I thought about an old movie with humans and cartoons, *Who Framed Roger Rabbit* from the late 80s.

The old shave-and-a-haircut knock, with the answer-back knock of two bits. Is it possible Nate would've seen this movie and known if I knocked five times, his answer would have to be a two-knock response?

With my fist held up, I said a tiny prayer, closed my eyes, and knocked, then waited.

I hadn't realized I was holding my breath when I heard the double knock as I expelled the air in my lungs. In a hoarse whisper: "Nate, is it you?"

"Raven? Are you okay?"

"Me? I'm fine. What about you guys? Anyone hurt?" M

My face was pressed against the pile of boards as I spoke, trying to keep my voice down but loud enough for them to hear me.

"Joe has a sprained ankle, and we have a few scratches, but yeah, we're good, and I'm damned glad to hear your voice."

I almost wept and would have if I had the time, but not now. Later, I'd let myself have a first-rate long cry.

First, I had to find out how to get them out.

"Where are you, in a room or what?"

"The floor gave way, and the room we're in has one door, but it's blocked on the other side, so we can't open it. I think we're in a rather large storage room. There are shelves, but whatever was here has been taken."

Nate looked around the room again. "It might have been an oversized pantry, but the only way out is up there. The doorway is blocked by debris, so you've got to uncover the wreckage to pull us out. Can you? Are you strong enough?"

With a nod, I evaluated the area and said, "Yeah, it might take a minute, but I think I can. If I were y'all, I'd stay away from the middle of the room, just in case anything falls from up here, okay?"

"Yeah, we'll plant ourselves in the corners and wait. Not much else we can do."

Silence.

"Hey!" he called up to me.

"Yes?"

"Be careful and keep your ears and eyes peeled. We saw German soldiers earlier. They were ransacking the back of this inn just before the floor caved in and more bombing started."

"I'm going to hurry," I responded, tears stinging my eyes.

My priority was to help them escape to prevent us from being caught and killed.

Captured!

If that happened, it wouldn't end well for me. I was unaware Nate had the same thought.

Under a pile of rubble, covering the hole they'd fallen into, was a man who'd already given me his heart; and he was praying for a chance to tell me in person.

*

Concrete and mortar dust crumbled downward as I moved boards and broken tiles from the heap.

Nothing was too heavy, but I wished a million times over for a pair of work gloves.

My nails cracked and chipped, and I was going to deal with a few nasty splinters.

The room was getting warm, so I shucked the long-sleeved shirt, tying it around my waist.

Down on my hands and knees, I clawed at the heap of dirt. After unburying a longer piece of lumber, I found it was attached by concrete to a rock column—too heavy for me to move.

My eyes stung with unshed tears.

"How's it coming up there?" Nate called up.

My cheeks became streaked with dirt as I rubbed away my tears.

"Slow but sure, but I've got a problem."

I squatted, balancing myself and shaking my head, trying to figure out what to do.

"What problem?"

"A rock column laying across the last layer of boards and crap, and it's too heavy, Nate. I can't move it."

The tears came, and I snuffled them up.

"Raven, please don't give up, you're the charmed bird," I heard Joe, his voice hoarse.

"No, Joe, I'm not giving up. I just need to figure a way to move this column, and..." I stopped, my heart rate sped up, and then I pressed my lips to the floor so they could hear, or I trusted they could.

"Keep quiet. I hear men coming. Nate, Joe, don't make any noise. I've got to hide. Nate, knock twice if you hear me."

Two knocks followed. After this, I got up and scurried to a nearby room, praying there was a safe place for me to hide.

It was the only moment in my existence I wished I spoke German, but no magic happened.

I could hear them but not understand them, relieved there were only maybe six men, not an entire unit.

My eyes rolled into my head.

Heck, even one man was one too many; a full unit or six made no difference to my predicament.

Would they be able to tell someone was moving debris?

Had I stacked it in a fashion that appeared to be haphazard?

Or had I neatly piled it?

I hadn't thought so, but I'd been trying to be quiet about moving about, afraid someone would hear and come to investigate.

Had that been what happened?

Was this my fault?

Heavens, here I was, crying again.

What was my darned problem?

I chalked it up to fear; and for the first time since this began, I was terrified our lives hung in the balance, and if I failed, Nate, Joe, and I would all die.

*

The crash was thunderous; it sounded like a cave-in inside the main room, and my heart stopped.

Had the soldier's weight caused them to cave in on top of Nate and Joe?

I had to look, even if it wasn't safe.

With cautionary steps, I snuck out, peering around the doorway to see the soldiers investigating the hole. The rock column moved over, and I knew they'd spotted Joe and Nate.

Courage or stupidity, not sure which. But I stepped from my hiding spot and let out a bloodcurdling scream. Then I ran as if the Devil himself was chasing me.

If I thought I'd run fast before, this was nothing compared to the speed my feet carried me.

I jumped piles of lumber, then skirted around mounds of dirt and trudged through a few ditches full of water.

They were yelling in German for me to halt or whatever, but nope—they'd have to catch me to get me still.

I'd lost them in a maze of smaller apartment suites, but I knew they wouldn't give up, so I kept sprinting until I saw the old Protestant church ahead.

After racing to the doorway, I went in, looking around, prancing like I had to pee, and that's when I saw the baptismal area behind the pastoral stage.

On the platform, I stood on tiptoes to see in.

No water and stairs on the end leading to the back side of the stage area.

Hands on the edge, I hauled myself over and dropped into the pit, and just in time, as I heard voices outside the main doors yelling in frantic German.

They stepped into the church, and one of them let off a round from his machine gun toward the pulpit area.

My heart stopped as I covered my ears and prayed.

38

"Mr. Johnson," the doctor began. "Your brother has regained consciousness."

"Does this mean he'll be alright?" Pete's face was wrinkled and older these days from worry.

"I'm not sure yet. His vitals are weaker than expected, but the surgery was a complete success. We'll keep monitoring him closely."

"Can I see him?"

"Yes, but make it brief."

Jon Little Bird stood next to Pete and patted him on the shoulder. "Go check on your brother. Give him my wishes to get well."

"I will, Jon, and if he's up to it, I'm sure he'd like to visit with you, too." Pete looked at the surgeon. "Can he?"

"After you've finished your visit, I'll let you know." The physician paused a beat, then, "And don't rile him, keep him calm."

Jon and the doctor watched Pete walk through the hospital's corridor, his shoulders slumped, his head bent.

Deep within his heart he knew his brother wasn't coming home, not to their brick-and-mortar home, but he'd be going home to the spirits in the sky. Just when was only known by a powerful spirit.

Jon's cell phone rang. It was Meda Clark.

"Any news?"

"Sam's conscious, but the doctor says very weak. Pete's with him now."

On the other end of the phone Meda sat, her face drawn in sympathy, knowing how hard this was to lose a comrade who long ago had been a fierce enemy.

"Will they let you see him?"

"If the doctor says so after Pete's visit."

"He's ready for this journey, so don't be sad," Meda spoke into the mouthpiece.

"I know, Soft Dove, but it still pains my heart."

Without further words, they disconnected the call.

———

The beeping of monitors, the clinical smells of the hospital room, and the white linen sheets Sam Johnson lay against had an eerie effect. Once a tall, muscular man with jet-black hair and eyes to match, lay a frailer-looking gent, his eyes closed and his hair more salt than pepper these days.

His arms lay outside the sheets and his hands rough and calloused from working cattle or in his beloved garden.

Old age had caught up with the once virile man who had lived the life of Sioux, hunted, fished, and protected what was his.

He had no regrets sans one; he'd never married and had no offspring.

The youngsters in their village were all his kids, and he loved them as if they were his own. For him, his lifetime had been full, and he had lived the best life he could.

Pete sat in the chair near his bedside. Reaching out he covered his brother's hand bowing his head.

"Pete, don't weep for me," Sam's voice groggy and tight as it pained him to know his brother was unhappy.

"Rest, Sam, and get well. I need you back home."

"I've traveled back to the motherlands, brother. Raven is on her way, so my work is almost done. Please don't be sad, for I'm ready to hunt the buffalo and visit the lands again."

His breathing shallow, he stopped speaking.

A tear slipped down Pete's face; he knew it was time, and he didn't want to say goodbye, but he also knew it wasn't forever, for one day he too would meet the spirits in the sky.

Sam's eyes fluttered open to see his brother. "Is my frenemy Jon here?"

Pete's chuckle sad. Yet he smiled.

His brother and Jon had a kinship that was by most accounts unheard of for a Hunkpapa Sioux and an Apsáalooke man.

"Yes. He's hoping your doctor will let him in."

"It's no longer up to her. This is my wish, and I wish to see Jon Little Bird of the Apsáalooke, once my enemy, but now my friend for life."

I n the small hospital room, Jon Little Bird sat in the chair next to Sam's bed.

Two men, once fierce adversaries in a past life were now as close as brothers.

Neither spoke for a few minutes, both understanding this would be the last time their physical bodies should meet.

Jon spoke first. "Soon you will ride high, my friend. Don't ride on the wrong side."

"Never," Sam's voice was faint. Then, "Will you sing with me?"

Jon's forehead crinkled in question. "The death song?"

Sam's eyes opened, then shut. "Yes, for I go into war. I still have one last spirit journey before I fly to the stars and meet the others who wait for my return to the fold."

"Do you not wish to do this with White Feather, for he's your brother?"

"By blood, yes, and we have already said goodbye, but you, Little Bird of the Apsáalooke Nation, are my spirit brother and it is with you I shall set my spirit free."

Two men sat from tribes that long ago despised one another, ready to kill or be killed if seen or rode upon.

Men who had passed the line of hate, who bore no ill will toward one another, hands clasped on top of a white hospital sheet, heads bent, eyes closed.

They chanted, one lowly with deep sadness, the other almost inaudible, but the words rang loudly in his heart. Together they sang the death song to send Sam into the afterworld of ancient spirits where men and the buffalo were free of their earthy bodies.

---

1 *940 Small Village Near Paris, France*

Although they'd stopped firing off rounds from their machine guns, they were still there, laughing and cutting up, and I could just imagine what they'd shot up.

Statues, beautiful stained-glass biblical scenes, the exquisite carved wooden pulpit, all because they didn't believe in an omniscient power other than the nasty man with the partial mustache, the man with mother issues.

I slowed my breathing and didn't move a muscle.

Were they ever going to leave or were they parking it for the night?

I had to get out of here and didn't want them to hear me, so with caution I rolled over on my belly, raising my head to the stairs leading out of the baptismal area.

There were five steps up and then out the back—only thing was I didn't know the layout, and this was a disadvantage; but then I was certain they didn't know the place either.

My hope was Joe's unit was searching for him and would find them before the Germans did. With that one thought, a tear slipped, and I had to suck it up.

If I started bawling, I'd be found, so I had to stop.

Something tickled my neck, and it startled me, and I put my hand to my throat and remembered Nate had given me this braided leather rope necklace of some sort.

I pulled the rope out from under my T-shirt, looked at the articles, and I smiled.

The pouch with the sage and elk's teeth. Sage to cleanse my thoughts. The teeth of an elk, divine protection from evil.

My fingers clutched the bag; I silently intoned, wishing for spirits to help, and deep in my soul a whirling began, and a hand touched my face, but I wasn't frightened.

"Raven, you can speak. Only I shall hear you."

All the air went out of my lungs, then I breathed in and opened my eyes.

"You have come for me?"

"It is on my way to where I go, so you may travel with me. Out of this land, away from the evil men." The apparition extended his hand, and I accepted it without hesitation, no longer afraid of the men with guns who were in the main sanctuary.

"No, I can't go, my friends are trapped."

"The allies will find them. Saved to do the deeds they are commissioned. You must ride the wind with me now, young Raven, for time grows short, and my spirit must move to the new place and be settled."

Like air, I floated up with him.

I felt safe as I looked down at the men who had meant to harm me and kill me, but they couldn't see me.

We soared into a hazy sky filled with smog from tanks and gunfire, and we rose about the clouds into an atmosphere I had never traveled.

Gliding along a trail of stars and rainbow waves, into the darkness and out again into a burst of bright twinkling lights. Into another realm and an older dimension.

The hand pulled me and below, I saw where there was nothing.

Then there were mountains, waters, and a magnificent array of colors.

"I must take my leave." He spoke in Lakota, then in Apsáalooke he said, "Goodbye, Jon Little Bird."

With those as his last words to me, he let go, and I watched his spirit glide out of sight, and I stayed suspended in air going nowhere.

My feet didn't work.

How would I get home?

Where was I to go next?

My hand was still gripping the small pouch, I couldn't let go, couldn't lose this, for it was Nate's and if I lost this, I'd lose Nate.

———

With a huge grunt, Nate said, "Push again."

They put every ounce of strength, using their entire body mass against the door. It gave an inch, but the opening wasn't wide enough for either man to slip through.

"It's no use, Nate, we aren't gonna move it and the only way out is the hole above us."

"You know they are chasing her, and if they catch her..." Nate couldn't bear to voice it aloud.

Joe knew and shuddered at the thought. He then sensed the ground shaking and put his hand on Nate's arm.

"Feel that?"

Nate's eyes went upward. "Yeah, feels like tanks moving closer, and not good for us if they plow through."

"We've got to get out of here. I need to locate my unit. I'm the only one with them who speaks Comanche."

Nate could hear the panic in the young man's voice, but he was just as stuck as Joe was.

The structure shook harder as the army tank rolled in and butted the outside walls.

"Stay flat against the wall, Joe. If the middle caves, if we're lucky, the heap of rubble will be our way to climb out."

"Or it'll bury us."

Nate glanced at Joe but said nothing, and then they braced themselves, both men praying.

The vehicle hit the structure again, they could hear crashing and splintering wood; and the concrete and mortar dust floated down, but no cave-in.

It had stopped but hadn't left, or they would've heard it retreating.

"You think it's the Germans?"

Nate lifted his shoulders, his eye cut up to the hole in the ceiling above them and shook his head.

One thing he was sure of—he wasn't supposed to die, not here and not now. Not that he had officially signed up for this; he was thrown into this ordeal because of his ancestors, and besides, magic was supposedly on his side, so where the heck was this supernatural power?

Nate placed his finger to his mouth and pointed to his ear.

There were men inside the dilapidated site, walking around but not talking, so they didn't know if it was Germans or Americans and couldn't give themselves away.

Army boots plodded across bits of tile— the crunching twofold signifying more than a few men were walking around above them.

Scooting up to Nate, Joe whispered, "You think if we make noise one of 'em will glance down here, then we hide and see who it is?"

"Hide where? Nothing to hide under, Joe," Nate said under his breath.

Footsteps came closer to the hole. Nate and Joe froze.

"Guess there was a cave-in. Wonder if anyone was inside when the sauerkrauts bombed it?"

Oh, Lord, he spoke English and referred to the German soldiers as sauerkrauts!

"Down here, hey, we're down here!" Joe called up and the guy stuck his head into the hole. "Little Fox?"

"Yeah, and I got another dude with me. He's American so don't shoot! Guys, are we happy to see y'all."

It didn't take long to get rope and pull both Joe and Nate to safety, make some quick introductions, and explain not a darned thing.

Joe said Nate was in France, gave no reason just he got caught at the wrong time.

These men would never believe in Native American magic or any of what they considered folklore, no sense in getting into that.

Anyway, they needed to beat feet and get back to Central Command.

A soldier stepped up and stuck his hand out to Nate. "I'm Gunnar Johnson. You ever ride in a tank?"

"Nope, it'll be my first time. Is there room inside?"

"No, only enough room for five men," the commander said, "but two men can ride atop. You and Joe are gonna ride inside."

Nate shook his head. "Nah, I don't mind riding on the outside. You get Joe inside, make sure he's safe."

Gunner Johnson looked at Nate, then he smiled.

"Here, we got an extra helmet. You'll need to wear it if you ride outside. Any chance you know how to use a gun, a machine gun?"

"Yeah, shot one a few times. Where you from, Gunner Johnson?" Nate asked, trying not to narrow his eyes in question, but there was something odd about this soldier who seemed vaguely familiar.

"Oh, small city outside of North Dakota. I own some land and cattle, got drafted, and here I stand."

He handed Nate an extra helmet. "Come on, let's get aboard."

A sudden calming peace rested within Nate's middle, and he slapped on the helmet and climbed onto the Sherman, taking his first ever as well as his last ride on an army vehicle.

The sound of the Army vehicle rolling along didn't keep Nate and Gunner Johnson from chatting, raising their voices a decibel or two. Nate answered some basic questions from the soldier and was surprised he hadn't asked for further explanation to why he'd ended up with the Private called Little Fox.

"You gotta girl?" His words vibrated as the Sherman rolled over wreckage bombed or flattened by other tanks, like the German Panzer.

"Not sure. I mean, I'd like it if I did, but don't know if she'd agree." Nate let out a hearty laugh.

Johnson laughed too, then sighed. "I had wished I had a girl, but got too busy with our ranch. Never took the time."

"Ah, shoot, you're still a young man. You've got time after you get home from the war," Nate supplied, eyeballing the guy.

Gunner Johnson shook his head. "No, young Cooper, my time is up and I shall fly with the spirits soon."

Nate's heart stopped. He knew this man, only he knew him from the future as an older man.

Sam Johnson, Running Elk.

"Cooper, you wonder about Raven?"

Nate Cooper's mouth dropped open, and all he could muster was a nod.

"She is safe and waits in the clouds until it is time. Soon I shall depart, as shall you, and the men inside will not recall us. Joe Little Fox will get the messages out saving hundreds of US soldiers, and the course of the war will change."

"How, I mean, *why* did I need to be here?" Nate asked.

"To keep Joe safe and from doing anything stupid. He might have taken off and gotten captured had you two not shown up and changed the course of his fate; otherwise, the Germans would've tortured him to get him to talk about the Comanche Code, and he would've been killed."

He gave Nate a look of satisfaction, his eyes twinkling. "Now he'll live to be an old man and be awarded the Congressional Medal of Honor posthumously, as all the Native American Code Talkers will be remembered."

"I'm privileged to have been part, then," Nate remarked.

Gunner Johnson saluted then he took on spirit form, looking like the older man Nate knew, and as he floated upward he said in Lakota, "We honor the fallen and the brave and salute those who go into battle to save our freedom."

B ack Home at Fort Yates Hospital, Minutes Later

The machine flatlined and Sam was gone.

No longer in his mortal body.

His unique spirit now flying amid the clouds with his ancestors from long ago.

Even the other tribes who he'd once made war with were spirits united by their earthly death.

Jon Little Bird let a tear slip, and he patted his dear old friend's still warm hand and in a hushed voice said, "In the next life, my friend, I shall see you again."

With much heartache, the elderly Apsáalooke gent rose to tell Pete 'White Feather' Johnson his brother was gone.

———

On the outskirts of Paris, France, 1941

Nate's eyes widened as he watched the fellow calling himself Gunnar Johnson vanish like an old magician's trick.

He sat alone his eyes surveying the damages of this quaint French village with no name, his own fate hanging in the balance.

What was next?

Where was Raven?

Would he see her again?

Sam said she was in a secure place, but where was that?

Where was her mare, Gypsy, the backpacks with the books, and the possible answers they needed?

Were they destined to go between worlds never landing in one to have a permanent home?

Deep inside, he sensed a tug, an unknown force pulling him upward.

Just as Nate drifted into a new realm, my body felt the force of an unseen energy pushing me down.

It felt as if I were falling, and unable to fight it, I fell and looking down, all I saw was space.

As dizziness washed over me, I thought, "Oh, no, not again, where..."

I didn't get the words out as I lost consciousness, dropping through another wormhole in time.

Any measure of time was useless for me, or for Nate, as we were both pulled forward and backward without our blessing and without warning.

39

Somewhere on the Frontier in 1779

My head ached, as did my neck and back. I tried to open my eyes, but I couldn't keep them open.

A cool cloth was pressed to my forehead, and it felt so nice, so I kept my eyes closed.

Under my head was a soft pillow, and I could tell a blanket covered me. I so hoped I was at home in my bed with my mom tending to me.

The quiet, only sparked by the sound of a cricket or the howl of an old coyote, sounded just like home, so I let myself drift back to sleep, hoping to wake to a new day at home with my parents.

Into a full sleep I went, and I dreamed.

"**H**ow do you feel?"

"Mmm, better rested, happy to be home."

"Raven, uh, we are a far cry from home. You need to open your eyes and sit up."

My eyes still closed, and my body stiffened. It was Nate talking, and if I opened my eyes, I sorta figured I might not be thrilled, so nope, I kept them closed and shook my head.

"Nu-uh, I wanna go back to sleep and wait for time to drop me back to my world."

A hand pushed at the back of my neck, then slipped under my shoulders, lifting me into an upright position.

"Get up. We must get going before someone sees us."

"Now where and when are we?" I droned.

"Beats the heck out of me. But I get a deep-seated feeling women aren't wearing Army slacks and drab olive-green T-shirts in this period."

"Fine, fine, fine," I harangued, opening my eyes and deciding Nate had a point.

We were in a field, and my head was laying in his lap. Heavens, was he my pillow? Well, I'd never tell him I'd thought that. Man, I must've hit my head hard!

As I focused my eyes, I saw, in the far distance, smoke and tipis.

Here we go again!

"We need to make tracks."

Nate took me by the hand, and we took off.

"Where're we headed?" I panted.

With his free hand, he pointed. "Up there, see the hill—up and over. It's the best idea I've got right now. Don't know if it's a friendly tribe or not, and we can never explain these clothes, so pick up the pace."

The other side of the hill was just that—the other side—other than trees with grassy prairie land. There was nothing. Not people, nothing. We were hidden behind the hill, but it still wasn't safe, so we had to keep moving.

"Which way do we go? You have any idea?"

Nate hunched his shoulders, looking in every direction. "Not sure, since all we can see isn't a darned thing but land."

"Over there,"—I pointed—"there's a small grove of trees. We can hide and think."

"Perfect." Without asking, he grabbed my hand again, and we ran.

I figured he was holding my hand so if something were to happen, we wouldn't be separated.

Or if a wormhole opened and took one of us, then we'd both go.

I didn't care either way, just happy to stay connected. If I were to say I didn't think it was romantic, that'd be a lie—because running for our lives together was romantic in a funny, scary kind of way.

Anyway, my thinking he didn't want to be separated from me was also an idealistic notion.

The grove of trees was larger than we'd thought, thrilled to have the shade and be able to stop to breathe. We took a position so we could see the tiny dots of tipis scattered about.

"Wonder what year this is?"

I took my boot off to rub my aching foot and found a nasty blister and winced. "If we had my books, we might be able to tell, and boy-oh-boy, sure would love it if Gypsy were here. It'd save our feet."

"Let me see," Nate said, grabbing my foot.

I pulled it back, but not in time.

He touched my bare foot after it'd been in a boot and was all nasty and sweaty. It was then I tried to recall the last time I'd bathed.

"Hey, uh, let me have my foot back. I haven't had a bath in, well, I don't know how long." I was embarrassed.

"I'm in the same boat, Rave, so don't worry. Some dirty feet are nothing." He grinned while I put my sock and boot back on, my nose wrinkling as if to say *yuck*.

Present Day, After the Death of Sam Johnson

At the ranch of Pete and Sam Johnson, on the outskirts of the Standing Rock Reservation, the wind blew out of the south, and a group walked to the family cemetery.

Each brother had a plot on either side of their parents. Pete was the last remaining from his immediate family; the rest had perished long ago.

Neither brother ever married. Had no children. Although down the line, there were cousins, third and fourth removed, and the last name Johnson would live on with any male relative of their clan.

Her steps slowed with purpose. Silver Moon walked to the piece of earth where Sam was interred the day before, and she held a lock of his hair in her hand, ready to begin the purifying ceremony.

She lit the sweet sage and held it in her hand to let it smolder while holding the lock of Sam Running Elk's hair over it, letting the sweet sage smoke filter through the tresses as she prayed to Wakȟáŋ Tȟáŋka—the Great Spirit.

Finished, she wrapped the lock of hair in a blessed and sacred piece of buckskin, the soul bundle, then handed it to Jon Little Bird.

"You are appointed soul-keeper and must keep this in a special place in your abode (for they no longer lived in tipis). You will vow to live a life of harmony for twelve moons. After this time, we will gather for a banquet and disperse gifts. Then you may release Running Elk's soul so it may travel the spirit path along the Milky Way to reach Mayá Owíčhapaha, the old woman who judges each soul."

Jon took the sacred soul bundle, tears in his eyes, nodding, too emotional to speak.

Pete Johnson patted the sad man on the back. "You loved him like a brother. I'm thankful."

He looked at the others. "I need to take my leave and rest. Thank you for being my family."

Pete, his face etched with sorrow for he'd miss his big brother, took his leave and headed to the house he'd once shared with Sam.

"Wakȟáŋ Tȟáŋka," a faint voice said, "we must focus on Raven and Nate now."

"Yes, and this I leave to you and Blaze, for it is your youthful power they will need. I am tired."

Blackie took Silver Moon's arm. "I'll take you and Meda home."

He looked at Hank. "You need to go with Blaze and Wakanda since you're an ancestral link to Nate. They'll need you."

He walked both women out to the Jeep while the others stayed to sort things out.

"I'll stay with Pete. He needs company," Jon spoke up.

"Me, too. I think it's best to have people with him," Bud Parker added.

"We'll need your help, Eli, as you're the most passionate dancer. The gods smile upon your ways," said Wakanda.

"Dakota and I will go into town and get supplies needed for Pete, and whatever Meda and Silver Moon need," Payton volunteered.

"Yeah, and we'll go to everyone's place to make sure all the livestock is fed and tended to. We can't neglect these things, even in the time of sorrow," Dakota rejoined.

"Eli, meet us at our ranch, out back, behind our house," Blaze said. "We have a place which has already been blessed and visited by Chief Black Raven. There is where we shall call up his powerful charms."

Then she kissed her husband Dakota, walked to the Jeep, hugged her aunt and Silver Moon, and left to prepare the area with sweet sage, cedar, and tobacco. She'd also have ready the peyote, the drums, and rattles for their ceremony, including her magical charm: a circle inside another circle and the two spheres that lapped one another from her Aunt Meda.

———

T he sun dropped, so there was a chill in the air. Blaze started a campfire as she and Wakanda sat, waiting for the others.

"I feel lucky that we've married brothers and are sisters-in-law," Wakanda remarked out of thin air.

Blaze laughed softly. "I think they're the fortunate ones to have snagged us and should count their lucky stars. According to Aunt Meda, our love was written in the stars—Dakota and I destined to be mates."

"Payton and I had a rocky start, I admit, because I thought he was so full of himself, but something changed one day. To be truthful, I think Silver Moon cast a spell over us; otherwise, we'd not be married, because I really didn't like him." She looked at Blaze. "Don't tell him I told you."

Blaze crossed her heart. "Your secret is safe with me. I can't lie, I thought the same about Dakota, and me having to go back over 130 years to find love, well, puts a new spin on matchmaking."

"Blaze," Wakanda said, "I was always a little jealous because you got to go back in time. I thought I was to be the one, but, well, here we are, right where we are supposed to be. Married to the men we would marry and have the children we'd have. I don't know about you, but I'm happy with my life."

"Me too, Kanda, yet I fear for our children. Old magic is powerful, but there are still many what-ifs that can happen."

Wakanda Kangee, whose name meant "magical," frowned in a sad sort of manner and said, "The past we learned about as children, never once questioning anything. Then somewhere the world's axis slips, and things get thrown off-kilter."

She paused, swallowed hard, and then asked, "Who knew our world would be swallowed by a black hole, and our people would disappear? Blaze, it was your purpose to travel back in time to that specific moment, and this powerful enchantment saved a man, the future father of a grander man. As his birthright, he would become a famous name in history, a hero for the Sioux people."

Blaze Clark Kangee nodded, her eyes focused on the ground before looking at her sister-in-law.

"As time marched forward, as it always does, the people destined for greatness came into being. My daughter does this now for multiple groups. For with Raven, certain legends will echo through time, a testament to our tribe and the Real People. These stories shall remain throughout history."

"Ah, yes," Kanda concurred. "Native American legends shall live forever. The Great Spirit has called upon us—Sioux, Cherokee, Crow, Cheyenne, and the Paiute. Even the Whiteman who has favor with the

Great Spirit can provide valuable assistance. Our combined powers will protect history."

Blaze's brows dipped. "I hear, but... but what?"

Kanda exhaled. "Understanding the history, we avoided changes that would have caused chaos. But, well, the future—that's very different. We have no way of seeing it so far ahead and don't know what will be wrong or what needs to be fixed or put right."

"And we never will, not until we are spoken to by the spirit. So?" Blaze gestured with a hand.

"Our son Chay, our tribe's Star Gazer, is my only child, and he lives in a place yet to be, and I worry. We have no magic book; we have no special medicine man for this. No one has lived it once before, and I fear for his safety."

"What does Paytah say?"

Kanda looked at Blaze, her chin up proudly.

"That our son will help make history, a significant history, and we shall be proud. But he won't do it alone. Paytah dreamed, and he saw Chay far into the future in a world not recognizable, and Chay was a celebrated warrior."

Blaze had more questions for Kanda, but they'd have to wait until the others had arrived, and it was time.

They could wait no longer, as the spirit night was strong, and Raven and Nate needed their magic.

40

I n the open field, the fire burned hot, and the blue, yellow, and red flames danced over the wood like fairies conducting a ceremonial ballet. As the sweet sage smoldered in the fire's corner, it circled the air, cleansing all evil or negative feelings, and Blaze took charge.

"Hank, with your ties to the Sioux through T. H. Cooper, Indian Agent, and honorable adopted brother of Chief Black Raven's clan, I hand you the dance stick of the horse. You shall begin the sun'ka wakan Wačhípi, the Dance of the Horse, so these powerful spirits will move the spirited animal through time to get to her owner."

Next, she turned to Dark Water Dan of the Cherokee. "You will sing the song which shall send a protector to Nate. Young Nate will need to be seen not as a Whiteman, but as a worthy warrior to be feared." Blaze handed him a staff holding the feathers of a red-tailed hawk.

Kanda pulled out a shirt from her pack and handed it to Eli Harris, Two Suns of the Paiute. "A blessed Ghost Dance Shirt," she said.

With reverence, he grasped it as his hand slid across the plain cotton shirt, adorned with the feathers of a raven, eagle, and owl. It was sewn with black thread and fringed along each side, the bottom, and under the arms.

A remnant of a past long gone.
But not of the dreams the Real People had to obtain what they'd lost.

His own people with the power and wisdom of a man called Jack Wilson—better known as Wovoka—spiritual leader and creator of the second Ghost Dance back in 1889. Although it was banned, the dance was the idea behind a ritual Two Suns had always believed in.

"Silver Moon traveled far for this blessing; this will be of help to Raven and to Nate for finding what they've lost."

"I'm here." Blackie Kangee trotted up to the group. "Silver Moon says I'll be needed for the fire dance. She and Meda will travel on a vision quest as we dance."

Wakanda took the rod Paytah had once plunged into the snowbanks in the North Dakota mountain region, sending Blaze back in time. Removing a vial from her pocket, she sprinkled it in a circle around the base of the pole, walking counterclockwise, and she sang about time, past and present, in Lakota. Then Blackie joined her.

Hank held up the horse dance stick, and he sang of the powerful beast that carried, fought, and hunted alongside man.

His song spoke of a wish for the magnificent beast to appear to those in need, while Two Suns danced wearing the Ghost Dance Shirt.

Blaze took the charms of both hers and Meda's two circles, and she too chanted lowly the song of joining.

Her song linked all the past to every present, including the future which had yet to happen.

*

In an Era Hundreds of Years Ago

Nate and I lay on our stomachs, looking out from the grove of trees, and saw nothing, so we were sure no one had seen us.

There were no plumes of dust rising from any riders on horseback, no sounds, human or animal.

Just as I turned to ask Nate a question, I found him staring at me.

Our eyes locked, and I diverted my stare first, feeling flushed and off-kilter, rolling over on my side so I could sit up.

Nate stayed flat, his head down, his eyes fixed on the ground, and he was silent.

I wasn't sure how long we stayed this way, but Nate sat up and faced me, his knees up same as mine, and they touched.

"Are you afraid of me?" he asked.

"No, I'm not," I reacted hastily. "Just afraid of what could get one of us hurt or worse in this unknown time."

"Nope, I don't buy it."

I frowned. "That's good to know, because I'm not selling it."

Scooching over on his rump, he sat next to me, arm to arm and shoulder to shoulder.

We both sat staring out into the uninhabited flatland of where we didn't know, and it didn't matter.

The truth of the matter was there were no cars, trains, or airports; no indoor toilets; no Super Walmart shopping centers or even a strip mall to be seen, much less heard of.

There were no cell phones, pagers, and who knew if the telegraph had been invented yet?

I could scream bloody murder, and no one would hear.

Thank goodness it's not how I felt.

I mean, I wasn't afraid of Nate; however, the man petrified me all the same.

The deal was I didn't want to feel anything for him or any other man, because this would mess up my life.

I had to focus on...

Focus on... what did I need to focus on?

Oh, yeah, my family's ranch, the cattle, and how to learn to run it when my mom and dad were too old and I had to care for them; this was what a dutiful daughter did.

I didn't have time for silly things like love. There were tribal matters that needed to be taken care of, and I knew I was in line to move up in the Council and had to be serious about...

My mother's voice sounded in my ear, and I looked over, expecting to see her; the voice was so real.

"Raven, release your emotions and follow your heart to find happiness. Your happiness enables you to connect with the past and rectify harm that could affect the Real People. Don't battle against fate; it will only bring you sorrow. If you opt to battle or neglect this, your future will remain stagnant, and you'll aimlessly wander in a loop of indefinite time."

I didn't speak aloud.

In my head, I asked myself, *Is this journey about finding love?*
Or is it about correcting history?
Which one is it?

"For you, my daughter, it is both; as it was for me, so shall it be for you."

"No way."

Nate poked me, and I thought he heard her voice too, and I was about to comment, saying he was right—no way was him and I gonna fall in love—but then I looked up to see the most wonderful sight ever—

Gypsy walked through the thicket, saddlebags, backpacks, and all.

"Oh, my stars, I can't believe it."

I jumped up and ran to her, and she whinnied, then bobbed her head and snorted.

Nate ran to her too and stroked her muzzle. "You lovely girl, so happy to see you!"

Gypsy snuggled her muzzle into Nate's hands like she'd known him all her life and missed him.

I was pissy because she was my horse, not his.

I took her reins, pulled her deeper into the thicket of trees, and checked her over.

She hadn't been galloping, for she was dry and not sweaty; her legs and hooves and everything looked perfect. Gypsy looked refreshed, like she hadn't been ridden hard in days.

She was well fed, watered, and brushed.

Just how could this happen? Was my horse cared for by mountain nymphs or elves?

In addition, I noticed something. Her harness was old and beaded in the geometrical design the Sioux were known for, and rhythm beads made from bones and shells intertwined with baubles around her neck.

"Okay, this is odd." I pointed to her harness. "This isn't mine. I've never seen it before."

Nate walked over to where I stood.

"Sioux beadwork. It's beautiful." His fingers stroked the old harness, and then he lifted a longer strap of leather from the end of the saddle blanket. "Look at this—wow."

It was three strips of leather, braided, then knotted every inch with beadwork, then more leather, and at the end dangled three feathers.

"Wonder what birds these feathers are from?" he asked, not expecting a reply.

"A raven, an owl, and an eagle," I responded.

He gazed at me with a question mark on his face.

"My dad taught me about birds and feathers, which ones are sacred and powerful—you know, Native American stuff no one else cares about."

I fingered the feathers, thinking about what they represented, and Nate asked me, "So tell me what they mean."

"Okay. So, an eagle feather is given because people believed in you and your achievements—so a chief with a war bonnet of eagle feathers is a symbol of power and authority. These feathers are given for significant accomplishments or feats of bravery; this must be earned. The owl plume can be an embodied spirit of the dead or associated with a spirit in some way, and if it's the feather of a great white owl, this could be a spiritual guide for that person."

"Ah, interesting. So what does the feather from the raven mean? I'm interested to know since you bear the name of the same bird."

He winked at me, and I exhaled, semi-rolling my eyes.

"The raven, called *kȟaŋǧi tȟáŋka* in Lakota, is considered a creature of metamorphosis and symbolizes change and/or transformation. In some tribes, not all of them, the raven is thought to be a trickster because of its transforming and changing characteristics."

I held up a hand. "Stop, before you say another word."

"I haven't said a thing yet." He smirked.

"Yeah, well, I know my name is Raven, but buddy, I'm not a trickster or evil, got it?"

"Not what I was gonna say. All I was gonna say is I've heard ravens are intelligent and can learn to talk. At least one thing is right. Here you are, right beside me, talking."

"You are just so hilarious, Nate, ha-ha-ha." I punched him in the arm, harder than I meant to, but I didn't care, and he hooted anyway.

"I guess you're pretty smart for a girl."

"Are you just trying to make me mad?"

"No, I'm not, but I'm glad to know you have feelings, or at least emotions."

"What in the devil is that supposed to mean? Of course I have feelings."

"Oh, then what you do is deny your feelings, is that it?"

"For crying out loud, I'm not denying anything. There's nothing to deny." My voice rose an octave.

"Sure there is, but you just don't see it." His words calm, he was unmoved, and this irritated me. Right now, I wanted to argue, but evidently he didn't.

"If there was something to see, I damned well would, but there's nothing but you and me working to get back home, then go our separate ways." Oooh! I wanted to stomp my foot, but didn't want to act out like a mad little girl.

"Sure, if that's what you think, then you are right. You are always going to be right, aren't you? What do you want to do then?"

He'd used the word *you* five times, and he'd emphasized it to a point, making me grit my teeth.

I used the word *me, me, me* a lot too, so maybe I acted self-centered and wasn't thinking about anyone else.

Nate had feelings too, and I wasn't validating his feelings, only my own.

Mutely, I stood there thinking about this, my hand stroking the neck of Gypsy. I was about to apologize for being so self-involved when he grabbed my arm.

"Come on, we need to go."

"What's the hurry?"

"I hear horses, and we don't know who's coming. Let's get outta here."

I didn't argue when he jumped on Gypsy and pulled me after him, and when he said, "Hang on tight," I did.

We escaped from the dense undergrowth on the other side, and Nate slapped the mare on her hindquarters, giving Gypsy her head.

He let her run, and she did, like the Devil himself was behind her with a fire-hot pitchfork.

As far as the eye could see was about three miles of flatlands, and up ahead of us were mountains in the foreground. They looked to be further than three miles, but I knew that's where Nate was headed.

We needed to be able to hide, and the mountains were our only chance.

41

The terrain was rough and steep.

I feared Gypsy would slip, but Nate was a remarkable rider.

As sure of himself as he was of the horse, he maneuvered her with ease at a fast pace over rocks and slopes, missing crevasses which might have caught her hooves or even caused a leg break had she stepped in one.

I admired him for his skillful riding.

While we rode higher into the mountains, he located a trail that wound around and up, and he guided the mare with caution.

I hung on tight, both my arms around his middle, my left cheek pressed to his back, and I saw everything on the right as we climbed higher.

As hard as Nate tried, he couldn't keep the bramble and the limbs from hitting him or me, so I dodged anything that might have poked out an eye and would worry about the scratches later.

"That's it, Gypsy, easy now," he spoke to the horse as she ambled slower over a pile of rocks that started to slip and scatter once her hooves came in contact, and with a light tap to her flanks, he pressed her forward.

Nate looked up front.

He saw the desired flat terrain, my view dominated by the intimidating sight of a steep mountainside and a perilous landscape below.

My grip tightened, and I locked my knees on the backside of my mare.

"Just a few more feet and we'll be on a level piece of land, but we can't stop, okay?"

"Why not?" I loosened my grip so I could turn my head to see behind us. "No one is following us, Nate."

"No, but look up."

I did what he asked, and I saw them.

Hawks and turkey vultures circled the area, so something had died, and whatever had been killed was big enough to garner lots of birds of prey.

If the dead animal was big, then whatever killed it was even bigger.

Could be a bobcat, mountain lion, or a black bear.

The possibility that it might be human crossed my mind, as hunting for food was a regular part of life during this period.

"Yep, I agree. Let's get past the birds of prey, and then we can pray it isn't a man hunting, or, uh..." I couldn't voice what I was just thinking.

And I didn't have to. Nate took the words out of my mouth.

"Yeah, let's pray it wasn't a man hunted by beast. Is that what you were gonna say?"

"Uh-huh, and I might add I hope we haven't come upon any sacred grounds, burial, or whatnot, either."

"Not this high up. Or I wouldn't imagine it would be, unless they've put the body in a tree. I'm sure you know about burial rituals, right?" he asked me.

Sure, I knew about tree burials, but hoped we wouldn't encounter one.

My heart just couldn't take coming upon a dead person in a tree scaffold and then knowing the animals had been consuming—I... oh, ugh.

I shuddered, gritting my teeth and squeezing my fingers into Nate's middle.

"Yikes, Raven, you're pinching the crud outta my love handles."

I spurted out a laugh, then snorted into his neck. "Sorry, I didn't mean to snort on you, Nate, but thanks—I needed a laugh."

We both became silent when we looked ahead and saw the carcass of a rather large elk.

It had been ripped to shreds, and part of it covered with grass, leaves, and rocks, which hadn't stopped the turkey buzzards.

All of this, though, didn't account for the winged predators above us, so there had to be another carcass nearby.

"It's a giant bull elk, so I'd be guessing a big cat—a mountain lion, I'd assume—and Lordy have mercy, I hope he isn't anywhere nearby," I stated, my eyes not leaving the bull elk's carcass.

"You know your wildlife, don't you?" he asked.

"On a ranch my entire life in South Dakota near mountain ranges, I've seen my share of the aftermath of a lion's kill or dealt with coyotes in our chicken coops." I snickered. "And my share of rabbits who get into my mom's garden, and how she hates it, but she also hates to kill a bunny."

"You ever go hunting?"

"You're joking, right? And if you think because I'm a girl I can't shoot, you'd better think again, Nate Cooper, because I'm a decent shot with a scope and a thirty-aught-six deer rifle. Matter of fact, I love deer hunting, and venison is spectacular meat."

"You are a paradox, girl—an absolute paradox."

I frowned, not knowing if that was a good thing or not, and I was just about to ask when something pounced off the rocks, scaring Gypsy, sending her rearing up and me on my butt.

Then she flew off like a frightened deer, taking Nate with her as I slid downhill, rump first, my hands grabbing at anything to stop my plunge downward as I toppled off the short incline, momentum carrying me.

The low-lying branch of a bur oak, which grew in two halves at an awkward angle, saved me from tumbling any further as I grabbed hold and pulled the limb as hard as I could to stop me from sliding.

When I stopped, I didn't let go. I pulled myself uphill and got proper footing before releasing the limb and looking down.

The mountain loomed above me, and below were the craggy rocks and hard ground, which would have been certain death had I continued to keep slithering down and picking up speed.

My heart raced.

I had scratches and scrapes on my elbows and hands. When I moved to get up, I felt a sharp pain.

"Ouch!"

Oh boy, I was thankful I had been wearing the 1940 Army slacks, socks, and boots, but the pant leg had rolled up, and a smaller cactus paddle stuck its thorny spine in my right ankle.

One might even say I was lucky because the barbs were not grown—just baby thorns—but all the same, they hurt like all get-out.

I tried to pull the spikes from my Army-issued sock, but pricked my finger, thus causing more pain, and it was a circle of never-ending pain as I tried repeatedly.

So, I sat in pain, looking up for anyone—Nate, Gypsy, anyone.

Then I wondered what the heck had pounced out and spooked Gypsy into her run.

My ankle throbbed when I stood, and my body hurt from the fall, but I didn't think anything was broken.

With effort, I crawled toward the big rock I had escaped from crashing my head into it. I sat leaning against it, and I searched my immediate surroundings.

No bobcats or mountain lions, and if it had been a bear, I would've seen such a large animal—I was sure.

My eyes dropped to the ground, searching.

Perhaps a snake had scared the hooey out of Gypsy, but there was nothing.

The stinging in my ankle grew worse, and I thought back if I'd ever heard cacti needles could be poisonous.

No, I didn't think so, but the discomfort was enough to cause tears to form, and I whimpered in silence for my pain.

Five minutes into my crying, I knew I wept for more than just the stupid fall or the cactus needles, and this was how he found me—crying, and feeling lost and lonely.

————

Against the rock, my head down, my hands covering my face, a hand reached out and touched my arm.

My first thought was that Nate was back.

"Thank God, Nate," I started, lifting my eyes, then recoiled.

It wasn't Nate.

It was a man dressed in a buckskin shirt and leggings, his hair long and in braids on either side of his head.

His facial expression was hard to read.

He frowned, but his eyes held a million and one questions about me as he menacingly loomed over me.

I spoke first in Lakota, hoping to have found an ally.

"I am Raven Kangee. I'm injured. Can you help me?"

He was silent, staring at me, and I wondered if he spoke Lakota, so this next time I repeated myself, but in as much Cheyenne as I had learned when we'd been with Kingfisher and She Who Sees Truth.

His eyes narrowed.

So, I tried again in Apsáalooke.

His eyes darkened, and he growled, but still said nothing.

"Well, dang, I don't know another language—at least other than English—so maybe you should say something so I'd know if I could understand."

My words spat out in English, and his eyes opened wider.

"Whiteman's words?" he responded in a dialect akin to Lakota, so he was Sioux, or part of the Siouan family.

I nodded, my brow puckered as I waited for him to continue.

I'd already shown him too much of my hand by speaking two other Native American languages, one being the language of his sworn enemy, the Apsáalooke, or more commonly known as the Crow Tribe.

My clothing had to have him believe I was from outer space.

This was if they knew about aliens and stuff.

He might even think me a witch.

He pointed to the bottom of my pant leg I had rolled up to expose the sock with the cacti thorns and commented it must hurt, and I replied with a nod.

The man turned on his heel and walked off, leaving me perplexed and speechless.

My only thought was I didn't pose a threat to him, being a mere female.

He wasn't the least bit interested in my so-called oddities in this era, like my clothing and footwear.

I looked Native American enough—my skin coloring and my hair long and braided.

He might even think he was seeing and talking to a genuine spirit or a mountain fairy.

Up on the mountain alone, he might have been on a spiritual vision quest.

My appearance could have resulted from his dehydration, fasting, or peyote.

I sat thinking about this and my next move and was grateful he hadn't taken me by the hair of my head and thrown me off the mountain or taken me as his captive.

Shame on me for not wondering if Nate was all right.

How selfish was I?

My self-involvement was so disgustingly obvious that it made me nauseous.

I hadn't started off that way, so what in the Sam Hill was my problem? Then it hit me.

It was self-pity—feeling sorry for myself for the predicaments I'd been thrown into without my consent.

I didn't mind the duties I had been called to fulfill, but deep down, I wondered what was in it for me.

At what juncture was I going to get to make a darned choice about my future?

That was the narcissistic part of me clawing to get out.

I knew deep, deep down it wasn't centered on me. But I wanted it to be about me, just a little.

As I sat there in all my self-wallowing, I heard a young female voice call out in Lakota, and my head jerked up.

"Woman, are you here?"

"Here, I am here," I rejoined.

The female who spoke walked around to the boundary of the rock I rested against.

Her appearance flabbergasted me.

She was about five foot six, wearing a buckskin dress with red, yellow, and blue beads, with dazzling designs depicting horses and arrows—the artwork stunning and precise. The symmetry was perfect, the colors vibrant.

On the bottom of each fringe were dentalium shells.

She wore thigh-high deerskin boots adorned at the top edge with what might be brown rabbit fur, and they laced up the front with strands of thin leather, either from the same deer or from a buffalo hide.

I guessed her age to be around eighteen or twenty; she was young, and she was beautiful.

Smooth, dark-brown complexion, a facial construction befitting a supermodel with prominent cheekbones and a well-shaped nose, dark-onyx eyes, and long lashes.

She smiled, and her teeth were nice—not straight, but clean—and she seemed very well groomed.

Here I was, judging her because they didn't have showers, dentists, beauty shops, and nail salons.

When had I become so judgmental and commercialized?

Lord have mercy, I was a jerk to the nth.

42

Covered and warm in a tipi, I woke, not recalling how I had arrived. My ankle was less painful, and I moved the buffalo skin covering me to find I wasn't in my Army clothing but in a nice, soft animal-hide dress, and my ankle tended to.

Under the large leaves, I could feel a wet poultice, the leaves bound with braided stalks of what looked like wheat.

As I wriggled atop the pelt I lay on, I was relieved to know whoever had taken my clothes off had left me with the undergarments I'd arrived in. My face flushed hot at this knowledge.

Someone unknown to me saw me half naked. I prayed it was the young girl, and her only.

I scooted back, lifting the upper half of my body into a sitting position, and looked around.

Mats woven out of cedar bark strips hung to my right, with other assorted blankets made of various animal skins. Varied baskets sat in a corner, with eating utensils made from the bones and horns of the bison.

Charred wood lay in the center of the tipi, encircled by medium rocks. On one section of the fire lay a larger, flat rock I believed was a cooking stone.

My mother, having also traveled back in time, had lived with Chief Black Raven's clan. She'd learned how they lived—lived life with them—and she'd taught me what she knew.

I was fascinated when she wove these tales, and now here I am with the opportunity to live the story firsthand.

My mom also said it was demanding work, yet in many ways rewarding. My first memory was asking her about food.

"Little Bird," she cooed, "you don't go to a supermarket. You had to go out and find it—picking berries, learning about the different roots and grass, searching for mushrooms and for other herbs we buy at the store. It was demanding work. All the men and older boys hunted and fished, and if you didn't find it or kill it, you starved. Water wasn't purified; there were no porta-potties, no two-ply toilet paper, no modern conveniences we take for granted—but the people were happy and lived decent lives, in general."

A sigh escaped my lips. I closed my eyes, remembering I asked her what "mostly" meant.

"The people had hard lives but were not unhappy—until things like gold, silver, and coal mining came into play. Everything changed."

"Momma, why did that matter if they didn't need gold? They didn't have stores anyway?"

This was a longer story for me to hear, but my mom didn't mince words, and she'd told me the truth.
I'd learned greed begat tremendous suffering for all the American Native tribes who never wanted the gold or silver, but just to live off the land and, well, just live.

These memories caused my emotions to soar and my heart to twist in pain.
How could anyone do this to another human—just take and take and take until there was nothing left, and continue to take?

A tear slipped down, then another, and I wept in silence for a past I could never change and for a future that was my destiny to put back on track.

"My dear daughter, you have a woman's heart."
The words rang in my ears, only I was alone.
It was then that I smiled.
No, I was never alone.
She Cougar, my smart mother's spirit, was always near. It was her voice that had sounded in my ears.

My eyes closed, and I pictured her smiling, her eyes dancing with mischief, as she touched her charm of two circles.
Her voice, soft and melodious, sang in my head—her breath on the nape of my neck as she spoke.

"You must also find your future, my dear daughter. Don't reject what's there. Always embrace everything."

A dizziness entered my head, and I felt weak and tired, so I lay back down, pulling up the hide to cover me, and I shut my eyes.

While I slumbered, an apparition of a man came to me while I slept.
He touched my heart, and I saw a woman who bore a daughter. The daughter wouldn't be a name many would know.

She would give birth to a courageous man, a champion of his people.

A man who'd become a name for all to say and be renowned for his leadership and courage, his determination and humility.

He was a man whose name would live on, his legendary spirit and his remarkable ability to overcome impossible obstacles etched into history.

One hundred eighty-four years later, his name would still ring out amongst his people, as well as the world.

*

I woke to a fire burning and the smell of fish cooking.

My gaze shot up and around to my surroundings, and then I recalled I was inside a tipi, covered with an animal pelt, and I'd drifted back to sleep.

I must have slept the sleep of the dead because I could tell it was dark outside, and I heard a hoot of an owl and a wolf bark, then howl, with the addition of other wolves answering in the distance—the nighttime sounds of being out on the open prairie.

"Ah, you wake. Now you must eat."

My head turned to see the lovely woman I had thought I hallucinated about on the mountain.

She sat on her knees, flipping over a fish on the cooking rock which sat in the fire, and she looked at me with a sideways glance.

"I, uh," I began in English, then reverted to Lakota. "Thank you for caring for me and not leaving me to the animals."

"You are Lakota, from which clan?"

She handed me a gourd with water, and I drank, then wiped my mouth with the back of my hand.

Her question hung in the air, and I sat pensive, my answer swirling in my mind.

I was from Chief Black Raven's clan—not a famous man in the world, but to my family he was an important man—a man who was magic and could see the future into the past and back again.

Someone who possessed the ability to depart from their physical form and allow their soul to drift among the clouds and through time.

If not for this chief, I wouldn't be here.

Would she believe me?

Or think me crazed and sick in the head with fever?

"Black Raven's clan." I decided to speak the truth, simply because I had no cause for dishonesty.

She took the fish off the cooking rock, and with a buffalo bone sharpened as a knife, cut into it, placed half on a woven mat nestled with pine needles, and handed it to me.

Next, she gave me a small bowl made from bone she'd filled with a mash-up of corn and red berries soaked in animal fats.

My host took a piece of her fish, dipped it into the bowl, and took a bite, so I followed her lead.

I chewed. The flavor—unexpected.

The fish had a charred flavor, like blackened fish, sprinkled with herbs and rolled in pounded dry corn. The berries were mixed with other unnamed herbs.

It reminded me of sweet-and-sour sauce, and I must have umm'd, because I saw her nod and smile.

"Is good?" She swallowed her last bite. "You wish for more?"

Not remembering the last time I ate, I shook my head.

If I ate too much of what I wasn't used to, it could make me sick.

"Will eat a morning meal."

I also didn't know whether they called it breakfast or not.

There was still a lot for me to learn.

She cleaned up and made me rest, then she sat cross-legged and faced me.

"Tribe calls me White Cow, sometimes Iron Cane. What do they call you?"

"They call me Raven."

I'd decided it was best she lead the conversation.

"On the mountain, you were alone?"

She tightened her eyes, watching me, and I felt she was like a human lie detector, so I wasn't about to lie.

I explained Nate loosely, and how the horse got spooked and took off with him, and they hadn't returned.

"Man wears same clothes as you? Horse gray and black color, with many bags?"

Okay, now I was listening carefully.

How would she know the coloring of Gypsy, and the bags had to be backpacks of assorted sizes and colors?

So had she seen Nate.

"You see this man?"

"From distance. He rode over the mountaintop. No return."

I had to let this sink in.

He rode off over the mountain.

Had he just left me there?

Or was this fate again, making me wonder what was next?

Or—my heart lifted a smidge, if I was fortunate—Chay would return and Nate would go to blazes after he sent my horse back to me.

"White Cow, you have husband?"

"Yes, Black Buffalo." She rubbed her belly. "Inside I have wakanjeja." (child)

"You are Lakota?"

"No, Miniconjou."

Miniconjou—another band of the Sioux Nation, I believed to be part of the Tetons—but this was a history lesson for when I got home to my own century and time.

"This is your dwelling? You and Black Buffalo? Where is your husband?"

I wasn't about to be a third party in this tipi with her and her hubby. My wish was a place with a single woman as a tipi-mate.

"You sleep here. Black Buffalo takes care of you. You are my sister, and you shall be his wife, too."

Okay—every sense in my being was alive and tingling, and I wasn't about to become wife number two, no matter what. So I had to think of something, and it had to be quick.

"The man over the mountain—he is my, uh—we are to be married. He's already paid a bride price, but we need to rejoin our, uh, people."

"Is good, then. Black Buffalo is to bring back your man, and then we wait together."

Her husband rode after Nate to bring him back.

My question was—why?

43

"Your first baby?"

"This is four." She patted her flat belly.

Four!

I wondered how she kept her youthful appearance but didn't ask.

If she were to tell me she used part of the innards of the buffalo or any other animal on her face, I might get sick.

Her not gaining weight, or keeping it off, meant she either had stupendous metabolism or the arduous work she did every day paid off.

"The other children. You have boys or girls?"

"Sons, One Horn and Lone Horn, and a daughter called Good Looking Woman. Girl sleeps with Unci (unh-chee—grandmother) and Gaka (gah-gah—grandfather). This child"—she rubbed her tummy—"sick a lot in morning, they help."

"Your children, how old?"

Her face lit up when she spoke of her offspring. "One Horn is man now, twenty winters, and Lone Horn nineteen winters. They ride on the hunt. Daughter is four winters, and a handful."

Okay, I wasn't prepared to hear that the woman's sons were nineteen and twenty, for she was well preserved. Although, in the age, females married young.

Hey, female to female, I guessed it was okay to ask her age.

"Your winter counts?"

Her eyes squinted just a hair. "Born in Ptaŋyétu (fall), Canwapekasna Wi (the Moon when the wind shakes off leaves). That winter, men with red coats and wigs fighting other wasi'chu (non-indigenous persons). These stories my Gaka (gah-gah—grandfather) tell me when I am old enough."

I dug into my brain to figure out what this meant, and a light popped on.

The Revolutionary War happened in 1775.

So, she'd been born the first winter the war began.

Amazing!

I was chatting with a real-life woman, born the same year the British started the war with the colonists—the war when General Washington's Army won the battle for independence for the United States.

She repeated stories her grandfather told her, and as much as I used to hate that sort of history in high school, she had me enthralled, drawn into every word.

I'd only read about this from long ago, but she'd been here in the flesh, even if only as a newborn.

This made it so much more real to me.

The other thing was her age.

If she was born in 1775 and had a son age twenty, another age nineteen, and a four-year-old, the woman had to be pushing forty!

White Cow looked remarkable. If I could get ahold of what she used and take it back with me to my world, I'd make a fortune.

I scolded myself: You're not here for self-serving purposes, so forget it.

White Cow Woman regaled me with the tales of the vision quests for both her sons, then of her daughter playing house and mimicking her.

She even told me about courtship and how Black Buffalo paid the bride price of ten horses to win her hand.

"We have great fun, play games with plum pits, and winter's fun when boys race down mountainside on a hohukazunta (bison rib sled)—much laughter, and sometimes much pain!"

The pure joy and love she had for family oozed from her pores, and the glee sparkled in her eyes, lighting her face into a rapturous glow.

This made me homesick.

Life on our ranch, much like here, was hard but rewarding, and it was the life I knew, lived, and loved.

Although I had no one bidding for my hand in marriage, I'd had a few suitors but pushed them away.

Some of them were now married to other girls and thrilled. I'd been glad for them, because I wasn't looking for love—or didn't think I was.

My gut clenched at the thought of a family.

Was I letting life pass me by?

"Your clan, where do they camp?" she asked, her eyes getting droopy, and I knew she was growing tired and needed rest.

"South of the Rosebud River."

No way I could say I lived on lands outside of Standing Rock Reservation, because conveying the reservations to White Cow would always be impossible for me, and my heart broke to think of what was in store for the Native Americans of this period.

Oh, I wished to change it all. My feelings became very real, and unexpectedly it wasn't about me; it was about every Native American and the lives of their ancestors.

———

Since Black Buffalo and Nate were not yet back, White Cow and I talked until she could no longer hold her eyes open.

I encouraged her to rest and said I needed to rest too, although I didn't sleep. I had slept straight for, I would only guess, about ten hours and wasn't tired.

My stupid brain wouldn't shut off, so I lay awake facing the opening of the tipi. The flap quivered when the wind blew, and I thought of a butterfly clapping its wings and how fast change happened, in the flutter of a wing.

Next, I thought about how to explain to Nate that he was my intended hubby and why I'd concocted the story.

Lie upon lie.

A sigh blew out of my partially closed lips, and I rolled onto my back.

My gaze went to the hole at the top of the dwelling to see blinking stars. I couldn't explain why, but I needed to see the night sky.

With unhurried movements, I rolled out from under the heavy hide. On my knees, I ducked out of the tipi.

After I got out, I peeked in to make sure White Cow stayed asleep, then stood in front of hers and Black Buffalo's lodging, looking about.

The camp settled down as all slumbered, horses' heads down, munching on prairie grass or sleeping.

I knew horses slept standing and only laid down to sleep daily for a brief time; I'd been around horses all my life, although I was no equestrian know-it-all.

If a dog was in camp, it slept inside with the family who cared for it.

Glancing at my ankle, which was no longer throbbing or stinging, I ventured my weight on it, then chuckled. It wasn't broken or sprained—just used as a pincushion to a willing cactus plant.

Plants and poultices. If I ever got back to my own time, I was going to do some research about this sort of stuff.

A large campfire glowed in the middle.

A community fire.

Each abode had fires inside, like White Cow's private lodge.

The main campfire's embers cooled, and a drifting wind blew bits of ash about, which swirled in the night air.

The sky was dark, yet bright, as city lights hadn't come into play, and the stars outshined themselves, with no manmade lights competing to dim their brightness.

As I watched the night stars shimmer, I noticed an odd twirl of thin clouds swirling amongst the twinkling tiny balls of fire.

I thought of an Etch A Sketch, and the image of a hand turning the knobs to bring a picture to life flashed in my mind. I watched the breathtaking phenomenon, mesmerized and unable to look away.

As the wispy white clouds shifted, they formed a picture of two large circles and four tiny dots arranged in a specific pattern.

I reached in and pulled up the chain lying at my breast, holding it up against the sky.

A perfect replica of my charm, in every sense.

I gasped, holding my breath.

The breeze intensified, and the wispy matter broke up as clouds do on a blistery day, then faded into nothingness.

A darker movement caught my eye just right of the North Star, and I glanced over.

I saw him—the old chief I'd seen on our back forty, the one who'd stood with the lone buffalo.

He regarded me with a nod, then disappeared.

My heart pounded, then slowed.

My very ancient grandfather, Chief Black Raven.

He was watching over me.

I knew I had nothing to fear.

44

Dawn broke.

I woke feeling refreshed and somehow invigorated.

Even though I was unsure of my purpose here, I'd soak up this life and learn. I might've grown up surrounded by the stories of the Lakota culture, with the tales of the old life, but never like this.

The dream book was off in la-la land once again, and I had no references to check into, no puzzle to read and solve, so I'd wing it the best I could. Though I did wonder about Silver Moon and Aunt Meda.

These two women had traveled and seen life behind them, and it had me wondering if they'd ever traveled to the days ahead, into the future. Aunt Meda met Pocahontas, for Pete's sake.

Did these women possess other abilities, like going into the future?

This was a splendid question to ask when I saw them again.

My arms stretched overhead. I looked over to where White Cow slept, but she was gone, and then I noticed the little bundle sitting in the corner.

Upright, I reached and pulled it over.

Tied in leather straps were the clothes I'd been wearing—pants, shirt, socks.

My eyes searched for my boots, and I spotted them sitting on the other side, where all the other footwear was, and I smiled at how neat and organized the interior of their shelter was.

The flap moved, and White Cow stuck her head through.

"Ah, you wake, come, time to eat. Hungry?"

"Yes, starved," I reacted. I stood, getting a full-on stretch with a shudder. "I uh, need to uh…" I was embarrassed.

"Private moment, go down to stream, and after, splash face, then come eat. Your man, he already ate."

My head jerked so fast I thought I might've cracked my spine.

"My man is here?"

I fumbled with my clothing, making sure the dress was down and not up around my waist, and for some unknown reason, I put a hand to my hair to smooth it down.

Then I ran my tongue across my teeth, the inside of my mouth tasting a bit like a buzzard's breath might smell.

After catching myself doing these movements, I stopped.

What had gotten into me?

It was just Nate, not like he was, oh, voted the sexiest man alive in any century.

Although I'd admit he was rather easy on the eyes.

Tall and fit, and his smile...

"Stop summing him up, you dunderhead," I hissed through gritted teeth, not thinking about her listening, and I looked up, with her startled on me.

In Lakota, she asked, "What is what you say?" then using English, she repeated the word, "Dunderhead?"

A small chuckle escaped me, and she frowned, not liking my laughing at her.

She'd caught me by surprise, and when I didn't answer, she stormed off.

"Raven Kangee, you most certainly are an idiot, dunderhead or whatever," I grumbled, tossing the buffalo hide off my feet, grabbing my Army boots, tugging them on.

I got ready to look for her; however, first I needed a private minute, or I'd need a new buckskin dress.

I didn't go to the stream. I made it to a clump of bushes just behind her lodge. No one was around, so I squatted to have my much-needed moment, and just as I'd finished, I heard voices.

In record time, I'd yanked up my drawers from the forties and pulled down the 1800s dress made of deerskin, and my head popped up over the bushes.

White Cow stood there with the same man who'd found me the first time on the mountain. She looked at me, then him, and she introduced me to him, then she stood back.

Her hand up and flat, she gestured to him. "Sapa Tatanka, Hiŋgnáku (Black Buffalo, husband)."

I was sure that right now wasn't the time to apologize to her and go into an explanation, so I smiled and nodded to him.

"Nice to meet you," I said in Lakota.

And his one eyebrow cocked up.

"You are Oglala, or Hunkpapa?"

"Hunkpapa."

"Humph, not like man." He turned and walked away.

I had no understanding of what he meant, so I had to ask her after I apologized first.

"Not laugh at you," I said. "Laugh at self for thinking silly things about how I look."

My words tumbled out, clueless about what I was saying, but she bought it and nodded her acceptance of my apology.

I let out a soft sigh, then asked, "Sapa Tatanka (Black Buffalo), what does he mean about not like man?"

"He say you not full Lakota, not like man. You have Whiteman eyes."

In my head, I processed this to mean he'd found a man, and it hadn't been Nate; it had to be Chay because he was full Lakota!

My heart jumped up and down with glee.

I looked beyond her to see if I could see him, and although I wanted to run back to the village, I stopped myself.

Crud.

I had told them Nate was my intended.

Would they think Chay was my intended?

Oh, yuck, yuck, yuck. I couldn't act lovey-dovey with my cousin; he was like a brother to me, and I shuddered in disgust at the thought.

"Come, eat, then we work."

Her hand came out and grabbed my elbow to guide me back.

"The man, my, uh, man," I asked as we walked.

"He ate. Now he sleeps. See him later, after he speaks with Chief and Council."

Okay, it sounded like Chay was going to be on trial or at least in a tipi interrogation.

I had to bite my lips in order not to smile or laugh thinking about how he'd feel or act.

By this time, knowing my cousin, wherever he'd been, he was most likely pissy and not in the mood to be pelted with twenty-one questions.

Oh, my, I just couldn't wait to talk to him, see what he'd been doing and where, and who he'd been with, and oh, my, was I ever eager to see him, to hug him.

I hadn't realized how much I'd missed him until this very minute.

Just as we got back to her lodge, it hit me.

Where was Nate?

Was he alright?

I was sure he was fine.

I mean, he was also in the vortex of my family's and the Council's magic, so I was sure he was safe.

But then, perhaps he wasn't, and something bad had happened in the mountains that no one could have foreseen.

My gut tightened up, the worry set in, and under my breath I prayed.

"Lord, please care for Nate."

This was when I felt it.

My heart flipped, and I thought to myself, what if I never see Nate again?

Our conversation prior to zooming off and up the mountain played in my head.

He accused me of denying my feelings, and I'd fervidly stated there was nothing to deny, and he'd come back saying I just didn't see it or wouldn't admit it.

If I'd felt something, would I have suppressed it?

I wondered to myself, then recalled his emphasis on using the word "you," like I was thinking I was all that—a bag of chips to boot.

His question, "What do you want to do then?"

His words rang in my ears, and I thought, I don't know what I want.

What I thought was he should've said, "Raven protests too much, me-thinks," just like the line in the Shakespearean play, *Hamlet*.

I'd just had this entire conversation in my head and eaten breakfast and wasn't sure of what I had eaten.

Not scrambled eggs and toast, I knew for a fact, so I took another bite using the spoon made from the bone of a bison and chewed.

Corn mush with—I chewed more—ah, hickory flavor, and uh, yeah, pine nut flavors—a nutty oatmeal of sorts—and it wasn't half bad at all.

I took a small length of the jerky and scooped out the mush and ate a bite with the jerky, and it was rather tasty.

It was probably healthy, too.

"Mmm. Good."

My head nodded at White Cow. I picked up the water-filled gourd and drank, and expecting it to be gritty creek water, I was pleasantly pleased to find it wasn't.

"How is water so clean?" I asked.

The woman looked at me as if I had snakes coming out of my ears and frowned.

"Your clan not use hot rocks or sand. Get dirt out?"

"Oh, yes, yes, this is just very good," I lied.

Purifying water was never a question I had asked about this era.

I just assumed it was all just creek or stream water.

My thoughts turned to waterfalls in the mountain area and melting snow and how it was probably purer in the present without all the man-made things which had been destroying our ecosystem.

She began cleaning up, and I attempted to help her, but she stopped me.

"No, sit, I do. You help me later, carry water and wood."

"No, I help now, you have baby, you need rest."

I patted my tummy, signifying her baby, not wanting to get too personal by touching her belly.

Without an argument, she let me do the work, and then I attended to the water-carrying and the toting of wood, and I felt good about the work.

Since Annie Shorey's, I had done nothing productive, and I needed to feel needed.

Okay, no watch, and no way to tell time except for the position of the sun. It was almost high noon, so where was Chay? I hadn't heard or seen him.

"The man," I hesitated to say my man. "He is awake now, and rested?"

"In Chief Smokes' lodge, they talk, smoke pipes, tell stories, eat, soon finish, he comes out."

"Chief Smokes?"

This wasn't a name I knew in my history, nor White Cow, either. I'm sure they'd played an important part in history, or I wouldn't be here.

"He is brother, and leads our tribe, smart, fair man. You meet soon."

Well, I thought, it's good for me.

I'm friends with the chief's sister, can't get any better.

And Chay was here!

Yay.

45

My basket packed with twigs and small kindling to start a fire or keep it going, I passed the lodge of Chief Smoke headed to White Cow's lodge.

I didn't see them exit when I felt a hand upon my shoulder and heard my name whispered in English. My heart skipped several beats as I turned.

"Lordy, Chay, I've..." I started and stopped all at once, my mouth gaping open. No words came out as I stared.

"You okay?" he asked.

Still, I didn't reply. I was stunned—stunned to think Black Buffalo said this man was more Lakota than me because this man was Nate!

"You can speak, can't you?" he frowned.

"I didn't know it was you. I thought it was my cousin Black Buffalo had found."

His frown didn't disappear; it intensified. "So sorry to disappoint you, but no, it's me, here in the flesh."

"Oh, my bad. It's just Black Buffalo said you were more Lakota than I, and I don't see how. I mean, look at you, I, uh..." I had to stop. I was shoving my foot so deep into my mouth I was going to choke to death.

"They all see me as a full-blown Native American, and I don't know why, but it might be advantageous—not so much for you as I see, but for me and not getting my butt kicked."

"Look at you. How do they see it and I don't? And you don't speak Lakota, or do you, and you've just been hiding this from me?"

"Huh, well, maybe you and only you can see I'm a Whiteman. And why would I hide the fact that I could or couldn't speak Lakota from you?"

There he went again, emphasizing the word *you*, and I tried to ignore it, not taking the bait.

"Fine, then. You've been able to speak and understand Lakota, I suppose, for a long time—making me seem stupid, is that it?" I dropped the basket at my feet and crossed my arms.

He looked away from me and around the camp. "Let's not draw attention to ourselves by raising our voices and arguing. Come on, we'll take a walk."

I glanced around. Everyone worked and weren't paying attention, except for a few older teens who had stopped what they were doing to stare at us.

"Fine. First let me take this to White Cow's tipi. It's what I've gathered for her."

"Terrific. I'll follow you, and we can go from there." His words pressed between clenched teeth as he followed me, stepping heavily on the ground in anger.

Once I'd dropped the basket of smaller kindling, he gave me a side glance and gestured sharply with his head. "This way. I know a private spot."

I shrugged. "Lead the way."

"Uh-huh, sure. My leading you anywhere is a big fat joke," he muttered under his breath.

"What did you say?" I asked.

"Nothing, never mind," he said clearer.

I came back with a stiff-lipped, "Fine."

We were over four blocks from camp, and I wondered if he'd brought me here to shout—or expected me to. Either way, I didn't give a donkey's behind.

Nate stopped near a large fallen tree, turned, and faced me, his arms crossed, eyes narrowed into slits, lips turned down like a marionette's mouth.

"You wanna tell me what your damage is, and why you treat me like I'm an insignificant piece of dog crap?"

I tried to talk, but he kept going, so I shut my mouth and listened.

"Since day one, I wasn't included in your travels, and just so you know, Miss High and Mighty Princess of the Sioux, I didn't ask to come along. I repeat... did not ask to be here. No one gave me the option to say no, and even then, I might have agreed to come. Still, after meeting you—I do mean the real you—I'd have emphatically said no, no way, nada. Don't put me five hundred years near that woman."

"Well, I gotta—"

He cut me off.

"I'm not finished. You've been disrespectful, opinionated, all-knowing, and think you're God's gift to horsemanship and the only freaking person whose magic works for, on, or about. Here's a truth for you, Princess: it ain't about you at all, or me, it's about these people."

He waved his hand, encompassing the area and the time. "This is about keeping history from swerving off track, changing things, and creating a domino effect that could go very wrong, something we'd never want to know—or find out about. That's the gist of what I interpreted all of this to be, at least for me."

He thumbed to himself. "As far as me speaking Lakota or Apsáalooke, magic has been very good to keep me in the loop of communication with the people of this era. Man, I'm so thankful your Aunt Meda and the old wise woman, Silver Moon, don't see me as you do."

All of this left me speechless. Nate was laying it out verbally, in a heated unplanned speech, no-holds-barred.

"Alright, tell me, how do you think I see you then?" I asked.

"A weak-minded little Whiteman with no reason for being."

"Oh, come on, Nate, no, I don't."

"Yeah, well, you thought I'd disappeared, and your cousin had replaced me. Until you saw me, you'd been happy. When it turned to disappointment, I saw it all over your face."

"I was just surprised, that's it. Also, because Black Buffalo said the man was more Lakota than me, so I figured it had to be Chay. My cousin recently made a disparaging remark about me not being a full Lakota, and, well..." I trailed off, palms up, meaning I didn't know what else to say.

He rolled his eyes, shaking his head. "You are the most exasperating woman, and I don't know why I even like you."

"You like me, and this is the way you show it?"

"Hey, little girl, you can like someone and not like them too. Don't push my not-liking-you buttons. I'll be honest—there are more of those to push than the I-like-you ones."

I exhaled and twittered nervously.

"That's funny? Really? Get this, I don't want to not like you because if that starts happening, the 'I can't stand you or the sight of you' buttons will be next. Then what, especially if we are traveling through time and space together for any lengthy period?"

"Well, you'd better get your 'I love you' face on for me, because I've sorta got you down as my intended. It's what I told White Cow."

"Why in the Sam Hill would you tell her this?" His face contorted into a holy-moses-what expression.

"Because she said I was now her sister and would live with her and Black Buffalo, and I was gonna be his wife too, and well..." I stopped at the pure delight that crossed Nate's face.

"You find this amusing?"

His head bobbed. "Yeppers. A romance would've been hard to play off with your cousin, don't ya think?"

"We'd have managed, I'm sure," I stated matter-of-factly.

"Really? All the romantic motions, verbalized or actions? You and Chay couldn't play the part convincingly."

"Again, we'd have worked it out."

"No one here is a fool, and you can't just play these people. You think because they're from this period they can't see what is or isn't true, and you can fake your way?"

"If they can see you as a full-blooded Lakota, then they'd think me and Chay were in love. Yeah, I'm sure it would've been no problem."

A quick burst of laughter blew from his lips like a horse snort.

"What did that snort mean?" I asked.

"Looks like it's just you and me pretending to be in love, since we didn't get any love potion, and I'm not feeling it."

"Fine, just pretend then," I waved my hands. Oooh, he was pissing me off.

"All I can say is I hope you have some talented acting chops," I added.

"I'm sure you've seen *An Officer and a Gentleman* with Gere and Winger, right?" he asked.

"Yeah, so what of it?" I asked, refolding my arms across my chest.

"The story goes that their love scenes were so hotly intense because they detested each other. I'm guessing we'll do alright too, since we are the unknown versions of those two famous people. Now come on, we need to return to camp before they come looking for us."

I followed Mister Smarty Pants back toward the camp. Through all this conversation, I hadn't asked him a few important questions.

"Hey, stop a minute."

"Ask nicely."

"Nate, please, will you stop a second?" I made a cheeky gesture, sticking my tongue out.

"What?"

"First, where is Gypsy and the backpacks?"

He inhaled. "I can't believe you're just now asking, but okay. I hid the backpacks in a hole, covered with bushes and rocks. Gypsy... I've got no idea what happened. Her saddle and the rifle too."

"In a hole?"

"No, sorry. Not a hole. A small cave, big enough for one single big bear—and nothing else. Thank goodness there was no bear."

"Gypsy?" I stared at him.

"I looked back. She was walking off—literally off the mountain. I chased after her. You won't believe me if I tell you."

"Oh, Nate, for goodness' sake. You don't think I'll believe you? Are you for real?"

"Shush, keep your voice down, geez, Louise! I got to the edge of where she walked off, and she was floating, then she just faded out of sight."

I didn't say a word because I believed him. I knew my dear mare wasn't lost—just waiting in another realm.

"You believe me, don't you?"

I nodded, then asked, "And you, how did you explain yourself to Black Buffalo when he found you?"

"Told him I was on a vision quest and headed back down the mountain when I fell and suffered a blow to my head. Didn't knock myself out, so I could prove the bump on my noggin. Anyway, it's all good because through magic I speak and understand Lakota. It scared me out of my wits when he snuck up on me."

"And what do they call you? I'm sure you didn't tell them, 'Hey, my name is Nate Cooper.'"

"Šuŋgmanitu Čikala."

"Your name is Little Wolf?"

"Okay, sue me. It's all I could come up with on short notice."

Nate turned, heading back, and I followed, uneasy about our new acting roles as lovers.

46

Nate and I agreed to act civil when we found ourselves alone, no more snapping or barking at each other. We were here and needed to deal with it as best we could until we left this era—something we both prayed would be soon. It was imperative we maintained a polite, if not romantic, attitude when in the presence of others.

We came from different clans, as we'd told them. This wasn't a falsehood, though it wasn't the complete truth either. I felt bad with all the lies we'd had to fabricate about who we were, where we came from, and our fake intended love and future together.

Nate explained to Chief Smoke he'd been on a vision quest, and that's how Black Buffalo found him.

Me? Well, I had to come up with a humdinger of a story.

I told them I'd left our camp alone to hunt for berries and nuts. Somehow, I'd wandered too far and lost my way. The clothes I wore were from a fur trader who had found me, captured me, then left me stranded after discovering the Crow Tribe was out on a hunt. But this fur trader didn't know one Native American from another and thought me to be Crow, so he left me to save himself when we stumbled too close to their camp.

"This Whiteman hurt you?" Chief Smoke asked.

With vigor, I told him no—I was only frightened.

"Is good? You chaste?" was his next question.

I blushed eighteen shades of red and purple, nodding that the man hadn't touched me.

"Is good. You and Little Wolf will soon marry. He needs right woman," he voiced to me during a Q&A session at his tipi.

"Yes, he does," I responded, though I thought to myself I wasn't going to be his woman—never would be.

"Go, then, to White Cow; you help her and others until we move closer to the herd. You and Little Wolf will search for your clan and join them before winter sets."

Chief Smoke dismissed me, and I left, wondering when this time would be. I hadn't noticed changing colors in the scenery, nor any weather changes. Time seemed unchanged. I woke with dread, knowing the new day was equivalent to the day before, and the one before that, and would be just like the next day or the one after—like the old movie, *Groundhog Day*.

Was it the same for Nate? I hadn't asked him because I only talked to him when necessary—a grunt here and there, or a "yeah," or "huh." Long days and longer nights.

I worked alongside White Cow every day, maintaining her lodge, toting water, and assisting her and the other Sioux women with the weeding and upkeep of the corn, bean, and squash crops. I did my part most days but never cooked. It was her home, and being the woman of her lodge, I didn't take charge of anything—I followed her lead or her orders.

One day, though, she asked me to cook something, and I looked at her like she was a woman with twenty pairs of eyeballs staring at me, and me with no tongue to answer.

"You no cook?" White Cow scowled.

"I... uh, no. No one teach me. I... uh... Mother not here."

I was at a loss for what to say. I didn't want to lie and say my mother was dead—bad karma.

"No other women teach?"

I shook my head.

"I teach. You cook, for man, and for children one day."

She tsked, clicking her tongue at my inadequacies at being a proper Sioux wife. The woman taught me how to make pemmican, cornbread, and corn porridge. How to tan hides, do quill work, and make cornmeal. White Cow guided me through the process of painting on a buffalo hide.

The woman farmed and told stories of her family to her four-year-old daughter while caring for her husband and two older sons. Her life was full—fuller some days than others—but never dull. A small basket by her side held shells, colored pebbles with holes drilled through them, various animals' teeth, bones from small birds, small feathers, and porcupine quills. She was teaching her four-year-old alongside me the art of beadwork and design.

"Put like this," she instructed her daughter.

Then she began showing her how to string the teeth and shells in a unique fashion, using the sinew of a buffalo slaughtered from their previous hunt. Sewing with tendons of an animal was amazing. Whoever thought it up was a genius. I suspect it was a Neanderthal man who first sewed.

My knowledge of such history wasn't paramount. I contended not to dwell on the whys or wherefores, but on the blissful use of plants, clay, and specific berries to transform items such as teeth, shells, and quills into beautiful works of art and jewelry.

"You can paint, too?" I asked, watching her take juices from a chokeberry, yellow from wildflowers, and red from clay sediment.

White Cow drew pictures of a horse and warrior with charcoal bits found near the mountains. She used ash from campfires as a shadowy wash. My admiration for her and the traditions of my native tribe grew. Theirs was a hard life, and after a full day you ended with decent night's sleep, waking to love and respect from your fellow humans. The family unit was top priority.

Several times I'd watch Nate, making sure he didn't catch me, and I wondered how he felt about all of this—these people and this life. Could it be he detested it? Or, like me, was he learning a valuable lesson about life?

———

Day Ten of My Arrival

I'd been marking the days on a flat section of hardened bark I'd found when gathering wood. I kept it under my sleeping hide.

What I found strange was that in ten days' time, White Cow had grown more pregnant. The first day, her tummy was flat. Today, she looked six or seven months along.

This morning, it was beneficial to speak to Nate—to get his take on how he saw things, to see if we were on the same page. I tapped him on the shoulder as he sat, laughing with a few of the other single men in the camp.

"Can we talk alone?"

A frown appeared as he looked up, then at his new friends, then back at me.

"Of course." He gazed at the others. "Private talk—we go behind the trees."

Nate wiggled his eyebrows, and the others yukked it up, teasing in jest. It still irritated me.

Side by side, a few feet apart, we walked, and I uttered out of the side of my mouth, "Gotta show off in front of your friends?"

"Nah, not showing off. Just being one of them—not acting all lovey-dovey, not displaying a sign of weakness."

"Weakness! Lord, Nate. Not one of them could consider you soft or, in this era, panty-whipped. We hardly ever talk; we never eat a meal together or spend any time alone. You're off hunting or fishing, doing men's work or talking and smoking with the chief or whatever."

"You telling me you miss me?" he asked offhandedly.

"Wait until we get to the stream. I don't want anyone to hear us."

Him and I spoke in Lakota only these days, and everyone knew what we were saying. We couldn't risk speaking English in front of the tribe—it would raise a red flag and could cause serious issues.

———

The stream was peaceful, the water bubbling quietly, and the birds sounded in the trees. A chipmunk—or perhaps a squirrel, I couldn't tell—ran up a tree chasing another. All the sounds of nature exploded in your ears if you took the time to listen, as I had these past few days. Crickets sang and chirped; at night, the hoot of an owl filled the air.

The atmosphere was fresh and unpolluted; the lands so wild, untamed, and glorious. If I'd tried to describe how it made me feel alive and invigorated me, it would've fallen on deaf ears to those born and raised here. They wouldn't know anything different, and I was a little jealous.

"I like it here."

It was all I said as he stood at the edge of the stream, wet grass under our feet, and the water sparkling clear.

"What?" His face was serious. "You want to stay here, not go back home to your own time? Do you even think you have a choice?"

"No, guess not, and haven't since this began. I've been shoved, pulled, pushed, and tossed into whatever was my planned destiny. Can we go sit somewhere?"

"Yeah." He pointed. "Over there, see the fallen log? We can stick our feet in the water."

I nodded and walked over first. He followed. I took off my moccasins, setting them atop a short juniper bush. Nate removed his deer-skinned boots.

Right as I climbed up on the log, I slipped a little. Nate's hand steadied me, surprising me too. He almost acted kind.

"Thanks. Don't feel like falling in, not today."

He shrugged. "No problem."

"How long do you think we've been here?"

I began swirling my big toe in the water, on the lookout for amphibious animals, as snakes were a huge worry.

"Not sure. Two weeks? Why?"

"I've counted ten days, so, yeah, two five-day weeks—not including weekends."

His foot came up to splash mine with water, and he shrugged.

"If you knew, why did you ask?"

Air expelled from my lips like a balloon.

"Because, in the last ten days, haven't you noticed White Cow is even more pregnant?"

Nate, being a guy, might not notice these things, so he closed his eyes and envisaged her from his first encounter up to today.

"You're right, she is larger, in a going-to-have-a-baby way. I guess I just hadn't noticed. So?"

"Oh, my stars, a woman isn't at the morning sickness level one day, then looks six to seven months pregnant ten days later. These past ten days have virtually been months, Nate."

"Doesn't feel like it, does it to you?"

He pulled up his foot, untangled some grass from his toes, then stuck it back in the water.

"No, but time is moving differently for us than it is for them. The other thing is nothing has happened which merits our being here unless you have done something and I haven't heard about."

"No, nothing spectacular or heroic, if that's what I'm expected to do. Our not talking—that's on you," was all he said.

He was silent, and so was I. Nate was right—I was the one who pushed him away. And now, what? I was missing him? What I was feeling was odd, and I couldn't explain it to him because I didn't understand it myself.

My hand reached over and covered his.

"I'm sorry for being disagreeable and mean. I'd like for us to be friends if we can."

"Sure, friends we can be. And as far as you being my intended, how about we step back and un-announce our engagement? Go back to single people still on the prowl. You game?"

"You mean, you want me to marry Black Buffalo?" I shuddered.

He was a nice man, but way, way, way too old for me—like hundreds of years too old. Even though it was none of Nate's business, I was chaste and didn't want my first time to be with a man who already had a wife, three kids, and a fourth on the way. Heavens to mercy, he put me in a nasty spot.

If I argued, he might make something out of it and think I had fallen for him. Then I knew he'd be smirking, thinking he had the upper hand.

"I don't expect you to marry him. Just tell them you want to go home to your clan. Or you just thought you loved me, but there's another young buck in our clan. You'd rather he paid your bride price."

I shifted my head from side to side, observing my toes in the water, lifting and dropping them. Ripples started from the center and worked outward each time while I considered his suggestions.

If my attitude was his justification, he had full authority to break it off because I had been a giant pill.

"Never mind, I'll think of something. Afterward, we can cut off our pretend relationship. Once that happens, I'll move in with another family who isn't looking to add a new wife."

"Fine by me. About the other issue, we can't do anything about how time is moving or not moving. We need to play this adventure out, so how about we get back? The other fellas are going to play some games, and I wanna join in."

Nate stood and held his hand out. I accepted it, and he helped me up and off the log onto solid ground, dropping my hand like a hot potato right after.

We donned our footwear and walked back—him smiling and me, well, depressed that it had been so easy to break it off.

We returned to camp.

The other young men were playing the first game of *Little Brother of War*, a version of lacrosse. Nate jumped right in when picked for the second game. These young men, including Nate, laughed and had a ton of fun.

I sat on the sidelines, watching the muscular, youthful men and their athletic prowess. Each man competitive, much like in my day, far into the future; competition hadn't changed amongst men who played sports.

Nate smiled at a young woman who seemed to be around our age; she glanced at him shyly from under fluttering eyelashes, then blushed, lowered her head, and giggled with her friend.

This did not go unnoticed by me. Nate gave her a nod and a look, then ducked his head and dove into the game once the wooden ball wrapped in deer hide was back in play.

The two young women weren't anyone I'd noticed until today. However, one of them had my full attention, just as she evidently had Nate's. It was the same no matter what year, time, era, or century; jealousy reared its ugly head, and my heart thudded at the thought that Nate might have eyes for another—and not for me.

47

That afternoon, I went to White Cow's lodge for a heart-to-heart.

"I don't love him, and it's not good for me. I'll be unhappy."

She sat, caressing her large baby belly, and aahed.

"Is not always for love. That we join a man. Woman needs a provider, a man she can do work for, and make healthy babies. Little Wolf is not the man for this?"

I'd gotten used to him being called Little Wolf.

"He is, but my heart..."

She put her finger to my lips to shush me.

"No, your heart speaks, and you do not hear because your eyes are closed."

My eyes narrowed a fraction; it made little sense to me, but I let her speak.

"He will provide and love, and you shall love him and provide to him children and a warm home. Many men take more wives, but in Little Wolf I see only one love, one woman. You, Black Bird, and the man's love for you to burn an eternal fire, never to be put out."

I gulped. It sounded like a romance novel being read aloud, and I nodded as she resumed.

"The fire in your belly is not like the fire in his. His burns and shines through his eyes. You have covered your fire, and it smolders, but it will soon burst forward and light the skies."

She patted my hand, then replaced it on the baby moving inside her belly, cooing in Lakota a song about an eagle and a fox.

"I must think on these words. But not consent to marry and will not let my father take a bride price," I said resolutely.

"Fire and love, you shall see, Little Black Bird, as Little Wolf runs after you."

I stood. "I shall leave you to rest and begin the fires outside for the evening meal."

She nodded, then, as deftly as she could, lay back, closing her eyes and still humming, resting her tired feet and achy back. Her time was near. I felt it.

———

The baby girl was beautiful, and ten days later, they named her.

"She is called Rattling Blanket Woman and will bear greatness one day," the old shaman proclaimed, his arms held up to the Great Spirit, Wakan Tanka, as he sang his songs.

Sage filled the air to purify, and tobacco was given to please the spirit. A blessed shaker was shaken over the child's head, the drum beating behind him.

The fire that night was large as the people sat around, and some danced at the naming ceremony of Black Buffalo and White Cow's new offspring. I sat behind her older sons, the four-year-old in my lap, and although I enjoyed the ceremony, my eyes kept darting to where Nate—Little Wolf—sat.

His eyes followed each movement of the young maiden called Dancing Flower, the daughter of Speckled Beak and Sits Quietly. Nate made no move on her nor spoke, but I caught them eyeballing each other at times, which discouraged me.

Tall, her skin a golden bronze, her hair reaching the back of her knees, her eyes a dark chocolate brown with a sparkle, her smile a Mona Lisa at times, bashful grin at others showing tiny dimples—she never spoke to me but regarded me with curious eyes. Her friends, two girls her age, watched me with more angry eyes than curious.

I suspected Dancing Flower fancied Nate, rather Little Wolf. I had to admit whatever magic they were doing back home had served Nate well, because if she knew he was a Whiteman, it would have been a giant disappointment for her, and her parents.

All of this didn't whitewash the fact I was envious, but hey, he'd come onto me more than once, so I wondered if this was a ploy to get my attention.

There was a problem, though: I'd already stuck my foot in my mouth, claiming I didn't want him for an intended, telling White Cow there was another buck I was interested in.

I wondered if any young men here liked me, or if, like modern men, they'd avoid going after someone else's "has-been girlfriend."

No matter how much you knew about a culture, there were always things about relationships you'd never understand—or maybe this was universal across all time periods.

I knew that in this era, men married more than one wife, sometimes sisters or cousins, to keep the green-eyed monster at bay. I, however, was altogether for monogamy and had no plans to share a husband.

My feet hurt from walking most of the day, after watching another game of Native American lacrosse and seeing Nate flirt with the pretty young gal. My mood was low, and I desired solitude.

It had been a month since we'd arrived: I was engaged, then broke up. White Cow's morning-sickness then had her baby three weeks later. I was still living in Black Buffalo's tipi, assisting White Cow with chores, the four-year-old, and the new baby—and thankful the idea of marrying Black Buffalo never came up again.

The cool water of the stream appeared inviting. I slipped off my moccasins, tied them together, and slung them over my shoulder, walking into the shallow stream.

"Oooh, that feels good," I aahed, letting the water flow over my ankles and watching for sharp rocks or sticks.

I walked about fifty yards, climbed out, and took a seat on the bank, pulling my knees up and staring into space, thinking.

The thing I couldn't wrap my head around was how all this had transpired in four weeks. Time seemed to stand still or moved hour by hour.

For Nate and me, nothing was unexpected—or at least nothing that didn't appear genuine. Okay, fine. It was unreal.

Anyone who knew our story would understand what I meant. The rest of the world would see it as fantasy, movie material. Alone in the wilderness of what I believed was South Dakota—or possibly Minnesota. I knew the Lakota were first in the Minnesota-Wisconsin area and were pushed to South Dakota due to conflicts with the Cree and Anishinaabe.

It had to be the Dakotas, because the Black Hills were a focal point—or they would be, if I could tell the difference.

I laughed aloud thinking if Mount Rushmore were here, I'd know for sure I was near the Black Hills.

"Hey there, what's so funny?"

I jumped a foot off the ground. Even though I heard it in English, I knew it was Nate. I wasn't prepared for someone to sneak up on me.

"Hey, a bit of a warning would have been nice. You just scared about twenty years off me."

My hand at my heart, I felt it thudding.

"Sorry, but my, don't you look good for a woman of what, nearing fifty? Or should we do subtractions since we've gone backward in time?"

"That would make us less than a spark in our parents' eyes," I replied monotone.

"Am I disturbing you?" he probed, taking a seat next to me without invitation.

"Don't you always try to?"

I heard his heavy exhale, knowing I frustrated him. He probably felt he was never on the winning end of our relationship.

Of course he was disturbing me, yet not in the way a person bothers you—this was emotional, and his nearness made me lash out.

I admit my counterattack to protect my feelings wasn't an excellent strategy, but it was automatic.

"Why are you out here this far from camp and alone? It's not safe."

"Just what makes you think it's not safe?"

I pulled my feet up and put my moccasins back on.

"Horses were stolen last night from the camp."

I sat up straighter.

"Someone came into the camp and took horses. Who?"

"A group of Pawnee warriors. One of them left their mark on the chief's tipi—like counting coup. We're on high alert here."

I jumped up, looking about, out in the middle of nowhere with no weapons or horses to flee on.

"We'd better get back, then."

"We're safe, Raven," he said, placing his hand on my arm. I tossed it off.

"We're flesh and blood, too. What makes you think that? Neither of us know enough about how this works. We don't belong here. What if we die here and never know our real lives? We are just passing through."

"Okay, sure, it makes sense, sort of. We do belong here, though, both of us, or we wouldn't be here." He nodded. "I know, I know, it's by strange magic, but we were chosen. I feel there's more to do, more for you to do, Raven."

His hand returned to my arm. This time I didn't shake it off and looked him in the eye.

"Nate, Little Wolf, you're not finished either, I would assume."

"Just what does that mean?"

"Shouldn't you see about drumming up a few horses to give Speckled Beak for the hand of his daughter, Dancing Flower?"

"What the...my Lord, are you nuts? Why in heaven's name would I do that?"

"I've seen the way she looks at you and you return her ardent looks. That's why. The girl fancies you, Little Wolf." My tone was harsh.

Nate began a low chuckle, which turned into a full-blown howl.

"I don't think this is funny, not one iota," I snapped.

I pulled my arm away and took a few steps back; my right moccasin slipped on wet grass, throwing me off balance.

I teetered backward, dumping myself into the creek, butt first, landing flat on my back.

Caught unaware, Nate stood watching, then thrust his hand out to grab one of mine and pulled me out, dripping wet.

"You okay?"

The frown on my face should have told him I wasn't.

"No, I'm not."

"Are you hurt anywhere?" He spun me around to check my head.

"I'm not hurt, Nate. I'm embarrassed, pissed off, and..."

I blubbered, tears for a lot of things that had transpired over these past days, months, or even years. I had no awareness of time anymore.

My tears were for Chay—I had no idea if he was safe. For Gypsy, my beloved mare. For my life back in the twenty-first century, my parents, and other friends, even if they were three times my age.

Last, I wept for a love I felt but would have to deny, as he loved another.

48

"Little Wolf, Chief looks for you," the unknown woman disclosed as Nate and I walked back into the camp, me still wet from my unplanned dip in the creek.

"I shall meet him in his lodge then."

She looked at me, a soft smile on her chubby, older, wrinkling face. Her eyes seemed familiar, only I couldn't place her. I watched her turn and walk away, her movements slower, and she limped.

"Who is she?" I spoke in English slowly from the corner of my mouth, and I saw him pressing his lips together to keep from grinning widely, but he didn't respond.

Instead, he called out to her, "Thank you, Dancing Flower, you beauty."

The woman stopped and looked back over her shoulder at him, and she beamed. "Little Wolf, you a devil. You not let Old Badger hear you flirt with me!" Then she went about her business.

My eyes widened, and Nate took his finger and closed my jaw shut, which had dropped open. Then, with his hand at my elbow, he marched me—or walked me, whichever way you want to say it—to the front of a lodge I wasn't familiar with.

"Go inside."

I narrowed my eyes, turning my head sideways to stare at him.

"Whose place is this?" I asked, prepared to tug the flap it open and enter.

"Ours, yours, and mine," he rejoined. He opened the flap and halfway shoved me in, then poked only his head through the gap.

"Get dry clothes on and wait here, and I mean it, Raven, wait so we can talk. Will you?"

Mutely, I nodded, and he left me dumbfounded inside a tipi we supposedly shared to go find the chief.

———

After I found a dry dress, I slipped off the wet one and hung it up. Most people dressed commando today, but some undergarments were available, like loincloths or breechcloths made from tree bark.

It was an amazing process I had helped White Cow with just months ago—or was it yesterday? My time equilibrium was out of synch.

I slipped on the softer undergarment and was pulling the dress back down when Nate returned, and I blushed vivid red.

"You've got pretty gams, something us guys in this era don't get to see often."

It was uttered matter-of-factly as he passed by and took a seat on a pile of furs stacked on a mound of hay—his bed, I assumed. Then I wondered where I slept if this was a lodge we shared and I fumed letting it sink in. My attitude turned crankier. I felt like I was being tossed straight into an episode of *The Twilight Zone*.

It would seem as if Nate were reading my innermost thoughts. Just as he saw me inhale and open my mouth, his palms came up in a fashion to calm me.

"Before you say anything or yell, please sit down and give me a chance to tell you a few things first. Okay?" His face set in a serious mode.

What was I to do—not listen, behave like a harpy or a screaming banshee, accuse him of taking advantage of me?

It appeared a lot had happened since my stupid walk, or while I had slept. I wasn't even sure anymore.

I plopped down, situated my legs to be comfortable, and then crossed my arms over my chest. Yeah, I knew it was a closed-off gesture, and right now his job was to win me over, convince me I had nothing to be angry about. My mouth set grimly, I gave him a curt nod and a tight-lipped, "Fine."

"While I was playing a game of Lacrosse with the fellas and you were off taking a walk, I'm gonna guess about twenty years have passed. Seems Dancing Flower married Old Badger and has four children with him, and Chief Smoke passed two years ago."

"Oh, no, he did?"

Nate nodded morosely.

I narrowed my eyes. "I'm going to let you continue to give me your update, but I have a question for you."

"And this is?"

"How do you know this and I don't? I don't understand."

"Beats the heck outta me. After the game, I washed up and then lay down to rest. I had a dream, and when I woke up, what I'd imagined in my sleep was true."

"Hmm. Aunt Meda and Silver Moon I suspect may have entered your reveries. Who is Chief now?"

"One Horn."

"Black Buffalo and White Cow's oldest son? Wow, they must be very proud."

Nate's silence spoke volumes.

"Please don't tell me they're dead."

"Black Buffalo is alive, but White Cow's death happened because of a rogue buffalo, a freak accident in this age. Happened eight years ago."

Tears streamed down my face as I mourned a woman who had taken me in and treated me as a family member, a sister, and mentor.

"And Rattling Blanket Woman, her baby?"

"A beautiful young woman of twenty winters now."

"Nate, I just can't wrap my head around this. I was only gone for a few hours, and just yesterday they did the naming ceremony."

His shoulders twerked upward, and only one word came out of his mouth. "Magic."

"Well, no, duh, but why? Okay, don't answer because you know the same things I do. I sure wish I had my books." My index finger patted my upper lip as I recalled he'd said he hid the backpacks in a cave. It was then I admonished myself under my breath, not articulating my words.

He eye-balled me. "What are you muttering? I can't understand you?"

"The backpacks. In all this time, why haven't we searched for them?"

"I forgot all about them until just now. So much has happened in such a brief span of time. Why are you just remembering?"

Nate did a thing you do with your eyes and eyebrows when you look at someone in question mode.

"Fantastic question, and I've got no answers either. Do you think you can find where you hid them?"

"Raven, this tribe has moved more than several dozen times since we got here, and honestly I've no clue where we are. I mean, I can try but not promise. A landmark might jog my memory bank."

"Of all the things we've been able to do since this began, we've been able to communicate in new languages we never studied. And you give off the persona of a Native American, and no one here can see you as a Whiteman, and this keeps you safe." I took a deep breath and didn't let him get a word in.

"Add in another crucial factor—we're not aging and no one notices. Time is speeding forward and we are at a confounded standstill. I should think we'd be able to find those darned books."

I paused, then huffed rather loudly. "And I would also like to think my mom, Aunt Meda, and Silver Moon are working at something to help us get home—or a plan to get us to the next whatever it is we are doing phase."

All these emotions had balled up, and the tears began. There was no stopping them as my body convulsed with my sobs.

Nate scooted over and put his arm around me, holding me.

"Shush, it's going to be alright. I promise I'll never leave you. You can depend on me."

I pressed my face into his chest, letting him stroke my hair and rock me, and I wrapped my arms around his neck and wept.

Once my crying slowed to a few tears trickling down my cheeks, I didn't let go. It felt right to be in his arms, so I lay against his chest as his chin rested atop my head.

We stayed like that for a while before I lifted my face to his and our eyes met.

His face close to mine, his lips moved to taste the salt from my tears, still wet on my face, then he uttered, "I'm going to kiss you."

I didn't move to resist, and with care, his lips pushed against mine.

I responded, my words muffled against his mouth. "Then kiss me, Little Wolf."

At first, it was soft, almost playful, his lips teasing mine, me teasing back, and then the fire inside us ignited. The kiss became more than a kiss; it was a dance—a hot, flaming dance consuming us to our core.

His hands held me tight; his mouth ran down the side of my neck and back up again.

Nate stopped, and with one hand splayed against my back, steadying me, he took his other hand, cupping my chin.

"Open your eyes."

With languid eyes, I did, and my stare connected with his.

"Keep them open. I want to look at you when I kiss you."

Just before he kissed me with a passion I'd never experienced, I saw myself in his eyes.

What I saw was a woman who would love with such fierce passion it would burn another to cinders if they didn't have the same fire.

In his eyes, I also saw Nate Cooper, the real man. A man with a burning desire matching mine, a man called Little Wolf in this lifetime who would withstand the heat of the flames we'd create as one.

Our movements unhurried, almost as if we'd practiced them day in and day out. Our bodies moved together slowly, smoothly, naturally. Nate lay me back on malleable hides, pushing my long black hair away from my face, and kissed me tenderly. His face searching mine. His forehead wrinkled.

"Raven, for the past twenty years, as my visions told me, we have lived together, but in reality we have had no physical relationship, so if you say no, I'll respect your answer and we'll continue to be tipi-mates, pretending to be married."

"The tribe thinks we're married?"

"Yeah, they do, according to my dream."

My brows dipped in thought. Sure, I had a ton of questions but wondered if they should wait.

Our discussion was becoming a buzzkill on what was the most erotic moment I'd ever experienced, and I wondered how much better it would be if I just shut up and let go.

I made up my mind, holding his face between my hands, looking deeply into his eyes with a soft voice and a relaxed posture.

"Can I ask questions later and take my chances I'll be okay with it all?"

Nate's voice raw, almost guttural, "You sure?"

"Very," I reacted, my voice a seductive whisper.

Deftly, he helped me remove my dress and my one undergarment. Then he discarded his moccasins and deerskin breeches and stood to look down at me as I lay in all my naked glory for him to see. I heard him catch his breath before lowering himself next to me.

We lay naked, skin to skin, facing front to front.

"Raven, you're so beautiful."

"So are you, Nate," I rejoined.

Nate brought his hand up to my shoulder to roll me on my back, then he hovered over me, looking intently at my face. He lowered his head to mine, our foreheads touching as were the tips of our noses, and said huskily, "I'm going to love you like no other man will ever love you," then his lips covered mine.

The Future World, Far From Here

Two older women sat, rocking and chanting. Reminiscent of the old days, a campfire burned in the backyard as the sounds of native drums played from a recording made at a Sioux festival they attended last fall. In the distance, an owl hooted as crickets chimed in with the singing.

Red-and-blue dancing flames of the fire crackled against a night sky filled with tiny glittering stars winking at each other as if they knew an enormous secret.

Silver Moon, the elder of the two, sat draped in an old bark-blast blanket: aged and worn, geometric patterns in yellow and blue decorated the cloth and the outer edge painted red with lines and arrows. She wore her long silver hair parted and woven in braids. In her hand, she held a magic power bag containing tobacco, cedar, sage, and sweet grass. Inserted and tied at the top was the feather of the snowy owl.

Her friend and tribal sister, Soft Dove, wore her salt-and-pepper hair the same. Over her shoulders, she'd draped a buffalo skin left to her by her great-grandmother from days long forgotten. Faded were the colors of chokeberry, clay, and black walnut dyes used to paint pictures telling the story of wars, and of the Real People. Hand drawings depicting buffalo hunts and the Black Hills of South Dakota.

On her ears dangled earrings created out of porcupine quills, tinted with the dyes of blueberries, and sewn together with the soft strong sinew of the massive buffalo.

In her gnarled hand, she held a shaker made of a dried gourd, filled with withered juniper berries, painted with symmetrical shapes in yellow and blue with dots of red. This shaker blessed for ceremonial use.

Silver Moon's shaky voice hummed as her head bounced with the beat to the drums. She'd lived many winters, too many, and was ready to meet the noble spirits. An old woman not afraid of the afterlife, ready to see her ancestors. In her heart, she knew her time was close.

Soft Dove's chair rocked to the rhythm of the drums as she chanted words of joining, songs of change, and verses of a new life. Her heart heavy knowing her time with her tribal sister, Silver Moon, was growing shorter by the day, yet understanding the life cycle must be completed.

Soft Dove closed her eyes to see what others couldn't see, and she saw them locked in each other's arms hundreds of years in the past:

Nate kissed Raven and then he took her, making her a woman, and she arched into him, joining his soul.

At that very moment, high above in the twenty-first century heavens, two stars collided, merging into a colossal fireball illuminating the skies with an overwhelming energy.

49

Nate and I couldn't get enough of each other.

This was unfamiliar territory, and I was enjoying the journey and prayed it would never change. Funny, our lives fell in step with this era.

We worked hard every day, Nate hunting, fishing, and me keeping our home fires burning. In the evening, we sat, laughing, and telling stories.

Let me rephrase this—I didn't tell tales; I listened. It'd been twenty years—yet only hours for me. Improvisation was Nate's forte.

Alone when everyone slumbered, we exploded, loving each other like it was the first time every night. I'd never had these feelings for one person as I did for Nate. My love for him was within an inch of desperation, a feeling that without him I wouldn't be able to breathe.

With a pained heart, I missed White Cow, but Rattling Blanket Woman, her daughter, and I became close friends.

Her younger sister, Look At It, who later in life would be called They Are Afraid of Her, was the newest member of the family. It felt odd to know I'd been around for her birth, but this was the first time I was meeting her.

How can anyone explain that?

"Just be agreeable to whatever is said. Don't challenge them or act surprised. They've known you for years or think they have."

My nose wrinkled. "Don't they find it strange I haven't aged?"

"Is it any stranger they see me as Native American, one of them with the same skin, and not a Whiteman?"

"Point taken."

He was right. This magical life we were floating around in was overwhelming and hard to keep up with.

"Wow, I'm glad I see the person I truly am in the water's reflection and not what they see because I've zero desires to see me as an old lady."

"Well, I'm going to love you no matter what."

My head jerked up, my mouth opened then shut, and Nate saw my weird expression.

"What? What's wrong?"

"You, uh, love me?"

"Uh, well, I..." He hesitated, then dove right into the deep end. "I, yes, in fact, I do. Are you okay with that?"

His arms crossed over his bare chest which had tanned to a golden brown.

A sad smile perched on my face, and he frowned.

"Raven, are you saying you don't love me back?"

I inhaled and quickly refuted his statement. "No, not at all. I love you too, Nate, but..."

"No, there are no buts. Either you do or you don't."

I held up my hand. "We are here in this time, this place, and things seem perfect, but what if later it all just disappears?"

"It won't. We can't let it."

"Nate, I took a walk to be alone, and you found me later, on the same day, and twenty years had passed and I was unaware. So much unaccounted for, and so many questions and no answers. For the past few days, if it has been days, might only be just hours, who knows, we've searched for my books and can't find them and without them we may not have a way back home to our own time."

"The Council knows we're here and they might not be able to just snap their fingers and make us reappear, but they won't abandon, and I won't leave you."

He hugged me and I didn't let him see the tear that leaked, swiping it away as quickly as it appeared.

Somewhere along the line, I'd lost my edge, and I wanted to get it back but didn't know how.

Her laugh was infectious and when I spent time with her, I forgot my own troubles and worries.

"I hope someday to marry and have lots of babies—boys—so they can be powerful warriors for our people."

"Huh, is there a special way to making boys?"

I kept picking the summer squash, filling my basket.

She put her hand to her mouth and her eyes widened.

"Some women say it is how you lie with a man, but I think just talk. Just women who brag and not know. Why does you and Little Wolf not have a baby?"

Uh-oh, boy, how was I going to answer this?

When I didn't answer, Rattling Blanket Woman laughed, and this took me by surprise.

"This is funny?" I frowned.

"My sister says you act like rabbits in your lodge, on honeymoon, baby will come soon enough, and you are young. "

Me, youthful? I was almost afraid to ask her how old she thought I was, then it occurred to me to wonder how her sister, Look At It, knew about mine and Nate's romantic encounters.

"Look At It says we act like rabbits? How does she know this?"

I got off the subject of my age, because by all rights I was minus 193 years old, give or take a few, heck, even Mom and Pop were in the negative numbers of age; none of us or the people we knew even existed, yet.

And babies. I sure didn't want to discuss this. I knew my mom got pregnant with me when she time-traveled and yeah, I was already born an old soul, however, I wasn't ready to be a mom, not yet. Nate and I discussed this, and we took what precautions we could, but we also knew there was no guarantee.

"She had to take a nighttime private moment and passed your lodge, she stopped when she discovered moaning, she thought something was wrong, then hears what kind it was."

Rattling Blanket Woman's expressions so wonderfully comical and tried as she did, she couldn't hold in her amusement at the mortification on my face, and after she began her riotous laughter, I joined in.

She told me the stories about other newly married men and women in the camp and embarrassing moments.

"Dancing Flower go to river to wash one evening and Old Badger followed her. Wants to sneak and surprise her. In stream, naked, washing when he swims underwater and pops up. She hit him strong in his man parts, and he scream so loud half camp come to see."

Rattling Blanket Woman had to stop because she was laughing so hard she couldn't catch her breath, and I laughed with her, not because the story was hilarious, but her laughter was delightful, and I needed this uplifting.

After harvesting squash, beans, and corn, she and I journeyed down to the stream to wash the food, and to strain water through sand for the evening meal. We gathered fire kindling and helped two new mothers with chores before the sunset.

Not that I couldn't see myself living in this era, but I'd already experienced the future and so wanted to go back.

As long as I had Nate, all was well, but a few what-if's ran through my head about that, and nope, I didn't want to be someone's second or third wife if Nate were gone.

These were my thoughts when Nate and Crooked Stick walked back into camp, a basketful of fish and a turkey strung to his back, and Crooked Stick's horse pulled a travois with a large deer atop.

"Good hunt," he raised his game, eyeing my thoughtful face. "Anything the matter?"

I shook my head, reaching for the basket of fish, and he leaned into my ear.

"I think I found the cave."

My heart jumped into my throat.

"Really? Can we go tomorrow?"

"No, I want to go tonight."

"After sunset? Won't it be too dangerous?"

"Crooked Stick showed me how to make a pine torch, so we'll have light."

"Are you in a hurry, Nate?"

"Aren't you?"

I let my eyes wander over the camp—the many tipis were families lived.

The kids playing a game of tug-of-war and a few others playing like they were on a buffalo hunt, while a gaggle of girls watched and snickered at their silly antics.

Women sat in front of their lodges, open fires, and cooking rocks with fish atop or a perhaps a small game animal on a stick rotating over the open flames.

Men sat playing a game of chance called Stone Plum and next to their lodge, five teen girls played the ring-and-pin game, with the high-pitched giggles associated with teen girls even in my future time.

"Yes and no. Their life is uncomplicated yet filled with uncertain danger and still they're happy. They live and love."

"Raven, you know the future. You know how it ends for them. I'm not saying we couldn't be happy here in this life, but don't we want our families to be involved in our futures, too?"

"When we get back you think we will still be us, or did you have another life you need to get back to?"

He pondered my words and was silent, which worried me. Did he have a girl back in the twenty-first century? I'd never asked him about his life in the future. Which was remiss of me.

"Look, Nate, you've made no promises to me, so..."

His hand rose to halt me.

"Yes, I have. I promised I'd never leave you..."

"I know," I butted in. "Here and now, you promised, but that doesn't extend to the future—"

I paused as soon as I noticed his scowl.

"What?"

"Are you implying that you only prefer me in this life and not in the future? Is that it, Raven? I'm fine for now, but won't be later?"

My brows dipped in anger.

"Not at all, but since you've not said one blessed word about our future, I figured you hadn't thought past the sex. Am I right?"

"Of all the stupid things for you to think, are you kidding me? You think I just want a physical relationship? Forget it. I see how it is, and I'll keep my hands to myself."

He untied the leather which bound the dead turkey to his back and tossed it at my feet.

"This isn't your first turkey, so I assume you know how to pluck and cook it. I need some time alone."

He turned and stalked off toward the back area of the encampment, back where the horses were held to be by himself and away from me.

Mad, I jerked up the enormous bird and flung it back on the ground, letting it smack against the dirt, then I clenched my fists and teeth, and growled.

"You try to kill bird who is already dead?"

Rattling Blanket Woman walked up behind me, startling the fire out of me, and I turned in a rush, tripping over the turkey's body and tumbling into her.

Tears of frustration balled up and flowed and as she caught me from falling. I held on as a flood of tears escaped my eyes as I experienced a complex array of emotions—anger, sadness, and confusion—yet above all, my tears were driven by an overwhelming frustration caused by my profound lack of understanding regarding my purpose for being there.

My interval here with these people was undetermined, and the reasons unclear. Time went on, never backpedaling, and left me behind.

The thing I feared most was what if I blinked, and found myself a feeble old woman whose love had died and I was alone?

A lot of what-if's flooded my head. What if Nate died, or he was jettisoned back to his real time and left me here alone?

I needed answers, and this meant I needed the books.

"Are you hurt? Is this why you weep, Raven?" Rattling Blanket Woman asked, her voice laced with concern.

"No, I'm fine, I'm just tired. Cry easy. You understand?"

She shook her head and clicked her tongue.

"Sleep, rest, then feel better in morning. I take care of turkey and fish for your man."

She shoved me into the tipi, giving me no opportunity to refuse.

I lay atop the hides, facedown, and I felt exhausted, so I closed my eyes.

The waterworks started all over and I sobbed in silence, until I exhausted myself and slept.

———

The howling of the wolves woke me, and I found Nate asleep on a pile of hides he moved to the far side of the lodge.

My heart dropped. I'd angered him, but it hadn't been my intention to do so.

His breathing deep and steady. As I lay awake, staring at his serene face I was missing his arms holding me, and keeping me warm and safe.

We never talked about what our future selves were doing before we met in this past lifetime.

Did he have a job?

Was he happy with his life?

Did he have a girl?

I was too self-absorbed, I suppose, and never asked, but then, he hadn't asked me any questions about my life either.

Boy, oh boy, I was at it again ... all about me.

I crawled to him, drew the hide to cover us, needing to be near him and slept without dreams.

Right before the dawn broke, I woke and Nate was gone.

Panic filled me.

Given the circumstances, he could have vanished entirely, perhaps to another dimension, or simply stepped away to the stream for some privacy.

I waited, covered up to my neck in buffalo fur, as a proverbial clock ticked down the minutes in my head. When I thought an hour had gone by, I got up, put on my moccasins, and wrapped myself in a hide to stay warm from the morning chill. I poked my head out, first to see if anyone was moving about yet.

No one, no kids, no dogs, no men ... nobody was awake yet, and no Nate, either.

Out of the tipi I passed each lodge headed toward the stream to find Nate. As I reached a clump of juniper trees, I caught voices of men and I stopped, tilted my head, and strained to listen to what they were saying.

Once I understood what they said, I clamped my hand over my mouth in panic and waited for them to leave. When I was sure they'd gone, I raced back to the camp and ran flat-dab face to face into Nate.

"Raven, for gosh sake, why are you in such a hurry?"

"I—uh ... come with me."

I grabbed his hand pulling him into the tipi. "Nate, I heard men near the stream's edge, Nate, they were saying...."

He cut me off.

"Who?"

"Pawnee, they said—"

He held up his hand.

"Wait-wait-wait. You speak Pawnee?"

I had to stop and think. Then I shrugged.

"I guess I do. But right now, I don't want to question how I can understand. It doesn't matter, does it?"

My eyes beseeched him and he nodded, his face grim.

"What did they say, exactly?"

"Something about stealing back horses. They think this clan stole from them, and then killing the men who were the thieves and anyone who got in the way. Nate, they mean to wipe this clan out. That's the gist of what I caught. Do you know anything about stolen horses?"

"No, no one has left the camp. Nothing I've gotten wind of. I've been meeting with the Council on a regular basis now. Our horse count hasn't changed. Crooked Stick is free with telling me stuff since we've been hunting together often and he's said nothing about it either."

"Nate, what do we do?"

I asked, then eyed the bundle in the corner which hadn't been there when I'd left to hunt for him.

"What's that?"

He stepped over to the bundle, untied it, and out fell my books.

"You found them!"

My heartbeat increased as I reached for the bundle.

"When did you go after them?"

"Early this morning, I didn't want you to be disappointed if I was mistaken and they weren't there."

"You could have wakened me. I'd have gone with you."

I opened a book looking at the pages.

"I figured after the way we'd left things last night it was best to get some distance."

Distance? Really? Had he not noticed I'd moved over and slept beside him, not touching him, but made the effort? I bit my bottom lip, wanting to tell him I was sorry, but not grovel.

"That's all secondary, and not important. Right now, we've gotta keep from getting ambushed by Pawnee."

He looked at me with a face that could have been either concern or fury after I said we weren't important, then slowly nodded his head.

"Yeah, the Pawnee coming in the middle of the night or early morning and us not ready for the attack—we'd all be dead, then you and I wouldn't matter any more or less than we do right now."

He stood and dusted off his hands and his backside.

"I'm going to talk to Chief One Horn. Tell him what we know. Why don't you check in your book of tricks, see what you can learn? Stay here until I get back."

"Is that an order, Little Wolf?" My sarcastic tone was obvious.

"Knock it off, Raven, do us a favor. Read one of your books to see what you can find out. I need to figure out a way to let Chief One Horn know you understand the Pawnee. He's gonna want to know how you can understand their language."

With that, he left me alone, and he was right. How would I understand Pawnee if I wasn't Pawnee?

This was going to be a huge issue.

I began skimming the book as quickly as I could, looking for anything helpful.

50

I skimmed through the books a dozen times and found nothing useful, and by the time Nate returned, my frustration—twofold.

"There's nothing here about this, Nate, or nothing I can find."

"We've got to talk to the Chief. If we're lucky, he'll believe you. You can be persuasive, can't you?"

"Like how? Tell him the truth? I don't think so, because I don't feel like getting dumped on the prairie alone to die."

"You won't die. I'll be with you, and we will survive, but if we let the Pawnee pull a raid on this camp and we could've stopped it, then perhaps we should be stuck here to live out the rest of our lives."

All I wanted was to be done with this and to be at home, in my comfy bed, with a bathroom.

Nate stood and stuck his hand out.

"Can I try?"

With an indifferent shrug, I handed him the books, then leaned back on my elbows and watched as he read.

My brain ticked on one fact I knew regarding the Pawnee and any stories I'd picked up.

One was regarding Nate's ancestor, T.H. Cooper, and a young Sioux woman named Laughing Maiden, the daughter of Chief Black Raven. She'd been taken by the Pawnee and later got back to her tribe but mistrusted men and wasn't considered bride material.

Cooper befriended her, and a romance ensued.

Well, dang. Now I absolutely understood Nate. It was his ancestor who was entangled with the Sioux and this magical time travel and history.

As I pondered this story, it occurred to me perhaps a member of Chief One Horn's family might be who I was there to ensure the safety of. The only person who came to mind was Rattling Blanket Woman, because we'd grown close.

My own mother befriended a chief's daughter when she journeyed back in time, and perhaps there were some story parallels I should focus on.

It was then a light flicked in my head, and I understood my task. I reached out and touched Nate's arm.

"I'll speak to the Chief and tell him I come from a family of wise and powerful shamans, and my heart doesn't lie. But we need to speak with him together. I need you to be supportive. Can you fake it until we're clear of any threat?"

My words were said sarcastically.

"Until we get clear of whatever this danger is, sure, I can be supportive, you bet, but afterward, we need to discuss separate tipis and find out how they do a divorce Indian style."

Nate's tone held a lilt of what I call dark humor, although I knew he was serious, but I figured he had every right to be a donkey's butt.

"I agree, but first things first. Let's go."

Without another word, he sprang up, exited the dwelling, and not too chivalrously dropped the flap on my face as I followed right after him.

I grimaced and gritted out, "Try to put on a face that says you like me still, even though you don't. We can't have Chief One Horn thinking we're not getting along, or he might think this is a ploy for you to get rid of me as a possessed or wicked wife."

"Huh, odd, isn't it?"

"What is?" I asked, trying to keep up with his fast-paced walk, him in a hurry to get to the chief's lodge.

"That in the future, the word 'wicked' would mean fantastic or impressive. Here in this era, it means what it is. You know—malicious, heinous, cheeky—and this isn't a wonderful thing, is it?"

"You saying I'm all those things?"

He turned, looking over his shoulder.

"Oh, and don't get me started on the word 'possessed.' If so, then the words 'controlling,' 'dominating,' and 'mad' come to mind."

"Well, Mr. Smarty Pants, there are some perfect words which come to mind, too, but right now isn't the time to quote words we remember from a modern-day thesaurus, so stop."

No matter how hard he might try to goad me into another fight, I bit my tongue, because now wasn't the time.

We reached the lodge of Chief One Horn, and Nate called out to him for permission to enter.

"Enter, Little Wolf."

"Raven accompanies me. May she too enter?"

"Ah, yes. Your Little Black Bird may enter as well."

With a snort, I rolled my eyes, because first, I was a little sick and tired of being called Little Black Bird, and foremost, I wasn't his Little Black Bird. I was my own person.

Although I clamped my mouth, my eyes glared at him just as he pushed open the flap and I followed, politely.

I knew—and so did Nate—a woman's work was not considered menial, but just as important as a man's. Women were revered, because without them, no new life could be brought forth to increase their clan's numbers or create more male warriors. Females gave birth as the chain of life must go on.

"Raven, will you tell us you will bear a child soon?" Chief One Horn was always joking with me, but not joking, wondering why I wasn't pregnant yet.

"May we sit and talk about important matters?"

"Yes, yes, Little Wolf, please."

The chief waved a hand over a pile of hides near his center fire and motioned for us to sit.

"You have news?" His serious Chief side read Little Wolf's expression, and he sat upright, his face contemplative, waiting to hear what his warrior had to say.

I was sure he was wondering why I was there. Only men spoke of things such as war and tribal issues.

Nate explained what happened and what I overheard. Chief One Horn eyed me.

"You know the Pawnee words—you understand?"

Whew, here we go...

"Yes, and I understand Lakota, Cherokee, Apsáalooke, Cheyenne, and Whiteman words."

I stopped to let him digest this information, and I waited.

One Horn never let it be known he too understood some words of his enemies. He tested me, asking me what means *Iichík Baalee*.

"Iichík Baalee, the First Creator," I rejoined in Apsáalooke.

The older man nodded, his head bobbing in thought. Then he asked me, "What word do the Pawnee use—Kȟaŋǧi Tȟáŋka—Raven?"

"Kaáka', Chief One Horn, and in Cherokee I'm called Ko-la-nv, and the Cheyenne call me He'heeo, meaning Black Bird. The Whiteman calls me Raven."

This didn't surprise the chief, and I was confused.

"You are from magical family—seers and shamans?"

The chief's stare penetrated my very core, and I physically gulped before answering.

"My Aunt Soft Dove is a prophetess."

I stopped there. I knew Silver Moon was also powerful. Then there was Chief Black Raven. Any knowledge about his birth date was nil.

I mean, there were plenty of Sioux tribes, but they all didn't know one another.

Chief One Horn's tribe was Miniconjou, one of the seven bands of the Sioux Nation.

For all I knew, Chief Black Raven was alive and well in another encampment.

All I knew was it was near the Grand River territory in South Dakota, nearer the Black Hills, and they were Oglala.

The Miniconjou were in the Nebraska/South Dakota territory. I could've name-dropped both Silver Moon and Chief Black Raven, but didn't think it would matter, especially if he had never heard of either of them, so I sat and waited for him to respond.

"Yes, Meda. This is her Christian name. Am I right?"

My heart raced, and as hard as I might try to keep the tremble out of my voice, I didn't manage very well.

"Y-y-yes, it is. And just how do you know this?"

"I have conferred with her spirit many times. Meda is still one with the woman known as Silver Moon?"

My jaw dropped.

"You're familiar with Silver Moon, too?"

His brow dipped.

"You know of her?"

I bypassed his question, asking one of my own.

"Chief Black Raven of the Oglala—you have knowledge of him?"

"Black Raven's spirit has floated overhead. A wise man, with much inner power."

I cut my eyes to Nate, then looked back at the chief.

Then I jumped into the deep end.

"And what of a maiden known as She Cougar and a brave called Wind Dancer?"

"Ah, yes, the creation of Black Raven's magic. His journal to turn back time, and if not for him, the story is that greatness will not be born. We are already an extraordinary people with importance, though."

The man's head bounced as he reflected on what he said, and then he continued his story.

"A boy child born into the Oglala family of Her Holy Door and Jumping Bull, ten winters now. They call him Jumping Badger, and they say he's already killed his first buffalo."

It was my turn to convey something he had yet to hear, because it wouldn't happen for four more years.

I told him how this boy, Jumping Badger, at age fourteen winters, would join a raid to take horses from a camp of Apsáalooke warriors.

"He will display much bravery and will be seen by other mounted Lakota warriors as counting coup on a surprised Crow warrior, and his father will celebrate him."

His face was pensive, and he was so still he looked like a marvelous statue who lived, and I was holding my breath, waiting for him to call out the others to come snatch me up and tie me to a tree to dangle till dead.

Nate sat, enthralled by our conversation, and I glanced at him, him watching the chief, and wanted to tear up, for I knew this was all ending.

One Horn stood.

"Come."

"Where are we going?" I asked, as I stood and Nate followed suit.

"We go speak with Toh-ki-e-to (the Stone Horns) and with a second chief of clan, Tchan-dee (Tobacco). As Council, we decide."

Then he was out of the flap, heading to the medicine man's tipi.

Passing a lodge, he motioned to the second-in-command, Chief Tobacco, to join.

Everyone followed.

Once we were all seated in the medicine man's lodge, he brought out the sage and burned it in the fire to purify the spirits which surrounded us.

One fact didn't elude me: as I was a woman, and females didn't partake in rituals such as this.

I knew the customs, so being present for this was surreal for me. As the circumstances were, they allowed me because I was, to them, a mystic.

Not once did they question Nate's involvement. I only guessed because he was with me and along for the ride.

Or so I thought.

Stone Horns, the only member of our group standing, his hand waving the smoke of the burning sage as it swirled inside the lodge, chanted quietly.

The songs of war, the songs of death, and a last song of victory crossed over the flames.

He sprinkled the fire with the ashes of the hair of a sacred white buffalo, and the heat intensified, with sparks hissing, and the red-and-blue fiery flames coiling and intertwining with the smoke lifting upward, then dying down in mere seconds.

His gaze was upon me when he spoke.

"You are who Chief Black Raven called the daughter of the first traveler. It is you. You will take women into the mountains tonight while our braves take horses to a safe place not to be found by the Pawnee warriors."

"And then what? They'll have no horses to steal. The tribe—won't you be in danger?"

All of this had me worried. Then I asked, "And you said women, not one? Which women do I take? Do you know?"

Stone Horns regarded me with a no-monkeying-around sort of look.

"You know her. I don't. The spirits do not tell me this. Noble Spirit say you take four women. One is special. You shall hide them in separate places. Chief Tobacco will find only three on the day of the next sun."

"And the last woman?" I asked.

"On the day when the fifth sun rises, a tribe of the Oglala will rescue her. This shall be her home until she returns to us on the moon day of the wolf."

I nodded my understanding, even though it made no sense to me, and I crinkled my brows in thought, but before I could speak, Chief One Horn added, "You go now, Raven, and ready for your travels tonight when the sun drops behind the mountains. Little Wolf will stay here."

Nate was staying.

Was I going alone?

The old medicine man's hand landed on Nate's shoulder, holding him down.

"You will be needed tonight when the Pawnee come. We need all warriors here to fight. Chief Tobacco take women and children to a place down below river, to be safe until this is over."

My gut pulled into a giant knot.

Fight?

War?

Heavens, this wasn't at all what I expected.

None of this was good.

Nate would be here with them, perchance being killed, and me, up in the mountains with four women, hiding them in different areas to be found later. And all the what-ifs filled my head—so many crammed in there I couldn't think straight.

"Go now, young Raven. You have a destiny to fulfill. Take with you the shaman's charm of power."

He knew about that.

Well, why not?

He knew who Silver Moon, Aunt Meda, and Chief Black Raven were; he had to know more than he was saying, didn't he?

How could I test him?

Then it occurred to me perhaps he didn't know about Nate not being a Native American. I pondered how to go about bringing this up, or if I should. He might let Nate go with me and not stay to get killed.

I spoke up. "Cooper, a man who joined Black Raven's tribe—you know of him, of this story?"

He almost smiled, if this was what his smile looked like, for he was a very serious man, a man without much humor.

"Ah, yes, Cooper, who befriended Laughing Maiden—a noble and fearless man."

His head bobbed in quick spurts, and his eyes cut over to Nate.

"You are much like him, Little Wolf—same eyes, same features of face, same kind heart. I know it here." He pointed to his own heart. "Good friend to Black Raven, honorable man who loved our people, bonded with the distinguished chief, and gained favor."

The looks on the other chiefs, One Horn and Tobacco, were amusing. They looked first at Nate, then at the old medicine man.

"Not Miniconjou?" One Horn asked, his eyes shifting from Nate to the shaman and then to me, and landed back on Nate.

Stone Horns lifted his hand, and his lips turned downward in a dismissal fashion.

"It matters not, for he is one of the Real People, deep within his heart. He fights alongside us and will to the death if this be his destiny."

Okay, everyone seemed fine with this except me, and a quick intake of a gasp sounded.

"To the death? Nate, you can't," I said in English, thinking they wouldn't understand.

At least that's what I thought until Stone Horns remarked, "Little Wolf has a destiny to fulfill, or he does not live the life he preordained to have. Go, Little Black Bird, and ready your own house," he said with authority, commanding me to leave and not look back.

With a heavy heart, I rose and looked at each man, my eyes lingering longer on Nate, Little Wolf.

I didn't speak.

I tried to let my heart say to him what my lips could not.

Come back to me, my love. No matter what era we shall travel to or end our lives in, I'll love you always.

I said no more, exiting the lodge of Chief One Horn, going to my own, too ready to leave as soon as the dusk set in.

51

Have you ever heard of the longest day?

Yeah, I knew there was a movie with this title, but I was living the longest day of my life, and I wasn't talking about just now. I was talking about it all.

From the first day I saw the buffalo on the back forty of my family's ranch land, and the old shed which had eerily appeared out of thin air; Kingfisher and his pregnant wife, She Who See Truth; and every other incident leading me to right here.

With no calendar, no timepiece, and other than the knowledge I'd had, I'd been tossed into the midst of World War II. I was unaware of what years I'd lived in or where I'd been since the United States was only broken into territories.

I might see a mountain range and think I knew, but like I'd said before, geography wasn't my strong suit.

Yep, it had either been the longest day ever a person had lived, or I'd lost days and months of my other life in the future I was born into.

In our tipi, I fretted about Nate and him not coming with me, and the what-if's ran rampant in my head.

There was a huge probability he might be slain by a Pawnee warrior, and if he died here in this time, would it mean he'd cease to exist in our future world?

My eyes searched the hides, and I spotted a corner of one of the books underneath the top hide, and I dove to them, plunking my butt down.

I took a deep breath, opened Meda's book first, and started with page one.

My index finger glided over each word I read, carefully, sometimes rereading it to make sure I wasn't missing a hidden meaning.

Midway through, as my neck became stiff from the same position, I lay flat, the book underneath me, my elbows propped up. I searched every word and found something which had me back upright, clenching the book.

I dreamed of a bird and a pony that shall become one on the mountaintop. Alone, but never alone, for the spirits fly with them. In my visions, I saw a man who is far away, and he brandishes his bow and arrow to shoot, hitting his target, but the bird does not fall; as yet another arrow from beyond pierces his heart, and never again will he be the same. I watched the little bird fly without him. His heart is wounded, for if he can never follow, then centuries shall pass, and they shall never meet again.

I stopped reading, because I was sure I was the little bird, but was Nate the man she was referring to?

What pony was this fantasy referring to?

It wasn't Gypsy, because my beloved grayish-black mare had long ago disappeared into the netherworlds, and I hoped she wasn't lost forever.

Turning my neck from side to side, I closed my eyes to work out the kinks. As I bent my head, my eyes caught the next sentence. The hand-writing was almost too faded to make out, as if it had once been erased, then penned and erased again, then rewritten.

The raven and the fox shall meet on the other side of time.

I sat back legs crisscrossed and laid the book in the open weave of my lap.

Was Aunt Meda not sure what she'd dreamed?

Were Nate and I destined to be together or not?

Even so, does it matter to this story, to these people here and now?

I was sure it didn't, and my job was to get Rattling Blanket Woman to a safe place. I still wasn't finding anything useful, so I grabbed the old journal of Chief Black Raven and set Meda's book aside.

Hard to decipher, the hieroglyphics and the Lakota words didn't seem to make any sense on some pages.

I was sure Meda or Silver Moon knew, but I was a novice at this type of reading, or so I thought, until I got to a certain page.

The Lakota words for passing time, the raven, and the fox jumped out at me.

A drawing of two orbs side by side.

On one side of the sphere, a bird, and on the far side, a stick-figure man.

At the top and bottom of the page were two smaller circles under the larger ones.

The top figures touched, but the ones on the bottom didn't.

My brow creased, and I pulled out my charm with the six round orbs.

Two next to each other, two smaller ones at the top and bottom.

My eyes widened.

The circles at the bottom were no longer touching. They'd moved and were now hanging under the larger spheres.

"What in the blue blazes? How could this happen?"

And, to use a word Chay always hated me to say, "Moreover, why has it happened?"

A tear slipped, then another.

Deep down, I knew it meant once we separated in this era, we might never meet again.

I swiped the tears away and grew a new resolve.

Somehow, I would change this future because it wasn't what I wanted.

And damn those who might think this was me being self-centered, because my future was with Nate Cooper, and no other man would ever take his place.

Outer Regions of Standing Rock Reservation

They met on land owned by members of the Council and other tribal members of the Sioux Nation who were not under twenty-first-century government.

"Your daughter has a powerful force," Kanda said, her eyes closed as she reached out her hands to feel the warmth of the fire.

"Yes, she does, and she is also stubborn." A small titter sounded. "Like me, I guess."

Kanda opened one eye, peering at her sister-in-law. "Yeah, I know, Blaze, and she has your courage, and you can call her stubbornness courage."

"Why, thank you, Kanda. Very nice of you to say."

Blaze was touched.

She and Kanda always got on well, and today, them together, performing old magic, strengthened their bond.

"Like you and Dakota, she and Nate will forge a wonderful life."

Hank Cooper stood, one hand in his back pocket, and he looked up at the stars. "I want to tell each of you how much it means for Nate and me to be included in your lives, and how proud we are to be called members of your clan."

Blackie sidled up to him, putting his big open palm on his shoulder in a brotherly gesture.

"It is we who thank you and your ancestors for befriending a wise chief captured by renegade Dragoons. If not for T.H. Cooper, Chief Black Raven may have perished, and his magic would've never been known."

Eli Harris chimed in, "And if not for Black Raven, many things wouldn't be as they are now, and the Real People wouldn't have what history was vitally important. Cooper, your ancestors have much to be proud of and will always be welcome in the arms of the Real People, all Real People."

"Appreciate that, Two Suns. Means a lot, and I hope down the line none of my direct ancestors ever fail our family."

Blackie grinned and snickered.

"What's funny?" Blaze asked.

"From what I know of Silver Moon's travels, she has not only traveled to the past, but she has moved her spirit, like Black Raven has, into the future."

"Oh, well, do tell."

Kanda took a seat, motioning for the others to sit. "The ritual is over. Let's gossip." She winked at Blaze. "Black Crow, why don't you enlighten us? We know you and Silver Moon have been as thick as thieves for years. I'm sure she's told you some fantastic tales."

"Yeah, and I'll tell you this much—I believed her, too."

"She's a cagey old woman but isn't a fraud." Eli stretched his legs, crossing one ankle over the other, settling in to listen.

"Will she care if you tell us?" Blaze eyeballed him.

Blackie exhaled. "No. I'm supposed to tell you some things tonight." He looked at Kanda, then at Payton. "She's traveled light-years forward and has a message for you two."

"Oh, she does, does she?" Payton winked at his wife.

"Yes. Chayton sends his love. Moon Beam is on the back forty on Uncle Dakota's ranch. Will you make sure she gets home?"

"Come on, Blackie, that horse has been missing for weeks now, same time Chay and Raven were sent back."

Kanda playfully slapped the older gent's knee, but when she saw Payton's face, she frowned.

"Payton?"

"When Dakota and I checked our livestock, we found Moon Beam with the herd, saddle and all."

All eyes turned to Blackie, who said, "Let me tell you a few more accounts of our precious Silver Moon's travels..."

Back in What We Call the Olden Times

The sun had started its slow descent, and I was a ball of raw nerves when Nate poked his head into the tipi.

"You ready?"

"Come in here." I beckoned with my hand, my face puckered in worry, tears in danger of spilling over.

He sat near the entryway across from me. "What's the matter?"

"What's the matter? Oh, for pity's sake, what do you think it is, Nate?"

My sudden urge to weep turned into a sudden urge to shriek, flailing my arms and legs and stomping my feet.

"You're scared, is that it? Because I'm not gonna be there to hold your hand?"

Of all the nerve—the audacity to think I was afraid for myself. I was darn well scared for him.

I sucked it up. If he wasn't afraid, then I wasn't either.

"No, not scared at all—worried, uh, about you, though. But I'll be danged if I let that upset me any longer. You're a big boy. Some might even call you a man."

I got huffy and tried to insult him, but saw the teeny, satisfied smirk on his face.

"What, did I hurt your feelings?"

"No, Raven, you didn't, and I don't believe you."

"Believe what?"

"That you think I'm a boy?"

"You are."

"That's not how you treated me several days ago when I made love to you."

This time I reddened as I bit my bottom lip in total embarrassment.

He was right. I knew very well he was a man in every way a man was a man.

"Have nothing to throw back at me? No more insults?" Nate scooched up, and his face was inches from mine.

He spoke, his breath warming my face. "You are every bit a woman, Raven Maka Kangee, and me, a red-blooded male. Circumstances threw us together; fear and the unknown pushed us into each other's arms. We did not plan this. The circumstances were forced upon us, and we only did what two people do when in strained situations. We joined, without thought, for strength and hope, clinging to each other to live. It was nothing more, so don't make a big deal out of it, okay, Raven?"

"Noth—"

I clamped my mouth shut, moving myself back to get distance, yet he stayed put. If it was nothing to him, then it was nothing to me, too.

"Sure, none of it meant a thing—just things which occur when emotions are high and you think it might be your last chance at..." I didn't finish because I was about to declare love.

"Love? Ha!" He sneered.

His face leaned toward mine again, and his hands came up to hold my upper arms. His nose almost touched mine, and my heart raced.

"We said the words of love in a moment of heated passion. They meant nothing, and neither does this." Nate took my lips with his, and I didn't resist, nor did I react—not because I didn't want to, but because I was stunned at first, then angry.

But he didn't let go, and his tongue invaded my mouth, and I responded—but only for a split second—then pushed him away.

"Stop, Nate." My lips stilled but pressed to his.

He stopped, stood, and looked down at me.

"Raven, I'm going to make a promise to you. I won't do that again—not until you ask me to, and not until after you've been honest with me about your true feelings."

Nate left me sitting alone in the tipi, stunned, with lips still tingling from his kiss.

Well, I thought, he'd better not hold his breath waiting for me to declare my love.

He was pompous and arrogant to think I would.

I wanted to release my anger, so I buried my face in the pile of buffalo hides.

Balling my fists, I screamed bloody murder, pounding the already poor, dead beast's fur.

Once I let it all out, I sobbed.

He'd left the ball in my court, only he wasn't in the game any longer.

My heart would mend, I told myself, and things could change once we moved hundreds of years forward—or I hoped it was true.

I waited, watching the sun touch the mountains and set. Following that, I'd travel alongside four Miniconjou maidens—Woman Who Carries Water, Noble Flower, She Throws Sticks, and Rattling Blanket Woman.

The last woman on my list was my quarry to save.

I was still unsure how I'd save her.

52

T hree women hidden.

Rattling Blanket Woman and I found a place to sit and rest.

It was a full moon tonight, perfect all the way around—good for us, so we could see as we navigated the mountain trails.

What lifted our spirits was the fact that the full moon thwarted a raid from the Pawnee. Too much light—no cover for the darkness. It was a huge risk they took trying to run a surprise attack, or even a sneaky attempt to steal horses.

"Pawnee not come in full moon," I remarked.

With shrugged indifference, Rattling Blanket Woman said, "No matter. Our men ready if they come, and horses hidden. Pawnee scout should see this and warn tribe."

Her voice was flat, sounding dejected, and I wondered why.

"You are sad?" I asked her.

"Why am I to hide from my people? Does my brother wish to rid himself of me?"

"Oh, no, no. He loves you. He just wants you safe."

"I am strong woman, can take care of myself, and can fight if I need to, for our tribe."

Well, I had no doubts about this.

I'd seen Rattling Blanket Woman carry another rather hefty girl who'd passed out at the river. She'd hoisted the gal over her shoulder and carted her to her tipi to administer care.

The girl had fainted from what I figured was heatstroke, and after resting underneath an awning weaved with bark strips, sipping cool water and her face being bathed with the same cool water, she'd felt much better.

"Can you fight what you cannot see?"

She angled her head. "What I cannot see... you speak of spirits?"

"Do you believe in magic?"

I avoided her question, questioning her instead.

"Sorcery, is this what you speak of? Am I to be bewitched?"

She chucked inside her throat at the thought.

"Pffuffh." The sound I made as I huffed air from between my partially closed lips before I spoke. "No, you are not bewitched unless this makes me a witch."

Her eyes grew round and wide, as her brows both popped upward into her forehead.

"You are witch, or prophetess—I think."

My turn to widen my eyes and extend my eyebrows into my hairline.

"Why do you say such things?"

"Raven, you good woman, but not like others. You have an aura. It tells me you are old but not old, and wise. This how I know not same as me. You have oldness surrounding you, do you not?"

Her words were very insightful.

I had oldness surrounding me—Silver Moon, Aunt Meda, my parents, and the entire Council. Except for my parents and my aunt and uncle, Kanda and Payton, the rest were aged sixty-plus. Silver Moon, I swear, was over a hundred, give or take five or so years either way.

"Do you know a woman they call Silver Moon?" I was curious.

"Ah, yes, but I know her as She Dreams Much, woman with deep eyes into our hearts. She visited many moons ago in my sleep."

I glanced up at the sky and saw a smattering of silvery-gray clouds beginning to build, then looked back at Rattling Blanket Woman.

"And what did you see as you slept?"

"A man saved me from wolves who attack. He cares for me and we marry."

"There's more," I asked, seeing her face.

"Yes. We create a boy who will become strong and he shall be known to all the world one day. And..."

Her voice faded off, and when I looked into her eyes there was such a deep sadness, I didn't want to know the rest, but she released a long breath, like the air from a balloon being deflated.

"She Dreams Much said my life is important, and I must be wise and not be foolish."

My temple puckered in thought.

"Do you understand what this woman means?" I asked.

She shook her head.

"Maybe one day I shall understand, or She Dreams Much will come to me again."

The clouds above moved in a circular motion and the wind picked up, and I knew it was time to leave.

"Up further, there's a trail to go down the side. We must go."

She didn't argue but followed.

In less than an hour, we were on the way down on the north side, headed for the cave where Nate found the books he'd stashed.

Inside the cave, I shuddered. It didn't feel right, and I was uneasy about leaving her here.

"No, not good. We must leave. Hurry."

I pushed her out the entrance, and I felt the mountain rumbling. I never recalled earthquakes being a thing in the Nebraska/South Dakota region, but something was happening, and it was coming fast.

"Take my hand." I stuck my arm out. "We have to stay together no matter what."

We felt the earth quavering and saw small rocks and dirt particles drop from the sides. The moon was now a blessing overhead because it lit our way as we scrambled down and away from rocks and rockslides.

I saw our chance and shouted, "Sit on your rump, hold onto me."

With her behind me, we slid down a trail trampled by whatever climbed this mountain besides men.

The wind picked up, and it howled like a pack of wolves, and the swirling clouds gathered speed.

I saw it, and my heart stopped.

I had never witnessed a real tornado, nor did I desire to.
The winds we felt were in front of us, and I was sure the force behind it was ferocious, but we had yet to feel the brunt of her sting.
I didn't want to, and I didn't know what to do but run from the situation as fast as we could.

She was about a mile away, and the moon illuminated her; the thing was unreal, like something out of a Hollywood movie.

"What's that?"

Rattling Blanket Woman's voice screamed, and I almost did not hear her over the forceful winds.
I didn't answer because I didn't have time to stop and give her a lesson about weather and tornadoes. Maybe I'd explain later.

I was never so happy to see the bottom of the trail, the flatland, I think. Anyway, the rain started, and we needed to make a mad rush somewhere.

As I looked around, my brain on super-think mode, we needed to get to a ditch or entrench ourselves inside a crevice in the mountainside.

The clouds were building, and the moon was no longer our friend of light.

I closed my eyes, a tear escaped, and I prayed into the wind, needing the spirit of time to send my words to the ears of those who loved me:

Momma, you are here, in my heart. Aunt Meda. Please, it cannot end this way. I've tried so hard. I must save this woman. If it is my destiny to die, then I'm fine with this, but please help me save this woman, for she is to carry and bear a legend for the Real People.

A sharp sound of lightning sizzled several times with such force in the sky.

As if a light switch had been flicked on and off three times, I saw what I needed to see.

Immediately, I grabbed her hand, and we ran through the mud and rain, and the noise of winds, which sounded like a freight train. We reached an area of the mountain with a fissure large enough for both of us.

I shoved her in, then squeezed in, my back toward her, and I watched through the opening as the weather began its terror across the lands.

She spoke behind me, into my ear.

"Pawnee not come; the winds will blow them away. I pray the Great Spirits will watch our clan."

I closed my eyes, and the tears flowed.

Please let them all be okay, let them get to safety, and then I remembered the other three women.

I prayed the places I'd hidden them were strong enough to save them from this wretched storm.

N o sounds, no wind, no rain... nothing but calmness.
I stepped out into the open air and breathed the smell of freshness from the heavy rain and tuned back to where she was.

Gone.

How could this be?

I was in front of her and would've had to move to let her out; this was impossible.

The crevice wasn't large and not deep, so she couldn't have gone the other way. This was ludicrous.

Tears formed at the back of my eyes, and I stood in front of the opening, turning in all directions to see if somehow she'd gotten out and was waiting for me.

I looked down and saw a torn piece of deerskin dress and blood, and I searched my own clothing—no tears, nor was I wounded.

Her dress? Was she hurt?

No... no... no... she had to be alright; she just had to.

I looked up, then down, and decided going up the mountain wasn't my best bet after the wild tornado. No telling what had been pulled up by the roots and flown over to block any path I might encounter.

I headed to the base of the foothills and would take my chances. If she'd gone down somehow before me, I might catch up with her. I prayed she wasn't hurt.

I'd gone about two miles or so and saw footprints—animal prints, and after all, I was a rancher's daughter. I knew my prints.

Wolves.

It had to be a pack; there were so many.

Then I spotted human footprints—smaller, made by moccasins.
Had to be Rattling Blanket Woman, and she'd been running.

Were the wolves chasing her?

Then She Dreams Much, or rather Silver Moon's, interpretation came to mind.
With quick steps, I followed the tracks and in a matter of minutes saw the other prints—larger, made by a man, perhaps two—and the smaller woman tracks, and then blood, realizing it wasn't human.

Deep down inside me, I knew someone had killed a wolf and the other animals had scattered.
She was safe. Rattling Blanket Woman was on her way to her destiny.

As I grew closer to the village, I noticed the land was peaceful, no signs of torrential rain or wicked winds which could blow a house down. A tornado could rip up a tipi, rip up poles, fire and all, sending it flying five territories over.

Nothing.

Was the storm in the hills only for me and her?

Had my strength and faith been tested?

———

C ould this have been the lesson I needed to learn about myself? To not
   care what happened to me and make sure the woman was saved at
all costs?

This was all swimming in my head when I saw the community—the tipis
all safe, the people normal, working, and not aware of the storms that had
nearly washed us away.

I wasn't even going to question how this could happen, for I knew
without a doubt supernatural things were normal in my life.

When I came to what I thought was the tipi Nate and I shared, something didn't feel right.

Instead of just barreling in, I called out in Lakota, "Little Wolf, are you
inside?"

I waited as I heard rustling and moving about, and a young maiden
poked her head out of the closed tipi flap.

"No one called Little Wolf lives here, only me and Black Cloud with new
baby."

Then she dropped the flap, going about her business for the early morning, and I suppose she was nursing her new baby with the lack of clothing
covering her topside.

Had Nate been made to move to another dwelling, or was he just gone?

My next stop was at the chief's lodge, hoping he was still there.

The chief's dwelling looked the same yet different—more worn, and
even the background and the land seemed different.

I stood back a few feet from the opening, pivoted, looking at the landscape and placement of each lodge, and where the horses were.

My eyes followed a trail, and I wondered if it was the same trail leading
to the river.

I'd been walking due south when I got here with the mountains immediately behind me, but now as I looked, I could see the massive hills were
now in the north, and flatlands lay to the south from where I stood.

Crazy.

And even though I knew this wasn't possible, I knew anything concerning me was possible.

I wasn't numb, just tired, and in my heart, I knew once I got an audience with Chief One Horn, I'd find he too was different. Would he know me, or would I be an apparition to him, only part of his imagination?

Again, I called out to see if anyone was home.

An older man's voice answered, "Yes, Little Black Bird, please come in and sit."

His calling me Little Black Bird was an excellent sign, so I entered, and stood at his fires looking down on him.

He sat cross-legged, his face older, more wrinkle-defined, in his lap a bowl of corn mush and in his hand a piece of buffalo jerky. He dipped the jerky, pulling up a mouthful and ate, as I stood still waiting for him to speak.

"Sit. Let me get you food. You must be hungry."

I was, so I nodded my thanks as he scooped up warm cornmeal porridge, short name mush. He handed me strips of dried buffalo jerky, and I ate as he did, scooping the cornmeal with the dried jerky, and I savored each bite.

"You are well, Raven?" he asked between bites.

"Yes. And thank you for the food. I was hungry."

"You are welcome. With a heavy heart, I must tell you..."

He took a bite and chewed, not finishing his sentence, and my heart pounded.

Anytime someone said, "with a heavy heart," not grand news.

My hand stopped before it reached my lips, and I couldn't take another bite.

"Bad news?" My innards quaked.

"Ah, yes, the shaman, Stone Horns. He has joined the majestic god in the sky. He said you were powerful, young Raven, and you are a good woman. You serve the Real People well in your journeys."

"He-he's dead? When... when did he die, how?"

He was in perfect health when I saw him just yesterday before I went into the mountains, so what had happened?

"Five, almost six winters he has passed," the chief stated as a matter of plain fact, like I should know this. "In my sleep time she told me time wouldn't be same for you as it was for us, and you wouldn't understand, but it is how it must be for you."

"And while you slept, who told you this?"

I had an idea, but I had to hear him say it.

"She Dreams Much, but you call her Silver Moon."

53

My enlightened conversation with an aging Chief One Horn left me spent.

Five, maybe six winters had passed, while it only felt like the next day for me.

I recall my mom's story, and hers was nothing like mine. She'd been sent back to a certain era and didn't move about in time as I had. She lived with her long-ago ancestors who were members of the Hunkpapa Lakota tribe. Her travels never varied from one year to the next, as she lived each day as it came.

Me, well, I felt like I was zooming in circles—forward and backward, up then down—never knowing if I'd land on my feet or my head.

I stopped at a lodge, and without a thought, I stepped inside feeling quite at home.

Comfortable and at peace, and exhausted, I lay on the pile of soft hides, squirming to get comfy, feeling a lump underneath me impairing my ability to relax.

I moved over, stuck my hand under the heavy buffalo pelts, and pulled out two worn books—Aunt Meda's dreams and Chief Black Raven's journal.

I clutched both to my chest and closed my eyes. No use reading now, for they'd yielded me little to no answers, so I drifted to sleep.

———

It was a sound, dreamless sleep, and when my eyelids fluttered open, I felt renewed—something I didn't think I'd felt in ages.

Ages, minutes, years, centuries—it was all the same to me.

I mean, I might stick my head out to find I was living in the 1920 Flapper years, or perhaps I'd been transported to the days of King Arthur and the Knights of the Round Table.

With a shrug, I got up, hid the books back under the pelts, stretched, yawned, and realized I was famished.

Outside, I saw others cooking at their campfires—the smell of fish and other small game cooking on cooking rocks—and kids scampering and playing. A few dogs barked, and in general, a community was living their daily lives.

Men were talking or playing a game of Native American dice. In the background, a horse whinnied, one snorted, and the rest were nibbling on grass.

"You are hungry?"

I turned at the female voice.

Her face seemed familiar.

Grasping her hem was a young boy of three.

A cute thing with dark, snapping eyes.

His complexion lighter than most Sioux, and his light-brown hair was filled with curls.

"I am hungry. Do you have enough to share?" I asked her, watching the young child who peeked out from behind his mother's legs.

"Come, we have plenty."

She turned, and the boy grabbed at the bottom of her deerskin dress and followed.

He checked if I was there, and I smiled once more.

At her lodge, a man sat, fashioning arrows from the limbs of an ash tree, readying them to attach to arrowheads he'd made from bones and rocks. He glanced up, and I nodded as the woman sat the small boy down, then asked me to help her.

"You are quiet, Raven. Are you ill?"

How did she know me?—I was confused.

"No, not ill. I spoke with Chief One Horn early, and it was a tiring talk. He had much to tell me, and after I rested…"

"Indeed, much has happened, hasn't it?"

"You know?" It was the only question I could think of asking.

"You saved me on the mountain five winters ago. Makes me happy. Outside, my husband sits with our boy. If not for you, there would be no husband, no boy, and no me."

"Rattling Blanket Woman?"

When she nodded, my jaw became unhinged.

She handed me a large, rounded bowl made from a small tree trunk, hollowed out and smoothed as shiny as glass on the inside, and a pestle made of an oblong rock with a knobby end.

I saw the basket of dried corn, grabbed two cobs, and began the process of taking the dried kernels off and depositing them into the bowl, pounding them into a dry powder to make cornmeal that Rattling Blanket Woman would fuse with herbs and berries.

Both of us worked in silence, lost in our own thoughts.

I broke the uncomfortable silence.

"Your son, how old is he?"

"Curly is three winters, last winter."

"He is a calm boy?"

She found this amusing. "He can be playful when he chooses."

"You call him Curly because of his hair?"

"And call him Light-Haired Boy, too."

"His father, what's his name?"

I sat the pounded corn down and reached for water to mix to make cornbread. I was thankful I sat it down, or I would've dropped the entire bowl on the dirt floor, spilling the contents everywhere.

"He is Oglala. His name is Tȟašúŋke Witkó."

"Crazy Horse?"

She nodded. "This was his father's name before him."

She handed me a mixture of berries to add to the cornmeal I was about to mix, and the sap from a maple boiled into a sugary matter.

"He likes his bread sweet, so does Curly."

I moved with automation, mixing berries, water, and maple sap into a doughy substance to be baked on a sizzling cooking rock in the fire.

Inside my head, I talked to myself.

Curly was her son, Crazy Horse was her husband, and I knew my Sioux history.

The famous Crazy Horse was sitting just outside this tipi.

He was only three winters old, with light-brown curly hair. His nickname was Curly, and sometimes his mother called him Light-Haired Boy.

Color me stunned.

I couldn't take my eyes off the young child, knowing how his life would affect the Sioux, and history in general.

He would grow into a brave man, joining forces with Chief Sitting Bull to lead his warriors. This toddler would become respected and adored by the Sioux Nation. He and his warriors would take down General Armstrong Custer in the battle at Little Bighorn, also known as Custer's Last Stand.

There was so much more to this man known in history, and how he fought devotedly to keep their way of life until he could fight no more.

Our evening meal finished, I thanked Rattling Blanket Woman for the food, then kneeled to speak to the toddler while she carried empty utensils down to the river to wash.

"It was nice to meet you. I love your curly hair."

My hand came up, and I stroked his curls, then placed my palm against his warm cheek.

"One day you will grow to be a strong and brave man. You shall do countless things."

I sat beside him, my hand on the shoulder of a renowned man who was yet just a child, and the emotions I felt were indescribable, knowing who I was meeting and how his life would impact many.

He was silent, staring up at me with his black inquisitive eyes, and I could see the wheels turning in his head as I spoke.

"Little one, you shall be a leader and the people follow you. Like your mother, who shared her food with me tonight, you shall be generous to your clan. You will fight to protect the Sioux way of life."

"I see you will be a skillful mother," Rattling Blanket Woman remarked when she saw me still chatting with her son.

"Curly, we must go wash in the river. Come," she beckoned to her young son, who rose, ever obedient. "You stay?" she asked me.

"No, thank you. I must visit with Chief One Horn again."

"Your time is up?"

Her eyes dug into my face, searching for answers to unasked questions. In her heart, she knew I was not part of them in this era, but part of them in the future.

"Yes, I must go. I hold you forever in my heart, and this time with you, forever in my memories."

"As I will you. One day we meet on the other side of the rainbow?"

Her hand came out to touch my arm. Her smile didn't reach her eyes. I knew from history in a fleeting time this wonderful woman would end her own life, and it saddened me.

My time there wasn't to change her future but to make sure her son, the young child standing at her knee, lived to see his destiny through.

"One day, yes, we shall meet again, I'm sure of it."

I hugged her, then kneeled to be eye-to-eye with the boy.

"And, one day, young Curly, you will be a famous war chief. Other warriors will call you one of the bravest men they have ever fought or ridden with."

I looked at him full face-on and saw what might've been construed as the tiniest of grins, with a light shining behind his dark eyes in a spark of understanding.

For whatever reason, I couldn't help myself—I hugged him, then kissed his warm, light-brown cheek.

Curly hugged me too, melting my heart.

Here I was, being embraced by a three-year-old who would one day become a famous chief named Crazy Horse.

I took my leave after my last goodbye.

I walked to the river to be alone before the sunset, but on my way, I stopped at my lodge to retrieve Black Raven's journal.

There was something I felt I needed to do, and his magic, if it worked for me, was my only way.

54

Alone, I walked downriver to be undisturbed and find a serene, secluded spot with a small mass of bushes and trees to hide in. My back pressed against a tree, with the bark cloth blanket I snagged on my way out draped over me like a shawl, I settled in.

I opened the book and began reading the words which had, on one other occasion, assisted me in letting my life-force travel across time continuums of space. I needed to find Chay.

Not knowing how much real time had passed in this loop I'd been wandering through, I wanted to know he was safe. In the beginning, I hadn't been as narcissistic. This happened after the first encounter with Kingfisher and She Who Sees Truth. It was then I realized I'd helped ensure a famous Cheyenne chief was born—Chief Dull Knife, once called Morning Star at birth.

At first, I thought this was about me pulling off some grand feats—all to save important people—and yes, this was part of it, but it was also about me becoming me. To be my best person, I needed to stop being so self-centered and focus on those around me who cared about me and loved me unconditionally. I wasn't talking about my parents.

Chay Kangee, also called Star Gazer, was one of those people I hadn't given a second thought to since we'd been separated by magic, time, and space. Selfish of me to just assume all was well and that he was fine. He was my only cousin, almost a brother. I'd just let the thought of him slip right out of my head.

It was time to make sure he was okay. I also felt Chay had things he needed to tell me. Afterward, I needed to find Nate—or go home and find him waiting for me—I wasn't sure. The journal opened, I read.

As night crept in, the moon was bright, just like a night lamp, and I could see perfectly. Yet another magical occurrence I would never be able to explain. I reread a passage over and over, then closed my eyes. Inside my head, I chanted the words the chief had penned, and the sincerity of what I felt filled my soul.

Within minutes, I felt my body growing heavy, but my spirit lifted to leave its fleshy entombment. When the chanting in my head grew weak, my eyes opened, and I looked down and saw my body, covered with a blanket, the book on my lap. My physical head bowed, my shoulders slumped as my earthly body rested into a deep slumber. Weightless. This was how I felt.

As I freely swooped over the trees, I saw the village—the people, tipis, and animals. Up ahead, the Black Hills. The land we called Mother Earth we survived on, and as I flew higher, I saw herds of buffalo darting in and out of trees and forest areas, and the other wildlife which fed the Real People. Fabulous.

However, I didn't want to see what was here, for I knew what was here. I wanted to find Chay, so I let my spirit glide as I chanted Chief Black Raven's time chant to carry me to him. Something deep within my being pulled me into a black hole through space. It was cold and dark, and I was blinded, then just as quickly it freed me, and once again I could see.

Odd. I was in a town that looked abandoned—a ghost town, perhaps. No signs of people, animals, or any breathing creature. My feet hit a flat area, and I was standing. I also wondered how a life-force could stand and walk since I wasn't in a human body form; perhaps I was, and didn't know it. Was this only a dream?

I walked a few feet, then touched the side of what I thought was a building and felt the brick substance. It was real. My fingers felt the rough texture. I was too afraid to call out, fearful I could be in danger. Where was I? Why was I here?

With caution, I walked along the perimeter of the building, then to another, then crossed a narrow road. Straight ahead, I saw an old barn. A feeling of nostalgia—or déjà vu—passed through me as I reached the barn and slid the rail to open the door. At first, it was dark inside. In the hayloft, I saw a small light, so I climbed up.

In the back corner sat a man with a gun draped over his lap, his head bent as if he slept. Small steps, I told myself, putting one foot in front of the other to reach the sleeping man. I squatted and was about to reach out to wake him when his head shot up—and so did the butt-end of his gun, which hit my chin, sending me flying backward.

My first thought—how did I feel that if I was only a wisp of my inner soul's essence? The second was—it hurt.

"Raven? Is it really you?"

I knew right away who he was. "Oh my God, Chay, Chay, it's you! Thank the Lord you're okay!" I was so thrilled the pain on my chin forgotten as I flung myself at him, embracing him.

He held me at arm's length. "Raven, why are you here? You shouldn't be here." His words stopped me dead. I pushed back, giving him space, and looked him in the eyes.

"Where is here, and what are you doing here?"

"Is your soul traveling?" he asked, ignoring my question.

I nodded wordlessly.

"Then you have completed your tasks and need to go."

"What about you? Are you all right? And what are you doing here? What's going on? I..." His hand came up to stop me.

"I'm doing what I was sent to do, and you're not part of this like I was on your travels. You're in a very different world here. It's not safe for you, so you must go."

"Chay, I..."

"No, Raven. Listen to me. When Annie Shorey was saved from those men, that was my part. Your part was to get me there."

"So, saving Annie Shorey was your purpose, not mine?"

"It was you who got us there. I would've never gotten there without you. Raven, you are a mighty conduit."

I changed the subject. "Chay, sad news back in our time—uh, Running Elk passed away. He came to me in a vision on a mountain after you vanished."

"Yes, I've heard."

I slanted my head, narrowing my eyes. "You've heard? How? Who?"

"My mom's magic, you know this. She and Silver Moon have come into my visions several times. Now, about this guy Nate, I think..."

I cut in. "What in the world about Nate? You know about him, too?"

This time, my spirit crossed her arms over her chest and became agitated. Okay, well, it was me doing this, but I hadn't any idea that an apparition of my inner self was able to do this or feel pain.

My hand reached back up and rubbed my jaw. "Sorry about clocking you in the jaw, but it won't leave a bruise."

He grinned, then frowned. "Nate. Go find him. He's part of who you are, part of your future, and you and he need one another to survive. You need not worry about me. When it's time, I can find my way home."

Something inside yanked at me, pulling me back. I had to hurry. "Alright, I'll try to find Nate. Thank you for being my best friend, even though you're my cousin. I can't ever imagine my life without you."

My words were out there as my life-force was pulled away, and his face grew distant. I saw his hand wave, he smiled with a wink, and I was gone.

As I drifted, I wondered why it wasn't safe for me to stay with Chay. He'd never said. But knowing Silver Moon and my Aunt Kanda were with him eased my worries some. Then Nate popped into my head. Chay knew about Nate... did he approve or not?

I woke, feeling drained, and I was still under the bark cloth blanket, the book on my lap, and darkness set in. My feet moved, and something akin to a spirit hand guided me safely back to the village and the tipi Nate and I once shared.

Right away, I slept a deep sleep, and I dreamed. It was a misty morning, and as I walked through the dewy grass, the silence enveloped me. A slight chill made me shiver as the fog rose from the warm ground into the cooler air. Whatever it was, it drew me to the large rock at the edge of the river, and I climbed up and sat, staring out over the water.

I saw gliding toward me a shadow, but I was not afraid. It woke me, telling me to go to One Horn.

The elderly chief sat outside, a tiny fire burning, wrapped in a buffalo hide, his eyes alert as if he expected me.

"You no sleep?" he asked.

"May we talk?"

He gestured. "Inside. And then our hearts may speak."

By his inside fires we sat, and he said nothing. I waited, for he took his time to ponder his words, always had and always would. This made him a shrewd chief. No respectable leader made knee-jerk decisions knowing everything needed to be thought out.

Time passed, and my weariness departed; my energy level rose. Odd, because I had felt so tired before.

"Your spirit's energy renews from your travels?"

My eyes crinkled in question. He was a wise one.

An older, larger hand came up, and with one finger he pointed at the book tucked under the blanket I'd twisted around my waist.

"Black Raven's?"

I nodded but didn't speak. I let him carry on our conversation.

"Wise and powerful. His daughter is wise; she was good to your mother. And your mother, another brave woman. She Cougar found herself and her future on her journeys. And you, Little Black Bird, what have you found?"

Chief One Horn sat, his spine straight, and he eyeballed me questioningly.

"There are others more important than I. That our history, if it is ever altered and not put back on track, changes would cause a ripple effect, which could cost many lives."

"Ah, young Raven, and if the past were never to be, then our futures would be unsure?"

I sat, and his words ran through my head on the spectrum of what-ifs. There was no way to know one way or another if life would've been better without these notable people: Chief Dull Knife of the Cheyenne, Chief Jon Ross of the Cherokee, Chief Plenty Coups of the Apsáalooke, Chief Crazy Horse of the Oglala Sioux, and a young man named Joe Little Fox of the Comanche Tribe. Each of these men were, in their time, men of vast importance for history.

Just trying to figure out what might have been, had they not lived, was useless because I knew our world would suffer to lose any man or woman of historical importance.

The women I'd been sent back to save were to ensure they bore these historical legends so each could fulfill their personal destiny. It would've been a travesty to have lost any of them, for these women, singularly, were strong, fearless, and in their own rights, legends. She Who Sees Truth, Annie Shorey, Otter Woman, and Rattling Blanket Woman were female legends no one spoke of, but if not for them, the men who became famous, born to each, would never have existed.

I had no hand in saving White Cow, the mother of Rattling Blanket Woman and grandmother to Chief Crazy Horse. It was she who taught me. Our saving Joe Little Fox of the Comanche Code Talkers saved thousands of men. This would've been a tragedy had he not been protected.

"My destiny was to make sure others lived their lives. Not to make things better, but to keep the process of history the same, moving it in the direction it was supposed to move."

"What about you, Little Black Bird?"

This was a hard question. I'd realized it was never about me but them.

All my life I'd been hemmed and hawed over by my parents, being their only child. In the community I lived in, I was seen by the elders and the older generation as a special soul. Being that I was conceived in the 1800s in my mom's time travel and born into the twenty-first century, I adapted to our Native language, knew my animals, and worked well with horses. A regular rancher's daughter who worked hard to help her family and stayed close to home.

My comfort zone was with the members of our Council. Men and women who were grandparent age—and I fit right in and was accepted more there than with my own generation. Me, I, mine—words I used a lot. Even with Chay, it was about me. Everything I felt, or wanted, it was all about me, putting myself first all the time, not intentionally, yet no one had stopped me. Not my parents or Aunt Kanda and Uncle Payton, Chay's parents. I bet he felt like my sad-sack lackey and second banana all the time.

I didn't know where Chay was, what era, or what was happening. The only thing he'd said was that it was dangerous for me to be there—and there again he was putting my needs first.

"Chief One Horn, I hope to travel once more and cross paths with you someday."

The old man's eyes crinkled in thought, and his eyes landed on mine. I saw his admiration... and shall I call it love?

"Take heed to my words, young Raven. You possess a pure spirit and have had a valuable contribution to the many eras you have traveled. Your spirit lives in all those souls you touched; your courage, strength, and determination affected each life. You share a kindred spirit with every legend you saved, and they too live inside of you. As your time here ends, there is one last task for you to finish. I ask, are you prepared?"

As I exhaled and nodded, one tear slipped out. His older gnarled hand came up, and with his index finger, he wiped that tear and the few others, then put that hand to his heart.

"I hold these tears, and you shall live here always, as will your devotion to the Real People, to your family, and to the way of life you love."

We stood, and I stepped up to this wise chief and hugged him. He reciprocated, patted my back, then put me away from him, and his eyes sought mine.

"Time to take wing, young Raven, and fly to your life, and to your love."

I nodded, then headed to my dwelling to gather what little belongings I owned. My possessions were two books and the necklace Nate had given me to hold, all of which fit in a pouch made of deerskin.

One last goodbye needed to be taken care of. I surveyed the inside of the tipi. Buffalo hides piled on a heap of soft hay for a bed, a burned-out fire in the center, a stack of kindling in one corner, with a cooking rock and gourd bowls and utensils made of buffalo bones and horns. No décor, save the painting on the inside walls, or the smoke stains from the fire. No modern conveniences whatsoever. This was life in its purest, simplest form; it had been heaven on earth for Nate and me.

We laughed, made love, and when the lovemaking was over, he'd held me as we whispered our dreams. Then we'd sleep, only to reawaken with passion that would once again take us to magnificent heights, afterward resting sedate in each other's arms until dawn. Most times he woke me, his lips brushing my neck, his hands caressing me and waking the inner fire in my belly. These desires rose, gurgling, and my heart raced at the memories.

A single tear escaped, and I let it ride the course down my cheek as the other eye dropped a tear, then a few more followed. My only fear was all I had were memories. Once I returned to my time, Nate might never feel the same.

55

"You must leave soon?" was the first question out of Rattling Blanket Woman's mouth as I approached her tipi.

"Yes, I must find my way home, but not without saying goodbye." My eyes searched for the tot.

"You seek my Light-Hair Boy?"

"Yes, I wish to say goodbye."

She called out her special call for him, and the tyke burst out of the dwelling and into her arms. This warmed my heart and made me sad, for I knew in a year's time or so, she'd take flight into the heavens by her own hand. This wasn't my purpose here; I'd completed my quests, so it was time to take my leave from this world.

I kneeled and faced this boy with the light curly hair, intensely curious dark eyes, and a whimsical smile that didn't reach his lips, but lay dormant behind those eyes that stared into mine.

Moving my head forward, I leaned into his tiny ear, whispering, "You will one day be a well-known chief, you will love your life and your people fiercely and will be a brave man. Others will follow you, and the world will remember you forever."

As I pulled back, his little arms wrapped around my neck and he hugged me, and in a low childlike voice said, "Thank you for saving me."

I caught my breath, then he let go and ran back into the tipi to sit with his father.

"Is good you came."

Rattling Blanket Woman broke my speechless moment, and I stood to face her. She continued, "And now you must fly back to your realm and find your soulmate, for he waits."

A questionable expression crossed my face, yet she smiled.

"Oh, he will be there, for Little Wolf only has a heart for you. Do you not know what you have of his?"

I had to think, then I realized. Nate had given me a braided leather rope necklace on which four objects dangled: one shiny copper and gray variegated rock, grayish flint shaped like a crescent moon, a gemstone with hues of rose, and a leather pouch containing teeth of an elk mixed with sage.

"Yes, and he said he'd ask for it back one day."

"Raven, he's asking now, and you must go to him. Worry not for me, for I don't fear my future, and you shouldn't fear yours either." Her voice sounded unfamiliar but familiar; then I noticed her eyes were fixed, unblinking, and knew it wasn't her who had spoken to me. The voice was that of my mother, who'd somehow embodied Rattling Blanket Woman's earthy body to speak to me.

Without hesitating once, I reached in and hugged her, then pulled back as I felt a shift in her spirit.

"We shall meet again one day?" It was a question, not a statement, and I knew my mother had vanished.

"No, I don't think we will, and this saddens me."

"Then I am pleased to have known you, young Raven, and wish you well on your journey."

It was then that I was torn with wanting to stay to see that she lived, but this wasn't mine to decide, for this history was already set and unchangeable. With a smile, I left, and she watched me walking away. I looked over my shoulder only once, I waved again, and I felt a shift in the earth as I did.

I headed back to the denser treed area where the horses were penned. My eyes searched for a particular colt. After I spotted her, I cajoled her over with a fistful of corn kernels. I flattened my hand, and she ate while I stroked her soft, light-gray muzzle. I'd always had a way with animals, especially horses.

With a clicking noise, she came alongside me, stepping away from the group clustered near the green, damp grass beside the riverbank. A thick tree break reinforced the back section, and a crude fence made from fallen trees bound by buffalo hair ropes kept them penned in. No longer the wild pony of the plains, they were content as a group to munch on grass and stay put.

At the end of the makeshift fence, I lifted the limb to an opening, coaxing her out. My eyes bore into hers, and I spoke to her in Lakota.

"I need you to take me into the mountains and not be afraid, for you and I will become one. You are strong where I am weak, and your feet swifter than mine if trouble comes."

Then I slipped off the rope halter from a jutted-out broken limb and walked her out a little further, draping it over her head as I did. My thoughts shifted to how they revered the horse in this age, making life much easier.

"Easier," the word stuck in my head, causing me to frown because I knew this life was anything but easy, but they didn't know of modern times, so to them, this was the life they knew and loved.

It was time. I climbed on her back, and without looking behind me, I kicked her flanks with my feet-clad moccasins, and she took off into the back area toward the mountains as I guided her head. My destination was as high as I could go without putting the pony in danger, then getting further up on my own. I wasn't fearful this colt would leave me; we'd connected and now shared a purpose.

This pony's calling was to grow to be ridden by a chief. My calling here had been to make sure the mother of this boy lived to give him life.

This side of the mountain was steeper than it had appeared as we plodded upward. I spoke to the young pony like a person spoke to another, calming her, cooing to her, telling her she was doing a brilliant job. Her unshod hooves clamored over the rocky terrain; not once did she lose her footing, nor have an ounce of fear as she took her steps, without my guidance, as if she recognized her way and had traveled this trail many times.

With this thought, I loosened my hold on the buffalo rope reins and permitted her to have control over the pace and to choose the path she wanted to follow. In my heart, I understood that whichever path she chose would not be done with her head, but with her instincts and her heart.

Clouds swirled overhead as we climbed higher, and the atmosphere changed—lighter air, less oxygen—but my heart raced. Above me I glimpsed a shorter overhang. Wanáyi headed that way. Wanáyi, the Lakota word for Ghost or spirit.

This beautiful two-year-old Appaloosa in her own right was a vision to behold, and just looking at her countenance as she strode upward, one saw she had a mightiness inside her life-force which would live forever.

Gypsy.

My steed was not an Appaloosa, but the black and gray variegations in her coat would've had one wonder if one wasn't a person who understood horses. To me, though, this was a sign and the reason I sought this pony. Pedigree or not, Ghost and Gypsy were free spirits, and both linked to me forever.

I'd let her take me to the top, or as far up as she could climb, and there wasn't much further to go. I was high enough. My journey ended there with her, and I slipped off. She made no move to leave, her stance still and serene, her head up and her eyes gazing into mine.

"Is this where you need to be?" No words needed, as I gave her a minuscule nod, and she backed up, standing strangely still, watching me.

With one hand I drew up the chain holding my four interconnecting circles, and in a small pocket area I'd sewn into the deerskin dress I wore, I pulled out the replica of the feathers of power, still encased in Plexiglas. Something I'd shown no one since Chay; and how on earth would I explain Plexiglas? I chuckled to myself.

As I regarded the replicas of an eagle feather worn by Chief Swift Eagle, the black feather of a raven worn by Chief Black Raven, and the hawk feather worn by warrior Dark Cloud, I reminisced on my journey here, to this date, time, and era alone.

The first leg on my journey was to meet and learn from White Cow. She had saved me, in an unexpected turn of events on the mountain when she and I met. An amazing woman who taught me the art of cooking on a cooking rock, how to make pemmican, cornbread with herbs and berries, and corn mush with maple sap sugar. Most importantly, she imparted to me an understanding about love, which was not just an emotion, but a fact of well-being: to be cared for and to care for someone other than yourself. To have multilayered feelings which would grow into love lasting forever. Sharing.

As did most women in this era who shared husbands, the work, and the care of the children sired by this one man. No, I'd never shared a husband, but I understood the loyalty and commitment these women must have to one man. Heck, that was what I wanted—to be able to commit like that.

Nate. Was he the one man? We had lived as two, loved as two, and fought as two who were committed to one another.

Ghost nickered, and when I looked back, she'd turned, facing the path back downward, looking over her broad shoulders, her head bobbing, and she reared up, whinnied, and snorted. Her one hoof pawed at the ground when she dropped to all fours, and her eyes sought mine, and we locked stares. She was on her way to being the warhorse for a small boy who would one day become a Sioux legend. I nodded, and she nodded back, then turned and vanished down the slope of the mountain, headed to her life as fate had intended.

Alone, I sought a flat place to sit at the edge of the mountain where I could see the beauty below me, and I was no longer afraid.

Next, I took out the feathers of power and my personal spherical amulet, then I fished into the deerskin sack, pulling out what Nate gave me, then Chief Black Raven's journal. Deep down, my heart whispered that we'd been connected by a shared bloodline, bound by the name of Raven.

In the book, as I thumbed through, I saw a diagram I had not noticed before: four objects, hand-drawn. One resembling a round flat disk, with lines of black and ash from a burned-out fire drawn across it. Next was an arrow, the form filled in with dark ash, almost flat gray. Then a jagged-looking rock, the color of faded red berries, and last, a picture depicting a pouch or a bundle.

Why had I never seen this before?

I read the words penned in Lakota aloud in English:
"A finding stone to find your way, to find your courage, the arrow to direct you or to pierce the heart of your enemy. A rose quartz to show you love, to fill you with compassion and to give you hope. In the pouch of power, you hold a cleansing herb and the teeth of the mighty elk, a protector of the worthy people. A symbol of divine protection from evil. The elk, symbolizing dignity, grants the wearers of its teeth the ability to navigate life's journey with compassion, always aiding those in need. They're life-giving spirits, full of masculine power and energy."

I looked at the objects, then I pulled out my amulet with all the circles, studying them all as they lay atop the book. My talisman seemed off-kilter. With no magnifying glass, I squinted at it so I could see how it had changed. The two larger hoops now crossed in the middle and created a larger space, and the two smaller ones had moved. They were no longer at the top but sat in the center of the gap where the two bigger spheres now crossed.

I closed my eyes, counted to ten, and opened them, looking out across the land. I blinked to clear my head as well as my eyes, then looked back at my necklace. Nope, it had changed, and even if I said that was impossible, I realized it wasn't. Nothing in my life was impossible. That was it. The words: nothing and impossible.

Unbraiding the leather rope necklace Nate had given me, I placed the finding stone and the arrow in my right hand, and in my left, I clutched the rose quartz next to my heart as I spoke into the wind.

In Lakota, I wailed, "Help me, noble spirit, to find my way home. Take me to my love, guide me and give me strength and courage to face my future with open arms."

I sat in complete silence, my eyes stayed closed, and I was aware of the rhythmic thumping of my heart pounding in my ears. Clenching my fists, I held onto each object, the books resting firmly on my lap.

The feeling of drifting overwhelmed me. I was lightheaded, and the urge to sleep was powerful. On my feet, the books slipped off and slid to the edge of the crag. My legs felt wonky, and my spirit felt as if it were fading as my breathing became shallow. Without the power to keep them open, my eyes closed.

"No, no, no, not again," I heard myself saying, knowing each time this had happened I'd ended up in the past, never headed home. Oh, spirits, I beg of you, send me home, were the last words I thought as I crumpled, my body teetering to the edge of the cliff.

The objects dropped out of each hand, and the books slipped off, falling down the side of the massive mountaintop, with me tumbling over seconds later.

Raven. No longer shall you live between the realms of time, for you have completed your tasks. Fly, Raven, you have earned your wings. Time to go home to those who love you. Fly.

Home. I'd rested and eaten and rested some more. A flight over the pond, or down under to Australia and back, would leave you with tremendous jet lag. That was nothing compared to time travel into hundreds and hundreds of years backward and forward and backward again, then home. I was toast.

The day I felt rested and alive, my mom said I'd been home for two months.

"Are you up to talking?" she asked as we sat at the breakfast table.

With a nod, I went into the story, but not in depth. I explained everything, except Nate and our interlude of passion—that was only for me.

"Silver Moon has been asking for you," my mom remarked.

"Why don't you tell her the story I told you, Mom? I'm not up to that just yet."

With a look in her eye that said she understood, she nodded.

"I'm going to visit her and Aunt Meda today, so I'll explain and give your apologies."

All I could muster was a soft, "Thank you."

My mom knew, as well as I did, that those two knew more than I was telling them; however, I was not ready to talk about Nate, not yet. He had not returned, and if he had, he hadn't tried to find me.

My life needed to heal.

It was time I went on with my life without him.

56

Several Months Later

Out in the pasture, the herd grazed as I watched my father riding up on his large chestnut gelding, his face all smiles.

Five of our heifers had calved. Now they were mama cows, no longer the maiden heifers they had been before breeding. Out of the calves born, three were bull calves, which pleased my father, who hoped for a prize bull from the one cow he'd bred with Pete Johnson's prize bull—winning the accolade twice in the past two years.

Being a member of the Council, Pete had given my father a fair price for his breeding rights, and in turn, my dad would let him have two of the calves to add to his fee.

"Herds grazing up along the south forty too, so in a few days, we'll get the vaccines ready and ride out that way, if you're feeling up to it."

"Sure, Dad, I'll be ready."

"Okay, tell your mom I'll be in for supper; gotta go check the other fence lines and fix the ones I saw a few days ago that need mending." With that, he turned his six-hand horse around, kicked his sides, and took off to be what he was—a rancher.

I stroked the mare's neck as I cooed, "Gypsy, you wonderful mare, let's go back to the house."

I guided her reins, turning her head, and we headed that way—not at a run, not at a trot, but a walk—enjoying the last days of what had been a scorching summer.

Everything looked the same, was the same, except Chay was gone, and no one would tell me where he was. They alluded to the fact that they did not rightly know.

I found this to be baloney, because Silver Moon or Aunt Meda knew—they just were not saying. I had been home for months but no longer took much stock in time, hours, or minutes; I'd lived several lifetimes, losing count of the days.

As Gypsy and I came to a crossroads, my hands robotically turned her head to the right, and we headed in another direction, away from the house.

We rode along this rock-strewn trail until it narrowed into a grassy path, abruptly surrounded by trees, bushes, and weeds—a pathway that led to a river. Once we reached the water, we crossed to the other side. In a few miles, we'd be off our ranch land and onto the land owned by our neighbor, Pete Johnson.

We galloped over the flatland, and it felt freeing.

Up ahead, I saw the Johnson's private cemetery. I tugged on the reins to slow the mare to a trot, stopped at the gates, slid off her back, hooked her reins to the gate, and reverently entered.

At the headstone of Sam 'Running Elk' Johnson, I dropped to my knees. He'd been in my life and in my visions, and he was missed by the community. Wildflowers grew abundantly, so I stepped outside, gathered a handful of yellow, blue, and purple flowers, and laid them near his headstone. Then I rocked back on my heels in thought.

Sam traveled in death to seek me in the past. He'd found me when I had needed him, and this was the ultimate design that linked us. My voice soft, I whispered, "Thank you, Running Elk, for comforting me in such a fearful time."

After saying a brief prayer in our native tongue and thanking him again for being a spirit guide, I latched the gate and hopped back on Gypsy.

As I rode, I thought how grateful I was that neither of my parents had battered me with questions about what I had told them.

I had no answers anyway—sans one.

If they asked if I pined for a love, I would've told them yes.

In my dreams, I saw Nate.

He spoke to me, and me to him. Each night I hoped to dream of him so we could sit by the river and talk. I hoped to feel his kiss and his touch, and any night I didn't dream, my smile would disappear.

Headed home, I prayed tonight Nate and I would once again meet in my dreams. I had no way of knowing if he was safe or where he was. It was no longer about me; it was about him—and about us.

I'd been back for six months with no word about him.

His uncle was in Alaska on a hunting expedition, and I had no way to contact him.

Nate had no siblings or other relatives I knew of. I kicked my mare's sides, sending her into a full gallop. As I rode, the wind that'd kicked up out of nowhere coursed through my hair, and I thought of the winds of time—and an idea formed.

Silver Moon and Aunt Meda knew time travel.

My question was, had they ever gone forward or back to the same time? And if so, could you change anything?

———

H er rocker creaked as she rocked, and I sat, waiting for an answer. Silver Moon always contemplated her answers—even her questions—before speaking. Aunt Meda sat in the high-backed armchair, and she too waited.

"I have been many places and met many people in my travels and in my dreams. As you have, I have lived many lives, and,"—she looked at Soft Dove—"so has your Aunt Meda. However, these are the pathways we must wander alone. You cannot go to where your mother and father have been, and we,"—again she looked at Meda—"cannot travel in your footsteps."

"Sure, I understand. But can I go back to a special time and change an outcome for myself?" Once I'd said the words, it made me feel nauseous. Here I was again using self-pronouns—me, mine, I, or myself.

Her rocker stopped. She eyed me curiously. "For yourself, no; for another, yes—but it cannot benefit you. Do you understand what I say?"

My heart heavy, I nodded, because my going back to make things right with Nate was my selfish desire. If I were to know that he needed me, then it would be beneficial for him first, then for me.

"Raven," Silver Moon said, "you need to purify your heart of all other things and wish not for yourself. Be happy for what you have, and your happiness will come to you."

"Raven," Aunt Meda said. "Your mother's travels were for her to accept who she was, find love, and ensure the legendary Chief Sitting Bull's lineage continued. Her last task was to bring you into this world from that world. Your task was to ensure many others lived to bear the prominent men of the past—or save lives as you did in France."

"And like my mom, find love?" My semi-frown crinkled my forehead. "Were you looking for love, or looking to fulfill your destiny for the Real People?"

I was silent, thinking about everyone I had met in my time-travel life, and how each one had somehow touched me, enriched me, made me a better person. Nate.

"No, not looking, but fell into."

"Ah. I see." It was all my Great Aunt said.

Silver Moon's feet scraped the floor as she pushed off the ball of her foot to begin her rocking again. "Do you know Nate Cooper's Sioux name?"

I replied, "He was called Little Wolf."

"Yes, in your travels that was his name, but here, in this world he is Red Elk. Do you know why?"

I shook my head, waiting.

"Nate's spirit animal protects upright people from evil and follows the right path, helping those with moral hearts. An elk is a masculine spirit, full of power and energy. The color red means he is full of passion and courage, and he holds a strong spiritual connection to our tribe, to the lands."

I let this sink in, but it was not said that he was connected to me—or that he ever would be. After a few minutes of silence, I had to ask, because I had to know.

"Have either of you ever moved your spirits forward into the future?"

A look passed between these two older women, and I saw Aunt Meda hesitate to reply, but Silver Moon dove right in.

"Yes, but it is not too good to know much about your future years ahead. Do you understand?"

My eyes closed. I rolled them up under the lids so they couldn't see. I'd seen the *Back to the Future* franchise, so you can imagine what I was thinking.

"You cannot go unless the spirits want you to see, and that is all we shall say about this." Silver Moon's lips were straight, her tone stern.

Then they changed the conversation, asking about the ranch and my parents, and if things were doing okay.

They talked about how Pete was doing after the death of Sam, and how it had been nice to see old friends.

We had tea and enjoyed the rest of our visit, and then it was time for me to leave. I hugged Silver Moon, who was tired and needed to rest.

Her frail fingers caressed my face, her voice low.

"We will forever see each other in your dreams. I will never be far, even when I am no longer."

She hugged me, then stared into my eyes. I saw it—the cloudless mountains—and then in my ears I heard the rushing of water and the call of the owl. Our eyes locked, and her headshake was barely discernible as she put her old fingers to my lips to keep me silent.

Silver Moon had seen two or three lifetimes and would continue to travel in the afterlife, I was certain. "In my dreams, then, until we meet again." I kissed her withered, timeworn face.

Aunt Meda walked me to the front door.

"Tell your mom not to be a stranger, and that I'd like some of her peach jelly."

I hugged her, wondering if she knew it was Silver Moon's time. She hugged me back, and when she let go, a tear rolled off her cheek.

"Yes, but we shall not talk about it."

Aunt Meda, with her uncanny ability to read minds, saw Nate pop into mine. Her eyes locked onto mine, and she asked, "Do you not realize what you possess that belongs to him?"

"Who?"

"Nate. You have something of his. He will come to retrieve it. Go now, and be happy."

She shut the door, leaving me there with more questions than I'd shown up with.

57

I'd forgone dinner and went to my room to be alone, to mourn for love lost. I took out the braided rope necklace Nate had given me to keep and lay down, my memories rolling through my head. He'd told me to keep it until he asked for it back.

Such a simple thing had me crying buckets of tears until I fell asleep, exhausted.

I slept, my dreams and nightmares jumbled together.
As I slept, my dream-self traveled everywhere.

First, I was on a mountain, then in a tunnel, and by a river.
Tossing and turning, next I was riding the open prairie, then in a tipi, under a mound of buffalo hides, chased by a pack of wolves.

I woke up sweating, my breathing labored.
My stomach was nauseous, my mouth dry, and my heart beat so hard I could see it thumping beneath my pajama shirt.

Minutes passed, then I lay back down, covering my eyes with my forearm, thinking on these dreams.

There had been a shadow behind me in every scenario—scary, but comforting. It had protected me from falling off the mountain and kept me from drowning in the rushing river waters. In the tunnel, it guided me out into the sunlight.
When the wolves were upon me, it sheltered me from their fangs.

On the prairie, as I rode the wide-open, untamed land, another rider—unseen—rode with me, and I never felt alone.
The dream of being in the tipi caused an ache in my heart, for the shadow had a name: Nate Cooper.

It was his spirit, Red Elk, which lived within this braided rope.

Without making too much noise, I went downstairs to get a drink of water, the braided rope around my neck, keeping Nate near me.

He'd been a part of my life. I had resigned myself to knowing my love for him was real and would never falter.

Unlike my mother, no one had to show me history to prove it wasn't only a dream—because this was real.

The window was open halfway, the curtains pulled back.
I could see the night sky—no clouds—and out in the country the stars shone and twinkled, unhindered by city lights.

The cool night air blew, the curtains fluttering like butterfly wings.
This was the north side of the house.
Outside the fenced-in yard, our pasture began.

My hands moved the curtains. I leaned in, my forehead against the cool glass, my eyes searching the dark. I couldn't see the land, but I could feel it. It was part of me—part of who I was.

The land of the Real People.
The land we still owned, that no one could take from us.
Land I would never let go of—never give up.

Something inside me burst, and a fresh wave of myself was born. At that very second, several shooting stars streaked across the sky, and I saw the old chief riding atop the majestic buffalo as he glided through the stars.
I'd gone full circle—from seeing Chief Black Raven on the north forty to seeing him one last time tonight.

A heavy sigh left me as I pulled the window shut and closed the curtains. In a whisper carried through the air, I said the words, "I love you, Nate Cooper."

Just as I was about to leave the kitchen, I heard a very light rat-tat-tat-tat on the back door.
Maybe it was Ben, our ranch hand, so I crept to the door and opened it.

"Raven."

My heart stopped. My vocal cords stopped working. My hands shook.
It wasn't Ben—it was Nate Cooper, in the flesh.

He'd come.

"You have something of mine, and I came to retrieve it."

With one hand, he lifted the braided rope from my neck. His other hand held my arm.
Our eyes locked.

I was still speechless.

"This is not all I've come for," he said, his voice deep, filled with emotion.

A hard swallow went down. I was without a voice.

"You have something else of mine. Do you know this?"

I shook my head, unable to move, afraid this was a dream—and that he would disappear.

As he pulled me against his chest, his other hand slid around my waist. He held me captive, our noses almost touching, so close that when he spoke, his warm breath filled my nostrils.

His mouth was dangerously close to mine, and just before his lips claimed mine in the fervent passion I'd dreamed would never again happen, he muttered:

"You have my heart—and I never want it back."

58

Six Years Later

Anniversaries. Not always happy, but they mark a time when something or someone begins or ends—

How is it possible that so many things could occur on the same date, but years apart?

I knew how.

Our family was magical.

It has been five years now since Silver Moon passed; the entire community continues to grieve the loss of the legendary woman who possessed an uncanny ability to understand us simply by looking into our eyes. I learned so much about our undocumented history from her, and knowing she still journeys through time, I long for the day I will see her again.

Four years ago, Great Aunt Meda passed, adding to the sadness. Although I miss her, my mother's grief is still ongoing. My father is a steadfast presence, providing strength for my mother. After all these years, I am still amazed at how their love continues to blossom.

Nate remained stuck in a time loop for months after my return—for that was his journey, not mine. This date is also the anniversary of Nate's return to our present and the beginning of our life together.

From the time I left to the time I returned, I had emotionally aged twenty years. Being conceived sometime around circa 1828 and born into the twenty-first century meant I was already an ancient soul.

Our children. The day of their births arrives, a poignant echo of the last cherished memories from this special day.

Fraternal twins—Rose and Jaden. Such a delight, as well as a major handful.

Rose Louisa Kangee Cooper, three minutes older than her brother, Jaden

Chay Kangee Cooper—our pride and joy. Long names, yes; however, they each have a special tribal name as well.

In Silver Moon's *Book of Knowledge*, written years before, she had already named my children. After her passing, I was given her book. I read:

Two shall be born and together will face future worlds. One shall be called Dark Star Maiden, the other shall be known as Black Wolf. They will join one who is known as the Time Warrior. The torch shall be passed to them to correct future wrongs.

We have raised our children in the culture of our people and the ways of the Whiteman; we wanted both our worlds to become one.

Before Silver Moon's death, I spent a great deal of time with her, and I can still vividly recall her last words to me.

"Raven, your wisdom runs deep, but until the time it will be needed, it will stay buried. But know this—this is not knowledge for you, but for children. When the time is right and the day comes, your stored wisdom will give them the powers they will need. Keep the books you have from us, then write your own. Save them for your children. Store away the amulets and talismans of power, as well as their father's, for one day they too shall be needed."

I heeded her words and have since written accounts of my life, carefully choosing only the noteworthy events. If I dreamed, I recorded it, and if Nate spoke of his reveries, I recorded those as well. We have both had many, so I have filled pages and pages for the future—for my children.

Dear Diary,

With my elbow resting on the windowsill, I watch my children and their father playing a game of kickball, the air filled with the sound of their laughter. Nate takes a dive for the ball, landing flat, and the kids pounce on him. The three of them lie in a pile of giggles. Although it makes me smile, it also makes me sad.

My cousin, Chayton Kangee, known as Star Gazer, is now where they shall go, for he has visited me in my dreams. In another book, I pen his dreams, for they are not for the light-hearted, and I am frightened for the future worlds.

As I end my writing today, I know Rose—our Dark Star Maiden—and Jaden—our Black Wolf—will have destinies they too shall fulfill. I will be there to advise, but not to interfere, for I have been warned it is not safe for me.

The End

Afterword

Thank you for purchasing one of my books and giving me the opportunity to entertain you through the written word.

Word of mouth is vital for any author to be a success, so if you enjoyed Protector of Legends: Raven's Story, would you please be so kind and leave a review online—anywhere you are able to do so? A single sentence, or global stars, could make all the difference in the world, and I would be very grateful.

Thank you, and as always, happy reading!

Acknowledgements

Who do you thank when you do not have a team of researchers or employees at all?

All my research was done via Google and reading about the Native American cultures searching through pages and pages of genealogy sites; and digging as far back as I could. I loved reading about history, piecing my story around facts and folklore. The research for the language of each tribe I dove into. If I have made any errors, I hope those who know the language of the Sioux, Cheyenne, Cherokee and the Apsáalooke (The Crow Nation), will forgive me.

I dug into all Native American tribunal laws and ways: researching how each culture lived, worked. Loved; how they hunted and how each tribe lived and survived the world and its ever-changing ways. A vibrant history that engrossed me so that at times I was reading more than I was writing.

I hope you enjoyed the story and perhaps learned a bit of history in the process.

DK

About the author

Protector of Legends: Raven's Story is the second of the YA fantasies penned by Deana King. Saving a Sioux Legacy: The Story of Blaze was the first, and she is planning a third book to complete her trilogy.

She is also the author of the Jack West series about a Houston Homicide Detective. And her latest release, "When Good Men Fall: A Kasper Bergman Novel" released February 2024, and the first book in her newest FBI series.

Deanna lives in Texas with her husband, Travis, and two feisty pups named Ruby and Daisy.

Reach out to her @ deannakingwriting.com